the evolution of mara dyer

VOLUME 2 OF THE mara dyer TRILOGY

the evolution of mara dyer

MICHELLE HODKIN

SIMON & SCHUSTER BFYR

NEW YORK LONDON TORONTO SYDNEY NEW DELHI

SIMON & SCHUSTER BFYR
An imprint of Simon & Schuster Children's Publishing Division
1230 Avenue of the Americas, New York, New York 10020
This book is a work of fiction. Any references to historical events, real people, or real places are used fictitiously. Other names, characters, places, and events are products of the author's imagination, and any resemblance to actual events or places or persons, living or dead, is entirely coincidental.

For information about special discounts for bulk purchases, please contact Simon & Schuster Special Sales at 1-866-506-1949 or business@simonandschuster.com.
The Simon & Schuster Speakers Bureau can bring authors to your live event. For more information or to book an event, contact the Simon & Schuster Speakers Bureau at 1-866-248-3049 or visit our website at www.simonspeakers.com.
Also available in a SIMON & SCHUSTER BFYR hardcover edition
Book design by Lucy Ruth Cummins
The text for this book is set in Caslon.
Manufactured in the United States of America
First SIMON & SCHUSTER BFYR paperback edition October 2013
14 16 18 20 19 17 15
The Library of Congress has cataloged the hardcover edition as follows:
Hodkin, Michelle.
The evolution of Mara Dyer / Michelle Hodkin.
p. cm.
Sequel to: The unbecoming of Mara Dyer.
Summary: Mara Dyer continues to unravel the mystery of her powers and her relationship with Noah.
ISBN 978-1-4424-2179-0 (hc)
[1. Supernatural—Fiction. 2. Love—Fiction. 3. Florida—Fiction.] I. Title.
PZ7.H66493Ev 2012
[Fic]—dc23
2012019195
ISBN 978-1-4424-2180-6 (pbk)
ISBN 978-1-4424-2181-3 (eBook)

To Martin and Jeremy Hodkin,

for always betting on me

Acknowledgments

This book would not exist without the extraordinary effort of many people, but there are four in particular who rise to the top of the list:

Courtney Bongiolatti: I learned so much from you and your time, talent, and limitless patience are appreciated beyond words. You made this one great, and you are missed.

Alexandra Cooper: In such a short time, you have brought so much to this book. I can't believe my good fortune in having won the editor lottery twice.

Barry Goldblatt: No matter how heavy things get, you never let me sink. Thank God you're on my side.

And last but not at all least, to Kat Howard. Kat, you helped me find the words I needed to write and you pulled them out of me one by one. You were with me every day even though we were thousands of miles apart. Thank you will never be enough.

Thanks also to Ellen Hopkins for helping me hear Noah's voice, and to Nova Ren Suma, for rescuing me again and again. You are both so gracious and wise, and I am lucky to call you friends.

To Justin Chanda, Paul Crichton, Siena Koncsol, Matt Pantoliano, Chrissy Noh, Amy Rosenbaum, Elka Villa, Michelle Fadlalla, Venessa Williams, and the entire team at Simon & Schuster, I am grateful for you all every day. And to Lucy Ruth Cummins for designing yet another stunning cover—you amaze me.

To Stephanie, Emily L., Sarah, Bridget, Ali, Anna, Christi, and Emily T., for everything Maggie and beyond, and to Rebecca Cantley, for taking care of my life when I can't be there to do it myself.

And as always, thanks to my family for their infinite love and support: Janie and Grandpa Bob, Jeffrey, Melissa, Uncle Eddie, Aunt Viri and Uncle Paul, Barbara and Peter, Nanny and Zadie, Z"L, Tante and Uncle Jeff and all of my cousins. Bret, thank you for *Dawson's Creek*, New Year's Eve, and for tolerating so much abuse. Yardana, I love you and can't remember what our family was like without you. Thank you for lending your professional expertise to this book; I could not have done my misfits justice without it. All of the psychological details that were accurate were accurate because of you, and any mistakes made were mine and mine alone.

Martin & Jeremy, you got the dedication. Don't be greedy.

Finally, thanks to my mother, Ellen, for always believing me. Even when she shouldn't have.

the evolution of mara dyer

"Can we become other than what we are?"

—Marquis de Sade, *Justine*

PREFACE

YOU WILL LOVE HIM TO RUINS.

The words echoed in my mind as I ran through clots of laughing people. Blinking lights and delighted screams bled together in a riot of sound and color. I knew Noah was behind me. I knew he would catch up. But my feet tried to do what my heart couldn't; they tried to leave him behind.

I finally ran out of breath beneath a leering clown that pointed to the entrance to the Hall of Mirrors. Noah caught up to me easily. He turned me to face him and I stood there, my wrist in his grasp, my cheeks wet with tears, my heart splintered by her words.

If I truly loved him, she said, I would let him go.

I wished I loved him enough.

1

LILLIAN AND ALFRED RICE PSYCHIATRIC UNIT

Miami, Florida

I WOKE UP ON THE MORNING OF SOME DAY IN SOME hospital to find a stranger sitting in my room.

I sat up gingerly—my shoulder was sore—and studied the stranger. She had dark brown hair that bled into gray at the roots, and hazel eyes with webs of crow's feet at the corners. She smiled at me, and her whole face moved.

"Good morning, Mara," she said.

"Good morning," I said back. My voice was low and hoarse. It didn't sound like my own.

"Do you know where you are?"

She obviously didn't realize that the floor directory was positioned directly outside the window behind her, and that from the bed, I had a clear view. "I'm at the Lillian and Alfred Rice Psychiatric Unit." Apparently.

"Do you know who I am?"

I had no idea, but I tried not to show it; she wouldn't have asked me if we'd never met, and if we *had* met, I should remember her. "Yes," I lied.

"What's my name?"

Damn. My chest rose and fell quickly with my breath.

"I'm Dr. West," she said evenly. Her voice was warm and friendly but not at all familiar. "We met yesterday, when you were brought in by your parents and a detective by the name of Vincent Gadsen."

Yesterday.

"Do you remember?"

I remembered seeing my father lying pale and wounded in a hospital bed after he was shot by the mother of a murdered girl.

I remembered that I was the one who made her do it.

I remembered going to the police station to confess to stealing my teacher's EpiPen and releasing fire ants in her desk, which is why she died of anaphylactic shock.

I remembered that it wasn't true—just a lie I would feed the police so they would keep me from hurting anyone I loved again. Because they wouldn't believe I wished my teacher dead and that not long after, she died. Choked to death on a swollen tongue, exactly the way I imagined she would.

I remembered that before I could tell anyone any of this, I saw Jude at the Thirteenth Precinct of the Metro Dade Police Department. Looking very much alive.

But I did not remember coming here to the hospital. I didn't remember being brought. After Jude appeared, I remembered nothing else.

"You were admitted yesterday afternoon," the stranger—Dr. West—said. "The detective called your parents when they couldn't get you to stop screaming."

I closed my eyes and saw Jude's face as he walked by me. Brushed past me. Smiled. The memory stained the backs of my eyelids, and I opened them quickly, just to see something else.

"You told them that your boyfriend, Jude Lowe, who you thought died in a building collapse in December, is alive."

"Ex," I said quietly, fighting to stay calm.

"Excuse me?"

"Ex-boyfriend."

Dr. West tilted her head slightly and employed her carefully neutral psychologist expression, one I recognized well since I'd seen it often on my psychologist mother. Particularly in the past few months.

"You said that *you* caused the abandoned asylum in Rhode Island to collapse, crushing your best friend, Rachel, and Jude's sister, Claire, inside. You said Jude sexually assaulted you, which is why you tried to kill him. And you said he survived. You said he's here."

She was perfectly calm as she spoke, which magnified my panic. Those words in *her* mouth sounded crazy, even though they were true. And if Dr. West knew, then so did—

"Your mother brought you here for an evaluation."

My mother. My family. They would have heard the truth too, even though I hadn't planned to tell it. Even though I didn't *remember* telling it.

And this was where it got me.

"We didn't begin yesterday because you were sedated."

My fingers wandered up my arm, beneath the short sleeve of my white T-shirt. There was a Band-Aid on my skin, covering what must have been the injection site.

"Where is she?" I asked, picking at the Band-Aid.

"Where is who?"

"My mother." My eyes scanned the hallway through the glass, but I didn't see her. The hall looked empty. If I could just talk to her, maybe I could explain.

"She's not here."

That didn't sound like my mother. She didn't leave my side once when I was admitted to the hospital after the asylum collapsed. I told Dr. West as much.

"Would you like to see her?"

"Yes."

"Okay, we can see if we can work that out later."

Her tone made it sound like that would be a treat for good behavior, and I didn't like it. I swung my legs over the bed and stood up. I was wearing drawstring pants, not the jeans I last remembered myself in. My mother must have brought them from home. Someone must have changed me. I swallowed hard. "I think I want to see her now."

Dr. West stood up as well. "Mara, she isn't here."

"Then I'll go find her," I said, and started looking for my Chucks. I crouched to look under the bed, but they weren't there.

"Where are my shoes?" I asked, still crouched.

"We had to take them."

I rose then, and faced her. "Why?"

"They had laces."

My eyes narrowed. "So?"

"You were brought here because your mother thought you may be a danger to yourself and others."

"I really need to talk to her," I said then, struggling to keep my voice even. I bit down hard on my bottom lip.

"You'll be able to."

"When?"

"Well, I'd like you to speak with someone first, and have a doctor come in, just to make sure you're—"

"And if I don't want to?"

Dr. West just looked at me. Her expression was sad.

My throat wanted to close. "You can't keep me here unless I consent," I managed to say. I knew that much, at least. I was a lawyer's daughter and I was seventeen years old. They couldn't keep me here unless I wanted to be kept. Unless—

"You were screaming and hysterical and you slipped. When one of our nurses tried to help you up, you punched her."

No.

"It became an emergency situation, so under the Baker Act, your parents were able to consent for you."

I whispered so I wouldn't scream. "What are you saying?"

"I'm sorry, but you've been involuntarily committed."

2

"WE HOPE THAT YOU'LL ALLOW A DOCTOR TO DO a physical examination," she said kindly. "And that you'll consent to our treatment plan."

"What if I don't?" I asked.

"Well, your parents still have time to file the appropriate papers with the court while you're here—but it would be really wonderful for you, and for them, if you cooperated with us. We're here to help you."

I couldn't quite remember ever feeling so lost.

"Mara," Dr. West said, drawing my eyes to hers, "do you understand what this means?"

It means that Jude is alive and no one believes it but me.

It means that there *is* something wrong with me, but it isn't what they think.

It means that I'm alone.

But then my racing thoughts trailed an image in their wake. A memory.

The beige walls of the psychiatric unit evaporated and became glass. I saw myself in the passenger seat of a car—Noah's car—and saw my cheeks stained with tears. Noah was next to me, his hair messy and perfect and his eyes defiant as they held mine.

"There is something seriously wrong with me, and there's nothing anyone can do to fix it," I said to him then.

"Let me try," he said back.

That was before he knew just how deeply screwed up I was, but even when the last piece of my armor cracked on marble courthouse steps, revealing the ugliness beneath it, Noah wasn't the one who left.

I was.

Because I killed four people—five, if my dad's client never woke up—with nothing more than a thought. And the number could have been higher—*would* have been higher, if Noah hadn't saved my father's life. I never meant to hurt the people I loved, but Rachel was still dead and my father was still shot. Less than forty-eight hours ago, I thought the best way to keep them safe was to keep myself away.

But things were different, now. Jude made them different.

No one knew the truth about me. No one but Noah. Which meant he was the only one who could possibly fix this. I had to talk to him.

"Mara?"

I forced myself to focus on Dr. West.

"Will you let us help you?"

Help me? I wanted to ask. *By giving me more drugs when I'm not sick, not with anything worse than PTSD? I'm not psychotic,* I wanted to say.

I'm not.

But I didn't appear to have much of a choice, so I forced myself to say yes. "But I want to talk to my mother first," I added.

"I'll give her a call after your physical—okay?"

It wasn't. Not at all. But I nodded and Dr. West grinned, deepening the folds in her face, looking for all the world like a warm, kindly grandmother. Maybe she was.

When she left, it was all I could do not to fall apart; but I didn't have time. She was immediately replaced by a penlight-wielding doctor who asked me questions about my appetite and other wildly mundane details, which I answered calmly with a careful tongue. And then he left, and I was offered some food, and one of the staff—a counselor? A nurse?—showed me the unit. It was quieter than I imagined a psych ward would be, and with fewer obvious psychos. A couple of kids were quietly reading. One watched TV. Another talked with a friend. They looked up at me when I passed by, but otherwise, I went unacknowledged.

When I was eventually led back to the bedroom, I was shocked to find my mother in it.

Anyone else wouldn't have noticed what a mess she was. Her clothes were unwrinkled. Her skin was still flawless. Not a single hair was out of place. But hopelessness trampled her posture and fear dulled her eyes. She was holding it together, but just barely.

She was holding it together for me.

I wanted to hug her and shake her at the same time. But I just stood there, cemented to the floor.

She rushed up to hug me. I let her, but my arms were chained to my sides and I couldn't hug her back.

She pulled back and smoothed the hair from my face. Studied my eyes. "I am so sorry, Mara."

"Really." My voice was flat.

I couldn't have hurt her more if I had smacked her. "How could you say that?" she asked.

"Because I woke up in a psychiatric unit today." The words were bitter in my mouth.

She backed up and sat on the bed, which had been freshly made since I was last in it. She shook her head, and her lacquer-black hair swung with the movement. "When you left the hospital yesterday, I thought you were tired and going home. So when the police called?" Her voice cracked, and she held her hand up to her throat. "Your father was shot, and then to pick up the phone and hear the police say, 'Mrs. Dyer, we're calling about your daughter?'" A tear fell from one of her eyes and she quickly wiped it away. "I thought you'd been in a car accident. I thought you were *dead*."

My mother wrapped her arms around her waist and hunched forward. "I was so terrified I dropped the phone. Daniel picked it up. He explained what was happening—that you were at the police station, hysterical. He stayed with your father and I rushed there to get you but you were *wild*, Mara," she said, and looked at me. "Wild. I never thought . . ." Her voice trailed off and she seemed to be staring right through me. "You were screaming that Jude is alive."

I did something brave, then. Or stupid. Sometimes it's hard to tell the difference.

I decided to trust her. I looked my mother in the eye and said, without any trace of doubt in my expression or voice, "He *is*."

"How would that be possible, Mara?" My mother's voice was toneless.

"I don't know," I admitted, because I didn't have a clue. "But I saw him." I sat down next to her on the bed, but not close.

My mom pushed her hair away from her face. "Could it have been a hallucination?" She avoided my eyes. "Like the other times? Like the earrings?"

I had asked myself that same question. I'd seen things before—my grandmother's earrings at the bottom of my bathtub, even though they were still in my ears. Classroom walls collapsing around me, maggots squirming in my food.

And I had seen Claire. I saw her in mirrors. I heard her voice.

"You two kids have fun."

I saw Jude in mirrors. I heard his voice, too.

"You need to take your mind off this place."

But now I knew that I had heard them say those same words twice. Not just in mirrors at home. In the asylum.

I didn't imagine those words. I *remembered* them. From the night of the collapse.

But at the precinct it was different. Jude spoke to an officer. I strained to remember what he said.

"Can you tell me where I can report a missing person? I think I'm lost."

I never heard him say those words before. They were new. And he said them before he touched me.

He *touched* me. I *felt* him.

That was not a hallucination. He was real. He was alive, and he was here.

3

MY MOTHER WAS STILL WAITING FOR AN answer to her question, so I gave her one. I shook my head fiercely. "No." Jude was alive. He wasn't a hallucination. I was sure.

She sat there immobile for just a beat too long. Then, finally, she smiled, but it didn't reach her eyes. "Daniel's here to see you," she said and stood. She bent to kiss the crown of my head just as the door opened, revealing my older brother. The two of them shared a glance, but as Daniel entered the room he expertly masked his concern.

His thick black hair was uncharacteristically messy and dark circles ringed his dark eyes. He smiled at me—it was too easy, too quick—and leaned down to wrap me in a hug. "I'm so glad you're okay," he said as he squeezed. I couldn't quite hug him back either.

Then he let go and added too lightly, "And I can't believe you took my keys. Where's my house key, by the way?"

My forehead creased. "What?"

"My house key. It's missing from my key ring. Which you took before driving my car to the police station."

"Oh." I had no memory of taking it, and no memory of what I did with it. "Sorry."

"It's okay. Not like you were getting into any trouble or anything," he said, squinting at me.

"What are you doing?"

"Giving you the side-eye."

"Well, it looks like you're having a stroke," I said, unable to help my smile. Daniel flashed one of his own—a real one, this time.

"I almost had a heart attack when Mom almost had a heart attack," he said, his voice quiet. Serious. "I'm—I'm happy you're okay."

I looked around the room. "Okay is a relative term, I think."

"Touché."

"I'm surprised they're letting you see me," I said. "The way the psychiatrist was acting, I was starting to think I was on lockdown or something."

Daniel shrugged his shoulders and shifted his weight, obviously uncomfortable.

Which made me cautious. "What?"

He sucked in his lips.

"Out with it, Daniel."

"I'm supposed to try to convince you to stay."

I narrowed my eyes at him. "For how long?"

He didn't say.

"How long?"

"Indefinitely."

My face grew hot. "Mom didn't have the guts to tell me herself?"

"That's not it," he said, sitting down in the chair beside the bed. "She thinks you don't trust her."

"*She's* the one who doesn't trust *me*. She hasn't since . . ." *Since the collapse,* I almost said. I didn't finish my sentence, but judging by Daniel's expression, I didn't need to. "She doesn't believe anything I say," I finished. I hadn't meant to sound like such a child, but I couldn't help it. I half-expected Daniel to call me out but he just gave me the same look he always gave me. He was my brother. My best friend. I hadn't changed to him.

And that made me want to tell him everything. About the asylum, Rachel, Mabel, my teacher. All of it.

If I told him calmly—not panicked, in a police station, but rationally, after a full night's sleep—if I explained everything, maybe he would understand.

I needed to be understood.

So I closed my eyes and took a deep breath, like I was preparing to launch myself off a cliff. In a way, I guess, I was. "Jude is here."

Daniel swallowed and then asked carefully, "In the room?"

I shot him a glare. "No, you ass. In Florida. In Miami."

His expression didn't change.

"He was in the police station, Daniel. I saw him. He was *there*."

My brother just sat there, mirroring our mother's neutral expression from just a few minutes before. Then he reached for his backpack and pulled something out of it. "It's the security footage from the precinct," he explained before I had a chance to ask. "Dr. West thought it would be good for Mom to show you."

"So why are *you* showing me?"

"Because clearly you *don't* trust Mom, but she knows you trust me."

I gave him a narrow look. "What's on it?"

He stood and popped the disc into the DVD player beneath the ceiling-mounted television, then switched it on. "Tell me when you see him, okay?"

I nodded, and then both of our heads turned toward the screen. Daniel fast-forwarded it and tiny people scurried in and out of the police station. The counter sped forward and I watched myself walk into the frame.

"Stop," I said to Daniel. He pressed a button and the footage slowed to a normal speed. There was no audio, but I watched myself speak to the officer at the front desk—I must have been asking where I could find Detective Gadsen.

And then I watched Jude appear in the frame. My heart began to race as my eyes lingered on the image of him, on his baseball cap, on his long sleeves. Something on his wrist caught the light. A watch.

There was a shiver in my mind. I pointed at Jude's figure on the screen. "There," I said. My hand trembled annoyingly. "That's him."

We watched as Jude spoke to the officer. As he brushed right by me. Touched me. I started to feel sick.

Daniel paused the image before Jude left the frame. He said nothing for a long while.

"What," I said quietly.

"That could be anyone, Mara."

My throat tightened. "Please tell me you're kidding."

"Mara, it's a guy in a Patriots cap."

I studied the screen again. The camera angle only captured the top of Jude's head. Which was covered by the Patriots cap he always wore. Which was pulled down low, shading his eyes.

You couldn't see his face at all.

"But I heard his *voice*," I said. Pleaded, really. My brother opened his mouth to say something, but I cut him off. "No, listen." I took a deep breath. Tried to calm down, to be less shrill. "I heard him—he asked that officer something and the officer answered him back. It was his voice. And *I* saw his face." I stared at the screen, squinting as I continued to speak. "You can't see it so well on the tape, maybe, but it's him. It's *him*."

Daniel looked at me for a few silent seconds before he finally spoke. When he did, his voice was distressingly soft. "Mara, it can't be him."

My mind rushed through the facts, the ones I knew, the ones I was sure of. "Why not? They couldn't get to his body to bury it, right?" The building was too unstable, I remembered, and it was too dangerous. "They couldn't get to him," I said again.

Daniel pointed at the screen, at Jude's hands. My eyes followed his finger. "See his hands?"

I nodded.

"Jude wouldn't have any. His hands were all they found."

4

HIS WORDS DRAINED THE BLOOD FROM MY FACE.

"They didn't find complete remains for any of the—for Rachel, Claire, *or* Jude. But they did find—they found his hands, Mara. They buried them." He swallowed like it was painful for him, then pointed at the video screen. "This guy? Two hands." Daniel's voice was gentle and sad and desperate but his words refused to make sense. "I know you're freaked out about what's been happening. I know. And Dad—we're all worried about Dad. But that isn't Jude, Mara. It's not him."

It would have been a relief to believe that I was *that* crazy, to swallow that lie and their pills and shake off the guilt that had hounded me since I finally remembered what I was capable of.

But I tried that before. It didn't work.

I took a deep, shuddering breath. "I'm not crazy."

Daniel closed his eyes, and when he opened them again, his expression was . . . decided. "I'm not supposed to tell you this—"

"Tell me what?"

"The psychologists are calling it a perceptual distortion," my older brother said. "A delusion, basically. That—that Jude's alive, that you have the power to collapse buildings and kill people—they're saying you're losing the ability to rationally evaluate reality."

"Meaning?"

"They're throwing around words like 'psychotic' and 'schizotypal,' Mara."

I ordered myself not to cry.

"Mom is hoping that, worst case scenario, this is maybe something called Brief Psychotic Disorder brought on by the PTSD and the shooting and all of the trauma—but from what I think I'm hearing, the main differences between that, schizophrenia, and a bunch of other disorders in between is basically duration." He swallowed hard. "Meaning, the longer the delusions last, the worse the prognosis."

I clenched my teeth and forced myself to stay quiet while my brother continued to speak.

"That's why Mom thinks you should stay here for a while

so they can adjust your meds. Then they can move you to a place, a residential treatment facility—"

"No," I said. As badly as I had wanted to leave my family to keep them safe before, I knew now I needed to stay with them. I could not be locked up while Jude was free.

"It's like a boarding school," he went on, "except there's a gourmet chef and Zen gardens and art therapy—just to take a break."

"We're not talking about Fiji, Daniel. She wants to send me to a *mental hospital.* A mental hospital!"

"It isn't a mental hospital, it's a residential—"

"Treatment facility, yeah," I said, just as the tears began to well. I blinked them back furiously. "So you're on their side?"

"I'm on *your* side. And it's just for a little while, so they can teach you to cope. You've been through—there's no way I could deal with school and what you've been through."

I tried to swallow back the sourness in my throat. "What does Dad say?" I managed to ask.

"He feels like part of this is his fault," he said.

The wrongness of that idea sliced me open.

"That he shouldn't have taken on the case," my brother went on. "He trusts Mom."

"Daniel," I pleaded. "I swear, I *swear* I'm telling the truth."

"That's part of it," he said, and his voice nearly cracked. "That you believe it. Hallucinations—that fits with the PTSD. But you knew when you had them that it was all in your head. Now that you believe it's real," Daniel said, his voice tight, "everything you told them yesterday is consistent with—psychosis." He blinked fiercely and swiped one of his eyes with the back of his hand.

I couldn't believe this was happening to me. "So that's it, then." My voice sounded dead. "Do I even get to go home first?"

"Well, once they admit you they have to keep you for seventy-two hours, and then they reevaluate you before they make a final recommendation to Mom and Dad. So I guess that'll happen tomorrow?"

"Wait—just seventy-two hours?" And another evaluation . . .

"Well, yeah, but they're pushing for longer."

But right now, it was temporary. Not permanent. Not yet.

If I could persuade them that I *didn't* believe Jude was alive—that I didn't believe I killed Rachel and Claire and the others—that none of this was real, that it was all in my head—if I could lie, and convincingly, then they might think my episode at the police station was temporary. That was what my mother *wanted* to believe. She just needed a push.

If I played this right, I might get to go home again.

I might get to see Noah again.

An image of him flickered in my mind, his face hard and determined at the courthouse, certain that I wouldn't do what I did. We hadn't spoken since.

What if I had changed to him, like he said I would?

What if he didn't want to see me?

The thought tightened my throat, but I couldn't cry. I couldn't lose it. From here on out, I had to be the poster child for mental health. I couldn't afford to be sent away anymore. I had to figure out what the hell was going on.

Even if I had to figure it out by myself.

A knock on the door startled me, but it was just Mom. She looked like she'd been crying. Daniel stood up, smoothing his wrinkled blue dress shirt.

"Where's Dad?" I asked her.

"Still in the hospital. He gets discharged tomorrow."

Maybe, if I could put on a good enough performance, I might get discharged with him. "Joseph's there?"

Mom nodded. So my twelve-year-old brother now had a father with a gunshot wound and a sister in the psychiatric ward. I clenched my teeth even harder. *Do not cry.*

My mom looked at Daniel then, and he cleared his throat. "Love you, sister," he said to me. "I'll see you soon, okay?"

I nodded, dry-eyed. My mother sat down.

"It's going to be okay, Mara. I know that sounds stupid right now, but it's true. It will get better."

I wasn't sure what to say yet, except, "I want to go home."

My mother looked pained—and why shouldn't she? Her family was falling apart. "I want you home so badly, sweetheart. I just—there's no schedule for you at home if you're not in school, and I think that might be too much pressure right now. I *love* you, Mara. So much. I couldn't stand it if you—I was throwing up when I first heard about the asylum. . . . I was sick over it. I couldn't leave you, not for a second. You're my baby. I know you're not a baby but you're *my* baby and I want you to be okay. More than anything I want you to be okay." She wiped at her eyes with the back of her hand and smiled at me. "This isn't your fault. No one blames you, and you're not being punished."

"I know," I said gravely, doing my best impression of a calm, sane adult.

She went on. "You've been through so much, and I know we don't understand. And I want you to know that this" — she indicated the room—"isn't you. It might be chemical or behavioral or even genetic—"

An image rose up out of the dark water of my mind. A picture. Black. White. Blurry. "What?" I asked quickly.

"The way you're feeling. Everything that's been going on with you. It isn't your fault. With the PTSD and everything that's happened—"

"No, I know," I said, stopping her. "But you said—"

Genetic.

"What do you mean, genetic?" I asked.

My mother looked at the floor and her voice turned professional. "What you're going through," she said, clearly avoiding the words *mental illness*, "can be caused by biological and genetic factors."

"But who in our family has had any kind of—"

"My mother," she said quietly. "Your grandmother."

Her words hung in the air. The picture in my mind sharpened into a portrait of a young woman with a mysterious smile, sitting with hennaed hands folded above her lap. Her dark hair was parted in the center and her bindi sparkled between her eyebrows. It was the picture of my grandmother on her wedding day.

And then my mind replaced her face with mine.

I blinked the image away and shook my head. "I don't understand."

"She killed herself, Mara."

I sat there, momentarily stunned. Not only had I never known, but . . . "I thought—I thought she died in a car accident?"

"No. That's just what we said."

"But I thought you grew up with her?"

"I did. She died when I was an adult."

My throat was suddenly dry. "How old were you?"

My mother's voice was suddenly thin. "Twenty-six."

The next few seconds felt like forever. "You had me when you were twenty-six."

"She killed herself when you were three days old."

5

WHY DIDN'T I KNOW THIS?

Why wasn't I told?

Why would she do it?

Why then?

I must have looked as shocked as I felt, because my mother rushed to apologize. "I never meant to tell you like this."

She never meant to tell me at all.

"Dr. West and Dr. Kells thought it was the right thing, since your grandmother had so many of the same preoccupations," my mother said. "She was paranoid. Suspicious—"

"I'm not—" I was about to say that I wasn't suspicious or paranoid, but I was. With good reason, though.

"She didn't have any friends," she went on.

"I have friends," I said. Then I realized that the more appropriate words were "had" and "friend," singular. Rachel was my best friend and, really, my only friend until we moved.

Then there was Jamie Roth, my first (and only) friend at Croyden—but I hadn't seen or heard from him since he was expelled for something he didn't do. My mother probably didn't even know he existed, and since I wasn't going back to school anytime soon, she probably never would.

Then there was Noah. Did he count?

My mom interrupted my thoughts. "When I was little, my mother would sometimes ask me if I could do magic." A sad smile appeared on her lips. "I thought she was just playing. But as I grew older, she would ask every now and then if I could do anything 'special.' Especially once I was a teenager. I had no idea what she meant, of course, and when I asked her, she would tell me that I would know, and to tell her if anything changed." My mother clenched her jaw and looked up at the ceiling.

She was trying not to cry.

"I wrote it off, telling myself that my mother was just 'different.' But all of the signs were there." Her voice shifted back from wistful to professional. "The magical thinking—"

"What do you mean?"

"She would think she was responsible for things she couldn't possibly be responsible for," my mother said. "And she was superstitious—she was wary of certain numbers, I remember; sometimes she'd take care to point them out. And when I was around your age, she became very paranoid. Once, when we were on the way to move me into my first dorm room, we stopped to get gas. She'd been staring in the rearview mirror and looking over her shoulder for the past hour, and then when she went inside to pay, a man asked me for directions. I took out our map and told him how to get where he wanted to go. And just as he got back in his car and drove away, your grandmother ran out. She wanted to know everything—what he wanted, what he said—she was wild." My mom paused, lost in the memory. Then she said, "Sometimes I would catch her sleepwalking. She had nightmares."

I couldn't speak. I didn't know what to say.

"It was . . . hard growing up with her, sometimes. I think it's what made me want to be a psychologist. I wanted to help . . ." My mother's voice trailed off, and then she seemed to remember me sitting there. *Why* I was sitting there. Her face flushed with color.

"Oh, sweetheart—I didn't mean to—to make her sound that way." She was flustered. "She was a wonderful mother and an incredible person; she was artistic and creative and *so* much fun. And she always made sure I was happy. She cared so much. If they knew when she was younger what they know now, I think . . . it would have turned out differently." She swallowed hard, then looked straight at me. "But *she* isn't *you*. You're *not* the same. I only said something because—because things *like* that can run in families, and I just want you to know that it's nothing you did, and everything that happened—the asylum, all of it—it is *not* your fault. The best therapists are here, and you're going to get the best help."

"What if I get better?" I asked quietly.

Her eyes brimmed with tears. "You will get better. You *will*. And you'll have a normal life. I swear to God," she said, quietly, seriously, "you'll have a normal life."

I saw my opening. "Do you have to send me away?"

She bit her lower lip and inhaled. "It's the last thing I want to do, baby. But I think, if you're in a different environment for a little while, with people who really know about this stuff, I think it'll be better for you."

But I could tell by the tone of her voice, and the way it wavered, that she wasn't decided. She wasn't sure. Which meant that I still might be able to manipulate her into letting me come home.

But it wouldn't happen during this conversation. I had work to do. And I couldn't do it with her here.

I yawned, and blinked slowly.

"You're exhausted," she said, studying my face.

I nodded.

"You've had the week from hell. The *year* from hell." She took my face in her hands. "We're going to get through this. I promise."

I smiled beatifically at her. "I know."

She smoothed my hair back and then turned to leave.

"Mom?" I called out. "Will you tell Dr. West that I want to talk with her?"

She beamed. "Of course, honey. Take a nap, and I'll let her know to stop by and check on you in a bit, okay?"

"Thanks."

She paused between the chair and the door. She looked conflicted.

"What's wrong?" I asked her.

"I just—" she started, then closed her eyes. She ran her hand over her mouth. "The police told us yesterday that you said Jude assaulted you before the building collapsed. I just wanted—" She took a deep breath. "Mara, is that true?"

It *was* true, of course. When we were alone together in the asylum, Jude kissed me. Then he kept kissing me, even though I told him to stop. He pressed me into the wall. Pushed me. Trapped me. Then I hit him, and he hit me back.

"Oh, Mara," my mother whispered.

The truth must have been evident on my face because before I decided how to answer her, she rushed back to me. "No wonder this has been even harder—the dual trauma, you must have felt so—I can't even—"

"It's okay, Mom," I said, looking up at her with glassy, full eyes.

"No, it isn't. But it will be." She leaned down to kiss me

again and then left the room, flashing a sad smile before she disappeared.

I sat up straight. Dr. West would be back soon, and I needed to get it together.

I needed to convince her—them—that I only had PTSD, and not that I was dangerously close to having schizophrenia or something equally scary and permanent. Because with PTSD, I could stay with my family and figure out what was going on. Figure out what to do about Jude.

But with anything else—this was it for me. A lifetime of psych wards and medication. No college. No *life.*

I tried to remember what my mother had said about my grandmother's symptoms:

Suspicion.

Paranoia.

Magical thinking.

Delusions.

Nightmares.

Suicide.

And then thought about what I knew about PTSD:

Hallucinations.

Nightmares.

Memory loss.

Flashbacks.

There were similarities and there was overlap, but the main difference seemed to be that with PTSD, you *know*, rationally, that what you're seeing isn't real. Anything with a schizo prefix meant, however, that when you hallucinate, you believe it—even after the hallucination passes. Which makes it a delusion.

I *did* legitimately have PTSD; I experienced more than my share of trauma and now sometimes saw things that weren't real. But I *knew* those things weren't happening, no matter how much it felt like they were.

So now, I just had to be clear—very clear—that I didn't believe Jude was alive either.

Even though he was.

6

THE CLOCKS IN THE PSYCHIATRIC UNIT TICKED away, counting down the hours that remained of my required seventy-two. It was going well, I thought on Day Three. I was calm. Friendly. Painfully normal. And when another psychiatrist named Dr. Kells introduced herself as the head of some program somewhere in Florida—I answered her questions the way she expected me to:

"Have you been having trouble sleeping?"

Yes.

"Have you been having nightmares?"

Yes.

"Do you have a hard time concentrating?"

Sometimes.

"Do you find yourself losing your temper?"

Every now and then. I'm a normal teenager, after all.

"Have you been experiencing obsessive thoughts about your traumatic experience?"

Definitely.

"Do you have any phobias?"

Doesn't everyone?

"Do you ever see or hear people that aren't there?"

Sometimes I see my friends—but I know they aren't real.

"Do you ever think about harming yourself or others?

Once. But I would never do anything like that.

Then she left and I was offered lunch. I wasn't particularly hungry but thought it would be a good idea to eat anyway. All part of the show.

The day dragged on, and near the end of it Dr. West returned. I sat at a table in the common area, as plain and impersonal as any hospital waiting room but with the addition of small round tables peppered with chairs. Two kids who looked to be around Joseph's age were playing checkers. I was drawing on construction paper with crayons. It wasn't my proudest moment.

"Hi, Mara," Dr. West said, leaning over to see my picture.

"Hi, Dr. West," I said. I smiled big and put down my crayon, just for her.

"How are you feeling?"

"Kind of nervous," I said sheepishly. "I really miss being home." I nudged the picture I was drawing just slightly—a flowering tree. She would read something into it—therapists read something into everything—and normal people love trees.

She nodded. "I understand."

I widened my eyes. "Do you think I'll get to go home?"

"Of course, Mara."

"Today, I mean."

"Oh. Well." Her brow furrowed. "I don't know yet, to be honest."

"Is it even possible?" My innocent-kid voice was driving me insane. I'd used it more in the past day than I had in the past five years.

"Well, there are a few possibilities," she said. "You could stay here for further treatment, or possibly transfer to another inpatient facility. Or your parents could decide that a residential treatment center would be the best place for you, since you're a teenager—most of them have secondary educational programs that would allow you to spend some time on coursework as you're working in group and experiential therapies."

Residential. Not ideal.

"Or an outpatient program could be the best thing—"

"Outpatient?" Tell me more.

"There are day programs for teens who are going through difficult things, just like you."

Doubtful.

"You work mostly with counselors and your peers in group therapy and in experiential therapies like art and music—with a bit of time devoted to schoolwork, but the focus is definitely on therapy. And at the end of the day, you go home."

Not so terrible. At least now I knew what to hope for.

"Or, your parents might decide not to do anything but therapy. We'll make our recommendation, but ultimately, it's up to them. Your mother should be stopping by soon, actually," she said, glancing at the elevators. "Why don't you keep drawing—what a lovely picture!—and then we'll speak again after I talk with her?"

I nodded and smiled. Smiling was important.

Dr. West left, then, and I was still attempting to make the falsely cheerful picture even more falsely cheerful when I was startled by a tap on my shoulder.

I half-turned in the plastic chair. A young girl, maybe ten or eleven, with long, unbrushed dirty blond hair stood shyly with her thumb in her mouth. She wore a white T-shirt that was too big for her over a blue skirt with ruffles to match her blue socks. She passed me a folded piece of paper with her free hand.

Sketchbook paper. My fingers identified the texture immediately, and my heartbeat quickened as I unfolded it, revealing the picture I gave Noah, *of* Noah, weeks ago at Croyden. And on the back were just three words, but they were the most beautiful words in the English language:

I believe you.

They were written in Noah's handwriting, and my heart turned over as I looked behind me, hoping by some miracle to see his face.

But there was no one here that didn't belong.

"Where did you get this?" I asked the girl.

She looked down at the linoleum floor and blushed. "The pretty boy gave it to me."

A smile formed on my lips. "Where is he?"

She pointed down the hallway. I stood, leaving the bullshit tree and my sketch on the table, and looked around calmly even though I wanted to run. One of the therapists sat at a table talking to a boy that kept scratching himself, and one of the staff members manned the front desk. Nothing out of the ordinary, but obviously, something was. I casually walked toward the restrooms—they were close to the hallway, which was close to the elevators. If Noah was here, he couldn't be far.

And just before I turned the corner, I felt a hand gently grab my wrist and pull me into the girls' bathroom. I knew it was him even before I saw that face.

I lingered on the blue-gray eyes that studied mine, on the small crease between them above the line of his elegant nose. My eyes wandered over the shape of his mouth, following its curve and pout, as if he was just about to speak. And that hair—I wanted to jump into his arms and run my fingers through that hair. I wanted to crush my mouth against those lips.

But Noah placed a long finger on mine before I could say a word. "We don't have much time."

His nearness filled me with warmth. I couldn't believe he was really here. I wanted to feel him more, just to make sure he really was.

I raised a tentative hand to his narrow waist then. His lean muscles were taut, tense beneath the thin, soft cotton of his vintage T-shirt.

But he didn't stop me.

I couldn't stop my smile. "What is it with you and girls' bathrooms?" I asked, watching his eyes.

The corner of his mouth lifted. "That *is* a fair question. In my defense, they're much cleaner than boys' bathrooms, and they do seem to be everywhere."

He sounded amused. Arrogant. That was the voice I needed to hear. Maybe I shouldn't have worried. Maybe we were okay.

"Daniel told me what happened," Noah said then. His tone had changed.

I met his eyes and saw that he knew. He knew what happened to me, why I was here. He knew what my family thought.

I felt a rush of heat beneath my skin—from his gaze or from shame, I didn't know. "Did he tell you what I—what I said?"

Noah stared down at me through the long dark lashes that framed his eyes. "Yes."

"Jude's here," I said.

Noah's voice wasn't loud but it was strong when he spoke. "I believe you."

I didn't know how badly I needed to hear those words until he said them out loud. "I can't stay here while he's out there—"

"I'm working on that." Noah glanced at the door.

I knew he couldn't stay, but I didn't want him to leave. "Me too. I think—I think there's a chance my parents might let me come home," I said, trying not to sound as nervous as I felt. "But what if they make me stay? To keep me safe?"

"I wouldn't, if I were them."

"What do you mean?"

"Any minute now . . ."

Two seconds later, the sound of an alarm filled my ears.

"What did you do?" I said over the noise as he backed up toward the bathroom door.

"The girl who gave you the note?"

"Yes . . ."

"I caught her staring at my lighter."

I blinked. "You gave a child, in a psych ward, a lighter."

His eyes crinkled at the corners. "She seemed trustworthy."

"You're sick," I said, but smiled.

"Nobody's perfect." Noah smiled back.

7

NOAH'S PLAN WORKED. THE GIRL WAS CAUGHT setting fire to my drawing, actually, but not before the alarm went off. They managed to override a full-scale evacuation and in the midst of the chaos, Noah slipped out. Just before my mother arrived. And she wasn't happy.

"I can't believe someone on staff would bring a lighter in here." Her voice was acid.

"I know," I said, sounding worried. "And I was working really hard on that picture." I shuddered for effect.

My mother rubbed her forehead. "Dr. West thought you should stay here for another week, to get your medications stabilized. She also thought you'd be a good candidate for an inpatient program, it's called Horizons—"

My stomach dropped.

"It's off of No Name Key, and I've seen the pictures—it's really beautiful and has an excellent reputation, even though they've only been operating for about a year. Dr. Kells, the woman who runs it, said she met you and that you'd fit in really well—but I just . . ." She sucked in her lower lip, then sighed. "I want you home."

I could have cried, I was so relieved. Instead I said, "I want to *come* home, Mom."

She hugged me. "Your father's been discharged and he's waiting downstairs—he can't wait to see you."

My heart leapt. I couldn't wait to see *him*.

"Should we get your stuff?"

I nodded, my eyes appropriately misty. I didn't have much with me, so I mostly milled around while my mother filled out a bunch of paperwork. One of the psychiatrists—Dr. Kells—clicked toward me in expensive-looking heels. She was dressed like my mother—silk blouse, pencil skirt, perfectly applied makeup and perfectly coiffed hair.

Her wide red lips pulled back to reveal a flawless smile. "I hear you're going home," she said.

"Looks that way," I said back, careful not to sound too smug.

"Good luck to you, Mara."

"Thanks."

But then she didn't leave. She just stood there, watching me.

Awkward.

"Ready?" Mom called out.

Just in time. I left Dr. Kells with a wave and met my mother by the elevator. As the doors closed, it took everything I had not to cheer.

"What do you think of her?" Mom asked me, once we were alone.

"Who?"

"Dr. Kells."

I wondered where she was going with this. "She's all right."

"There's an outpatient program that Dr. West recommended—it's actually run by her as part of Horizons. They do a lot of group therapy work—teens only—and art and music therapies, that type of thing."

"Okay . . ."

"I think it would be good for you."

I wasn't sure what to say. Outpatient was better than inpatient, certainly—and I had to act like I wanted that brand of help. But dropping out of school was a big deal. I needed a minute to think.

Luckily, I got it. Because the elevator doors opened and there was my father standing in the lobby, looking healthy and invincible. I knew better than anyone that he wasn't.

"Dad," I said, with a smile so wide it hurt my cheeks. "You look good." He really did; the pale skin we shared had some color to it, and he didn't seem tired or haggard or thin, despite what he'd been through. In fact, standing there in khakis and a white polo shirt, he looked like he was heading out to play golf.

He flexed one of his arms and pointed at his biceps. "Man of steel."

My mother shot him a withering look, and then the three of us walked out into the sub-Saharan humidity and into the car.

I was happy. So happy that I almost forgot what landed me in the hospital in the first place. What landed my *father* in the hospital in the first place.

"So what do you think?" my mother asked me.

"Hmm?"

"About the Horizons Outpatient Program?"

Had she been talking? Had I not noticed?

Either way, I was out of time. "I think—I think it sounds okay," I finally said.

My mother let out a breath I hadn't noticed she'd been holding. "Then we'll make sure you start ASAP. We're *so* happy you're coming home, but there are going to be adjustments. . . ."

There's always another shoe.

"I don't want you home alone. And I don't want you driving, either."

I bit my tongue.

"You can leave the house as long as Daniel's with you. And if you come back without him, he'll have to answer for it."

Which wasn't fair to him. Which they knew.

"Someone will take you to and from the program every day—"

"How many days a week is it?"

"Five," my mother said.

At least it wasn't seven. "Who's going to take me?" I asked, peering at her. "Don't you have work?"

"I'll take you, sweetheart," my dad said.

"Don't *you* have work?"

"I'm taking some time off," he said lightly, and ruffled my hair.

When we pulled up onto our street, I was surprised to find myself annoyed. It was the picture of suburban perfection; each lawn meticulously edged, each hedge carefully trimmed. There wasn't a single flower out of place, or even a stray branch on the ground, and our house was just the same. Maybe that was what bothered me. My family had been through hell and I was the one who put them there, but from the outside looking in, you'd never know.

When my mother opened the front door, my little brother rushed into the foyer wearing a suit, pocket square and all.

He smiled with his whole face, threw his arms wide open and seemed like he was just about to launch himself at me, but then stopped. He teetered on his toes. "Are you staying?" he asked cautiously.

I looked to my mother for an answer.

"For now," she said.

"Yes!" He wrapped both arms around me, but when I tried to do the same he jumped away. "Watch the suit," he said, glaring.

Oh, boy. "Have you taken over the operation of some Fortune 500 company while I was gone?"

"Not yet. We're supposed to dress up as the person we most admire and write a speech from their point of view for school."

"And you are . . ."

"Warren Buffett."

"I didn't know he was partial to pocket squares."

"He isn't." Daniel appeared from the kitchen, his fingers wrapped around a very thick book, the title of which I couldn't read. "That was Joseph's special touch."

"Wait, isn't it Sunday?" I asked.

Daniel nodded. "It is. But even with the entirety of spring break to practice, our little brother doesn't appear to want to wear anything else."

Joseph lifted his chin. "I like it."

"I like it too," I said, and ruffled his hair before he ducked away.

Daniel grinned at me. "Glad to have you back, little sister." His eyes were warm, and I'd never felt happier to be home. He ran a hand through his thick hair, creating a gravity-defying mess. I cocked my head—the gesture was unusual for him. It was more reminiscent of—

Noah glided out of the kitchen before I could finish my thought, holding his own massive book. "You're completely wrong about Bakhtin—" he started, then looked from my parents, to me, to Daniel, and then back to me.

Scratch that. I'd never felt happier to be home until *now*.

"Mara," Noah said casually. "Good to see you."

Good did not do my feelings justice. All I wanted was to pull Noah into my room and pour out my heart. But we were under observation, so all I could say was, "You too."

"Mr. Dyer," he said to my father, "you're looking quite well."

"Thank you, Noah," my Dad said. "That gift basket you brought kept me from starving. The hospital food nearly killed me."

Noah's eyes met mine before he answered, "Then I'm thrilled to have saved your life."

8

NOAH SPOKE TO MY FATHER, BUT HIS WORDS were meant for me.

An unsubtle reminder of what he did for me after what *I* did to my father, and it stung. Everyone kept talking but I stopped listening, until my mother pulled me aside.

"Mara, can I speak to you for a second?"

I cleared my throat. "Sure."

"You guys figure out what you want for dinner," she called out, then led me down the long hallway into my room.

We walked by our own smiling faces on the wall, past the gallery of family pictures. When I passed my grandmother's portrait, I couldn't help but look at it with new eyes.

"I want to talk to you about Noah," my mother said once we were in my room.

Stay cool. "What's up?" I asked, and slid onto my bed until my back leaned against the navy wall. Despite everything, I felt oddly relaxed in my room. More like myself in the dark.

"He's been spending a lot of time here, which I know you know, but also after you were—gone."

Gone. So that's how we were going to refer to it.

"Noah's become one of Daniel's close friends, and he's great with Joseph, too, actually, but I also know you're . . . together . . . and I have some concerns."

She wasn't the only one. Noah came to the hospital today because he knew about Jude. He knew I was in trouble. He came because I needed him.

But was he there because he *wanted* to be? I didn't know yet, and part of me was afraid to find out.

"I'm nervous," my mother continued. "With all of the pressure you're already under—I'd like to speak to Noah about your . . . situation."

My face flushed with color. Couldn't be helped.

"I wanted to ask your permission."

A conundrum. If I said no, she might not let me see him. He was the only person on the planet who knew the truth, so being cut off from that—from *him*—was not an uplifting prospect. And if she didn't let me see him, and he still wanted to see *me* after we had the chance to actually talk, sneaking around would be tough.

But my mother talking to Noah? About my precarious mental health? I could almost feel myself shrinking.

My fingers curled into my fluffy white quilt but I don't think she noticed. "I guess," I finally said.

My mother nodded. "We all like him, Mara. I just want to set some parameters for you both."

"Sure . . . " My voice trailed off as my mother left and I waited in near-agony. Words like "schizotypal disorder" and "antipsychotics" would surely come up. Any sane boy would surely run.

But after a few minutes, I realized that I could still hear my mother's voice—were they talking in Joseph's room? It was only two rooms away. . . .

I stood, and leaned out of my doorway and into the hall to listen.

"Are you sure about this?"

Not my mother's voice. My father's.

"I'd rather them both be here where we can watch them; his parents are in and out all next week, and there's no supervision there anyway—"

My mother wasn't talking to Noah—she was talking to my father, *about* Noah. I edged out farther into the hall and slipped into my brothers' bathroom—right next door to Joseph's room—so I could eavesdrop properly.

"What if they break up, Indi?"

"We have bigger problems," my mother said bitterly.

"I just don't like thinking about what something like that would do to her. Mara's really—she scares me sometimes," Dad finished.

"You think she doesn't scare *me*?"

Maybe I didn't want to hear this conversation after all. In fact, I was becoming rather certain that I didn't, but I appeared to be rooted to the spot.

My mother raised her voice. "After watching what my mother went through? This scares the *hell* out of me. I am *terrified* for her. My mother was mostly functional, thank God, but if we knew then what we know about mental illness now? Maybe I would've realized it was more serious before it was too late—"

"Indi—"

"Maybe I could have gotten her the help she needed and she could have had a more fulfilling life—she was so *alone*, Marcus. I mostly thought she was eccentric, not delusional."

"You couldn't know," my father said softly. "You were just a kid."

"Not always. I wasn't always a kid. I—" My mother's voice cracked. "I was too close to see it—that there was something really wrong. And the one time I said something to her about talking to someone? She just—she just *shifted*. She was so much more careful around me after that; I wanted to think—I wanted to think she was getting better but I was too preoccupied with my own—in college, sometimes I went months without hearing from her, and I didn't—"

A long pause. My mom was crying. My insides curled up.

After a minute, she spoke again. "Anyway," she said, quieter now, "this is about Mara. And it's scary, yes, but we can't act like she's an ordinary teenager anymore. The same rules don't apply. I didn't—I didn't see the Jude thing coming."

My shoulder was pressed against the bathroom wall and it began to hurt, but I found I couldn't move.

"She's a complicated—she's complicated," my mother finally said.

She's a complicated case was what she *almost* said.

"And you really think Noah being here, you think that's helpful?"

"I don't know." My mother's voice was stretched and thin. "But I think trying to keep them apart will only create a unit: them versus us. She'll run in the opposite direction."

True.

"And if Noah's here, then Mara will want to be here, and that will make her easier to watch."

Also true, unfortunately.

"She's not in school anymore, she doesn't have any friends here that I've met—it's not normal, Marcus. But it *is* normal for a teenage girl to want a boyfriend. Which means that right now, Noah's the most normal thing in her life."

Little did they know.

"She's comfortable around him. He pulled her right out of that depression on her birthday—I think he helps keep her in the here and now, and we need her to stay there. My mother was so *isolated*." Her voice cracked on the word, and there was another long pause. "I don't want that for her. It's good for her to have someone her own age who she can talk to about things."

"I wish she had someone female," my father mumbled.

"He won't take advantage."

Oh, really?

"I've talked to him," Mom added.

Kill me.

"Come on, he's a teenage boy. I just don't see what he's getting out of this—"

Thanks, Dad.

"Mara isn't really allowed out, they won't be together at school—"

My mother interrupted him. "If you expect the worst from people, that's exactly what you'll get."

"I wonder what his family thinks about him spending so much time here." A diplomatic change of subject. Well played.

Mom made a derisive noise. "I doubt they've noticed; they're a mess. His father is some kind of business mogul and from what Noah's said, he sounds like a raging asshole. The stepmother is always out because she can't deal with it. The kids basically raised themselves."

I'd met Noah's stepmom—and she seemed nice. Like she cared. Noah's father, on the other hand . . .

"Wait—a business mogul—not *David* Shaw?"

"I didn't ask his name."

"It must be," my father said, and let out a low whistle. "I'll be damned."

This I wanted to hear.

"You know him?"

"Know *of* him. There were some federal indictments handed down a year ago for the executives of one of his mega-corporation's subsidiaries—Aurora Biotech? Euphrates International, maybe? There are dozens, I don't remember which."

"Maybe he needs a white-collar defense lawyer?"

"Har har."

"It would be safer."

"That depends." Dad's voice was louder now. He must have opened Joseph's bedroom door to leave.

"On?"

"Who you're getting into bed with," he answered, and left the room.

9

I EDGED AWAY FROM THE DOOR AND WAITED FOR my parents' footsteps to disappear. The way they talked about me—what they *thought* of me—

Especially my father. I couldn't stop thinking about what he said.

"I just don't see what he's getting out of this."

He thought I had nothing to offer Noah. That he had no reason to want to be with me.

Even as I rebelled against the idea, a tiny, miserable part of me wondered if he might be right.

I eventually pulled myself together enough to stave off a good cry—at least until I was back in my room. But much to my surprise, it was already occupied.

Noah's long legs straddled my white desk chair, and his chin rested lazily on his hand. He wasn't smiling. He didn't look anxious. He didn't look *anything*. He just looked blank.

You are my girl, he had said at the courthouse.

Was it still true?

Noah arched an eyebrow. "You're staring."

I blushed. "So?"

"You're staring warily."

I didn't know how to frame my thoughts, but something about Noah's coolly indifferent tone and his languid posture kept me from moving closer. So I just closed the door and hung against the wall. "What are you doing here?"

"I was discussing Bakhtin and Benjamin and a thesis about *de se* and *de re* thoughts as relevant to notions of self with your older brother."

"Sometimes, Noah, I feel an overwhelming urge to punch you in the face."

An arrogant grin crept across his mouth.

"That doesn't help."

He glanced up at me through those unfairly long lashes, but didn't move an inch. "Should I leave?"

Just tell me why you're here, I wanted to say. *I need to hear it.*

"No," was all I said.

"Why don't you just tell me what it is that's bothering you?"

Fine. "I didn't expect to see you here after . . . I didn't know if we were still . . ." My voice trailed off annoyingly, but it took several seconds for Noah to fill the silence.

"I see."

My eyes narrowed. "You see?"

Noah unfolded himself and rose then, but didn't approach. He backed up against the edge of my desk and leaned his palms against the glossy white surface. "You thought after hearing that someone who hurt you—someone who hurt you so badly that you tried to kill him—was alive, that I'd just leave you to deal with it on your own." He was still calm, but his jaw had tightened just slightly. "That's what you think."

I swallowed hard. "You said at the courthouse—"

"I remember what I said." Noah's voice was toneless but a hint of a smile appeared on his lips. "I would say you'll make a liar out of me, but I was one long before we met."

I couldn't wrap my mind around his words. "So, what, you just changed your mind?"

"The people we care about are always worth more to us than the people we don't. No matter what anyone pretends." And for the first time in what felt like a long time, Noah sounded real. He was still as he watched me. "I didn't think you had to make the choice you said you made then. But if I *did* have to choose between someone I loved and a stranger, I would choose the one I love."

I blinked. The choice I *said* I made?

I didn't know if Noah was saying that he didn't *care* about what I'd done, or if he no longer believed that I did it. Part of me was tempted to push him on this, and the other part—

The other part didn't want to know.

Before I could decide, Noah spoke again. "But I don't believe you have the power to remove someone's free will. No matter how much you might want to."

Ah. Noah thought that even if I did somehow put the gun in that woman's hand, I *didn't* make her pull the trigger. And so in his mind, I wasn't responsible.

But what if he was wrong? What if I *was* responsible?

I felt unsteady, and pressed myself more tightly against the wall. "What if I could?"

What if I did?

I opened my eyes to find that Noah had taken a step toward me. "You can't," he said, his voice firm.

"How do you know?"

He took another step. "I don't."

"So how can you say that?"

Two more. "Because it doesn't matter."

I shook my head. "I don't understand—"

"I was more worried about what your choices would do to *you* than what the consequences would be for anyone else."

One more step, and he'd be close enough to touch. "And now?" I asked.

Noah didn't move, but his eyes searched mine. "Still worried."

I looked away. "Well, I have bigger problems," I said, echoing my mother's words. I didn't need to elaborate, apparently. One glance at Noah's suddenly tense frame told me he knew what I meant.

"I won't let Jude hurt you."

My throat went dry when I heard his name. I remembered the frozen frame on the psych ward television, the blurred image of Jude on the screen. I remembered the watch on his wrist.

The watch.

"It's not just me," I said, as my heart began to pound. "He was wearing a watch, the same one you saw in your—in your—"

Vision, I thought. But I couldn't quite say it out loud.

"He had the same watch as Lassiter," I said instead. "The *same one.*" I met Noah's eyes. "What are the chances?"

Noah was quiet for a moment. Then said, "You think he took Joseph."

It wasn't a question, but I nodded in assent.

Noah's voice was low but strong. "I won't let him hurt your family either, Mara."

I inhaled slowly. "I can't even tell my parents to be careful. They'll think I'm just being paranoid like my grandmother."

Noah's brows knitted in confusion.

"She committed suicide," I explained.

"What? When?"

"I was a baby," I said. "My mom told me yesterday; she's even more worried about me because we have a 'family history of mental illness.'"

"I'm going to have some people watch your house."

Noah seemed calm. Relaxed. Which only added to my frustration. "My parents would probably notice, don't you think?"

"Not these men. They're with a private security firm and they're very, very good. My father uses them."

"Why does your father need private security?"

"Death threats and such. The usual."

It was my turn to be confused. "Doesn't he work in biotech?"

A wry smile formed on Noah's lips. "A euphemism for 'playing God,' according to the religious and environmental groups that hate his subsidiaries. And you've seen our house. He doesn't exactly maintain a low profile."

"Won't *he* notice?"

He shrugged a shoulder. "They don't all work for my father, so I doubt it. What's more, he wouldn't care."

I shook my head in disbelief. "It's amazing."

"What?"

"Your freedom." Even before everything happened—before the asylum, before Rachel died—my parents had to know everything about my life. Where I was going, who I was going with, when I was coming back. If I went shopping, my mom had to know what I bought and if I went to the movies, she insisted on talking about what I'd seen. But Noah floated in and out of his family's palace like air. He could go to class, or not. He could spend money like water or obstinately refuse to drive a luxury car. He could do anything he wanted whenever he wanted, no questions asked.

"Your parents care about you," Noah said then. His voice was soft, but there was a rawness to it that shut me up. Though he said nothing else and though his expression was still glass-smooth and unreadable, I heard the words he didn't say: *Be grateful you have them.*

I wanted to smack myself. Noah's mother had been murdered in front of him when he was just a kid; I knew better than to ever act like the grass was greener on the other side. I *was* grateful to have my parents, even though the hovering was out of control, even though they didn't believe me when I told them the hardest truth there was to tell. It was a stupid thing to say and I wished I hadn't said it. I looked up to reach for Noah, to whisper I was sorry against his skin, but he had pulled away.

He sprawled out on my bed and returned the subject to Jude. "If we can find out where he lives—"

I took Noah's former place and leaned against my desk. "Wait, where *is* he living? He's legally dead. It's not like he could just get a job and rent an apartment."

Noah raised his eyebrows.

"What?"

"It's Miami," he said, as if it was obvious.

"Meaning?"

"Meaning there's no shortage of methods by which to acquire money and housing without a social security number. But I do wonder. . . ."

"You wonder . . . ?"

"Might he have gone back to his parents? After the collapse?" Noah stared at my ceiling.

"You think they know he's alive?"

He shook his head. "If they did, they'd have told others by now, and we'd have heard."

My voice turned quiet. "Daniel said his hands were cut off."

"He told me."

I gripped the edge of my desk. "It doesn't make any *sense.* How did he survive? How is that possible?"

Noah bit his thumbnail as he leaned back against my pillow. "How is any of this possible?" he asked under his breath.

How *was* it possible? How could Noah heal? How could I kill?

The room had grown dark, and the subject made me uneasy. I peeled myself away from my desk and edged carefully onto my bed. Closer to Noah, but not quite touching.

I looked down at him. Not even a week ago, I was lying next to this disarmingly beautiful boy, feeling his heart beat against my cheek. I wanted to be there now, but I was afraid to move.

So I spoke instead. "You think he's like us?"

"That, or the remains they found weren't his."

I shook my head. "Wouldn't they do DNA testing?"

Noah's eyes narrowed as he stared at nothing. "Only if they had reason to believe it wasn't him. Regardless, records can be fabricated and lab rats can be bought." There was an edge to his voice now, one that wasn't there before.

"Who would—?"

My question was cut off by Daniel calling our names.

"Be right there!" I called back.

Noah swung his legs over my bed, carefully avoiding my body and my eyes as he rose. "I don't know, but we aren't going to find out in your bedroom."

"And I'm not allowed to go anywhere without a babysitter." I couldn't help but sound bitter. "So you're on your own."

Noah shook his head and then, finally, looked at me. "I'm not leaving you any more than I have to." He was on edge again. "Not like this."

I wished it was because he didn't want to be apart more than because he thought we had to stay together.

"So . . . how long are you staying?" My tone was more tentative than I intended. Much more.

But my favorite half-smile appeared on his mouth. I wanted to live in it. "How long do you want me?" he asked.

How long can I have you? I thought.

Before I could say anything, Daniel called us again.

"Alas," Noah said, glancing at the door. "I'm afraid that's my cue. Your father wanted to spend your first night back as a family."

I might have sighed.

"But your mother knows all about my cold and empty home life, and she's taken pity on the motherless urchin you see before you."

"Well, you are quite pitiful," I said, unable to help my smile.

"I told her that my enormous mansion will be terribly lonely this week in particular, so I expect I'll be here quite a lot. Unless you object?"

"I don't."

"Then I'll see you tomorrow," Noah said, and moved to the door. "And I shall formulate a plan to work on your father as well."

"My dad?"

Noah cracked a smile. "We bonded in the hospital a bit, but I think he enjoys playing the benighted father; 'I was a teenage boy once too, I remember what it was like,' et cetera." But Noah spoke with affection.

"You *like* them," I realized.

Noah's eyebrows lifted in question.

"Like, as people."

"As opposed to . . . furniture?"

"They're my *parents*."

"That is my understanding, yes."

I made a face. "It's weird."

"What is, exactly?"

"I don't know," I said, trying to find the right words. "Knowing that you've, like, talked to them without me there?"

"Well, if you're worried about your mother showing me your most embarrassing childhood pictures, don't be."

Thank God.

"I've already seen them."

Damn it.

"I'm a particular fan of your fifth-grade haircut," he deadpanned.

"Shut up."

"Make me."

"Grow up."

"Never." Noah's grin turned devious, and I matched it despite myself. "They'll relax, you know," he said then. "They'll get complacent. As long as you keep improving."

I raised my eyebrows. "Is that your way of telling me to keep my shit together?"

At this, Noah closed the distance between us. He leaned down until his lips grazed my ear. My pulse raced at the contact and my eyes closed at the feel of his five o'clock shadow on my cheek.

"It's my way of telling you that I can't bear to look at my bed without seeing you in it," he said, and his words made me shiver. "So do try to avoid a lockdown."

I felt him withdraw, and I opened my eyes. "I'll get right on that," I breathed.

One final wicked smile. "You'd better."

10

After Noah went home, my father cracked bad jokes at dinner, Joseph talked at fifty thousand miles a minute, my mother watched me too closely, and Daniel seemed like his lovably pretentious self. It almost felt like I'd never left.

Almost.

When we finished, my mom watched me take the multiple antipsychotics I was now on but didn't need, and then everyone went to their respective rooms before bed. I passed by the first set of French doors in the hallway but stopped short when I thought I saw a shadow move outside.

The air left my lungs.

The street lamps cast an unusually bright glow on the backyard, which was covered in a thin fog. It didn't *look* like there was anything there, but it was hard to see.

My heart was pounding so loudly I could hear it. Just last week, I would have dismissed it as nothing; just my misbehaving mind ruled by fear. I would have hurried into my bedroom and burrowed under the covers and whispered to the dark that it wasn't real. I was afraid of only myself then; what I might see, what I might do. But now, now there was something real to be frightened of.

Now there was Jude.

But if he wanted to hurt me, why show up at Croyden once and then leave me alone? Why appear at the Cuban restaurant and disappear seconds later? If he did take Joseph, my brother was still unharmed when we found him. And why would he walk into the police station, close enough for me to see, close enough for me to touch, just before walking out?

What was the point? What did he *want*?

I stood still in the safety of my house, my breath quick as my eyes searched for Jude behind the glass. The darkness revealed nothing, but I was still afraid.

I clenched my jaw as I realized that I would always be afraid. Now that I knew Jude was alive, that he was here, I wouldn't be able to walk into the bathroom without wanting to throw back the shower curtain to make sure he wasn't behind it. I wouldn't be able to walk down a dark hallway without picturing him at the end. Every snap of a twig would turn into his footstep. I would imagine him everywhere, whether he was there or not.

That was what he wanted. That was the point.

So I unlocked the door and stepped outside.

I was enveloped by the dull roar of crickets the moment my foot touched the patio. It was a rare cool night in Miami; the earlier rain became mist and the night sky was completely obscured by clouds. If it weren't March in Florida, I would have thought it was about to snow.

I breathed in the damp air, one hand still on the door handle as the wind shook a few stubborn raindrops from the trees. Someone might be out there—*Jude* might be out there, but my parents were inside. There was nothing he could do.

"I'm not afraid of you," I said to no one. The breeze carried my words away as it raised the hair on my skin. He might be alive but I wouldn't spend *my* life in terror of him. I refused. If fear was what he wanted from me, I would make sure he didn't get it.

A mosquito hummed by my ear. I dodged it, and stepped into something wet.

Something soft.

I backed up toward the house, fumbling for the outdoor lights. They flickered on.

I gagged.

The still body of a gray cat lay inches from where I'd been

standing, its flesh torn open, its fur streaked with red. My feet were soaked in blood.

I covered my mouth to trap my rising scream.

Because I couldn't scream. I couldn't make a sound. If I did, my parents would come running. They would ask what happened. They would see the cat. They would see me.

They would want to know what I was doing outside.

I heard my mother's voice in my mind.

"She was paranoid. Suspicious."

That's what my parents would think of me if I told them someone was out there. That I was paranoid. Suspicious. Sick. They would be worried, and if I wanted to stay home, stay free, I couldn't afford that.

So I turned off the lights and ducked back inside. I left a trail of bloody footprints in the hall. I grabbed toilet paper from my brothers' bathroom and rubbed at the blood staining my feet until I was clean. Then I cleaned up the floor. Checked all of the locks on all of the doors. Just in case.

And then, finally, I escaped to my room.

Only then did I realize I was shaking. I looked down at my feet. I could still feel the soft, wet, dead fur—

I rushed into my bathroom and threw up.

My hair was pasted to the back of my neck and my clothes were damp against my skin. I slid down to the floor and hugged my knees to my chest, the tile cool beneath me. I let my eyes drift closed.

Maybe the cat was killed by an animal. Another cat. A raccoon, maybe.

That was possible. More than possible; it was *likely*.

So I brushed my teeth. Washed my face. Forced myself to get into bed. Told myself that everything was fine until I actually found myself starting to believe it.

Until I woke up the next morning and looked in the mirror.

Two words were written there, scrawled in blood:

FOR CLAIRE

The room tilted. I heaved into the sink.

And then I cried.

Jude knew what happened that night. That I was the one who brought the asylum down. That I was the one who killed Claire. That was why he was here.

I wanted to scream for my parents. To show them the cat, the message—proof that Jude really was alive and that he was here.

But it wasn't proof enough. My hands trembled but I steadied myself against the sink and blinked hard. I willed myself to ignore the panic scratching at the surface, threatening to shatter my carefully constructed lies. I forced my feet to move. I checked the windows in my bedroom and checked the rest of the house too. All of the doors were locked.

From the inside.

I squeezed my eyes shut. If I showed them the message, they might think I wrote it myself.

They might think I killed the cat myself, I realized with horror. They would sooner believe *that* than they would believe that Jude was alive.

The thought stole the last bit of hope from my heart. Jude was in my *bedroom*. He left a dead animal outside my house and a bloody message on my mirror, and I couldn't tell my parents. I couldn't tell them anything or I'd be caged in a mental hospital while Jude taunted me through the bars.

Without Noah, I would be truly, completely alone in this.

My father might be right. If I lost Noah, I might just lose my mind.

11

I WAS JACKED UP ON ADRENALINE THAT GRAY MORNING and couldn't stop moving, afraid that if I did, I'd crack. I washed away the blood on my mirror. I forced myself to eat breakfast, to smile at my parents as they got ready to drive me to the program. The air was oppressive; it had poured again overnight. Before we left, I checked outside to see if I left any footprints on the patio, leading from the cat back to the house.

The cat was gone.

The car seemed to contract around me and even though I managed to stay engaged in their conversation, I couldn't remember what my parents said. Nausea gnawed on the remains of whatever was left in my stomach and I was drenched in sweat.

I willed myself to hold it together as my mother wrestled with snarls of traffic, and by the time she pulled into a non-descript strip mall in South Miami, I succeeded. The three of us headed toward a storefront sandwiched between a Weight Watchers and a Petco, and my mother squeezed my arm in what I assumed was meant to be a reassuring gesture. As long as they thought I was nothing worse than nervous, I'd be okay.

A man who looked oddly like Santa Claus was waiting for us just inside the door. "Marcus Dyer?" he said to my father as we stepped in.

Dad nodded. "Sam Robins?

The man gave a wan smile and extended his arm, stretching the fabric of his red polo shirt tight across his belly. "Welcome to Horizons," he said cheerfully. Then he spoke to me. "I'm the admissions counselor. How was I-95?"

"Not too bad," my mother said. She looked past the man and into the space behind him. "Is Dr. Kells here?"

"Oh, she'll be along for the intake evaluation," he said with a smile. "I'm just here to get you all acquainted. Come on in." He waved us inside.

The interior was much brighter than I expected, and modern, from what I could see of it. Horizons was all white walls and sleek furniture, dotted with a few calming pops of blue-hued abstract art. And even though I couldn't see much of it from where we stood, I could tell it was huge. It might've been a gym in its former life.

Mr. Robins pointed out several walled-off areas and named them as we passed: the common room, the art studio, the music studio, the dining room, et cetera. He seemed proud of the fact that it mirrored the structure of their inpatient place, complete with a little meditative Zen garden in the center. Something about "familiarity" and "consistency" but I didn't pay much attention because I didn't care. I was already counting down the seconds until I could see Noah, until I could tell him what happened. What I found.

What Jude had left.

But the adults looked at me expectantly, waiting for me to say something. So I said the first thing that came to mind.

"Where is everyone?" I hadn't seen any other teenagers since we walked in.

"They're in Group," Mr. Robins said. "You probably didn't get much of a chance to read over our materials, did you?"

Between my involuntary commitment and finding the mutilated cat? "No."

"Well, it's not a problem, not a problem at all. We'll get you up to speed in no time. Just follow me, and I'll get you all set up." He glanced over his shoulder. "You're a psychologist, Dr. Dyer?"

"Yes," she said as we followed him down the strangely claustrophobic hall. The ceiling yawned over us, but the spaces we walked through felt tight.

"What's your specialty?"

"I work with couples, mostly."

"That's wonderful!" He skipped right over asking my father the same question. I imagined he already knew—anyone who watched the news probably did.

Mr. Robins finally ushered my parents into an office in the back, which clearly wasn't his. A stack of papers towered precariously on the glass desk.

He indicated a bench just outside the door. "All right, Mara, you can have a seat out here while I talk some things over with your parents, okay?" He winked.

If I hadn't been freaked out, I would have rolled my eyes at the condescension. Maybe I wouldn't have to deal with him much, after today. A girl could hope.

The door to the office closed with my parents inside then, and I sat on the horribly uncomfortable plank of wood across from it. There wasn't much to see, and I found myself idly staring at the ductwork in the exposed ceiling when something soft hit me in the shoulder, then bounced to the floor.

I flinched—it was that sort of morning—but it was just a crumbled piece of paper. I opened it to find a crudely drawn picture of an owl, with a speech bubble that said:

!!!

I whipped around.

"Well, schmear my bagel, if it isn't Mara Dyer."

12

JAMIE.

Minus the dreadlocks and taller, but definitely, unmistakably Jamie. I smiled so widely my face hurt; I jumped up to hug him but he raised his hands defensively before I could.

"Can't touch this."

"Don't be an ass," I said, still beaming.

Jamie's expression mimicked mine, though he appeared to be trying not to show it. "I'm serious. They're strict about that," he said, giving me a once-over.

I did the same. Without his long hair, Jamie's cheekbones seemed higher, his face more angular. Older. His jeans were uncharacteristically well-fitted and his T-shirt clung to his frame. On his shirt was an image of what appeared to be ancient Greek men linking arms in a row and kicking their legs like Rockettes. He was so strange.

At the exact same time we both asked: "What are you doing here?"

"Ladies first," Jamie said with a little bow.

I looked up at the ceiling as I thought about what to say. "PTSD," I decided finally. "A few hallucinations here and there. Nothing to write home about. You?"

"Oh, my parents were persuaded that it would be a wise preemptive measure to send me here before I shot up a school." He dropped onto the bench.

My mouth fell open. "You're not serious."

"Unfortunately, I am. Our best Croydian friends made sure that's what the all-knowing adults would think when they planted that knife in my backpack."

Anna and Aiden, those assholes. At least I'd no longer have to see them on a daily basis. Lucky me.

Lucky them.

I sat back down on the bench and Jamie went on. "Unable to comprehend the idea that my earlier threat to give Aiden Ebola was made in jest," he said, "I was considered a two-time offender and was therefore labeled 'at risk' by the guidance department, those ultimate arbiters of wisdom. They in turn scrawled that all over my record." His mocking tone changed, then. "Words have power. And I may be privileged and have a higher IQ than any of our former teachers, but when people look at me? They see a black, male teenager. And there is nothing quite as frightening to some folks as an angry young black man." He popped a piece of gum into his mouth. "So. Here I am."

I offered a small smile. "At least we're together?"

He grinned. "So it seems."

My eyes rested on his shorn head. "What happened to your hair?"

"Ah." He ran a hand over it. "Once overanxious parents are told that their child is 'at-risk', they decide that all 'at-risk' attributes have to go. Good-bye, long hair. Good-bye, rebellious music. Good-bye, delightfully violent video games." He exaggerated a lip quiver. "Basically, I'm allowed to play chess and listen to smooth jazz. That is my life now."

I shook my head. "I hate people."

He nudged me with his elbow. "That's why we're friends." Jamie blew a small turquoise bubble and then sucked it back into his mouth. "I actually saw Anna last week when my mom dragged me to Whole Foods. She didn't even recognize me."

"Did you say anything to her?"

"I politely suggested she drive off a cliff."

I grinned. I felt lighter just being with him, and I was so glad to not have to endure this ridiculousness alone. I was about to tell him so when the office door opened in front of us and Mr. Robins peered out.

He looked back and forth between Jamie and me. "We're ready for you, Mara."

Jamie stood. "And I'm going to be late for electroshock therapy!" Then he faced me and said with a wink, "See you 'round, Mara Dyer." He saluted Mr. Robins, turned on his heel, and left.

I bit my lip to keep from smiling and entered the office appropriately somber.

"Have a seat," Mr. Robins said, closing the door behind me.

I slid into an uncomfortable plastic chair next to my parents and waited to hear the proclamation of my sentence.

"I just want to explain a few things and then we'll have you sign some paperwork."

"Okay . . ."

"The Horizons Outpatient Program, or HOP, as I like to call it, is part of an overall behavioral evaluation that your parents are enrolling you in. You will be expected to be here five days a week, from nine a.m. until three p.m. without fail, barring an excused absence accompanied by a doctor's note. Your success here will depend entirely on your participation in your activities and in group therapy, and—"

"And academics?" I wasn't a Daniel-level student, no, but there had never been a future for me that didn't include college. I didn't like thinking about how my adventures in psychotherapy would affect it.

"You'll be completing coursework under the guidance of

tutors, but the emphasis at Horizons, Mara, is not on academic achievement but on *personal* achievement."

Can't wait.

"As I was saying, your participation is integral to your success. After a period of two weeks, there will be a reassessment to determine whether this is the right place for you, or whether it would be prudent to move you to our residential treatment facility."

So this was a test, then. To see whether I could make it here in the real world without any . . . problems. I looked up at my parents' hopeful faces as the word *residential* echoed in my mind.

It was a test I needed to pass.

13

When Mr. Robins finished his lecture, he held out a pen.

My parents had explained this part to me—the "informed consent." I had to agree; Horizons required it. And I didn't mind the idea in the abstract, but sitting here in this weird place on this hard little chair staring at that pen, I hesitated. After a few uncomfortable seconds, I forced myself to take it and signed my name.

"Well!" Mr. Robins said, clapping his hands together. "Now that that's settled, I've set you up for a tour with Phoebe Reynard, another student at Horizons. Yes," he said, nodding meaningfully, "everyone is a *student* here. A student of *life*."

Oh, God.

"Each of you is assigned to a buddy, and Phoebe will be yours. That means she'll be your partner for most of your exercises. Not so different from a normal school, right?"

Sure.

"She should be along any minute. In the meantime, did you bring a bag with you today?"

I had, in fact. I toted my school bag along with me out of habit, even though this definitely wasn't school. I nodded at Mr. Robins.

"Can I see it?"

I handed it over.

"It will have to be thoroughly checked every time you enter the front door. Everything you bring in has to be cataloged, and contraband removed."

"Contraband like . . ."

"Drugs, cigarettes, alcohol, cell phones, laptops. We do allow portable music players, as long as they don't have Internet access. So your iPod," he said, nodding at the earbuds dangling out of the kangaroo pocket of my hoodie, "should be fine. I'll get your bag checked and make sure it gets back to you ASAP," he said with a toothy grin. "Got anything else in your pockets, Mara?"

I blinked. "Um, string or nothing?"

"Excuse me?"

I raised my eyebrows. "*The Hobbit?*"

He looked concerned. "A what?"

"It's a book," my father piped up. He met my gaze and winked.

Mr. Robins looked from my father to me. "You have a book in your pocket?"

I tried very hard not to sigh. "There's nothing in my pockets, is what I meant."

"Oh," he said. "Well then, you won't mind emptying them."

It wasn't a request. That would take some getting used to. I emptied my pockets to find some change, a packet of sugar, a receipt, and of course, my iPod. "That's it," I said with a shrug.

"Great!" He indicated that I could take everything back.

Just as I finished, a tall girl with lank, dyed black hair peeked in through the doorway. "Mr. Robins?"

"Ah, Phoebe. Phoebe Reynard, meet Mara Dyer, your new buddy."

I extended my hand. The girl eyed me warily, her eyes deep set in her wide moon face. She had a perfect ski slope nose that didn't quite match the rest of her features; it seemed lost, like it had wandered onto the wrong face.

After inspecting me for what felt like an hour, Phoebe took my hand and gave it a limp, sweaty shake, then dropped it like I was on fire.

Awkward. Phoebe's eyes darted back to Mr. Robins.

"All right, I'm going to send you two off," he said, "while I speak to your parents for a bit, Mara, and introduce them to some of the staff. Phoebe—you know what to do."

Phoebe nodded, then walked out without a word. I gave my parents a low thumbs-up and then followed Phoebe out.

She led me down a different hallway that was sparsely decorated with unironic motivational posters. I kept waiting for her to say something as we passed different partitions within the space, but she never did. Awesome tour.

"So . . ." I started. How to break the ice? "Um, how are you?"

She stopped short and faced me. "What did they tell you?"

Oh, boy. "Nothing," I said slowly. "I was just making conversation."

Phoebe glared at me. Continued to glare at me. But just as I was about to scurry back to my parents, Jamie reappeared. He stood at attention.

"I've come to rescue you," he announced.

"You're not supposed to be here," Phoebe mumbled.

"Now, now, don't be testy, Phoebe." His eyes never left her, but his next words were for me. "Has Sam come back for you yet?"

"Nope," I said.

"Then you have the next ten minutes free. Want to make them count?"

I looked over at Phoebe; she was ignoring both of us. Her lips moved, but no sound came out.

"Is that a rhetorical question?" I asked him.

Jamie grinned. "Would you like to join us, Phoebe?"

"I'm busy."

His brows drew together. "With what, pray tell?"

Phoebe didn't answer. Instead, she sank down to the floor and stretched out like a plank. I found this to be highly alarming, but Jamie just shrugged.

"There's no point," he said to me. Then, "Don't forget Group, Phoebe," before we headed out.

"So where are we going?" I asked him.

"Does it matter?"

I followed him into an open area with sleek white leather couches. He swept his hand in front of him. "The common room. Where we share our *feelings*."

I sank onto a couch. I remembered meeting Jamie on my first day at Croyden; it wasn't that long ago but it might as well have been a million years. He decoded the social hierarchy, he showed me around. I was lucky he was here.

"What's with the face?" he asked.

"Was I making one?"

"You were looking all wistful-like."

"Just a touch of déjà vu."

Jamie nodded slowly. "I know. It's like we just did this."

I smiled, and looked at his bizarre T-shirt again. I tilted my head at the image of the ancient Greek Rockettes. "What is it?"

He looked down and stretched the picture out. "Oh. A Greek chorus."

"Ah."

He leaned back against the leather couch and flashed a grin. "Don't worry, nobody gets it."

"Mmm." I cocked my head to the side, considering him. "It's weird that we're both here, right?"

A noncommittal shrug.

"Well, of all the behavioral modification programs in all of Florida, I'm glad I walked into yours," I said with a smile. Then flashed a knowing look. "Must be fate."

Jamie stroked his chin. "A nice thought, but there aren't *that* many. Not as swank as this, anyway." He gestured to the sleekly blank room. "This is where the privileged send their screwed-up progeny; no gluing macaroni to construction paper for us." He paused meaningfully. "They only let us *create* with *ricciolini* here."

"I don't even know what that is."

"It's very fancy, I assure you."

"I'll take your word for it," I said as teenagers began to file into the room. Jamie added a comment under his breath with each one. "Phoebe's the psycho," he said, when she walked in. "Tara's the klepto, Adam's the sadist, and Megan's the 'phobe."

I raised an eyebrow. "And you?"

He pretended to ponder my question. "The wise fool," he finally said.

"That's not a diagnosis."

"So you say."

"And me?" I asked.

Jamie tilted his head, considering me. "I haven't figured out your fatal flaw yet."

"Let me know when you do," I said, not entirely kidding. "What about everyone else?"

He shrugged. "Depression, anxiety, eating disorders. Nothing fancy. Like Stella," he added, nodding in the direction of a girl with strong features and curly black hair. "She could almost pass for normal."

"Almost?" I asked as I heard my name called behind me.

"There you are!" Mr. Robins said. He approached with my parents and Dr. Kells in tow, who was as expensively and impeccably dressed as ever. "Mara, you've met Dr. Kells," he said. "She's the director of clinical psychology here."

She smiled. Her matte makeup made the lines around her mouth seem deeper. "It's good to see you again."

Not exactly. "Nice to see you, too."

Mr. Robins handed me back my messenger bag. "All clear," he said as I slung it over my shoulder. His gaze circled the room. "So, did Phoebe show you around?"

Before or after she spread out on the floor? "Yeah," I lied. "Very helpful."

"And you've met Jamie," Mr. Robins said, his eyes resting on my friend. Who had promptly abandoned our couch for an armchair on the far side of the room.

"We knew each other at Croyden," I said.

"Ah. What a coincidence!"

My mother leaned down to brush a strand of hair from my face. "I have to get to work, sweetheart."

"And you have to get to Group," Dr. Kells said to me with a smile. "I'm looking forward to getting the chance to know you better."

That made one of us.

My parents hugged me good-bye, Mr. Robins made his excuses, and Dr. Kells said, "I'm really happy to have you here," once more before she left. I forced a smile in answer, and then faced my peers alone.

There were fourteen of us, some draped on couches, some settled in armchairs, some seated on the floor. I settled into a chair and dropped my bag at my feet. A freckled, grinning woman bedecked in a bronze headscarf with horn-rimmed glasses and a multilayered long skirt was perched on the arm of one of the sofas. She clapped her hands with authority and the bangles on her wrist clinked.

"Are we ready to get started?" the New Agey counselor asked.

"Yes," everyone mumbled back.

"Great! Today we have someone very special with us," she said, beaming in my direction. "Would you introduce yourself to the group?"

I raised my arm in an awkward half-wave thing. "I'm Mara Dyer."

"Hi, Mara," the chorus replied. Just like in the movies.

"We're so glad you're here, Mara. I'm Brooke. Now, just to get to know you a little better, I'd love for you to tell us where you're from, how old you are, and one special, secret wish of yours. We'll all go around the room and share after you. Sound good?"

Phenomenal. "I'm from a city outside Providence." I was met with thirteen glazed stares. "Rhode Island," I clarified. "I'm seventeen," I added, "And I wish I didn't have to be here," I finished. I couldn't resist.

My secret wish earned a chuckle from Jamie but he was the only one who shared my sense of humor, it seemed. No one else even cracked a smile. Oh well.

"We understand how you feel, Mara," Brooke said. "It's a big adjustment. Now then, let's move clockwise." She pointed to a boy sitting in an armchair to my left. He began to speak but I didn't hear what he said, because Phoebe slid into the seat next to me and I was distracted by the smell of her breath in my face. She slipped a folded piece of paper into my lap.

A love letter, perhaps? Could I be so lucky? I opened it.

Not a love letter. Not a letter at all. The piece of paper was a picture of me, lying in my bed. In the pajamas I wore last night. I faced the camera, but you couldn't see my eyes.

They'd been scratched out.

14

I WENT SLACK WITH FEAR, AS IF I WERE A PUPPET AND Phoebe had cut my strings.

"It fell out of your bag," she whispered.

I stared blankly at the picture until I heard my name called. I shoved it in my pocket and asked to use the bathroom. Brooke nodded. I grabbed my bag and fled.

Once inside, I hid in a stall and rifled through it. I took out an old paperback I'd found in the garage and decided to read—one of my father's, I think, from college—along with the sketchbook I hadn't been in the mood to draw in and a few charcoal sticks and pens.

And my digital camera. The one my parents gave me for

my birthday. I didn't remember putting that in my bag at all.

My pulse raced as I withdrew the picture from my back pocket and stared at it. I turned on the camera, pressed the menu button, and waited.

The last picture taken appeared on the screen. It was the same photo in my hand.

The picture before that was also of me asleep, in the same clothes I wore last night, my body in a different position. And the picture before that. And the picture before that.

There were four of them altogether.

Horror weakened my knees but I braced myself against the stall. I had to keep standing. I had to see if there was something, anything, any way I could prove that Jude took the pictures, that he was alive and in my room and watching me sleep. I thumbed through the camera's features as I forced myself to breathe.

The camera had a timer.

My bag had been searched; whoever checked it would have seen the printed picture, but to them, that's all it would look like. Just a picture of me asleep. They might think I scratched my eyes out myself.

And if I showed the digital camera to them, or to my parents, they might think that I took all of the pictures myself; that I used the camera's timer to set up the shots. The *why* didn't matter; I just came back from an involuntary stay at a psych unit. *Why* would never matter again.

I stifled the screams I wanted to yell but couldn't. I put the camera and the picture back in my bag. I went back to the common room and it was all I could do to sit still. Phoebe the psycho stared at me the whole time.

I ignored her. I detached. I was being tested, Mr. Robins said, evaluated to see if I could hack it in the outpatient world, and I needed to prove that I could.

So when the session finally ended, I seized on Jamie—I needed the distraction.

"Do you miss Croyden?" I asked, my voice falsely light.

"Sure. Particularly when they make us do positive self-talk with *Chariots of Fire* blasting in the background."

Thank you, Jamie. "Tell me you're kidding?"

"I wish. At least the food's good," he said, as we lined up for lunch.

I was about to ask what we were having when a piercing scream sounded from the front of the line. I was already on edge and that nearly sent me over. I watched, frozen, as a blond girl with a delicate doll face separated herself from the group.

"Megan," Jamie said in my ear. "The poor kid's afraid of everything. This happens a lot."

Megan was now backed up against the opposite wall, pointing at something.

A large, cartoonishly handsome "student" was walking in the direction of her extended forefinger. He crouched down low, just as I rose up on my toes to try and see.

"It's a ring snake," he called out. He lifted it with both hands.

I exhaled. No big—

Megan screamed again as the boy ripped the snake apart.

I was paralyzed for a second, not quite believing what I'd seen. The cat last night, and now this—anger rushed in and I seized it. It was better than fear. I couldn't do anything about the cat, but I could do something about this.

I pushed past the people in line as the boy, who more accurately resembled a Cro-Magnon man, dropped the mangled pieces on the white carpet with a satisfied look.

He towered over me but I looked him in the eye. "What is *wrong* with you?"

"You seem upset," he said evenly. "It's just a snake."

"And you're just a douchebag."

Jamie appeared by my side and looked down at the mess. "I see you've met Adam, our resident sadist."

Adam pushed Jamie into the wall with one arm. "At least I'm not the resident fag."

There was cheering and chanting of the "Fight! Fight! Fight!" variety, which mingled with a counselor's high, hoarse voice shouting, "Break it up!"

But Jamie wasn't remotely fazed. He was smiling, actually, and stared directly at Adam, who had pinned him against the wall. "Hit me," he said. His voice was low. Compelling.

And Adam looked all too happy to oblige. He pulled back

his fist, but a heavyset counselor in a wrinkled, too-tight dress shirt reached him first and wrestled his arms back. The veins in Adam's arms and neck bulged, making the tattoos on his forearms appear to twitch. He had a short, military buzz cut and his scalp was completely red beneath it. It was kind of comical, honestly.

"Wayne," Brooke said, waving to the counselor, "help Adam calm down. Jamie, you and I are going to discuss this later."

"Discuss what?" Jamie asked innocently. "I wasn't doing anything."

Another adult, a guy with a ponytail, said to Brooke, "He instigated it."

Jamie turned to him. "I did not instigate anything, dear Patrick. I was calmly but indignantly standing here as Adam needlessly ended a reptilian life."

"Two o'clock," Brooke said sharply. "You'll miss drama therapy."

"Shucks."

I snorted. People whispered around us, stealing looks. Jamie seemed to enjoy it.

"That was ballsy," I said to him as we moved up in line.

"Which part?"

"The part where you acted like you wanted him to hit you."

Jamie looked thoughtful. "I think I actually did. Funny thing: It's like coming here has made me *more* combative."

"Hmm," I murmured.

"What?"

"You just made me think of something my dad sometimes says."

He raised his eyebrows in question.

"Put a petty criminal in maximum security prison and he'll come out knowing how to rape and pillage."

"Precisely," Jamie said, nodding. "My urge to hit things is directly proportional to the cheeriness of the staff. And I find everything ultra-annoying lately. And everyone." As we neared the end of the line, I watched Wayne hand little paper cups to each of our peers in front of us. I glanced at Jamie.

"Meds first, then food," he explained.

"For all of us?"

"Part of the package," Jamie said as the line moved forward. "Drug therapy in conjunction with talk therapy, yadda yadda yadda." And then it was his turn. He took two little paper Dixie cups from the counselor, the one who broke up the almost-fight.

"Hi, Wayne," Jamie said cheerfully.

"Hello, Jamie."

"Bottoms up." Jamie tossed the contents of one cup back, then the other.

Wayne glanced at me then. "You're next."

"I'm new—"

"Mara Dyer," he said, handing me two cups. I peered into them. One was filled with water, the other with pills. Unfamiliar pills; I recognized only one.

"What are these?" I asked him.

"Your meds."

"But I'm not on all of these."

"You can talk to Dr. Kells about that later, but for now, you gotta take 'em."

I narrowed my eyes at him.

"Rules are rules," he said, shrugging. "Go on, now."

I tossed them back and swallowed.

"Open your mouth," he said.

I did as I was told.

"Good work."

Do I get a gold star? I didn't say it, but I wished I had. Instead, I trudged after Jamie and we ate together. Miraculously, I even laughed.

Just as I was beginning to think this place might not be so terrible, Dr. Kells appeared in the corner of the room and called my name.

"Good luck," Jamie said as I rose from our table.

But I didn't need luck. Despite my bad night and worse morning, I knew the script well. I could pull this off.

As I left the dining room, though, fingers tightened around my wrist and pulled me into a niche. My eyes followed them up to Phoebe's face. I glanced behind me; we were out of view.

"You're welcome," she said tonelessly.

I wrenched my arm away. "For what?"

Phoebe's face was a blank mask. "For fixing your eyes."

15

So Phoebe the psycho scratched my eyes out. Not Jude.

I was relieved and angry at once. Jude took the pictures and made sure I found them today, and that was terrifying and awful, yes.

But I was glad he hadn't scratched out my eyes. I didn't know quite why, but I was.

Phoebe drifted away before I could say anything else. I took a deep breath and followed Dr. Kells down the long corridor, but it felt like the walls were closing in. Phoebe had unbalanced me, and I had to get control.

After what seemed like a ten-mile walk, I reached an

open door near the end of the hall. Dr. Kells had already gone inside.

The room was white like all the others, and the only furniture in it was a blond wood desk and two white chairs dwarfed by the open space. Dr. Kells stood behind the desk, and a man was by her side.

She smiled at me and gestured to one of the chairs. I obediently went to sit but almost missed it. Weird.

"How did your tour go?" she asked me.

"Fine," I lied again.

"Wonderful. I'd like to introduce you to Dr. Vargas." The man next to her smiled. He was young—in his twenties, probably, with curly hair and glasses. He looked sort of like Daniel, actually.

"Dr. Vargas is a neuropsychologist. He works with some of our students who have suffered from head trauma and other acute illnesses that are causing them problems."

"Nice to meet you," I said.

"You too." Still grinning, he moved behind me toward the door. "Thank you, Dr. Kells."

"My pleasure."

He closed the door, and then she and I were alone. Dr. Kells rose from behind her desk and sat in the chair next to me. She smiled. She didn't have a pen or paper or anything with her. She just . . . watched.

The air felt heavy and my thoughts became slow as seconds

stretched into minutes. Or maybe they didn't; time was elastic in the giant empty room. My eyes darted around, searching for a clock, but there didn't seem to be one.

"So," Dr. Kells finally said. "I think we should begin by talking about why you're here."

Showtime. I reached into my memory to recall the symptoms of PTSD to make sure whatever I divulged mimicked *that* diagnosis and not schizophrenia. Or worse.

"I'm here," I said carefully, "because I survived a trauma. My best friend died." Meaningful pause. "It's been really hard for me, and I keep thinking about it. I've had hallucinations. And flashbacks." I stopped. Would that be enough?

"That's why your family moved to Florida," Dr. Kells said.

Yes. "Right."

"But that's not why you're here in this program."

I swallowed. "I guess I'm still not over it." I tried to sound innocent, but I just sounded nervous.

She nodded. "No one expects you to be. But what I'm asking is whether or not you understand why you're *here*. Now."

Ah. She wanted to hear about Jude—that I believed he was alive. I had to answer her, but it was a dangerous tightrope to walk. If I spoke too carefully, she'd realize that I was manipulating her. But if I spoke too candidly, she could decide that I was crazier than I actually was.

So I said, "My father was shot. I—I thought he might die. And I freaked out. I went to the police station and just started screaming. I wasn't—I didn't feel like myself. It's been a lot to deal with." My stomach churned. I hoped she'd move on.

She didn't. "At the police station, you mentioned your boyfriend. Jude."

I hated hearing his name. "Ex," I said.

"What?"

"Ex-boyfriend."

"Ex-boyfriend," she repeated, giving me that same look I'd seen on Dr. West's face a few days ago. "You mentioned your ex-boyfriend, Jude. You said that he's here."

The words *FOR CLAIRE* appeared in red on the white wall behind Dr. Kells's head. I felt a jolt of terror before I blinked them away.

"The information in your file says that your boyfriend, Jude—ex-boyfriend, I'm sorry—and your friends Rachel and Claire died in the collapse of the Tamerlane State Lunatic Asylum in Rhode Island."

"Yes." My voice was a whisper.

"But you said that Jude's here," she repeated.

I said nothing.

"Have you seen him since that night, Mara?"

I was stone. I modulated my voice. "That would be impossible."

Dr. Kells rested her elbow on her desk and her chin in her hand. She looked at me with sympathy. "Do you want to know what I think?"

Dazzle me. "I can't imagine."

"I think that you feel guilty about your best friend's death. About your boyfriend's death."

"Ex!" I screamed. Shit.

Dr. Kells didn't flinch. Her voice was calm. "Did something happen with you and Jude, Mara?"

I was breathing hard but I hadn't realized it. I closed my eyes. *Control yourself.*

"Please tell me the truth," she said softly.

"What does it matter?" A tear rolled down my cheek. Damn it.

"It's going to be so much harder to help you otherwise. And I really do want to help you."

I was silent.

"You know," Dr. Kells said, leaning back in her seat. "Some teens have been in this program for years; they started here and then moved to our residential center, and they've been there ever since. But I don't think you need that. I think this is just a way station for you. To help you get back to where you're supposed to be. You've been derailed by everything that's happened in the past six months—and that's *understandable.* You survived a catastrophic accident."

Not an accident.

"Your best friend died."

I killed her.

"You moved."

To try and forget what I did.

"Your teacher died."

Because I wanted her to.

"Your father was shot."

Because I forced someone's hand.

"That's more trauma than most people are faced with in a lifetime, and you've experienced it within six months. And I think it will help you to talk about it with me. I know you've seen other therapists before—"

Ones I liked better.

"But you're here now, and I think that even though you don't *want* to be here, you might find that it isn't a waste of your time."

The tears were flowing steadily now. "What do you want me to say?"

"What happened with Jude?"

My throat felt raw, and my nose itched from crying. "He—kissed me. When I didn't want him to."

"When?"

"That night. The night he—"

Died, I almost said. But he didn't die. He was still alive.

"Did he do anything else?"

"He tried to." And so I told Dr. Kells about that night, and what Jude tried to do.

"Did he rape you?" she asked.

I shook my head fiercely. "No."

"How far did it go?"

My face flooded with heat. "He pushed me against the wall but . . ."

"But what?"

But I stopped him. "The building collapsed before anything else happened."

Dr. Kells cocked her head to one side. "And he died, and you lived."

I said nothing.

She leaned forward just slightly. "Does Jude ever tell you to do things you don't want to do, Mara?"

I wanted to shake her. She thought he was some imaginary devil sitting on my shoulder, whispering evil thoughts in my ear.

"Do you think Jude is alive?" she asked again.

I wanted to take her by the collar of her perfectly pressed silk blouse and scream, "He *is* alive!" in her face. It took a mammoth force of will just to say the word, "No."

Dr. Kells sighed. "Mara, when you lie, I have to adjust your course of treatment for that. I don't want to have to treat you like you're a pathological liar. I want to be able to trust you."

She wouldn't trust me if I told her the truth, but at the moment, I wasn't convincingly lying. "I don't think he's alive," I said, steadily. "I know he isn't. But sometimes . . ."

"Sometimes . . ."

"Sometimes it scares me, you know?" I hedged. "The idea

that he might be? Like a monster hiding in my closet, or under the bed." There. Maybe that would give her what she wanted without making me sound like too much of a lunatic.

She nodded her head. "I understand completely. I think your fear makes sense, and it's something I'd like to work on during your time here."

I exhaled with relief. "Me too," I lied again.

"Let's say, hypothetically, that Jude didn't die in the asylum."

I didn't mean I wanted to work on it *today*. "Okay . . ."

"Let's say he's in Florida."

"Okay . . ."

"What do you think he'd be doing here? What's your fear?"

I was in dangerous territory, but I didn't know how to evade the question. "That he's—that he would be stalking me." Which he was.

"Why would he want to come all the way to Florida just to stalk you?"

The mutilated cat. The words on my mirror, written in blood. The pictures. My pulse spiked when I thought of them. "To make me afraid," I said.

"Why would he want that?"

Because I tried to kill him. Because I killed his sister.

Those were the answers that came to mind, but of course I couldn't voice them. I shook my head instead and asked, "Why would he assault me in the first place?"

"Those questions are different, Mara. Rapists—"

"He didn't rape me."

Dr. Kells stared at me a beat too long.

"He didn't. I—" I stopped him before he had the chance. "He didn't," was all I said. "What were you saying?"

"I was saying that rape is about power, not sex," she began. "It's about using force or the threat of it to take control over another person."

"So maybe, if he were alive, which he isn't, he'd stalk me to show that he can control me. That he can make me afraid." That fit.

Dr. Kells looked at me intently. "You've told me a lot of things, today, Mara. And I'm going to be thinking about them for a while. But if you're interested, I can tell you what I'm thinking right now."

I was about as excited for her insight as I would be for an enema. "Sure."

"When you were at the police station," she said, "you told the detective that you killed Claire and Rachel."

Here it comes.

"That makes me think that you feel very guilty, very responsible for the death of your best friend. For moving your family to Florida. For everything that has happened to your family since. I think that you've experienced two traumas—the sexual assault by Jude, and then the collapse—and I think that, in some way, it makes you feel more powerful to imagine that *you* stopped Jude from doing what you thought he was going to try to do. And that for every negative event or coincidence that has happened since, imagining that you triggered them, that you made them happen makes you feel like you possess a degree of control that you don't have. But subconsciously, you believe that you *don't* have control; and that's manifesting in your fear that Jude is actually alive."

I wasn't sure how I would manage staying sane while I was constantly being told that I was crazy. "That's really interesting," I said slowly.

"Can I ask you something, Mara?"

Do I have a choice? "Sure."

"What do you want?"

I tilted my head. "Right now?"

"No. In general."

"I want . . . I want." I tried to think. What *did* I want?

To go back? To when my biggest problem was that Claire was trying to steal my best friend? To rewind to before I even *met* Claire? And Jude?

But that was also before Noah.

I saw him in my mind, kneeling at my feet. Tying my shoelaces. Looking up at me with those blue eyes, flashing that half-smile I loved so much.

I wouldn't want to go back to before him. I didn't want to lose him. I just wanted—

"To be better," I said finally. For my family. For Noah. For myself. I wanted to worry about things like early admission, not involuntary commitment. I would never be normal but maybe I could figure out how to live a somewhat normal life.

"I'm so glad to hear you say that," Dr. Kells said, and stood up. "We can help you be better, but you have to want it, or there's nothing we can do."

I nodded and tried to stand too, but stumbled. I tried to lean against the desk to steady myself, but my synapses were slow, and I just hunched.

Dr. Kells rested a hand on my back. "Are you feeling ill?"

I heard an echo of her words—in someone else's voice.

In my mind.

I blinked. Dr. Kells's eyes were full of concern. I managed to nod but the movement blurred my thoughts. What was wrong with me?

"What's the matter?" Dr. Kells asked. She looked at me curiously and I felt strange. Like she was waiting for something to happen.

I felt paranoid. Suspicious.

As I tried to speak, she shifted out of focus.

"Water?" she asked, and I heard an echo again, from far away.

I must have nodded because Dr. Kells helped me sit and said she'd be right back. I heard the door open behind me, then close.

And then I blacked out.

16

BEFORE

Calcutta, India

I RESTED MY CHEEK AGAINST THE OPENING OF THE carriage and peeked out from behind the curtain at the creamy wax blossoms that sprouted from the trees and the thick green growth that clung to their trunks. Creepers hung from the branches above us, low enough for me to touch, but I did not care to. I knew that world, the green world of moss-covered rocks and glistening leaves, the jewel colored world of jungle flowers and sunsets. It no longer interested me. It was the tiny world of this carriage that was fascinating and new.

"Are you feeling ill?"

I heard the white man's words, the question in them, but I did not understand their meaning. His voice was weak from deep within the carriage. I did not care to look at his face.

The carriage jerked, and my small fingers sank deep into the plush seat. *Velvet,* the man said when I first ran my fingers over it in wonder. I had never felt anything so soft; it did not exist in the world of fur and skin.

We moved at a slow pace, much slower than the elephants, and we crept forward relentlessly, for several days and nights. Eventually the wet forest gave way to dry earth and the green gave way to brown and black. The sharp smell of smoke filled the air, mingling with the scent of sandalwood in the carriage.

The horses slowed, and I peeked outside again. I was shocked by what I saw.

Huge, still beasts—larger than any I had ever seen—rose from the water. Their skinny trunks stretched up to the sky and they swarmed with men though they themselves did not move. There were noises I had never heard, foreign and strange. The taste of spices coated my tongue, and my nostrils filled with the scent of wet earth.

The white man reached up to point out at the large beasts. "Ships," he said, and then dropped his trembling arm. His muscles were slack and weak, and he sank back into the shadows, his breathing heavy.

Then we stopped. The door to the carriage opened, and a kind-faced man in bright blue clothing held his arm out to me.

"Come," he said to me, in a language I understood. His voice felt like sun-warmed water. I was not afraid of him, so

I went. I waited for the white man to follow behind me as he had when we left the carriage on our journey, but he did not. He did shift toward the door, though his face was still in shadow. He held out a small black pouch to the man in blue, his arm shaking with the effort.

"Return here on the last day of each week and my clerk will fill it, so long as the girl is with you."

The Man in Blue took the pouch and bowed his head. "The Raj is generous."

The white man laughed. The sound was weak. "The East India Company is generous." He beckoned me back to the carriage. I moved closer. The white man gestured for me to open my hand.

I did. He placed something cold and gleaming into it. I was repulsed by the dry texture of his skin.

"Let her buy something pretty," he said to the Man in Blue.

"Yes, sir. What is her name?"

"I do not know. My guides have tried to coax her into telling, but she refuses to speak to them."

"Does she understand?"

"She will nod or shake her head in response to questions asked in Hindi and Sanskrit, so I do believe so, yes. She has an intelligent eye. She will take to English quickly, I think."

"She will make a lovely bride."

The white man laughed, stronger this time. "I think my wife would take exception. No, the girl will be my ward."

"When will you return for her?"

"I sail today for London, and business there will keep me occupied for at least six months. But I do hope to return soon after, perhaps with my wife and son." The man coughed.

"Water?"

The white man's coughs grew violent, but he waved his hand.

"Will you be well enough for the journey?"

The white man did not answer until his fit had ended. Then he said, "It is just the River Sickness. I need only clean water and rest."

"Perhaps my wife could make a tincture for you before you go?"

"I shall be fine, thank you. I studied medicine after the Military Seminary at Croydon. Now then, I must be off. Do look after yourself, and her."

The Man in Blue nodded, and the white man withdrew back into the darkness. The door of the carriage closed.

The Man in Blue walked to the front then, to the horses, and spoke to the man seated at the top in his own language. Ours.

"Make for him a mixture of dried garlic, lemon juice, honey, tamarind, and wild turmeric. Have him drink it four times each hour." He then handed the man two shining circles from the black pouch. *The coachman*, the white man had called him. He nodded once and lifted the reins.

"Wait." The Man in Blue held up his hand.

The coachman waited.

"Were you present when they found the girl?"

The coachman's black eyes shifted to mine, then darted away. He shook his head slowly. "No. But my friend, a porter in their group, was." He said nothing more but extended his hand to the Man in Blue, who sighed and placed two more silver discs on the coachman's calloused palm.

The coachman smiled, revealing many missing teeth. His eyes flicked to mine. "I do not like her listening."

The Man in Blue turned to me. "You may go explore," he said, and urged me toward the ships.

Yes, I nodded, and pretended to leave. I made myself flat against the other side of the carriage instead. They could not see me. I waited and listened.

The Man in Blue spoke first. "What did you hear?"

The coachman's voice was low. "They were hunting a tiger a few days' journey from Prayaga. They followed it into the trees on the backs of their elephants, but without warning, the beasts stopped. Nothing could urge them forward—not sweets or sticks. This fool," he said, tapping on the carriage, "insisted they continue on foot, but only three men would accompany him. One was a stranger—the white man's guide, perhaps. Another was the cook. The last was a hunter, the brother of the porter, my friend."

"Go on."

"They followed the tracks of the animal into a sea of tall grass. All hunters know tall grass conceals death, and the brother, the hunter, wanted to turn back. The other man, the stranger, urged them forward, and the white man listened. The cook followed them, but the hunter refused and left alone. He was never seen again."

"What happened?" The Man in Blue sounded curious, not afraid.

"The three men followed the tracks of the tiger for hours, until they vanished in a pool of blood."

"From a recent kill?"

"No," the coachman said. The horses stamped and snorted uneasily. "If it had been a tiger's kill, there would have been tracks leading *out* of the pool of blood. There would have been bones and flesh, skin and hair. But there was nothing. No carcass. No hide. And no flies would touch it. They circled the pool and examined the grass. That was when they saw the footprints. A child's footprints, soaked in blood."

"And they led to this girl?"

"Yes," the coachman said. "She was curled up in the roots of a tree, asleep. And in her fist was a human heart."

17

MY EYES FLEW OPEN. THE VIVID COLORS OF MY nightmare were washed away by whiteness.

I was in bed, staring at a ceiling. But I wasn't in *my* bed; I wasn't at home. My skin was damp with sweat and my heart was racing. I reached for the dream, tried to catch it before it drifted away.

"How are you feeling?"

The last traces of it dissolved with the voice. I let out a slow breath and leaned up on stiff, creaky elbows to see who it belonged to. A man with a brown ponytail edged into my field of vision. I recognized him, but didn't remember his name.

"Who are you?" I asked cautiously.

The man smiled. "I'm Patrick, and you fainted. How are you feeling?" he asked again.

I closed my eyes. I'm feeling sick of feeling sick. "Fine," I said.

Dr. Kells appeared behind Patrick then. "You scared us, Mara. Do you have hypoglycemia?"

My thoughts were still slow but my heart was still racing. "What?"

"Hypoglycemia," she repeated.

"I don't think so." I swung my legs over the side of the hard little bed. I shook my head but that only intensified the ache. "No."

"Okay. The blood work will let us know for sure."

"Blood work?"

She glanced at my arm. A piece of cotton was taped to the crook of my elbow; someone had taken off my hoodie and draped it over the foot of the cot. I pressed my hand against the sensitive skin there and tried not to look freaked out.

"It was an emergency. We were concerned about you," Dr. Kells felt the need to explain. Which meant I apparently *did* look freaked out. "We called your mother—she sent your father here to pick you up early. I'm sure it's nothing, but better safe than sorry."

I stewed in silence until he arrived. He smiled widely when he saw me, but I could tell he was worried. He hunched down.

"How're you feeling?"

Upset that they drew blood. Angry that I fainted. Scared it will happen again, because it happened before.

It happened before a flashback at the art exhibit Noah brought me to, and after a midnight hunt for my brother. It happened after I drank chicken blood in a Santeria shop that no longer seemed to exist. And each time I fainted, the borders of reality blurred, leaving me confused. Disoriented. Unsure of what was real. It made it hard to trust myself, and that was hard to bear.

But of course I couldn't tell my father any of this, and he was waiting for an answer. So I just said, "They drew blood," and left it at that.

"They were scared for you," he said. "And it turns out your blood sugar *was* low. Want to go for ice cream on the way home?"

He looked so hopeful, so I nodded for his benefit.

He cracked a smile. "Fantastic," he said, and helped me up off the cot. I swiped my hoodie and we moved toward the exit; I looked for Jamie on the way out but he was nowhere to be found.

My father leaned over a hutch by the front door and pulled out a thick-handled umbrella from a bin. "Cats and dogs out there," he said, nodding through the glass. Sheets of rain battered the pavement and my dad struggled with the umbrella as he opened the door. I hugged my arms across my chest, staring out at the parking lot from our haven beneath the overhang. I wondered what time it was; the only other car in the lot besides my father's was an old white pickup truck. The rest of the spaces were empty.

My dad made an apologetic face. "I think we're going to have to make a run for it."

"You sure you can run?"

He patted the spot beneath his rib cage. "Fit as a fiddle. Are *you* sure you can run?"

I nodded.

"Otherwise you can have the umbrella."

"I'm good," I said, staring into the rain.

"Okay. On the count of three. One," he started, bending his front knee. "Two . . . Three!"

We dashed out into the deluge. My father tried to hold the umbrella over my head but it was pointless. By the time we threw open our respective car doors, we were soaked.

My dad shook his head, scattering droplets of rain onto the dashboard. He grinned, and it was infectious. Maybe ice cream was a good idea after all.

He started the car and began to pull out of the parking lot. Reflexively, I checked my refection in the side mirror.

My hair was plastered to my face, and I was pale. But I looked okay. Maybe a little thin. A little tired. But normal.

Then my reflection winked. Even though I hadn't.

I pressed the heels of my palms into my eyes. I was seeing

things because I was stressed. Afraid. It wasn't real. I was fine.

I tried to make myself believe it. But when I opened my eyes, a light flashed in the mirror, blinding me.

Just headlights. Just headlights from the car behind us. I twisted in my seat to see, but the rain was so heavy that I couldn't make out anything but the lights.

My father pulled out of the lot and onto the road, and the headlights followed us. Now I could see that they belonged to a truck. A white pickup truck.

The same one from the strip mall parking lot.

I shivered and huddled into my hoodie, then reached out and turned on the heat.

"Cold?"

I nodded.

"That New England blood is thinning out fast," my father said with a smile.

I offered a weak one of my own in return.

"You okay, kid?"

No. I glanced into the fogged glass of the side mirror. The headlights still hovered behind us. I twisted around to see better through the rear window, but I couldn't see who was driving.

The truck followed us onto the highway.

I felt sick. I wiped my clammy forehead with my forearm and squeezed my eyes shut. I had to ask. "Is that the same truck from the parking lot?" I tried not to sound paranoid, but I needed to know if he saw it too.

"Hmm?"

"Behind us."

My father's eyes flicked to the rearview mirror. "What parking lot?"

"At Horizons," I said slowly, through clenched teeth. "The one we left ten minutes ago."

"Dunno." His eyes flicked back to the road. He obviously hadn't noticed, and didn't think it was a particularly big deal.

Maybe it wasn't. Maybe the stress of the pictures, of the interview, triggered the fainting, which triggered my hallucination of a disobedient reflection in the mirror. Maybe the truck behind us was just an ordinary truck.

I checked the side mirror again. I could've sworn the headlights were closer.

Don't think about it. I stared ahead at nothing in particular, listening to the hypnotic, mechanical swoop of the windshield wipers. My father was quiet. He reached to turn on the radio when we heard a squeal of tires.

Our heads jerked up as we were bathed in light. My father spun the steering wheel to the left as the pickup truck behind us swung into the right lane, nearly swiping the rear passenger side.

My father was yelling something. No, telling me something. But I couldn't hear him because when the truck pulled up next to us, my mind blocked out everything but the sight of Jude behind the wheel.

I screamed for my father. He had to look. He had to see. But he was screaming too.

"Hold on!"

He'd lost control of the car. A black wave of panic threatened to pull me down with it as the car spun out beneath us on the rain-slick pavement. The truck cut across several lanes and raced ahead. My heart thundered against my rib cage and I gripped the center console with one hand. Bile rose in my throat—I was going to throw up. We were going to crash. Jude followed us and now we were going to crash—

The second I thought it, we were plunged into silence.

"Asshole!" my father yelled. I glanced over at him—sweat had beaded up on his forehead, the veins in his neck were corded.

That's when I noticed we weren't moving.

We weren't moving.

We didn't crash.

We sat motionless in the far left lane—the carpool lane. Cars veered around us and honked.

"No one knows how to drive in this goddamned city!" He slammed his fist on the dashboard and I jumped.

"I'm sorry," he said quickly. "Mara—Mara?" His voice was brittle with worry. "Are you okay?"

I must have looked awful, because my father's expression morphed from fury to panic. I nodded. I didn't know if I could speak.

My father didn't see him. He didn't see Jude. I was the only one who had.

"Let's get you home," he muttered to himself. He started the car and we crawled the rest of the way. Even the retirees in their powder blue Buicks honked at us. Dad couldn't have cared less.

We pulled into our empty driveway and he rushed to open my door, holding the umbrella above our heads. We hurried to the house, my father fumbling for his key before finally opening the front door.

"I'll make some hot chocolate. Rain check on the ice cream?" he said, with a smile that didn't reach his eyes. He was seriously worried.

I forced myself to speak. "Hot chocolate, yeah." I rubbed my arms as a shudder of rain lashed the giant living room window, startling me.

"And I'll turn off the air—it's freezing in this house."

A fake smile. "Thanks."

He grabbed me then and hugged me so tightly I thought I might break. I managed to hug him back, and when we broke apart he headed for the kitchen and began to make a lot of noise.

I didn't go anywhere. I just stood there in the foyer, rigid. I glanced up at the gilt mirror that hung above the antique walnut console table by the front door. My chest rose and fell rapidly. My nostrils were flared, my lips pale and bloodless.

I was seething. But not with fear.

With fury.

My father could've been hurt. Killed. And this time it wasn't my fault.

It was Jude's.

18

MINUTES OR SECONDS LATER, I PEELED MYSELF away from the mirror and marched to my room. But when I opened my bedroom door, I was highly disturbed to find eyes staring back at me.

A doll sat placidly on my desk, its cloth body leaning against a stack of my old schoolbooks. Her sewn-smile curved happily. Her black eyes were unseeing, but strangely focused in my direction.

It was my grandmother's doll, my mother had told me when I was little. She had left it to me when I was just a baby, but I never played with it. I never named it. I didn't even *like* it; the doll took up residence beneath a rotating assortment of other toys and stuffed animals in my toy chest, and as I grew up, it moved from the toy chest to a neglected corner of my closet, to be obscured by shoes and out-of-season clothes.

But now here she was, sitting on my desk. She didn't move.

I blinked. Of course she didn't move. She was a doll. Dolls don't move.

But she *had* moved, though. Because the last time I saw her, she was packed away in a box, propped against stacks of old pictures and things from my room in Rhode Island. A box I hadn't opened since—

Since the costume party.

I reached back to the memory of that night. I saw myself walk to my closet, preparing to slip off my grandmother's emerald-green dress, only to find an opened cardboard box on my closet floor. I didn't remember taking it down. I didn't remember opening it up.

I rewound the memory. Watched myself walk backward out of the closet, watched my mother's heels fit themselves back on my feet. Watched the water in the bathtub flow backward into the faucet—

The night I saw the doll was the night I was burned.

The skin prickled on the back of my neck. It had been a bad night for me. I was stressed about Anna and felt humiliated by Noah and I raced back even earlier, to when I first arrived home. I saw myself reach out to unlock the front door but—

It swung in before I touched it.

I thought I was hallucinating that night—and I had. I imagined my grandmother's earrings at the bottom of the bathtub when they were in my ears the whole time. I assumed I forgot taking the box down from my closet too.

That was before I knew Jude was alive. If he was in my room last night, he could have been in my room *that* night.

My hands curled into fists. *He* took the box down from my closet. *He* opened it up.

And he wanted me to know it. That he was going through all my things. Watching me as I slept. Polluting my room. Polluting my house.

And when I left it, he chased my father and me back.

I was shivering before, but now I was feverishly hot. I felt out of control, and I couldn't let my father see me like this—he was panicked enough. I bit back my anger and fear and shed my waterlogged clothes, then threw them in the sink. I turned on the shower and inhaled deeply as my bathroom filled with steam. I stepped into the hot water and let it course over my skin, willing my thoughts away with it.

It didn't work.

I tried to remind myself that I wasn't alone in this. That Noah believed me. That he was coming over later and when he did I would tell him everything.

I repeated the words on a loop, hoping they would calm

me. I stayed in the shower until it ran cold. But when I emerged, I looked at my desk to find that the doll was no longer smiling.

It was leering.

My skin crawled as I stood there, wrapped in nothing but a towel, facing off with her as my heart beat wildly in my chest.

No, not her. *It.*

I snatched the doll off my desk. I walked to my closet and stuffed it back in one of my boxes. I knew, I *knew* the doll's expression had not changed. My mind was playing tricks on me because I was stressed and panicked and angry, which was what Jude wanted.

I opened my desk drawer, ripped off a length of scotch tape, and taped the box shut, imprisoning the doll inside. No, not imprisoning. Packing. Packing the doll back inside. And then I dressed and made my way back to my father as if nothing had happened at all, because I had no other choice.

Time was supposed to heal all wounds, but how could it when Jude kept picking the scab?

It was early afternoon and Daniel, Joseph, and my mother had all come home. They talked loudly to one another as my father leaned against the pantry cabinets, holding a cracked mug with both hands.

"Mara!" My mother rushed over and wrapped me in a hug the second she noticed me.

Daniel set down his glass. Our eyes met over my mother's shoulder.

"Thank God you're okay," she whispered. "Thank God."

The hug lasted for an uncomfortably long time and when my mom released me, her eyes were wet. She quickly wiped the tears away and dove for the refrigerator. "What can I get you?"

"I'm okay," I said.

"How about some toast?"

"I'm not so hungry."

"Or cookies?" She held up a package of premade cookie dough.

"Yeah, cookies!" Joseph said.

Daniel made a face that I interpreted to mean: *Say yes.*

I forced a smile. "Cookies would be great."

The second the words left my mouth, Joseph withdrew a cookie sheet from the drawer beneath the oven. Also the tinfoil. He grabbed the package of cookie dough from my mother and preheated the oven before she could get to it.

"How about some tea?" my mother asked, grasping for something, anything to do.

Daniel nodded his head yes, staring at me.

"I would love some," I said, following his cue.

"I made hot chocolate," my dad reminded her.

My mom rubbed her forehead. "Right." She pulled out a mug from the glass-front cabinet and poured the contents of a saucepan into it, then handed it to me.

"Thanks, Mom."

She tucked a strand of her short, straight hair behind her ear. "I'm so glad you're okay."

"Miami has the world's worst drivers," my father muttered.

My mother's lips formed a thin line as she busied herself by making a pot of coffee. My eyes flicked to the kitchen window and searched our backyard through the rain.

I was searching for Jude, I realized with an accompanying sting of shame. He was making me paranoid. And I didn't want to be.

"Hey, Mom?" I asked.

"Hmm?"

"Did you take out my doll?" There *was* a chance that she, not Jude, had moved it, and I had to be sure.

My mother looked up from the coffeepot, confused. "What doll?"

I exhaled through my nose. "The one I've had since I was a baby."

"Oh, Grandma's doll? No, honey. Haven't seen it."

That's not what I'd asked, but I had my answer. She didn't touch it. I knew who did, and this could not go on.

I glanced at the microwave clock, wondering when Noah would get here. I had to behave normally until he did.

"So how was Day One of spring break?" I asked Daniel between sips of hot chocolate. The liquid was warm, but didn't warm me through.

"We went to the Miami Seaquarium."

I almost choked. "What?"

Daniel shrugged a shoulder. "Joseph wanted to see the whale."

"Lolita," I said, setting down my drink.

My father shot my brother a look. "Wait, what?"

"It's the name of the killer whale," Daniel explained.

"How was it?" Mom asked.

Joseph shrugged. "Kind of sad."

"How come?" Dad's forehead creased.

"I felt bad for the animals."

My turn. "Did Noah go with you?" I didn't honestly care. I just wanted to know the answer to my real question without actually having to ask it or call him. Namely, where was he now, and was he coming back?

"Nope, but he'll be over in an hour," Daniel said. "Mom, can he stay for dinner?" He winked at me behind my mother's back.

Thank you, Daniel.

"How come you ask her and not me?" my dad asked.

"Dad, can Noah stay for dinner?"

He cleared his throat. "Doesn't his own family want to spend some time with him?"

Daniel made a face. "I don't think so, actually."

"Who wants cookies?" Mom asked. I caught the look she exchanged with my father as she opened the oven and the smell of heaven filled the kitchen.

My dad sighed. "It's fine with me," he said, and handed me his cell. "Go call him."

I backed slowly out of the kitchen, then raced to my bedroom. I dialed Noah's number.

"Hello?"

His voice was warm and rich and *home* and my eyes closed in relief at the sound of it. "Hi," I said. "I'm supposed to tell you that you're invited for dinner."

"But . . . ?"

"Something happened." I kept my voice low. "How soon can you get here?"

"I'm getting in the car right now."

"Noah?"

"Yes?"

"Plan to spend the night."

19

An hour later, Noah still hadn't shown. I was restless and didn't want to be in my tainted room.

Daniel caught me lurking in the living room, pretending to read one of my parents' books from college I had found in the garage. I was waiting for Noah, but there was no need to be obvious.

"What goes on, little sister?"

"Nothing," I said, staring at the yellowed page.

Daniel walked over to me and took my book in his hands. Flipped it right side up.

Damn.

"You had one heck of a day," he said softly.

"I've had better," I said. "And worse."

"You want to talk about it?"

I did, but I couldn't. Not to him. I shook my head and clenched my teeth to hold back the ache in my throat.

He sat in the squashy black-and-gold-patterned armchair opposite me. "Don't worry about the key, by the way," he said casually.

I looked up from the book. "What key?"

"My house key?" He raised an eyebrow. "The one that was on my key ring you took without permission? The one I asked you about when you were in the . . . while you were away?"

"Your key was missing," I said slowly.

"That is what I've been attempting to communicate, yes. But Dad had it copied today, so no big. Why'd you take it off the ring, though?"

But I wasn't listening to him anymore. I was thinking about the pictures taken with my camera. The doll on my desk, taken from its box. The writing on my mirror.

The doors locked from the inside.

I didn't take Daniel's house key. Jude did. That was how he came and went without breaking in, and he could do it whenever he wanted now. The thought tore at my mind and the horror must have shown on my face because Daniel asked if I was okay.

The way he asked, like all he wanted to do in the world

was help me, nearly broke me down. He was my big brother; he helped me with *everything*, and I so wished I could have his help with this. Daniel was the smartest person I knew—if only I could have his brain on my side.

But then this expression settled over his face. Tentative. Unsure. Like he didn't know what to say to me. Like I was freaking him out.

It snuffed out whatever spark of hope I might have had. "Yeah," I said with a tiny smile. "I don't remember about the key." I shrugged sheepishly. "Sorry."

I *hated* lying to him, but after I did, Daniel visibly relaxed and that made me want to cry. Daniel cocked his head. "Are you sure you don't want to talk?"

No. "Yeah," I said.

"Suit yourself," he said lightly, and returned to his notebook. Then he began to write. Loudly.

And started to hum. I snapped my book shut.

"Am I bothering you?" he asked innocently.

Yes. "Nope."

"Good." He went back to his scribbling, scratching his pencil furiously against the paper, flipping pages of his book with an unparalleled level of noise.

He was clearly not going to let me stew in solitude. I gave up. "What are you writing?"

"A paper."

"About?"

"The self-referential passages in *Don Quixote*."

"You're on spring break."

"It's due next week," he said, then looked up. "And it amuses me."

I rolled my eyes. "Only you would find homework amusing."

"Cervantes comments on the narrative within the narrative itself. I think it's funny."

"Hmm," I said, and reopened my book. Right side up, this time.

"What are you not-reading?" he asked.

I tossed my book over to him in answer.

"*The Private Memoirs and Confessions of a Justified Sinner: Written by Himself,* by James Hogg? Never heard of it."

"That's not something I hear often." And despite everything, it brought a smile to my lips.

"Indeed," he said, studying the book. He turned it over, then started reading the summary on the back. "'Part gothic novel, part psychological mystery, part metafiction, part satire, part case study of totalitarian thought, *Memoirs* explores early psychological theories of double consciousness, blah blah blah, predestination theory, blah blah blah—James Hogg's masterpiece is a psychological study of the power of evil, a terrifying picture of the devil's subtle conquest of a self-righteous man.'" He made a face. "Where'd you find this?"

"In the garage. It looked interesting."

"Yes, you're clearly riveted." He stood up and handed it back to me. "But that's not what you should be reading."

"No?"

"No. Don't move." He disappeared into his bedroom and returned a minute later, carrying a book. He handed it to me.

I made a face as I read the title out loud. *"One Thousand Obscure Words on the SAT?"*

"Better get cracking," my brother said. "They're only a couple of months away."

"Are you serious? I was just pulled out of school."

"Temporarily. For health reasons. Which, by the way, is how Dad got the principal to change your F in Spanish to an Incomplete, so this Horizons thing is not a total loss. You can start your SAT prep now and take them in June, just in case you want to retake in October."

I said nothing. Things like grades and SATs seemed utterly alien compared to my current problems. And I hated that we could talk so easily—so *normally*—about books and school and anything but what was *really* going on with me. I watched my brother write, the words flowing from his pen without hesitation. Give Daniel an abstract problem, and he can solve it in seconds.

Which gave me an idea.

"You know," I said slowly, "there is something I wanted to talk to you about."

He lifted his eyebrows. Put his notebook down.

"Don't move," I told him, then bolted to my room. I grabbed a notebook and a pen off of my desk and ran back to the living room. I couldn't tell my brother about my real problems because my brother didn't believe they *were* real.

But if I told him they *weren't* real, maybe he could actually help.

20

I WALKED BACK INTO THE LIVING ROOM AND GLANCED out the enormous picture window. Still no sign of Noah's car. Good. He'd never go for this.

I sat down on the couch and positioned the spiral notebook conspicuously on my lap. "So," I said to my brother casually, "At Horizons, they gave us this assignment," I started, my lie beginning to develop. "To, uh, fictionalize our . . . problems." That sounded about right. "They said writing is cathartic." Mom's favorite word.

My brother broke into a smile. "That sounds . . . fun?"

I raised my eyebrows.

"Okay, so maybe fun's the wrong word."

"'Stupid' would be more appropriate," I said, adding an eye roll. "They want us to work things out in a safe, creative space. I don't know."

My brother nodded slowly. "It makes sense. Sort of like puppet therapy for little kids."

"I don't know what that is, and I'm glad."

Daniel chuckled. "Mom told me about it once—the therapist uses a puppet to indirectly address the kid's feelings in an impersonal way; the child transfers her feelings to the puppet. Your assignment sounds like the teen version."

Sure. "Exactly. So, now I have to write this story thing about *me* but not me, and I need help."

"It would be my utmost pleasure." Daniel hunched forward and rubbed his hands together. He was into it. "So. What's your premise?"

Where to begin? "Well . . . something weird is happening to this girl. . . ."

Daniel placed his hand in his chin and glanced up at the ceiling. "Fairly standard," he said. "And familiar." He grinned.

"And she doesn't know what it is."

"Okay. Is it something supernatural weird, or something normal weird?"

"Supernatural weird," I said, without hesitation.

"How old is she?"

"A teenager."

"Right, of course," he said with a wink. "Does anyone else know what's happening to her?"

Just Noah, but he was as lost in this as I was. And everyone else I tried to tell didn't believe me. "She's told other people, but no one believes her," I said.

Daniel nodded sagely. "The Cassandra effect. Cursed by Apollo with prophetic visions that always came true, but were never believed by anyone else."

Close enough. "Right."

"So everyone thinks your 'protagonist' is crazy," he said, making air quotes with his fingers.

Everyone does seem to. "Pretty much."

A smile appeared on Daniel's lips. "But *she's* an unreliable narrator who happens to be telling the truth?"

Seems that way. "Yep."

"Okay," he said. "So what's really happening to you—I mean, her?"

"She doesn't know, but she has to find out."

"Why?"

Because she's a murderer. Because she's losing her mind. Because she's being tormented by someone who should be dead.

I studied my brother. His posture was relaxed, his arms draped casually over either side of the patterned black and gold armchair. Daniel would never believe that the things that were happening to me, the things I could do, were *real*—aside from Noah, who would?—but it was important to make sure he thought *I* didn't believe they were real either. I had to make sure he didn't think I believed my own fiction, or I would set off his alarms.

So I lolled my head back and looked at the ceiling. Stay casual, stay vague. "Someone's after her—"

"Your antagonist, good . . ."

"And she's getting worse. She needs to figure out what's going on."

Daniel leaned his chin on his hand and raised his eyebrows. "How about an Obi-Wan slash Gandalf slash Dumbledore slash Giles?"

"Giles?"

Daniel shook his head sadly. "I hate that I never managed to persuade you to watch *Buffy*. It's a flaw in you, Mara."

"Add it to the list."

"Anyway," he went on, "throw in a wise and mysterious character to swoop in and help you—I mean, your heroine—along on her quest, either by offering much-needed guidance or by taking her on as his pupil."

I should be so lucky. "There's no Dumbledore."

"Or go really old-school and pull a Tiresias," he said, nodding to himself. "From *Oedipus*."

I shot him a look. "I know who Tiresias is."

But Daniel ignored me. He was getting excited. "Make him blind but able to 'see' more than she can. I like that."

"Yeah, Daniel, I get it, but there's no mysterious figure."

He waved his hand dismissively. "You just started working on it, Mara. Make one up."

I clenched my teeth.

"Wait a second," Daniel said quickly, rubbing his hands together. "Are you going to make her an orphan?"

"Why?"

"Well, if you don't, you can have her family help," he said and grinned. "You could give her a profoundly insightful and knowledgeable older brother."

If only my profoundly insightful and knowledgeable older brother believed me. "I think that might be a little too transparent," I said, growing frustrated. "It's a creative writing assignment, not a memoir."

"Picky, picky," he said, rolling his eyes. "Write the requisite Google scene, then."

I could see it now: Searching for "kids with powers" would generate about a billion hits about X-Men and derivative novels and movies.

"She wouldn't even know what to Google," I said, and sank back against the couch. This wasn't turning out the way I'd hoped.

Daniel rubbed his chin, squinting. "How about a significant and portentous dream?"

Sure, I'll just snap my fingers. "That's a little . . . passive?"

"That's fair. Is not-Mara a vampire or a creature of some kind but just doesn't know it yet?"

I seriously hope not. "I don't think so . . . she has, like . . . a power."

"Like telepathy?"

"No."

"Telekinesis?"

I don't think so? I shook my head.

"Prophecy?"

"No." I didn't want to tell him what she—what *I* did. "She doesn't know the extent of it yet."

"Have her test it out. Try different things."

"It would be dangerous."

"Hmm . . . like she shoots lasers out of her eyes?"

I smiled wryly. "Something like that."

"So she could be a superhero or supervillain. Hmm." He folded one leg beneath him. "Is it a Peter Parker or a Clark Kent situation?"

"What do you mean?"

"Like, was your character born with this thing *à la* Superman or did she acquire it like Spider-Man?"

An excellent, excellent question—which I didn't know how to answer.

"The weirdness started—"

When? When *did* it start? My seventeenth birthday wasn't when this began—it was just when I remembered what I did.

What I did at the asylum.

So was the asylum the beginning? When Rachel died? When I killed her?

I heard her voice in my mind, then.

"How am I going to die?"

The hair rose on the back of my neck. "She played with a Ouija board."

"BOOM!" Daniel fist-pumped. "Your character is possessed."

My throat tightened. "What?"

"You should have told me earlier, the Ouija board changes everything."

I rubbed my forehead. "I don't understand."

"Ouija boards are a conduit to the spirit world," Daniel explained. "They are always, always bad news. If your protagonist played with one and then weird stuff started happening to her, she's possessed. You've seen *The Exorcist*. You," he said, pointing, "have a horror story on your hands."

I shook my head. "I don't think she's possessed—"

"She's possessed," Daniel said knowingly. "I like it. She'll get way worse before she gets better—*if* she gets better. Lots of conflict, and you can hit all the genre tropes. Good way to deal with the superhero-slash-supervillain issue too." Headlights appeared in our driveway and Daniel stood up.

"What do you mean?" I asked quickly. I needed to hear this.

"If she's a hero, she'll use her powers for good and defeat it. If she's a villain, she'll give in to it. Become it. And whoever the hero is will probably defeat *her*." He tucked his notebook under his arm. "But you should probably go for the hero angle—otherwise your therapists might worry about you—I mean, *her*." He glanced out the window. "Looks like *your* hero has arrived," he said with a smirk just as his phone rang. He held it up to his ear. "Hello?"

"Wait—"

"It's Sophie—I'll help more later, okay?" Daniel turned to leave.

"The girlfriend before the sister?"

Daniel waved and winked, then disappeared into his room.

I stood there, paralyzed, still trying to process everything my brother said when his head popped out from the doorway.

"You should write it in first-person present tense, by the way—then no one will know whether she survives the possession, although that creates a problematic narratological space." He vanished again.

"But she's not possessed," I said loudly.

"Then she's a vampire," my brother called out from his room.

"She's not a vampire!"

"Or a werewolf, those are popular too!"

"SHE'S NOT A WEREWOLF!"

"LOVE YOU!" he shouted, then closed his door.

I watched Noah walk up to our house, his gait languorous despite the rain. I was at the front door before he could even knock, and the second I saw him, I pulled him inside.

He stood there in the foyer, with wet hair curling into his eyes and droplets of rain falling from his soaked T-shirt onto the glossy hardwood floor. "What happened?"

I didn't answer him. I led him into my bedroom instead. Opened my messenger bag and handed him the picture of me, the one Jude took. And then I began to talk.

21

Noah went tense as he listened to me, his muscles visibly rigid beneath his soaked T-shirt. He ran his hand roughly through his wet hair, pushing it back and twisting it up as he studied it. I showed him the camera, too, and he scrolled through each photo. When Noah finally spoke, his voice had a dangerous edge. "Where did you find these?"

"At Horizons today. The camera was in my bag. The picture, too."

"They're from last night?" he asked, not looking up.

"Yeah."

"Were the doors locked? Your windows?"

I nodded. "But he has a key."

"How?"

I looked at the floor. "There's almost a whole day I don't remember," I said. "I had Daniel's keys with me at the police station, but after that, I'm blank." I was growing angry, now, but with myself. "He could've taken the house key there, on the way to the psych unit, *at* the psych unit . . . I don't know."

Noah looked down at the pictures. "This one was taken from the foot of your bed," he said mechanically. His eyes rested on my closet. "He must have been standing there."

I edged closer to Noah and stared as he studied the image, then scrolled to the next one. It was me in profile, my arm tossed above my head, my blanket down by my waist.

I spoke, this time. "He was standing at my window when he took this one." The words, the thought, filled my veins with ice. How long had Jude been standing there? Watching me?

Noah opened my bedroom door. He pointed at one of the sets of French doors in our hallway, just five feet away. "That's probably where he—Mara?"

I looked up at him. His eyes were dark with concern. "Are you all right?" he asked.

It was only then that I realized I wasn't quite breathing. A fist squeezed my lungs.

Noah drew me back into my room and closed the door. He settled me against it, placing his strong hands on my waist. "Breathe," he whispered.

I tried to. But with the pressure of his fingers against my skin, with his storm-gray eyes staring into mine, with his warmth and nearness just inches away, I was finding it difficult for other reasons. I nodded anyway, though.

And then Noah pulled away. "I called the security firm after I left yesterday, but the person I wanted for you was on assignment until tomorrow. I didn't think—" He closed his eyes, quietly furious. "I should never have left."

"It's not your fault," I said, because it wasn't. "But I'm glad you're staying tonight."

He looked at me, and there was something hard about his stare. "Did you really think I wouldn't? After what you just told me?"

I shrugged.

"I'm a bit bothered by your uncertainty," Noah said. "I said I wouldn't let Jude hurt you, and I meant it. If you didn't want me in the house, I'd be sleeping in my car."

His words drew a smile from my lips. "How did you manage to convince my parents to let you stay?"

"I'm taking Joseph fishing tomorrow. It's all been arranged."

"That's it?" I asked.

"At five-thirty in the morning."

"Still," I said, giving him a long look. "I'm impressed."

"By?"

"You have my mom wrapped around your little finger—"

"I do well with older women, it's true."

"And everyone else adores you," I said.

At this, Noah paused. "I think your father actually likes me less with each passing day."

"He doesn't know you saved his life."

Noah didn't respond; he went back to studying the pictures instead. "Your eyes in this one . . ."

Ah. Phoebe's handiwork. "That wasn't Jude," I said. "There's this girl at Horizons—she's seriously crazy, Noah, not just, like, neurotic or manic or whatever—she said the picture fell out of my bag, and then handed it to me just like that."

He held the photograph up against the light of my grandmother's white chandelier. "You're certain she's the one who scratched them out?"

I nodded. "She admitted it. She said she 'fixed' them."

"That is rather disturbing," he said and paused. "Is it awful there?"

I shrugged. "Jamie helps."

"Wait—Jamie . . . Roth?"

"Yup. He was banished there post-expulsion."

"Intriguing," Noah said, before I continued recounting everything that had happened. I watched him intently as I told him about the dead cat, the writing on my mirror, the near-accident, and the doll. But after his initial reaction to the pictures, he now seemed . . . impassive.

Carefully so.

And by the time I relayed my conversation with Daniel, including the fact that my brother thought I was possessed, Noah seemed *light*.

"Possessed with . . . emotion?" he asked slowly.

I narrowed my eyes at him. "*Possessed*, possessed."

"And he believes this, why, exactly?" He turned to my bathroom. "May I get a towel?"

"Sure," I said, dropping down onto my bed as Noah disappeared. "I told him what's happening to me."

He emerged with his head bent, rubbing a towel through his hair. When he stood up straight, I saw that he was shirtless.

The architecture of him drew my eyes like a magnet. Noah was built with clean lines and strong ones; his jeans hung low, exposing fine hip bones that made me want to touch.

I'd seen this much of him before, but not in my room, not like this. It brought a rush of heat to my skin.

"I thought we decided against that to avoid a lockdown scenario?" He hung the towel on the knob of my bathroom door. "May I borrow a shirt?"

It took a few seconds to collect myself before I could answer. "I don't think mine would fit you," I said, my eyes still lingering on his lean frame. "Ask Daniel?"

Noah's gaze slid to my bedroom door. "I would, but I don't think it would be wise to leave your room like this."

Right. "Right," I said. I left, came back, and tossed Noah one of Daniel's shirts. He stretched it over his head and his slender muscles moved beneath his skin and I was riveted.

"So," he finally said, unfortunately clothed and leaning back against my desk. "You told your brother what's been happening?"

"Kind of . . . I said Horizons gave us a stupid assignment to fictionalize our problems and then described what was happening to my fake protagonist."

"Oh, good," Noah said, nodding seriously. "I was afraid you'd be obvious about it."

I rolled my eyes. "He bought it *because* it's obvious. Fictionalizing my problems for therapeutic purposes is believable. Me having the ability to kill people with my mind, less so."

Noah inclined his head. "Fair point."

"Anyway," I went on, "his conclusion is that I'm possessed and I think there's something to it, Noah."

He ran his fingers through his chaotic hair once again. "Mara, you're not possessed."

"But I'm losing time and I played with a Ouija board."

"*I* never played with a Ouija board," Noah said.

"But *I* did. And it predicted Rachel's death."

It predicted I would kill her.

Noah slid into my desk chair and listened.

"Rachel asked it how she was going to die six months before the asylum collapsed," I explained. "And *it spelled out my name.* I didn't even *think* about it then."

"Dramatic irony."

I narrowed my eyes at him.

"Mara," he said lazily. "There are a million explanations for the scenario you just described."

"A million?"

"All right, not a million. Two. One being that Claire, Rachel, or both of them moved the piece themselves."

"I thought Claire was doing it too—"

"The other being that perhaps you moved it yourself."

I crossed my arms over my chest. "Why would I do that?"

Noah shrugged a shoulder. "Maybe you were upset with Rachel, and subconsciously you spelled your own name."

I said nothing, but my expression must have been murderous because Noah drew himself up and moved on. "Anyway, there's some fuckery afoot, clearly, but I don't think you're possessed."

"Why not?"

"For several reasons, the most obvious one being that with said fuckery happening to both of us—albeit with different manifestations—if I am not possessed, then you, too, are likely not possessed."

I lifted my chin. "What's your theory, then?"

"I've considered several."

"Try me."

Noah affected a bored tone as he rattled them off. "Genetic mutation, toxic waste, radioactive isotopes, growth hormones in milk—"

"But not possession?" My eyebrows lifted. "What about reincarnation?"

"Please," he said with amused contempt.

"Says the person who just tried to pin this on growth hormones in milk. Seriously?"

"I didn't say they were *good* theories. And they're more likely than either of yours."

I flopped down on my back and stared at my ceiling. "Who'd have thought Daniel would be more helpful than you?"

We were both silent as rain drummed on the roof. "All right," Noah finally said. "What else did he have to say?"

I turned my head to look at Noah. "He suggested I have a wise and mysterious figure help my character on her quest."

"Brilliant, save for the fact that there appears to be no wise and mysterious figure. Next?"

"Wait," I said as an idea dawned. Remembering the Ouija board from Rachel's birthday made me remember what I did on mine. I remembered—

"Lukumi," I said slowly.

"The priest? The Santeria priest? We're back there, are we?"

"You sound skeptical."

"Well, I do have doubts, yes, but I suppose I should have seen that one coming."

"I remembered what I needed to remember, Noah. Just like he said I would."

"Which could be explained by the placebo effect."

I held Noah's gaze. "I think we should look for him."

"We did, Mara," he said calmly. "We went back to Little Havana, and we didn't find any answers there."

"Exactly," I said, leaning forward. "The shop *disappeared*. Something's up with him."

"I was curious about that myself," Noah said, his legs stretched languidly out in front of him. "So I looked into it. Botanicas are often fly-by-night operations, because of animal cruelty issues. If proprietors think there might be a bust, they clean up and vanish. Hence the stray chickens wandering throughout Hialeah. Satisfied?"

I shook my head, growing more and more frustrated. "Why do you keep reaching for science?"

"Why do you keep reaching for magic?"

"We should look for him," I said again, and petulantly.

"Santeria isn't exactly the Catholic church, Mara. Asking locals, 'Pardon me, might you have that witch doctor's mobile number?' is likely to prove fruitless."

I was about to retort when Daniel pushed the door open. He looked back and forth between us.

"Uh, I was going to invite you guys out to dinner with me and Sophie, but the vibe in here's a little intense. Everything cool?"

"Where are we going?" I asked quickly. I needed to get out of this house.

"Sophie was thinking Cuban," Daniel said warily.

Noah and I broke into twin smiles. Then he met my eyes and said, "I know just the place."

22

Before we left, my mother made Daniel and Noah both swear to watch me every second and made me take my father's cell phone too, for good measure. She would have fitted me with an ankle monitor if she could have, but I didn't care—I was just glad to go.

We picked up Sophie on the way to the restaurant; she practically bounced into the car and kissed Daniel on the cheek. He totally blushed. She totally beamed. They were adorable together, I had to admit it.

The perfect pair talked about some concert some famous violinist was giving at the Center for Performing Arts next week, and I leaned my cheek against the cool window of Daniel's Civic.

The drenched roads rushed by us. Street lamps cast yellow cones of light on the houses below them, which went from expensive in Sophie's neighborhood to run-down as we neared the restaurant. At a red light, I noticed a cat watching us from the roof of someone's parked car. When it saw me, it pulled its gums back in a hiss.

Maybe I imagined it.

The restaurant was lit with white Christmas lights outside, and the smell of frying dough invaded the damp air.

"Whatever that smell is," Sophie said as we went inside, "that's what I'm having."

"Churros," Noah said. "It's a dessert."

Sophie tucked her short blond hair behind her ears. "I don't care. That smell is *crazy*."

"So's the line," Daniel said, eyeing the assembled crowd. Dozens of people were standing, laughing, talking—all waiting for a seat.

"It's always busy," I said.

"You've been here?" Sophie asked.

"Twice." Once on my birthday. And then the first time—the first time Noah and I went out. I smiled at the memory, just as Noah said, "I'll be right back."

The crowd pressed us against the bar. "Oh my God," Sophie squealed, looking at a display of the restaurant's green and white promotional T-shirts behind the counter. "Those are so cute."

"You want one?" Daniel asked her.

"Would it be cheesy if I said yes?"

"Yes," my brother said, but he was smiling.

She wrinkled her nose. "I love cheese."

So did I, in small doses.

I discreetly inched away from them and toward the glass dessert case. I didn't care about the food; my eyes roamed over the wall next to it, over to the fliers tacked on a giant bulletin board. That was how I first found Abel Lukumi. Maybe I'd get lucky again.

I scanned hundreds of words as quickly as I could when Daniel appeared back at my side. "Table's ready," he said. "Come on."

"Give me a second." My brother sighed and went off to sit with Sophie. But as promised, he didn't leave me alone.

"Find anything?" Noah's voice was velvet and warm next to my ear. I shook my head, but then four letters caught my eye.

kumi.

They peeked out from under the corner of another flier. I folded the top one over, feeling a rush of hope—

The full word *was* Lukumi, but as I squinted to try and read the small type, I realized I was having trouble understanding the sentence. Either the context was off, or my Spanish was already fading from disuse.

"It's a church," Noah said, reading the text along with me. "Church of Lukumi."

I bit my lip. "Well, he's a priest . . . maybe it's his church?"

Noah withdrew his iPhone and typed something in. "Of course," he said, sounding resigned.

"What?"

He showed me the screen. There were hundreds of thousands of hits—mostly referring to the Church of Lukumi and a Supreme Court case bearing its name.

"It's another name for Santeria," he said, and met my eyes. "For the religion. Whatever that man's name was, it wasn't Abel Lukumi."

He had used a fake name.

I tried not to let my disappointment show as I ate, but it was hard. Sophie didn't appear to notice, though, and Daniel pretended not to. When we finished dinner, we left the building loaded with Styrofoam boxes full of plantains and beans to spare.

"That was *incredible*," Sophie said, her voice dreamy. "I can't believe I've lived twenty minutes away and never knew about it."

"Good choice," Daniel agreed, chucking Noah on the shoulder. We all climbed back into the car, and Sophie put her iPod into the dock and played some tense, obscure piece she wanted Daniel and Noah to hear. But just as the music swelled to a crescendo, something small hit our windshield and slid down.

Sophie screamed. Daniel screeched to a stop.

The wheels skidded slightly on the wet pavement, and we found ourselves under a pool of light. The streetlamp illuminated a bloody smear on the glass and the windshield wipers swooped, spreading the stain.

We hadn't even turned off of Calle Ocho, but it was late and rainy and there was no one behind us, so my brother got out of the car. Noah followed right behind him.

The car was silent but my heartbeat roared in my ears. They were outside for less than a minute before the car doors creaked open again.

"It was a bird," Noah said, slipping into the backseat beside me. He laced his fingers between mine, and I began to calm down.

"A crow," my brother clarified. He sounded drained and guilty.

Sophie reached over and put her hand on his arm. "I'm sorry," she said softly.

My brother just sat there, idling in the lane. He shook his head. "I've never hit anything in my whole—"

His sentence was cut off by another soft thump, this time on the roof.

This time, the car wasn't moving.

"What the—" Daniel started.

But before he could finish his sentence, the thump was followed by dozens more. And not just on our car but also on the road, on the parked cars that lined the street.

We were shocked into silence as a murder of crows fell from the sky.

23

After we dropped Sophie off, Daniel and Noah exchanged theories on the way home. The storm. Disease. There were a bunch of scientific possibilities, but a feeling gnawed at me.

A feeling that it was something else.

Seconds seemed like lifetimes as I waited for Noah to come to my room that night. I stared at the clock on my nightstand, but the hours passed and he didn't show. He didn't tell me he would, but I assumed it.

Maybe I assumed wrong.

Maybe he fell asleep?

I threw off the blanket and slipped out of my room. The guest room was on the other side of the house, but I was confident I could silently make my way over and see if he was still awake. Just to check.

I stood outside the guest room door and listened. No sound. I pushed it open a crack.

"Yes?" Noah's voice. Wide-awake.

I opened the door the rest of the way. A small lamp was on a circular accent table in the corner of the room, but Noah was painted in shadow. He was still dressed and he was reading, his face entirely obscured by a book. He lowered it just enough to reveal his eyes.

"Hi," I said.

"Hello."

"Hi," I said again.

Noah lowered his book farther. "Is everything all right?"

I stepped inside and closed the door behind me. "I just came to say good night."

"Good night," he said, and returned to the book.

I had no idea what was going on, but I didn't like it. I half-twisted toward the door, then stopped. Glanced back at Noah.

He arched an eyebrow. "What?"

I'm just going to say it. "I'm just going to say it."

He waited.

"I thought you were coming to my room."

"Why?"

Well, that stung. I reached for the door.

Noah sighed. "I can't, Mara."

"Why not?"

Noah set down the book he was reading and crossed the room. He stopped next to me but stared out the window. I followed his eyes.

I could see the ridiculously long hallway that led to my bedroom from here, and the three sets of French doors that spanned its length. The hall light was on, which made it nearly impossible to see anything outside. But if someone went *inside*, Noah wouldn't miss it.

Was that why he didn't come? "You can keep an eye out on my room from my bed too, you know," I said.

Noah lifted his hand to my cheek; I wasn't expecting it and my breath hitched. He then ran his thumb over my skin and under my jaw, tilting my face up, drawing my eyes to his.

"Your mother trusts me," he said quietly.

A mischievous grin curved my mouth. "Exactly."

"No, Mara, she *trusts* me. If I'm caught in your bed, I won't be allowed to be here. Not like this. And I *have* to be here."

I tensed, remembering words I said to him not even a week ago, before I knew that Jude was alive. Back when I was only afraid of myself.

"I want a boyfriend, not a babysitter."

The circumstances had changed, but the sentiment hadn't.

"You don't *have* to be here," I said. "You don't have to do anything you don't want to do."

"I want to be here."

"Why?"

"I can't let anything happen to you."

I closed my eyes in frustration. Either Noah didn't understand what I was trying to say, or he was ignoring it. "Should I go?" I asked.

His hand was still on my face, and his touch was impossibly soft. "You should."

I wasn't about to beg. I broke away from him and reached for the door.

"But don't," he said, right when I touched it.

I faced him and stepped back into the room. He pushed the door closed behind me. My back was against the wood and Noah was almost against me.

I went in search of Noah with every intention of just sleeping when I found him. But now the beat of my blood, of my wanting, transformed the air around us.

I was consumed by the slow lift of the corner of his mouth and the need to taste his smile. I wanted to dip my fingers under the hem of his shirt and explore the soft line of hair that disappeared into his jeans. To feel his skin under my teeth, his shadowed jaw on my neck.

But here, now, with him only inches from me, and nothing to stop us, I didn't move.

"I want to kiss you," I whispered instead.

He angled his face closer, lower down to mine. But not to my mouth. To my ear. "I'll allow it."

His lips brushed my skin and suddenly it was too much. I grabbed a fistful of his shirt and pulled him against me as close as I could but he was still not close enough. My hands were trapped between the hard ridges of his stomach and my softness and I was almost breathless with wanting, trembling with it.

But Noah was still.

Until his name fell from my lips in a soft, desperate groan. And then his hands were on my hips and his mouth was on my skin and he lifted me and I wrapped myself around him. I was backed against the door and the copper buttons on Noah's jeans pressed against me and the ache was delicious and not enough, not at all. His rough cheek electrified the curve between my neck and shoulder and I leaned back, completely senseless. He gripped my waist and he shifted me up and then his lips brushed against mine. Soft. Tentative. Waiting for me to kiss them.

A memory flickered of us together in his bed, a tangle of limbs and tongues and hair. Noah wrapped around me as he unwrapped me with his mouth. Our mouths were fluent in the language of each other and we moved with one mind and shared the same breath. Until Noah stopped breathing. Until he almost died.

Like Jude should have.

Like I wished he had.

I shuddered against Noah's mouth and my heart thundered against his chest. I did not imagine him almost dying. I *remembered* it. And I was afraid it would happen again.

Noah slid me down.

I was breathless and unsteady on my feet. "What?"

"You're not ready," he said as he backed away.

I swallowed. "I was thinking about it. But then you just—stopped."

"Your heartbeat was out of control."

"Maybe because I liked it."

"Maybe because you're not ready," Noah said. "And I'm not going to push you."

After a minute passed in silence, I finally said, "I'm scared."

Noah was quiet.

"I'm scared to kiss you." I'm scared I'll hurt you.

Noah gently smoothed my hair from my face. "Then you don't have to."

"But I want to." It had never been more true.

His eyes were soft. "Do you want to tell me what you're afraid of?"

My voice was clear. "That I'll hurt you. Kill you."

"If you kiss me."

"Yes."

"Because of that dream."

I closed my eyes. "It wasn't a dream," I said.

I felt Noah's fingers on my waist. "If it wasn't a dream, then what do you think happened?"

"I told you already."

"How would that work?"

I studied his face, searching for any trace of amusement. I didn't find it. "I don't know. Maybe it's part of . . . *me*," I said, and I knew that *he* knew what I meant.

"Just kissing?"

I shrugged.

"Not sex?"

"I've never had sex."

"I'm aware. But if I recall correctly, you didn't seem to be worried about it that night in my room." The tiniest hint of a smile lifted the corner of his mouth.

I knew exactly which night he meant. It was the night he finally realized what I could do, when I killed every living thing in the insect house at the zoo, everything but us.

I thought I should leave him then, to keep him safe. I thought I should leave everyone I loved. But Noah wouldn't let me and I was grateful because I didn't want to let him go. I wanted him close, as close as he could possibly get. I wasn't thinking clearly. I wasn't thinking much at all.

"I don't know," I said, backing down onto the bed. "How am I supposed to know?"

Noah followed my steps and unfurled on the mattress,

drawing me down with him. My spine was pressed up against his chest; the silver pendant he always wore was cold against my skin, exposed in my tank top. The beat of his heart steadied mine.

Noah traced the length of my arm and held my hand. "We don't have to do anything, Mara," he said softly as my eyes began to close. I wanted to curl up in his voice and live there. "This truly is enough."

I had one final thought before I slipped into sleep.

Not for me.

24

BEFORE

India. Unknown Province.

THE MAN IN BLUE LOOKED DOWN AT ME AS THE horses drew the carriage away, kicking up dust. "What is your name?"

I stared at him.

"Do you understand me?"

I nodded.

"I do not know what your guardian has told you, but you are in my care for now. We will have to give you a name."

I was silent.

He let out a small sigh. "We have a journey ahead of us. Are you feeling well?"

I nodded again, and our journey began.

I was sad to leave the ships. We traveled by foot and by elephant back into the forest and still it was nearly sunset when we reached the village. The earth beneath my feet was dry and the air was quiet and still. I smelled smoke; there were many small huts that stretched out over the land, but there were no people.

"Come inside," the Man in Blue said, and waved me into one of the huts. My eyes wrestled with the dark.

Something moved near me; a figure emerged out of the dimness. I could see only smooth, brown, flawless skin attached to a slight slip of a girl. She was taller than I, but I could not see her face. Ribbons of black hair fell limply below her shoulders.

"Daughter," the Man in Blue said to the girl. "We have a guest."

The girl stepped into the light, and I could finally see her. She was plain, but there was a kindness, a warmth in her clean face that made her pretty. She smiled at me.

I smiled back.

The Man in Blue rested his hand on the girl's shoulder then. "Where is Mother?"

"A woman went into labor."

The Man in Blue looked confused. "Who?"

The girl shook her head. "Not from here. A stranger, the husband, came for Mother. She said she would return as soon as she was able."

The Man in Blue's eyes tightened. "I must speak with you,"

he said to her. Then he turned to me. "Wait here. Do not go outside. Do you understand?"

I nodded. He drew the girl away, out of the hut. I heard whispers but I could not understand the words. Moments later, the girl entered again. Alone.

She did not speak to me. Not at first. She took a step toward me, then turned up her palms. I did not move. She took another step, close enough now for me to catch her scent, earthy and intense. I liked it and I liked her warmth. She extended her arm then, and I let her touch me. She crouched in a corner and sat me down next to her. The girl drew me against her clean shift with the familiarity of someone who knew just the way I would fit. I wriggled, trying to get comfortable.

"You must not go out there," she said, misunderstanding my movement.

I stilled. "Why?"

"So you can speak," the girl said with a tiny smile. "It is not safe," she added.

"It is too quiet."

"People are sick. The noise hurts them."

I did not understand. "Why?"

"Haven't you ever been sick?"

I shook my head.

She smiled and shot me a sly look. "Everyone gets sick. You are full of mischief."

I did not understand her meaning, so I asked, "The Man in Blue, he is your father?"

"The Man in Blue?" she asked, her eyes glittering. "That is what you call him?"

I said nothing.

The girl nodded. "Yes, he is. But you may call him Uncle and my mother Aunt, when she returns." She paused. "And you may call me Sister, if you like."

"Did my father and mother get sick?" I asked, even though I did not remember my father or mother. I did not remember having either.

"Perhaps," the girl said quietly, and pulled me back against her. "But you are with us now."

"Why?"

"Because we will take care of you."

Her voice was gentle and soft, and suddenly I was frightened for her. "Are you sick?"

"Not yet," she said, then stood.

I followed quickly. She was not like the others. I wanted her to stay.

She glanced back. "I was not leaving," she assured me.

"I know," I said, but followed her anyway.

We did not go far. We simply turned into another small room, this one with several mats on the caked straw floor. The girl ducked down behind one and held a bundle of fabric in her hand, as well as a needle and thread. She removed a jar full of something dark and withdrew a puff of it in her fist. She folded the cloth around the fluff and hummed a simple song—it consisted of only a few notes—as she began to sew.

I was hypnotized by her hands. "What is that?"

"A present. Something for you to play with, so you will never feel alone."

I felt something like fear. "I want to play with you."

She smiled, warm and bright. "We can all play together."

This made me happy and I settled down on the mat, lulled by the melody and the rhythm of her fingers. Soon, the shapeless form in her hands became something else; I found a head early on, then two arms and legs. It grew eyes and eyelashes and a thin black smile, then rows of stitches of black hair. Then the older girl made a shift for it, and slipped it on over its stuffed head.

When she finished, I settled back into the crook of her arm.

"Do you like your doll?" She held it up to a shaft of light. There was a spot of red on the underside of its arm, where she held it. Where its wrist would have been.

I did not answer her. "What is that red?" I asked instead.

"Oh." She handed me the doll and examined her finger. "I pricked myself." She drew her finger to her mouth and sucked.

I was afraid for her. "Are you hurt?"

"No, do not worry."

I held the doll close.

"What is her name?" the girl asked me gently.

I was silent for a moment. Then said, "You made it. You choose."

"Her," she corrected me. "I cannot choose that for you."

"Why?"

"Because she belongs to you. There is power in a name. Perhaps once you know her better, you will be able to decide?"

I nodded, and the older girl stood, lifting me with her. My stomach made a noise.

"You are hungry."

I nodded.

She caressed the crown of my head, smoothing my thick, dark hair. "We are all hungry," she said quietly. "I can add more water to the soup. Would you like some before supper?"

"Yes."

She nodded and considered me. "Are you strong enough to fetch water from a well?"

"I am *very* strong."

"The handle is *very* heavy."

"Not for me."

"It is a *very* deep well. . . ."

"I can do it." I wanted to show her, but I wanted to be outside as well. The close air of the hut was pressing in, and my skin felt tight.

"Then I will tell you the secret to get there, but you must promise not to go any farther into the trees."

"I promise."

"And if you see someone, you must promise not to tell them where it is."

"I promise."

The girl smiled, and nudged the doll back into my hand. "Take her with you, wherever you go."

I clutched the doll tightly and brought her to my chest before the girl showed me out. Her eyes followed me as I ran into the fading sunlight. The scent of charred flesh singed my nostrils, but the smell was not unpleasant. A thick haze of smoke hung in the air and stung my eyes even as it rose among the trees.

I followed the path I was told. The well *was* quite far, and nearly hidden by thick brush. It was large, too; I had to stand on my toes to peer down into it. It was dark. Bottomless. I had an urge to throw the doll in.

I did not. I set it down beside the worn stone and my thin arms began the work of drawing up the water when I heard a cough.

Close.

I was so startled I dropped the handle. I picked up the doll and gripped it tightly as I crept to the other side of the well.

An old woman sat propped up against the trunk of a date palm, her wrinkles deep, folding in on themselves. Her black eyes were unfocused and watery. She was weak.

And not alone.

Someone was crouched over her, a man with waves of black hair and perfect, beautiful skin. He held a cup to the old woman's lips and water dribbled down her chin. She coughed again, startling me.

His obsidian eyes flicked to mine, and something flashed behind them. Something I did not know or understand.

The woman followed his gaze and focused on me. Her stare pinned me to the ground as her eyes widened, the whites showing around her irises. The man placed a calming hand on her shoulder, then stared back at me.

I felt a roll of sickness deep in my belly and doubled over. Red swirled at the edges of my vision. My head swam. I gulped for air and slowly, slowly rose.

The woman began to tremble and whisper. The man—surprised, curious, but not afraid—leaned his head in to hear her. Without realizing it, I took a step nearer too.

She whispered louder and louder. It was the same word, just one word, that she repeated over and over again. Her frail arm rose, her finger pointed at me like an accusation.

"Mara," she whispered, again and again and again. And then she began to scream.

25

"MARA," A VOICE SAID, WARMING MY SKIN.

My eyes opened, but the trees were gone. The sunlight had vanished. There was only darkness.

And Noah, next to me, his fingers resting on my cheek.

A nightmare. Just a nightmare. I let out a slow breath and then smiled, relieved, until I realized we weren't in bed.

We were standing by the guest room door. I had opened it—my hand rested on the knob.

"Where are you going?" Noah asked softly.

The last thing I remembered was falling asleep beside him, even though I shouldn't have. My house was tainted, but in Noah's arms, I felt safe.

But I left them during the night. I left *him*.

I had been sleepwalking.

The details of the dream hung low in my mind, thick as smoke. But they didn't fade with consciousness. I didn't know where I was going in my sleep or why, but now that I was awake, I needed to see something before I forgot to look.

"My bedroom," I answered him, my voice clear.

I needed to see that doll.

I pulled Noah along behind me and we crept silently to my room. Noah helped me unpack the doll from the box I had entombed it in, no questions asked. I said nothing as I looked it over, my skin feeling tight as I held it.

Its black smile was a little faded—from wear or washing, I didn't know—and the dress it wore was newer, but still crude. Definitely handmade. Otherwise? Otherwise it was eerily similar to the doll in my dream.

Maybe more than similar.

I remembered something then.

There was a spot of red on the underside of its arm, where she held it.

I lifted up the doll's sleeve.

"What is that red?" I had asked the older girl.

"Oh," she said, and handed me the doll. She examined her finger. *"I pricked myself."*

Looking at the doll now, I saw a dark brownish red spot on the underside of its arm. Where its wrist would have been.

My flesh felt dead where my skin met the doll's. I didn't know what the dream meant, if anything, but I didn't care. I was starting to hate this thing and wanted to get rid of it.

"I'm throwing it out," I whispered to Noah. He looked confused. I'd explain in the morning. We couldn't get caught, and the more we talked, the more we risked it.

He watched as I slipped on shoes, went outside, and threw the doll on top of the swollen garbage bags in the bin my father had already brought out to the curb. It would be taken away soon, and then I wouldn't think about it or dream about it or be tortured with it by Jude again.

We went back to Noah's bed; the doll and the nightmare made me uneasy, and I didn't want to sleep alone. I rested my head against his shoulder and my eyes closed, lulled by the feel of his silent, even breathing beneath my hands. When I woke again, it was still dark. But Noah was still next to me, and we were still in bed.

I was tired but relieved. "What time is it?"

"I don't know," Noah said, but his voice wasn't thick with sleep.

I drew back to look at him. "Were you awake?"

He pretended to stretch. "What? No."

I rolled over onto my side and smiled. "You totally were. You were watching me sleep."

"No. That would be creepy. And boring. Watching you shower, perhaps . . ."

I punched him in the arm, then snuggled deeper under the covers.

"As much as I'm enjoying this," Noah said, as he rolled over me, leaning on his arms, "and believe me, I am," he added, looking down into my eyes as a mischievous smile formed on his lips, "I'm afraid you have to go."

I shook my head. He nodded.

"It's still dark." I pouted.

"Fishing. With Joseph. You have to get back to your room before he wakes up."

I sighed dramatically.

"I know," he said, his smile growing wider. "I wouldn't want to sleep without me either."

I rolled my eyes and scooted out from beneath him. "Now you've ruined it."

"Just as I intended," he said, leaning back against the pillows. His eyes followed me to the door.

Torture. I pulled it open.

"Mara?"

"Noah?"

"Do wear those pajamas again."

"Ass," I said, grinning. Then left. I padded to my room, passing the French doors in the hallway, the night still black beyond them. I quickened my pace, hating to be reminded of what I couldn't see.

Of *who* I couldn't see.

It was nearly dawn, though. Jude wouldn't risk breaking in so close to daylight. The thought reassured me and I slipped into my bed, my parents none the wiser. I closed my eyes. I had no trouble falling asleep.

The trouble began when I woke up.

At around eight, my father knocked on the door to make sure I was awake. I poured myself out of bed and over to my dresser to pick out clothes for Horizons.

But when I opened my underwear drawer, my grandmother's doll was inside.

It was all I could do not to scream. I backed away from the dresser and locked myself in the bathroom, sliding down the tiled wall to the cold tiled floor. I pressed a fist against my mouth.

Was Jude watching me last night? Did he see me throw it away? And then put it back in my room while I was asleep in Noah's?

Goose bumps pebbled my flesh and my skin was slick with sweat. But I couldn't let my father know anything was wrong. I had to dress and look and act like everything was normal. Like I was healthy and Jude was dead and none of this was happening.

"Get up," I whispered to myself. I stayed on the floor for one more second, then stood. I turned the faucet on, cupped my hand under the stream of water and brought it to my lips, glancing at my reflection in the mirror as I straightened.

I froze. The contours of my face seemed strange. Subtly unfamiliar. My cheekbones were sharper, my lips were swollen as if I'd been kissing, my cheeks were flushed, and my hair stuck to the back of my neck like paste.

I was transfixed. The water slipped through my fingers.

The sound of it hitting the porcelain sink brought me back. My throat ached—I turned the faucet back on and cupped another handful of water and greedily drank it from my palm. It cooled me from the inside out. I looked in the mirror again.

I still looked different, but I felt a little better. I was tired and scared and angry and frustrated and obviously stressed out. Maybe I was getting sick, too. Maybe that's why I looked strange. I rolled my neck, stretched my arms above my head, and then drank again. My skin prickled, as if I was being watched.

I glanced at my dresser. The doll was still inside.

"Almost ready?" Dad called out from the hallway.

"Yeah," I yelled back. I turned away from the mirror and put on clothes. I threw one last look at my dresser before I left my room.

The doll had to go.

26

"GOOD MORNING," MY FATHER SAID WHEN I FINALLY appeared in the kitchen.

"Morning." I grabbed two granola bars and a bottle of water from the pantry, gulping half of it down while Dad finished his coffee. We headed for the car together.

He rolled down the windows once we were inside. It was unusually gorgeous out—blue and cloudless and not hot yet at all, but the inside of my skin burned, anyway.

"How're you feeling, kid?"

I shot him a glance. "Why?"

"You look a little tired."

"Thanks . . ."

"Oh, you know what I mean. Hey, you know what movie I rented?"

"Um . . . no?"

He paused meaningfully. *"Free Willy,"* he said with a giant smile.

"Okay . . ."

"You loved that movie—we used to watch it all the time, remember?"

Like when I was six.

"And Joseph is up in arms about the plight of orcas now, so I thought we could watch it together, as a family," he said. Then added, "I bet Noah would like it."

I couldn't help but smile. He was clearly making an effort. "Okay, Dad."

"It's uplifting."

"Okay, Dad."

"Transformational—"

"*Okay*, Dad."

He grinned and turned on the classic rock station and the two of us sat in silence. But being back in his car again, I found myself reflexively glancing back in the side mirror. I was looking for the truck, I realized.

I was looking for Jude.

I spent the whole drive to Horizons worrying I would see him behind us, but I didn't. Dad dropped me off and I was warmly welcomed by Brooke, who introduced me to the art therapist I'd be working with a few days a week. She had me draw a house, a tree, and my family—some kind of test, definitely—and once I did so to her satisfaction, it was time for Group. Half of the students had to share their fears.

I was very glad to be in the other half.

Phoebe kept her distance from me that day, and Jamie made me laugh the way he always did. The hours passed unremarkably but I found myself sneaking glances outside at every opportunity, waiting for the white truck to appear in the parking lot.

It never did.

When my father and I pulled up to the house that afternoon, Mom's car was already in the driveway. More importantly, so was Noah's.

I felt a burst of relief. I needed to tell him about the doll in my room this morning, about *Jude* in my room last night while we slept. I nearly dove out of the car while it was still moving.

"Tell your mom I'm off to work on her list," Dad said, rolling his eyes. "I'll be back soon."

I nodded and shut the door. He didn't drive away until I was inside the house.

Machine gun fire erupted from our family room, and I entered it to find Noah and Joseph slouched on the floor with controllers in their hands, their eyes glued to the TV.

Our conversation would have to wait.

"How was fishing?" I asked, in a casual voice that did not suit my mood. I walked through the archway into the kitchen and opened the fridge. I was hungry, but nothing looked good.

"We did not, in fact, go fishing," Noah answered, still squinting at the screen.

"What? Why?"

Joseph rocked forward, gripping his controller fiercely. He didn't speak.

"Joseph didn't want to kill any fish, though he seems to have no problem killing—you bastard."

Something exploded loudly and my brother dropped the controller, raising both hands in the air. "The champion is undefeated." He flashed an obnoxious smirk at Noah.

"Good for you," I said.

Noah shot me a look. "Where's the loyalty?"

"I meant about the fish, but for the game, too." I high-fived my brother and then I flashed an obnoxious smirk of my own. "Blood over boys."

"You're both evil."

"I'm going to be a vegetarian," Joseph told me.

"Mom will think I put you up to it." I hadn't eaten meat since the Santeria birthday show; every time I looked at it, I tasted blood in my mouth.

I dropped onto the couch. "So what did you guys do if you didn't fish?"

"We went out on the boat and watched for dolphins," Joseph said.

"Jealous. Did you see any?"

Noah nodded. "A small pod. We had to go out pretty far."

"The boat was so cool," Joseph said. "You can come with us next time."

I grinned. "That's very generous of you."

"Well," Noah said, standing up and stretching. His fingers touched the ceiling. "I don't know about you, but after letting your brother win, I'm quite famished."

Joseph slit his eyes at Noah. "Liar."

"Prove it," Noah shot back.

"I *can* prove it."

"All right," I said, "this rivalry is getting a little intense. Yes, Noah, I'm hungry."

"Then if you'll pardon me, nemesis," he said to Joseph. "We will rematch another day."

"You'll still lose."

The corner of Noah's mouth lifted as he walked to the kitchen. I joined him and watched him rummage in the refrigerator.

"Fancy a . . . cucumber?" he said, holding one up.

"You're not very good at this."

"Right, then. Takeout it is."

I looked behind us, toward the hallway. "Where's my mother?"

Noah shook his head. "One of her friends picked her up for coffee, I think?"

"Daniel?"

"Out with Sophie. I'm responsible for everyone's welfare until she returns."

"God help us," I said with a grin, but I was glad. I lowered my voice. "So last night—"

"Pizza!" Joseph called out.

"Must we?" Noah yelled back. He turned to face me. "What do you want?"

"Not pizza," I agreed. "I feel kind of gross."

"Gross. Indeed. Can you think of any food item in particular that would make you feel less gross?"

I shrugged. "I don't know—soup?"

"Pea soup, perhaps?"

"I hate you."

"But you make it so easy. Chinese?"

I shook my head and glanced out the window. I didn't really care. I just wanted to talk.

"Never mind, you're making this quite difficult. Joseph!" Noah called out.

"What!"

"Where are Daniel and Sophie?"

"Avigdor's!" my brother shouted.

Noah looked at me with raised eyebrows.

"Fine with me," I said.

"What kind of food is it?" Noah asked.

"Israeli!"

"Do they have soup?"

"Sushi too!" Joseph yelled.

"Enough with the yelling!" I shouted, then sank into a kitchen chair. I put my head in my hands while Noah ordered and texted Daniel to bring the food home with him. Eventually, Joseph abandoned the video game and went to his room.

Leaving us alone. I opened my mouth to speak but Noah interrupted me before I could.

"What did you do at your place today?"

"We shared our fears. Listen, last night—"

"That sounds appropriately hellish."

"I didn't have to go, they split the group in half. It's my turn tomorrow—"

"Daniel's anxious to see it," Noah said, interrupting me again. "He said he's going to a family therapy thing in a few days? Should be delightful."

"Yeah," I said. "I mean, no. Noah—are you staying tonight?"

"Actually, I've arranged for us to meet with your new guardian. Why?"

"I was going to suggest you sleep in my room, this time."

Noah gave me a sly look. "Not that I'm necessarily opposed, but why?"

The words *Jude was in my room* congealed on my tongue.

When I finally spoke them, my voice sounded different. Terrified. I hated it.

I hated that I was afraid of him. And I hated the way Noah tensed when he saw it.

So I swallowed hard. Then lightened my voice. "He left me a little present in my underwear drawer," I said casually, working hard to fake it.

Noah's eyes never left mine, but his frame relaxed just slightly. "Dare I ask?"

"The doll," I explained. "He must have seen me throw it out."

"Mara—"

I shook my head. "He was probably watching creepily from some bushes or something."

"Mara," Noah said louder.

"The neighbor's hedge is really tall," I went on. "What is *wrong* with him?"

"Mara."

"What?"

"It wasn't Jude," Noah said quietly.

"What wasn't Jude?"

"The doll in your bedroom. He didn't put it there."

I blinked, not getting it. "Then who did?"

It felt like forever before Noah finally spoke.

"You."

27

"What are you talking about?" My voice was quiet. Shaky. "I threw it away."

Noah nodded. "And then later you woke up and got out of bed. You didn't say anything, so I assumed you left to get a drink or something, but given recent events, when you didn't come back, I followed you. You left through the back door."

Invisible fingers tightened around my throat. "Why didn't you wake me up?"

"I thought you *were* awake," Noah said, his voice measured and even. "I asked what you were doing and you said you made a mistake—that you threw away something you wanted to keep. You seemed completely with it; you walked outside and I watched you take the doll from the waste bin and bring it back inside. You went to your room and then nearly came back to bed when I suggested you wash your hands first. You laughed, you did, and then you came back to bed and promptly fell asleep. You don't remember any of this?"

I shook my head because I wasn't sure I could speak. Nothing like this had ever happened before; I had nightmares, sure, and I blacked out before, yes. But this was new.

Different.

Like my reflection in the mirror.

I swallowed hard. "Do I look different to you?"

Noah's brow furrowed. "What do you mean?"

"This morning, after—after I found the doll in my drawer," I said. *After I put it there*, I didn't say. "I looked in the mirror and I feel like—like I look different." I glanced up at Noah, wondering if he saw it, but he only shook his head. "Look again."

Noah took my face in his hands then and drew me close. So close I could see flecks of navy and green and gold in his eyes as he studied mine. His stare was incisive. Piercing.

"Right?" I asked under my breath.

Noah said nothing.

Because I was right. "I'm right, aren't I?"

His eyes narrowed until all I could see were slits of blue. "You don't look *different*," Noah said. "Just . . ."

"Just *different*." I pulled away. I was frustrated. Anxious. I glanced in the direction of my bedroom, in the direction of the doll. "Something's happening to me, Noah."

He was distressingly silent.

Noah knew I looked different. He just refused to say it. I didn't know why and at that moment, I didn't even care. There was one thing on my mind and one thing only. I stood up. "Where are your keys?"

"Why?" he asked, drawing out the word.

"Because I want to burn that doll."

My parents would be disconcerted if they saw me light a fire in our backyard and burn a doll I've had since I was a baby, so we needed somewhere else to do it.

"You have a fireplace, right?" I asked him as I headed toward the front door.

"Several, but we can't leave."

I closed my eyes. "Joseph." Damn.

"And you. If we're not here when your parents get back—I'm sure I needn't remind you of your recent psych ward stint."

As if I could forget.

Noah ran a hand over his jaw. "They trust me *here*, with Joseph, for an hour, maybe. But I can't take you out alone."

"So I'm trapped here indefinitely."

"Unless . . ."

"Unless what?"

"Unless we bring them along."

I stared at Noah, waiting for the punch line.

That was it, apparently. "You can't be serious."

"Why not? An invitation to the Shaw abode would go a long way with your mother. She's desperate to meet my family—Ruth can distract her while we light fires and chant."

"Not funny."

A half-smile appeared on Noah's lips. "Yes it is," he said. "A little," he added as my eyes narrowed to slits. "But if you'd rather they didn't meet, I could burn the doll for you—"

"No." I shook my head. Noah didn't get it, and it didn't even matter to him. He was game for anything, as always. But I needed to see with my own eyes that it was gone. "I want to be there."

"Then it's the only way," Noah said with a shrug.

"You're not worried about losing the sympathy card?"

"Pardon?"

"If your parents charm *my* parents, you might not be allowed here as much."

An unreadable expression crossed Noah's face. "Your mother's clever," he said, his voice low. "She'll see things for what they are." He stood and withdrew his cell from the back pocket of his jeans. "I'll have Ruth invite her over tomorrow. For a ladies' tea."

"Your dad won't be there?"

Noah arched an eyebrow. "Highly doubtful. And if he is, I'll make sure we reschedule."

"But I want to meet him."

"I wish you didn't," he said as he scrolled through his iPhone.

"Why? Are you embarrassed?"

There was a bitter twist to Noah's smile, and he answered without looking up at me. "Absolutely."

I started to feel a bit uneasy. "By me?"

"By *him*."

"That bad?"

"You have no idea."

When my mother came home, Noah instructed me to ask her if I could go for a walk with him. I shifted my weight under her stare as she considered me.

"Be back in half an hour," she said finally.

I grinned, surprised. "Okay."

"And don't leave the block."

"Okay."

My mother handed me her cell. "I'm trusting you," she said quietly.

I nodded, and then Noah and I left. He loped gracefully ahead; his stride was so long, I almost had to jog to keep up.

"So where are we *really* going?"

"For a walk," he insisted, staring ahead.

"Yeah, I caught that. Where?"

Noah pointed down the street at a black car parked under an enormous live oak tree. "There's someone I want you to meet."

As we approached, an average-looking man exited the driver's seat of the car. He flashed a bland smile at us.

"John," Noah said with a nod, "I'd like to introduce you to your assignment."

John held out his hand. "Mara Dyer," he said to me as I shook it, "glad to meet you."

Noah faced me. "John's been working with a security firm so secure that it doesn't have a name for—how long, again, John?"

"Since before you were a concept," the man said, still smiling.

His answer surprised me—he didn't look *that* old. And he wasn't tall or broad or bodyguard-ish in any way. Everything about him was unremarkable, from his forgettable clothes to his forgettable face.

"He's going to be trading shifts with his partner. Between them, they've protected four presidents, seven members of the Royal Family, and nine Saudi princes."

"And now you," John said.

Noah slid one hand around my waist and lifted the other to my neck, my cheek, tipping up my chin with his thumb.

His voice was soft when he spoke. "They won't let anything happen to you," he said.

I won't let anything happen to you, he meant.

And he might have been right, if Jude were all I had to worry about. But no one could protect me from myself.

28

NOAH OFFERED TO FIND AN EXCUSE TO STAY over that night but I was wary of abusing my parents' benevolence. He couldn't stay over *every* night, obviously, but more importantly, I needed to know that I would be okay on my own.

And that night, I was. I slipped into bed and stayed there until morning. Nothing was out of place when I woke up. The ordinariness lifted my mood; Noah had taken my grandmother's doll with him before he left and later today it would be gone forever. John was watching my house. Noah trusted John and I trusted Noah, and even though I hated to admit it, that morning was the first time without him that I actually felt safe.

I checked for Jude only once on the way to Horizons, and I was uncharacteristically cheerful as the counselors put me through my paces. The day rushed by in a blur of blissful near-mundanity, considering my situation wasn't remotely mundane, and I was actually able to worry about something relatively normal for once. Namely: my mother and Noah's stepmother having tea.

He'd been right about the invitation; Mom really couldn't wait to meet Ruth. On the way to Noah's house that afternoon, his parents were all she could talk about. It did not escape my notice that she was more pressed and polished than usual. It almost made me feel guilty for using her as a diversion.

Almost.

My mother went quiet just as I had that thought. I turned to see what warranted the silence, and was unsurprised to find that we had entered Noah's neighborhood.

My mother's eyes roamed over each mansion we passed, one completely distinct from the next. When we reached the scrolled iron gate that heralded the entrance to Noah's house, I told her to drive up. A small camera swiveled in our direction.

My mother shot me a look. "This is Noah's house?" It wasn't quite visible behind the trees, not until the tall gate swung open and we drove through.

"Wow," she breathed. It was the right word. The lush

lawn was bordered by white statues and anchored by a huge fountain in the center: a Greek god clasping a girl who seemed to become a tree. Tiny, low hedges sprouted off into paths, forming intricate designs against the grass.

And then there was the house. Large and imposing, architecturally beautiful and grand. My mother was rapt, but I didn't quite see it the way she did, not now that I knew how much Noah couldn't stand it.

We pulled up to the landing where Albert, the Shaw butler or valet or whatever he was called, greeted us with a prim smile to match his prim suit. I half-expected Noah to be waiting by the door for us but lo, it was Ruth herself.

"Dr. Shaw," my mother said, smiling widely.

Noah's stepmother shook her head. "Please, call me Ruth. It's such a pleasure to meet you," she gushed. Ruth smoothed the linen dress that covered her petite frame and ushered us inside as my mother assured her that no, the pleasure was all hers.

No further formalities were exchanged, however, because the second my sneakered feet touched the patterned marble floor, I was charged by Ruby, the vicious Shaw pug. Who was apparently vicious only to me. The snarling fur-covered sausage ignored my mother completely, but even after Noah swooped in and scooped her up in his arms, she continued to growl at me.

"Bad girl," Noah said affectionately. He kissed her on

the head as she bared her tiny, crooked teeth.

I stood a healthy distance away. "Where's Mabel?" I asked. It would be nice to see her again, all happy and healthy and safe.

"Occupied," he said lightly.

Hiding, he meant. Hiding from me.

My mother didn't appear to notice anything amiss, however, not even as the dog strained for my jugular; Noah's stepmother and his house had her full and undivided attention. "I've heard so much about you," she said to Ruth as we passed beneath a giant chandelier dripping with crystals.

Ruth raised an eyebrow. "Only good things, I hope?" She adjusted a vase filled with bursting white roses on a stone accent table that likely weighed over a thousand pounds. "Never mind," she said archly. "Don't answer that."

Mom laughed. "Of course," she lied, as easily as I usually did. Impressive. "It really is such a pleasure to be able to finally meet Noah's family. We love having him around. Is your husband here?" she asked innocently. Knowing full well that he wasn't.

Ruth's smile didn't falter, but she shook her head. "I'm afraid David's in New York at the moment."

"Maybe another time, then."

"He would love that," Ruth said. She lied as well as Noah.

Noah leaned over and said, "You know, this is rapidly becoming as painful as you indicated it would be."

“Told you.”

“Right, then,” Noah said loudly. “I’m sure you ladies have much to discuss and would rather do so in privacy, yes?”

Ruth looked at my mother for a cue.

Mom waved at us. “Go on.”

Noah handed the wriggling dog off to Ruth. “I’ll give you the tour,” she said, and led my mother away.

I had no idea how long the tour or their conversation or this meeting would last, so I urged Noah up the wide, curving staircase and raced behind him to his room, taking no time to enjoy the view.

Once we arrived, though, I couldn’t help but stare. At his low, simple modern bed, an island in the middle of a neat sea of books. At the floor-to-ceiling windows that splashed amber sunlight onto the shelves that lined his room. It felt like forever since I was last in here, and I missed it.

“What?” Noah asked, when he noticed I hadn’t moved.

I stepped inside. “I wish I could live here,” I said. I wished I could stay.

“No, you don’t.”

“Fine,” I said, my eyes drawn to all the spines. “I wish I had your room.”

“It’s not a terrible consolation prize, I’ll admit.”

“I wish we could make out in your bed.”

Noah sighed. "As do I, but I'm afraid we have a ritual burning to conduct."

"It's always something."

"Isn't it though?" Noah retrieved the doll from his desk in the alcove, and I finally tore my eyes from the books, ready to get this show on the road. Noah led me to one of probably a dozen unused sitting rooms; the walls were mint green and dotted with ornate brass sconces; there was some furniture, but it was all covered in sheets.

Noah handed me the doll and began to search the room. I immediately set it down on the arm of what appeared to be a chair. I didn't want to touch it.

"What are you doing?" I asked him.

"I am preparing to start a fire." He was opening and closing drawers.

"Don't you still smoke?"

"Not around your parents," Noah said, still rummaging. "But yes."

"You don't have matches on you?"

"A lighter, usually." Then Noah looked up, mid-crouch. "My father had the fireplaces rewired for gas. I'm looking for the remote."

The statement dashed my fantasy of throwing a match onto the crude doll and watching it burn. Until I approached the fireplace, that is. The logs looked awfully real.

"Um, Noah?"

"What?"

"You sure it's gas?"

He walked to the fireplace then and removed the screen. "Apparently not. Shit."

"What?"

"They might smell an actual fire all the way down there. I don't know."

I didn't care. I wanted this over with. "We'll think of something." I picked up the doll from the chair with two fingers, pinching its wrist. I held it out in front of me. "Light it up."

Noah considered it for a moment, but shook his head and turned to leave. "Wait here."

I dropped the doll on the floor. Luckily, I didn't have to wait long; Noah returned in short order with lighter fluid and kitchen matches in arm. He approached the fireplace and struck a match. The smell of sulfur filled the air.

"Go on," he said, once the fire was set.

Showtime. I picked the doll up off the floor and threw it into the flames, swelling with relief as they consumed it. But then the air filled with a bitter, familiar smell.

Noah made a face. "What is that?"

"It smells like . . ." It took me a few seconds to finally place it. "Like burning hair," I finally said.

We were both quiet after that. We watched the fire and waited until the doll's arms melted into nothing and the head blackened and fell off. But then I noticed something curl up in the flames. Something that didn't look like cloth.

"Noah . . ."

"I see it." His voice was resigned.

I took a step closer. "Is that—"

"It's paper," Noah said, confirming my fear.

I swore. "We have to put it out!"

Noah shrugged languidly. "It'll be gone by the time I bring back water."

"Go anyway! Jesus."

Noah turned on his heel and left as I crouched over the fireplace, trying to see more clearly. The paper inside the doll was still burning. I leaned in even closer; the heat lit my skin, bringing color to my cheeks as I moved closer—

"Move," Noah said. I drew back and Noah doused the flames. Steam rose and hissed from the logs.

I immediately reached toward the dying embers, hopeful that maybe some part of the paper escaped unscathed, but Noah placed a firm hand on my waist. "Careful," he said, drawing me back.

"But—"

"Whatever it was," he said firmly, "it's gone now."

I was stung by regret. What if it was something important? Something from my grandmother?

What if it had something to do with me?

I closed my eyes and tried to stop punishing myself. There was nothing I could do about the paper now, but at least the doll was gone. I wouldn't have to look at it anymore and Jude wouldn't be able to scare me with it anymore. That was worth something.

That was worth a lot.

Finally, the fire died out and I stood over it, satisfied that nothing was left. But then something caught my eye. Something silver in the ash.

I peered closer. "What is that?"

Noah noticed it, too. He leaned down to look at it with me. "A button?"

I shook my head. "There were no buttons." I reached for the thing, whatever it was, but Noah pulled back my wrist and shook his head.

"It's still hot," he said. But then Noah crouched down and reached for the ashes himself.

I moved to stop him. "I thought it was still hot?"

He glanced back over his shoulder. "Have you forgotten?"

That he could heal? No. But, "Doesn't it hurt?"

An indifferent shrug was my only answer as Noah stuck his hand into the dead fire. He didn't flinch as he sifted through the ashes.

Noah carefully extracted the shining thing. He placed it in his open palm, brushed off the soot and stood.

It was an inch long, no bigger. A slim line of silver—half of it hammered into the shape of a feather, the other half a dagger. It was interesting and beautiful, just like the boy who always wore it.

Noah was impossibly still as I pulled down the collar of his T-shirt. I looked at the charm around his neck, the one he never took off, and then stared back at the charm in his hand.

They were exactly the same.

29

W HAT THE *HELL* WAS GOING ON?

"Noah," I said, my voice quiet.

He didn't answer. He was still staring.

I needed to sit down. I didn't bother with furniture. The floor would do just fine.

Noah hadn't moved.

"Noah," I said again.

No response. Nothing.

"Noah."

He looked at me, finally. "Where did your pendant come from?" I asked him.

His voice was low and cold. "I found it. In my mother's things."

"Ruth?" I asked, though I already knew the answer.

Noah shook his head, just as I expected him to. His eyes locked on the pendant again. "It was just after we'd moved here. I'd claimed the library for my room and had taken my guitar up when—I don't know." He ran a hand over his jaw. "I went back downstairs feeling like I had to unpack, even though I was jet-lagged and exhausted and planned to pass out for a week. But I headed directly to this one box; inside was a small chest filled with my mother's—Naomi's—silver. I began setting the silver aside for absolutely no reason at all and then took the chest apart. Beneath the drawer that held the knives, there it was," he said, nodding at the charm. "I started wearing it that day."

Noah reached down—to hand me the charm, I thought—but instead pulled me up from the floor and onto the sheet-covered sofa next to him. He handed me the pendant. My fingers curled around it, just as Noah asked, "Where did you get that doll?"

"It was my grandmother's," I said, staring at my closed fist.

"But where did it come from?"

"I don't—"

I was about to say that I didn't know, but then remembered the blurred edges of a dream. Hushed voices. A dark hut. A kind girl, sewing me a friend.

Maybe I did know. Maybe I watched while it was made.

Impossible though it was, I told Noah what I remembered.

He listened intently, his eyes narrowing as I spoke.

"I never saw the charm, though," I said when I finished. "The girl never put it inside."

"It could have been sewn in later," he said, his voice level.

With whatever that paper was too. "You think—you think it really happened?" I asked. "You think the dream could be real?"

Noah said nothing.

"But if it was real, if it really happened . . ." My voice trailed off, but Noah finished my sentence.

"Then it wasn't a dream," he said to himself. "It was a memory."

We were both quiet as I tried to wrap my mind around the idea.

It made no sense. To remember something, you have to experience it. "I've barely left the suburbs," I said. "I've never seen jungles and villages. How could I remember something I've never seen?"

Noah stared at nothing and ran his hand slowly through his hair. His voice was very quiet. "Genetic memory."

Genetic.

My mind conjured my mother's voice.

"It isn't you. It might be chemical or behavioral or even genetic—"

"But who in our family has had any kind of—"

"My mother," she had said. *"Your grandmother."*

That was just before she recounted my grandmother's symptoms.

Grandmother's symptoms. Grandmother's doll.

Grandmother's memory?

"No," Noah said, shaking his head. "It's nonsense."

"What is?"

Noah closed his eyes, and spoke as if from memory. "The idea that some experiences can be stored in our DNA and passed down to future generations," he said. "Some people think it explains Jung's theory of the collective unconscious." He opened his eyes and the corner of his mouth lifted. "I'm partial to Freud, myself."

"Why do you know this?"

"I read it."

"Where?"

"In a book."

"What book?" I asked quickly. Noah took my hand and we headed for his room.

Once inside, he scanned his shelves. "I don't see it," he said finally, his eyes still on the bookcases that spanned the length of his room.

"What's it called?"

"*New Theories in Genetics.*" He tipped out a thick book, then replaced it. "By Armin Lenaurd."

I joined in the search. "You don't alphabetize," I said as my gaze traveled over the spines.

"Correct."

There was no order to any of the titles, at least none I could discern. "How do you find anything?"

"I just remember."

"You just . . . remember." There were thousands of books. How?

"I have a good memory."

I tilted my head. "Photographic?"

He shrugged a shoulder.

So that was why he never took any notes in school.

The two of us continued to search. Five minutes passed, then ten, and then Noah gave up and dropped down on his pristinely made bed. He lifted his guitar from its case and began aimlessly playing chords.

I kept looking. I didn't expect the book to have all the answers, or any, really, but I wanted to know more about this and was mildly annoyed that Noah didn't seem to care. But just as my back began to ache from crouching to read the titles on the bottommost shelf, I found it.

"Score," I whispered. I tipped the volume out with my finger and withdrew it; the book was astonishingly heavy, with faded gold lettering on the clothbound cover and spine.

Noah's brow creased. "Strange," he said, watching me rise. "I don't remember putting it there."

I carried the book to his bed and sat beside him. "Not exactly light reading?"

"Beggars can't be choosers."

"Meaning?"

"It was all I had on the flight from London back to the States."

"When was this?"

"Winter break. We went back to England to see my grandparents—my father's parents," he clarified. "I accidentally threw the book I was reading in with my checked luggage, and this was in the seat pouch thing in front of me."

The book was already growing heavy on my lap. "Doesn't seem like it would fit."

"First class."

"Of course."

"My father took the jet."

I made a face.

"I would wholly embrace and mirror your disdain, but I have to say, of all the useless garbage he bleeds money on, that's the one I'm not at all sorry about. No lines. No security misery. No rush."

That actually did seem worth it. "You don't have to take off your shoes or your jacket or—"

"Or be fondled by an overzealous TSA agent. You don't even have to show ID—my father employs the pilot and crew. We literally just show up at the private airport and walk on. It's extraordinary."

"Sounds like it," I murmured, and flipped open the book.

"I'll have to take you somewhere, sometime."

I heard a smile in his voice, but all it did was frustrate me. "I'm not even allowed to come to your house without adult supervision."

"Patience, Grasshopper."

I sighed. "Easy for you to say." I began turning pages, but my eyes kept landing on jargon. "What else does Mr. Lenaurd think?"

"I didn't bother to read the whole thing; it was terminally dull. What you said just reminded me of it—the author believes that some experiences we've never had can be passed down genetically."

I blinked slowly as a key fit into place. "Superman," I said to myself.

"Beg your pardon?"

I looked up from the pages at Noah. "When Daniel was trying to help me with the fake Horizons essay, he asked if the thing my fake character has—the thing *I* have—was acquired or if it existed from the time she—I—was born. Spider-Man or Superman," I said, and snapped the cover closed. "I'm Superman."

Noah seemed amused by this. "As delightful as I find that concept, I'm afraid that our unnatural attributes must have been acquired."

"Why?"

He set his guitar down on the floor, and then met my eyes.

"How many times have you wished someone dead, Mara? Someone who cuts you off on the highway, et cetera?"

Probably more than I should think about. I answered with a noncommittal, "Hmm."

"And when you were little, you probably even screamed to your parents that you wished they were dead too, yes?"

Possibly. I shrugged.

"And yet they're still here. As for myself, my ability couldn't have gone unobserved when I was a kid; I had to get shots and things like everyone else. Surely someone would have noticed I could heal, no?"

"Wait," I said, leaning forward. "How did *you* realize you could heal?"

The change in Noah's demeanor was subtle. His languid posture stiffened even though he was stretched out on his bed, and there was something distant about his eyes when I met them. "I cut myself, and there was no trace of it the next day," he said, sounding bored. "Anyway," he went on, "it has to be acquired. Otherwise we would have noticed long before now."

"But you said you've never been sick—"

"What we *should* be thinking about is why the hell the same rather unusual pendant would be in my mother's chest of silver and sewn into your grandmother's creepy doll."

Noah's face was smoothed into an unreadable mask, the one he reserved for everyone else. There was something he wasn't telling me, but pushing him now would get me nowhere.

"Okay," I said, letting it go for the moment. "So your mother and my grandmother had the same jewelry."

"And hid it," Noah added.

I withdrew the silver charm from my back pocket and placed it flat in my palm. The detail was intricate, I noticed as I examined it. Impressive, considering the size.

I looked up at Noah. "Can I see yours?"

He hesitated for maybe a fraction of a second before slipping the fine black cord over his head. He placed it in my hand; the silver pendant was still warm from his skin.

I compared them both with an artist's eye; the lines of the feather, the contours of the dagger's half-hilt. The two pendants *looked* the same, but something bothered me. I turned the charm—my charm—over, and then I realized what it was.

"They're mirror images."

Noah bent over my open hand, then looked at me from under his lashes. "They are indeed."

"And they're not identical," I said, pointing out the slight imperfections that distinguished one from the other. "They look handmade. And the design is a little—it's a little crude, right? It kind of reminds me of the block printed illustrations you find in old books. And the symbols—"

"Fuck," Noah said, leaning his head back against his headboard. His eyes had closed and he was shaking his head. "Symbols. I didn't even think."

"What?"

"I never bothered to think about it in that context," he said, rising from the bed as I handed him back his pendant. "I just saw it, knew it was my mother's, and wore it because it was hers. But you're right, it could mean something—especially since there are two." He headed for the alcove.

"I was just going to say it reminds me of the symbols on a family crest."

Noah stopped mid-stride, and turned very slowly. "We're not related."

"I know, but—"

"Don't even think it."

"I get the picture," I said as Noah slipped his laptop off of his desk and brought it to his bed.

What was it Daniel had said about Google?

"So, the preponderance of hits for 'feather symbol meaning' bring up the Egyptian goddess Ma'at," Noah read. "Apparently she judged the souls of the dead by weighing their hearts against a feather; if she deemed a soul unworthy, it was sent to the underworld to be consumed—by this bizarre crocodile-lion-hippopotamus creature, it seems." He moved the screen so I could see it; it was, in fact, bizarre. "Anyway, if the soul was good and pure, congratulations, you've earned passage into paradise." Noah typed in something else.

"What about 'dagger comma symbol?'"

"Opened another tab already but alas, said search has generated not much."

"Did you try 'feather and dagger symbol' together?"

"Indeed. Nothing there, either." Noah snapped his laptop shut.

"How many hits did you say the feather thing brought up?"

"Nine million or so. Give or take."

I sighed.

"But most of the first ones were all to the Egyptian goddess," Noah said cheerfully. "That's something."

"Not . . . really."

"Well, we're further ahead than we were yesterday."

I raised my eyebrows. "Yesterday when I woke up to find that I'd been sleepwalking."

"Point."

"Yesterday when I was ready to blame my should-be-dead stalker for the creepy doll-in-underwear-drawer incident."

"I see where you're going with this."

"Good," I said, handing my grandmother's pendant to him. "I was starting to worry you didn't care."

"Is that what you think," Noah said coolly. Then, "Why are you giving me this?"

"I don't want to lose it," I said. But I didn't want to wear it, either.

Noah studied me carefully, but his fingers closed around the charm. "I have someone looking into the Jude issue," he said then, his voice level. "A private investigator my father's worked with. He's trying to find out where he lives, which is proving difficult since he's completely off the grid, and apparently isn't stupid enough to use the illegal immigration channels for help."

I rubbed my forehead. "He *was* kind of stupid."

"Well, he's not acting like it."

"Maybe he has help?"

Noah nodded. "I've considered it, but who besides you even knows he's alive?"

"Another question," I groaned. I flopped down on the bed and then turned my cheek to face Noah. "Why didn't you tell me you were looking for him?"

"I don't tell you everything," he said indifferently.

The words stung, but not as much as the way he said them.

"In any case," he said, "about the pendant, at least now we know that at some point, your grandmother and my mother crossed paths through whoever made them. I'll look through her things and see if I can find anything else."

I was quiet.

"Mara?"

I shook my head. "I shouldn't have burned the doll, Noah. I should have looked for a seam or something—"

"You couldn't have known."

"There was a piece of paper, too."

"I saw."

"It could have been the answer to *all* of this."

Noah lightly tucked a strand of hair behind my ear. "There's no point worrying about it now."

"When would be a good time to worry about it?"

Noah shot me a look. "No need to get snippy."

I bit my lip, then let out a breath. "Sorry," I said, looking up at his ceiling, following a pattern of swirls in the plaster. "I just—I'm worried about tonight." My voice tightened. "I don't want to go to sleep."

I didn't know where I'd be when I woke up.

30

NOAH STOOD UP SUDDENLY THEN, AND CROSSED the room. He locked his door as he met my eyes.

"Risky," I said.

Noah was silent.

"What about our parents?"

"Never mind them." He moved back to his bed and stood beside it, looking down at me. "I don't care about them. Tell me what to do and I'll do it," he said. "Tell me what you want and it's yours."

I want to close my eyes at night and never be afraid that I'll open them up and see Jude.

I want to wake up in the morning safe in my bed and never worry that I've been anywhere else.

"I don't know," I said out loud, and my voice had this awful, desperate tinge. "I'm afraid—I'm afraid I'm losing control."

I'm afraid I'm losing myself.

The idea was a splinter in my mind. Always there, always stinging, even when I wasn't conscious of it. Even when I wasn't thinking about it.

Like Jude.

Noah held my gaze. "I won't let that happen."

"You can't stop it," I said, my throat tightening. "All you can do is watch."

It was a few seconds before Noah finally spoke. "I have been, Mara." His voice was aggressively blank.

My eyes filled with infuriating tears. "What do you see?" I asked him.

I knew what I saw when I looked at myself: A stranger. Terrified, terrorized, and weak. Was that what he saw too?

I drew myself up. "Tell me," I said, my voice edged with steel. "Tell me what you see. Because I don't know what's real and what isn't or what's new or different and I can't trust myself, but I trust you."

Noah closed his eyes. "Mara."

"You know what?" I said, crossing my arms over my chest, holding myself together. "Don't tell me, because I might not remember. Write it down, and then maybe someday, if I ever get better, let me read it. Otherwise I'll change a little bit every day and never know who I was until after I'm gone."

Noah's eyes were still closed and the planes of his face were smooth, but I noticed that his hands had curled into fists. "You cannot fathom how much I hate not being able to help you."

And he couldn't fathom how much I hated needing help. Noah said before that I wasn't broken but I was, and he was learning that he couldn't fix me. But I didn't want to be the injured bird who needed healing, the sick girl who needed sympathy. Noah was different like me but he wasn't *broken* like me. He was never sick or scared. He was strong. Always in control. And even though he'd seen the worst of me, he wasn't *afraid* of me.

I wished I wasn't afraid of myself. I wanted to feel something else.

Noah stood beside his bed, his body taut with tension.

I wanted to feel in control. I wanted to feel *him*.

"Kiss me," I said. My voice was sure.

Noah's eyes opened, but he didn't move. He was considering me. Trying to gauge whether or not I meant it. He didn't want to push me before I was ready.

So I had to show him that I was.

I pulled him fiercely into his soft bed and he did not protest. I rolled beneath him and he braced himself above me and his arms were a perfect cage.

We were forehead to forehead. From this angle, it was impossible to ignore the length of his lashes, the way they skimmed his cheekbones when he blinked. It was impossible to ignore the shape of his mouth, the curve of his lips when he said my name.

It was impossible not to want to taste them.

I arched my neck and my hips and stretched my body up toward his. But Noah placed one hand on my waist and very gently pushed me back down.

"Slowly," he said. The word sent a thrill through every nerve.

Noah leaned down slightly, just slightly, and let his lips brush my neck. My pulse raced at the contact. Noah drew back.

He could hear it, I remembered. Every heartbeat. The way my breathing changed or didn't. He thought my heart was pounding with fear, not desire.

I had to show him he was wrong.

I arched my neck off of the pillow and angled my lips toward his ear and whispered, "Keep going."

To my complete shock, he did.

Noah traced the line of my jaw with his mouth. He was braced above me and touched me nowhere else. Then he hooked one finger under the collar of my T-shirt and pulled it down into a slight V, exposing a triangle of skin. He kissed the hollow at the base of my throat. Then lower. Once.

I was spinning. Pinned to his mattress by the space between us but I was desperate to close it—desperate to feel his mouth on mine.

"Now?"

"No," he whispered against my skin.

His mouth made me ache, sweet and furious. It was impossible to keep still, but when my body instinctively curved toward his, he drew away.

"Now?" I breathed.

"Not yet." His lips found my skin again, this time beneath my ear.

Just when I thought I couldn't possibly take any more, Noah lowered his mouth to the curve of my shoulder, and his teeth grazed my skin.

I was ignited, on fire, flooded with heat and ready to beg.

I thought I saw the smallest hint of a half-smile on his mouth, but it was gone before I could be sure. Because Noah's gaze dropped from my eyes to *my* mouth, and then his lips brushed mine.

The kiss was so light I wouldn't have believed it happened if I hadn't watched. His lips were cloud soft and I wanted to feel them more. Harder. Fiercer. I ran my fingers through his perfect hair and wrapped my arms around his neck. Locked them there. Locked him in.

But then he unbound them. Pulled away and kneeled back until he was at the foot of the bed. "I'm still here."

"I know," I said, frustrated and breathless.

A smile lifted the corner of his mouth, lazy and sublime. "Then why do you look so angry?"

"Because," I started. "Because you're always in control."

And I'm not. Not around you.

I felt and probably looked like a wild thing while Noah kneeled there like an arrogant prince. Like the world was his, should he choose to reach out and take it.

"You're so *calm*," I said out loud. "It's like you don't need it." Need me, I didn't say. But I could tell by the way his delinquent smile softened that he knew what I meant.

Noah moved forward, toward me, next to me then, the slender muscles in his arms flexing with the movement. "I'm not sure you can appreciate how much I want to lay you out before me and make you scream my name."

My mouth fell open.

So why won't you? I wanted to ask. "Why don't you?"

Noah lifted a hand to the nape of my neck. Trailed one finger down my spine, which straightened at his touch. "Because part of you *is* still afraid. And I don't want you to feel that. Not then."

I wanted to argue that I wasn't afraid anymore. That we kissed and he was still here and so maybe I *did* dream that he almost died, maybe it *wasn't* real. But I couldn't say any of those things, because I didn't believe them.

This kiss was nothing like that one. When we kissed before, I didn't know enough to even *be* afraid. Of myself. Of what I could do to him. I didn't know enough to hold myself back.

Now I was too aware, hyperaware, and so the fear chained me.

And Noah could tell. "When you're frightened, your pulse

changes," he said. "Your breath. Your heartbeat. Your sound. I can't ignore that and I won't, even if you think you want me to."

It was excruciating, the wanting and the fear, and I felt hopeless. "What if I'm afraid forever?"

"You won't be." His voice was soft, but certain.

"What if I am?"

"Then I'll wait forever."

I shook my head fiercely. "No. You won't."

Noah smoothed the hair from my face. Made me look at him before he spoke. "There *will* come a moment when there's nothing you want more than us. Together. When you're free of every fear and there is nothing in our way." Noah's voice was sincere, his expression serious. I wanted to believe him.

"And *then* I'll make you scream my name."

I broke into a smile. "Maybe I'll make you scream mine."

31

A slow, arrogant smile formed on Noah's lips. "Gauntlet thrown." He drew away and unlocked his door. "I do so love a challenge."

"Shame it isn't the only one."

"Agreed." He tipped his head toward the hallway. "Come on."

I rose, but before leaving his room, I grabbed the book. "Can I borrow this?"

"You can," he said, holding his door open for me. "But I should warn you that I fell asleep on page thirty-four."

"I'm motivated."

Noah led me down the long hall, our footsteps muffled by

the plush Oriental rugs beneath our feet. We turned several corners before he finally stopped in front of a door, withdrew something long and thin from his back pocket, and then proceeded to pick at an old-looking lock.

"That's handy," I said as it clicked.

Noah pushed the door open. "I have my uses."

We stood before a small room that actually seemed more like an enormous closet. There were stacks of temporary shelving and boxes that lined the walls.

My gaze slid over the piles. "What is this stuff?"

"My mother's things," Noah said, pulling a cord that hung from the ceiling. An antique milk-glass light fixture lit up the space. "Everything she owned is somewhere in this room."

"What are we looking for?"

"I'm not sure. But she left the pendant for me, and your grandmother left the same one for you—maybe we'll find something about it in a letter or a picture or something. And if there's a connection between your ability and your grandmother then perhaps . . ."

Noah's voice trailed off, but he didn't need to finish his sentence because I understood.

There might be a connection between his mother and *him*. I could tell he hoped it was true.

Noah opened a box and handed me a sheaf of papers. I began to read.

"What are you doing in here?"

I was startled by the unfamiliar English-accented voice. The papers fluttered to the floor.

"Katie," Noah said, smiling at the girl. "You remember Mara."

I certainly remembered Katie. She was equally as gorgeous as her brother—with the same dark mane, shot through with gold, and Noah's fine boned, elegant features. Lashes and legs for days. *Arresting* was the word that came to mind.

Katie gave me a slow once-over, and then said to Noah, "So *that's* where you've been spending your nights."

His expression hardened. "What is wrong with you?"

Katie ignored him. "Aren't you in a mental hospital or something?" she asked me.

I was speechless.

"Why are you being like this?" Noah asked sharply.

"What are you doing in here?" she volleyed back.

"What does it look like?"

"It looks like you're digging through Mom's shit. Dad's going to kill you."

"He'd have to come home to do that, though, wouldn't he?" Noah said, his tone disgusted. "Go eat something, we'll talk later."

She rolled her eyes. Then waved at me. "Lovely to see you again."

"Wow," I said once she was gone. "That was . . ."

Noah ran his hand roughly through his hair, twisting the

strands up. "I'm sorry. She's always been a bit snotty, but she's been insufferable these past few weeks."

So that's where you've been spending your nights.

"You've been away a lot these past few weeks," I said. Maybe I wasn't the only one who needed Noah around.

He ignored the implication. "*She's* been spending a lot of time with your best friend *Anna* these past few weeks. It's not a coincidence," Noah said tonelessly. "She's not acting out because I've been with you."

But I felt a twinge of guilt anyway.

"My family . . . isn't the same as yours," he said.

"What do you mean?"

He paused, measuring his words before he spoke. "We're strangers who happen to live in the same house."

Noah's voice was smooth, but there was an ache behind the words that I could feel, if not hear. However he felt about his family situation, it couldn't be helping that he was gone so much. And no matter what he said, we both knew that I was the reason.

"You should stay at your house tonight," I said.

He shook his head. "Not because of that."

"You should stay here for a few days." It cost me, but I didn't want to admit it.

Noah closed his eyes. "Your mother won't allow me to stay over during the week once Croyden starts up again."

"We'll figure something out," I said, though I didn't quite believe it.

And then I heard an all-too-familiar voice call me from downstairs.

"Ready to go, Mara?" my mom shouted.

I wasn't, but I had no choice.

My mother was quiet on the ride home, which was immensely frustrating because for the first time in a long time, I actually wanted to talk to her. But each question I asked earned me the briefest of answers, verbal and otherwise:

"Did Grandma ever leave me anything besides that doll?"

A head shake.

"Did she leave you anything when she died?"

"Money."

"What about . . . stuff?" Didn't want to be too obvious.

"Only the emerald earrings," she said. "And some clothes."

And the pendant I left with Noah, that my mother didn't seem to know anything about. "No letters or anything? Notebooks?"

Another head shake as she stared at the road ahead of us. "No."

"What about pictures?"

"She hated pictures," my mother said softly. "She never let me take any. The one in the hall is the only one I have."

"Of her on her wedding day," I said, an idea dawning.

"Yes."

"When she married my grandfather."

A pause. "Yes."

"Did *he* really die in a car accident?"

My mom inhaled sharply. "Yes."

"When?"

"When I was little," she said.

"Did you have any aunts or uncles?"

"It was just my mother and me."

I tried to imagine what that would be like. *Lonely* was the word that came to mind.

It was strange, realizing how little I knew about my mom's life before us. Before Dad, even. I felt guilty for having never really thought of her as anything but Mom. I wanted to know more—not just because of the weirdness with my grandmother, though that was the catalyst.

"We're strangers who happen to live in the same house," Noah had said about his family.

My mother felt a bit like a stranger too. And right now, I didn't want her to be.

But when I opened my mouth to ask her another question, she cut me off before I could.

"It's been a long day, Mara. Can we talk about this stuff another time?"

"Okay," I said quietly, then tried changing the subject. "What did you think of Noah's stepmother?"

"They're . . . sad," was all she said, and left it at that.

I was impossibly curious, but she was clearly not in a

sharing mood. The obscenely heavy *New Theories in Genetics* crushed my lap; I tried to start reading it in the car, but grew nauseous. It would have to wait, but that was okay.

Everything felt okay, oddly enough. Yes, Katie was rude. Yes, the necklace thing was weird. But Noah and I kissed.

We *kissed*.

He wouldn't spend the night, but I'd see him tomorrow after Horizons. And then it would be the weekend, and we could spend it looking for answers together.

And also maybe kissing.

When we pulled onto our street I almost missed John walking a terrier mix down the block. Seeing him made me feel even lighter.

Jude wanted to scare me, and he had, but that was over now. He'd have to find something else to occupy his second life.

32

OKAY, EVERYONE," BROOKE SAID, CLAPPING HER hands twice. "We're finally going to finish this round of sharing with Mara, Adam, Jamie, Stella, and Megan. Let's all take out our fear journals."

The unenthusiasm among my Horizons compatriots was palpable, but I was the queen of apathy today. Noah was theoretically roaming Little Havana in search of answers and digging through his mother's things. I wanted to be with him but instead I was here, and it annoyed me.

Some students withdrew composition notebooks from small bags they had with them. Others walked over to the bookshelf to retrieve theirs. Phoebe was one of the walkers. She sat down next to me.

I felt the urge to move.

"Who wants to go first?" Brooke asked, glancing at each of us in turn.

Don't make eye contact.

"Oh, come on!" She wagged her finger. "You're all going to go eventually."

Resounding silence.

"Mara," Brooke said. "How about you?"

Of course. "I'm still . . . unclear . . . about the . . . parameters of this . . . exercise," I said.

Brooke nodded. "It's a lot to process, I know, but you've been doing great these past few days! Don't worry, I'll walk you through this. So what we're going to do is make a list of situations that make us anxious or fearful. Then we rank them—one for things that make us very slightly anxious, and ten for situations that make us extremely anxious." Brooke stood up and walked to a low bookshelf in the corner of the room. She took out a composition notebook. "And with exposure therapy, we confront our fears little by little. That's why we keep journals with us, to write about our feelings and anxieties so that we can see how far we've come from where we started, and to find common ground with our peers during Group," Brooke finished. She looked at my lap, then at the messenger bag beneath my chair—freshly combed for contraband and not found wanting. "Where's your journal?"

I shook my head. "I never got a journal."

"Of course you did. On your first day, don't you remember?"

No. "Um."

"Check your bag."

I did. I rummaged through it and saw the small sketchbook I kept with me for art therapy along with a few spiral notebooks, but not a composition one.

"Are you sure?" she asked me.

I nodded, looking through it again. Nothing was out of place, except a stray piece of paper at the bottom.

Brooke sighed. "Okay, well, take a blank notebook for today," she said, and handed me one along with a pen. "But do try to find it, please?" Then she turned back to the group.

"All right, guys," she continued, "I want you to flip to the most recent page in your fear journal. Mara, since you aren't sure where yours is, just start listing some anxieties and rank them the way I described, okay? In fact, let's all take five minutes to look over our lists and see if we can find anything else we want to say."

Adam coughed, and it sounded a lot like "bullshit."

"Was there something you wanted to say, Adam?"

"I said this is bullshit. I did it at Lakewood. It's stupid."

Brooke rose and tipped her head, indicating that Adam should get up and follow her. He did, and they moved off to the side. Brooke spoke quietly and patiently, but I couldn't make out her words.

I wished Jamie was sitting closer so I could ask him what Lakewood was. Sadly, he was on the opposite side of the room.

But Stella was right beside me.

"She could almost pass for normal," Jamie had said about her.

Which made her more normal than me. Maybe I could make a new friend.

I leaned over to her and asked, "What's Lakewood?"

"A lockup," she said, cracking her knuckles.

I stared at her blankly.

"A secure residential treatment center?"

Still nothing.

She sighed. "You know how this place is a feeder for the Horizons inpatient program?"

"Kind of?"

"We're assessed here, in the day program, and then they tell our parents whether they think we're sane enough to hack it out here or whether they think our issues are serious enough to need inpatient treatment." She twined a strand of curly hair around her finger. "The Horizons RTC is inpatient, but you get to move around, to come and go from your room and stuff—the retreat's coming up, you'll see. Anyway, that's a normal RTC. At the *secure* RTCs, you're basically locked in your room unless they come get you. You're followed everywhere. Lakewood's in the middle of nowhere—practically all RTCs are—but without the good food and counselors who actually care. It's pretty much the last stop before state institutionalization." She cocked her head to the side. "You're new to this troubled teen thing, aren't you?"

I looked over at Adam with new eyes. "Apparently."

"Veteran," Stella said, and shrugged.

I was curious what she was in for, but she didn't volunteer and this wasn't exactly prison.

"Well, Adam," Brooke said loudly. "If you don't want to participate, I'm going to have to let Dr. Kells know and you'll have to do it with her."

"He doesn't belong here," Stella said quietly as Adam and Brooke walked back into our circle. I wanted to ask her more, but Brooke was ready to move on.

Back to me.

I successfully avoided mentioning any of my real (and valid) fears of the Jude and supernatural varieties by rattling off a bunch of benign, normal ones like bugs and needles. Jamie attempted to ruffle Brooke's patience with answers like "intellectual bankruptcy," and "sea monkeys," while Megan earnestly volunteered every phobia I'd ever heard of and several I never knew existed ("Doraphobia" is the fear of fur).

This earned an obnoxious comment from Adam, who Jamie then accused of having a fear of "physical inadequacies" of a very private nature, which resulted in what I thought was an unjust scolding from Brooke and also caused another Jamie-Adam confrontation. I was rooting for Jamie to land a well-deserved punch to Adam's brutish head but the face-off ended before it got too exciting. Stella managed to get by without participating at all. Lucky girl. I unintentionally caught a glance at her fear journal but saw only one word ("voices") before I quickly looked away.

Hmm.

When we were finished, we all handed our notebooks back to Brooke and she then asked for volunteers for a "flooding session." Megan's hand went up, bless her, and I had the non-pleasure of watching the poor girl's big, brown eyes go wide with terror as Brooke talked her through scenario after scenario in which she would encounter and then be confined in small spaces. Brooke talked her through it; first Megan sat there and imagined approaching a closet. Then she imagined walking next to it. Then in it. Then Brooke guided her closer and closer to one in real life. When the fear threatened to overcome her, she said a word that told Brooke she couldn't take it anymore, and then they backed up. Megan was committed, though; a True Believer. She really did seem to want to improve. Admirable.

When the session ended, we all applauded and offered our encouragement: "Way to go!" "Great job!" "You're so strong!" Exclamation points included.

We broke for snack time then—just like kindergarten!—and I pulled out my sketchbook to work on an asinine project I'd been assigned: pick an emotion and draw it. I *wanted* to draw a raised middle finger, but I would draw a kitten instead. Normal people love kittens.

But when I reached inside my bag for my sketchbook, my hand closed over that stray piece of paper.

I withdrew it. Unfolded it. I read what it said as the hair rose on the back of my neck:

I see you.

33

JUDE, MY MIND WHISPERED, AS MY VEINS COURSED with fear.

I whipped around; my eyes searched for him of their own volition.

He wasn't here.

He couldn't be. And he couldn't have been in my house last night—not with John watching it.

Then I remembered my first day at Horizons. Phoebe stealing the picture from my bag. Blacking out my eyes.

She'd sat next to me in Group today.

Jude didn't write the note. It was her.

But why?

Scratch that. She was insane. That's why.

I took the note and shoved it angrily in my back pocket, and waited for Group Part II to resume, leaning back in my chair and pressing the heels of my palms into my eyes. My life was screwed up enough without adding Phoebe's bullshit to the pile. Wayne came around with meds for some of us—myself included—and I downed them in the little paper shot glass. The aftertaste was bitter but I didn't bother washing it away. I just watched the clock and counted down the seconds until I'd get the chance to confront her.

Brooke breezed back in with a mug full of what was probably organic, fair trade coffee and a stack of worksheets. She began handing them out as we all found our chairs, Phoebe included. She eyed the room and pointedly sat as far away from me as she could.

I took the paper from Brooke just a tad too fiercely. It had rows of ridiculous cartoon faces on them, contorted into various exaggerated expressions and, I supposed, their corresponding "feelings." A squinty kid sticking his tongue out of one corner of his mouth as he smirked, with an unruly spike of hair to connote "sneaky"; a placid-faced, blond-pigtailed girl with closed eyes and folded arms above the word "safe." There was a preponderance of stuck-out tongues and googly eyes. Brooke began handing out markers.

"I want you all to circle the face and feeling that best describes your mood today." She looked at me. "It's called a feelings check-in. We do this twice a week."

I whipped the cap off of the marker and started circling: mad, suspicious, furious, enraged. I handed her back the sheet.

My feelings must have been evident on my face because I was the focus of over a dozen stares. Not Phoebe's, though. She was staring at the ceiling.

"It seems like you have a lot of interesting feelings right now, Mara," Brooke said encouragingly. "Do you want to share first?"

"I'd *love* to." I lifted my hips and pulled the note out of my back pocket. I handed it to Brooke. "*Someone* put this in my bag this morning," I said, speaking to Brooke but staring Phoebe down.

Brooke opened the note and read it. She maintained her calm demeanor. "How do you feel about this?"

I narrowed my eyes. "Wasn't that the point of the feelings check-in? Why don't you tell me what *you* think about it?"

"Well, Mara, I think it's something that has clearly upset you."

I laughed without humor. "Yes, clearly."

Adam raised his hand. Brooke turned to him. "Yes, Adam?"

"What's it say?"

"I see you," I said. "It says 'I see you.'"

"And what do you think about that, Mara?" Brooke asked.

If Phoebe wasn't going to admit to it, I would call her out and let the chips fall as they may. "I think Phoebe wrote it and put in my bag."

"Why would you think that?"

"Perhaps because she is *batshit crazy*, Brooke."

Jamie slow-clapped.

"Jamie," Brooke said calmly. "I'm not sure that's productive."

"I was applauding Mara for her extraordinarily appropriate use of the term 'batshit crazy.'"

Brooke grew annoyed. "Do you have anything you'd like to share, Jamie?"

"No, that pretty much covers it."

"My elbow hurts," Adam chimed in.

"Why'd you write it, Phoebe?" I asked.

She looked as squirrely as ever. "I didn't write it."

"I don't believe you," I said.

"I didn't write it!" she shouted. Then she dropped to the floor and began rocking back and forth.

Fantastic. I rubbed my hand over my face as Brooke moved over to the wall and pressed a button I'd never noticed before. Phoebe was still rocking on the floor, but when Brooke's back was turned, she glared at me.

Then smiled.

"You little shit," I whispered under my breath.

Brooke turned. "Did you say something, Mara?"

I narrowed my eyes at Phoebe, who had covered her ears now. Ponytail Patrick had appeared and was trying to coax Phoebe up off of the carpet.

"She's faking it," I said, still staring at her.

Brooke glanced down at Phoebe, but I could tell she didn't believe me. She looked up at the clock. "Well, we don't have much time left anyway. Patrick," she asked him, "will you take Phoebe back to Dr. Kells?" And then in a lowered voice, added, "I can page Wayne if you think she needs to relax."

And look at that. Phoebe was off the floor. Magic.

"Everyone else, grab your journals and take a few minutes to write about your feelings. We're going to talk more about what happened today later, all right? And don't forget—tomorrow's family day. You should all be working on your list of ten things your family doesn't know about you but you wish they did."

And with that, everyone stood and retrieved their journals to write. I only pretended to. I was still furious. Phoebe could fool Brooke and Dr. Kells and the rest of them—I knew from experience it wasn't that hard—but she could not fool me. She wrote the note, and I would make her admit it.

And just before the end of the day, I got my chance.

I found her in a small lounge area, writing something in *her* journal with robotic, bloodless focus.

I looked around. There was no one in the hall, but I didn't want to be too loud. I kept my voice low. "Why'd you do it?" I asked her.

She looked up at me, all innocence. "Do what?"

"You wrote the note, Phoebe."

"I didn't."

"Really," I said, my temper flaring. "You're really not going to cop to this? I don't even care—God knows you have enough problems—I just want to hear you say it."

"I didn't write it," she said robotically.

I grabbed the door frame with one hand and squeezed it. I had to go or I'd lose it.

"I didn't write it," Phoebe said again. But her tone had changed; it made me face her. She was staring directly at me, now, her eyes focused and clear.

"I heard you."

Phoebe dropped her eyes back to her journal. A smile inched across her lips. "But I did put it there."

34

MY BLOOD RAN COLD. "WHAT DID YOU JUST SAY?"

Phoebe began to hum.

I walked right up next to her and crouched so that I could look her in the eye. "Tell me what you said. Right now. Or I'm going to tell Dr. Kells. Right. Now."

"My boyfriend gave it to me," she said in a singsong voice.

"Who's your boyfriend, Phoebe?"

"You are my sunshine, my only sunshine, you make me happy, when skies are gray," she sang, and then reverted back to her humming.

I wanted to smack her head off of her spine. My hands

curled into fists. It took everything I had right then not to hit her.

I almost, *almost* wanted to kill her.

I closed my eyes. After a minute of paralysis, I turned around and walked away. Let's call it progress.

I was very ready for the pointless day to be over. When I got home, I wanted to try and decipher *New Theories in Genetics,* and also see if Noah had any luck scouring Calle Ocho on his own. But Joseph roped me into a video game war before I made it to my room, and when I called Noah after I lost thrice, he sounded strange.

He asked if I was all right. I said yes, and then immediately attacked him with questions. But he cut me off quickly, saying we'd talk tomorrow.

I hung up feeling a bit uneasy and I hated myself for it, for feeling insecure. We'd been spending nearly every moment together and I was even the one who suggested he spend more time at his house, more time apart. But his voice sounded so off and we were dealing with so much—*I* was dealing with so much—that part of me couldn't help but wonder if my baggage might be getting too heavy for him to want to carry anymore.

When the last day of my first week at Horizons arrived, I found myself about to unpack some of said baggage in front of my older brother. It was Family Therapy Day and I was completely unenthused about having Daniel bear witness to the whole psycho-sister scenario in full color. We were greeted by Counselor Wayne, who led us to the common area where we were divided into mini-groups. Most people brought parents, but a select few, like me, brought older or younger siblings. And when they sorted us into smaller rooms, and Jamie walked in followed closely by an older, freckled, very chill-looking girl I didn't recognize, my mouth fell open when I realized Jamie was one of them.

The girl behind him must be the infamous sister. The one Jamie said Noah defiled in some kind of twisted revenge game.

This could be interesting.

Jamie sat down in a plastic chair, his newly long legs stretched out in front of him. His sister sat beside him with an identical posture. I smiled even though Jamie kept glancing at the door.

Because of the way they split us up, there was a chance we'd end up with Wayne or someone else to "facilitate" today, and I hoped we did. Brooke was ditzy but relentless.

"Hi, everyone!" Brooke waltzed in.

Alas, no luck.

"Horizons students—what a wonderful morning! Family members, thanks *so* much for being here. Let's *all* go around in a circle and introduce ourselves—sound good? Because we're *all* family here."

I glanced over at Daniel. He seemed to be giving Brooke the side-eye. I loved him so much.

She pointed at Jamie first. "Why don't you start us off?"

"Hi, I'm Jamie!" he said, mocking her enthusiasm.

"Hi, Jamie!" Brooke said, not realizing it.

His sister—if that's indeed who she was—sucked in her lips in what I assumed was an attempt not to laugh.

"Who have you brought with you today, Jamie?"

The girl answered and lifted her hand in a wave. "Stephanie Roth. I'm Jamie's very lucky sister."

"Hi, Stephanie," we all said.

And so it went until we all introduced ourselves and our people. Brooke had us each read from our lists of things we wished our present family members knew about us but didn't. Mine was pretty much crap, which is why I was so surprised when Daniel began to read his. Apparently, our family people had been tasked without our knowledge with creating an identical list.

"I wish Mara knew that I'm jealous of her."

I whipped around to face him. "You can't be serious."

Brooke shook her finger. "No interruptions, Mara."

My brother cleared his throat. "I wish she knew that I think she's the most hilarious person on Earth. And that whenever she's not home, I feel like I'm missing my partner in crime."

My throat tightened. Do not cry. Do not cry.

"I wish she knew that *she's* really Mom's favorite—"

I shook my head here.

"—the princess she always wanted. That Mom used to

dress her up like a little doll and parade her around like Mara was her greatest achievement. I wish Mara knew that I never minded, because she's my favorite too."

A chin quiver. Damn.

"I wish she knew that I've always had acquaintances instead of friends because I've spent every second I'm not in school studying or practicing piano. I wish she knew that she is literally as smart as I am—her IQ is ONE POINT lower," he said, raising his eyes to meet mine. "Mom had us tested. And that she could get the same grades if she weren't so lazy."

I slouched in my seat, and may or may not have crossed my arms over my chest defensively.

"I wish she knew that I am really proud of her, and that I always will be, no matter what."

"Tissues?" Brooke handed me a box.

Nooooooo. I furiously blinked back the tears that blurred my vision and shook my head. "I'm fine," I said hoarsely.

Oh, yeah. Just fine.

"That was wonderful, Daniel," Brooke said. "Why don't we all clap for Mara and Daniel?"

Insert scattered applause here.

"And we can take a short break to give us a sec to catch up with our feelings."

SO AWFUL. I bolted for the bathroom. I splashed some water on my face and when I dried it, Stephanie Roth was leaning against the counter.

She smiled. "Hey," she said. "I'm—"

"I know who you are," I said. My voice was still hoarse. I cleared my throat. "I know."

"Right, the intros."

Not exactly. "I've heard a lot about you," I said instead, realizing after the fact that a) it wasn't true and b) what I had heard wasn't necessarily flattering.

"And I you, Mara Dyer," she said, flashing a cryptic smile. "Jamie told me you're Noah Shaw's girlfriend."

I raised my eyebrows. "He said that?"

"Actually, his exact words were 'Noah's new piece.'"

I grinned and threw the paper towel away. "Sounds more like him."

"Good for you."

Uh-oh. "Um . . ."

"I mean, about Noah."

I narrowed my eyes at her. "Is that sarcasm I detect?"

She shook her head. Her expression was serious. "No."

"Because Jamie, like, hates him."

She tied her blond hair back into a ponytail. "I know."

I wondered how far I could push this, because I sure as hell was curious. "He hates him because of what Noah . . . did to you," I finally said.

And then her expression changed. Stephanie looked wary, all of a sudden. Her posture straightened and she said, "Did Noah tell you what happened?"

"Jamie did."

"But not Noah?"

"I asked him if I should believe Jamie, and he said yes."

Stephanie gave me a slow, lingering look. "But you didn't." Stephanie crossed her athletic arms as she considered me. I was completely unsure of what to say next.

So I tried to flee. "See you in there, I guess," I said as I headed for the door.

But Stephanie held out her arm to stop me. "I had an abortion."

"Um." I was positive I was giving off that deer-in-headlights look. I glanced desperately at the door. "I'm not really qualified to—"

"Noah came with me."

I froze. "Was he—"

Stephanie shook her head vehemently. "No. It wasn't him. But that's kind of . . ." She paused, glancing up at the ceiling. "That's kind of what started it."

I said nothing. I mean, what *can* you say?

"Noah asked me out," she started. "He was only fifteen, even though he didn't look it, and I thought it was kind of hilarious, so I went even though I'd been dating this other guy at another school for a while. Once we were together, Noah totally admitted that he asked me because he thought Jamie was messing with *his* sister. You screw with my family, I screw with yours; that kind of thing."

I nodded cautiously. That fit with what I knew.

"And, I don't know, I thought Jamie shouldn't really be making out publicly with an eighth grader—they were the same age, but still. So I went along with the game, which didn't actually involve anything but pretending to fawn over Noah to Jamie over dinner and stuff. But I was with this other guy. Let's call him Kyle," she said, and her voice turned sharp. "We'd been dating for, like, six months in total secret. My parents would've hated him," she said, almost under her breath. "And we were having sex. Which my parents also would've hated." She glanced at the bathroom door. "Long story short, at some point I probably missed a pill, then I was late, then boom, two pink lines. I told Kyle, who said it wasn't his problem—I was easy, and must have been 'sleeping around.'" She rolled her eyes. "A winner, clearly."

"Sounds like it," I said quietly.

She half-smiled. "I *knew* I wasn't ready for a baby and that adoption wasn't for me; I knew what I wanted, I was sure, but I just felt—alone." She leaned back against the wall and stared at me. "I didn't trust my friends to keep the secret, my parents would have lost it if they found out, and the idea of going to Planned Parenthood by myself was excruciating. Holding it all in just made me feel—I felt screwed up." Her eyes hardened and she looked at the floor. "Noah saw me crying by the vending machines at school—I was such a mess that I just blurted everything out to the poor kid." She smiled at the memory. "But he was really great. He used his connections and had an appointment made with a private ob-gyn and he went with me. Anyway, I cried a lot after—I hated feeling like it was this ugly secret even though it was what I wanted and I was *relieved*." Her lips thinned into a hard line. "Noah saw me on the way to lunch a few days later and asked how I was and I just burst into tears. Jamie walked by, Noah walked away, Jamie drew his own conclusions and thought Noah dumped me, and I was too upset to correct him."

I couldn't stay quiet anymore. "So you just let everyone think he screwed you over? After he helped you?"

Stephanie shook her head. "I called Noah as soon as I got home that night, telling him I'd tell Jamie something else, make up a different lie, but he said he didn't care and the *way* he said it? I believed him. It's funny," she said, though she didn't smile. "I think part of him actually *wants* to be hated. He only ever shows you what he wants you to see. He's so closed off—it made me feel like he'd never tell."

"He never did tell," I said slowly. "But why are you telling *me*?" Not that I didn't appreciate it, because I did.

Her Mona Lisa smile appeared again. "Sometimes the biggest secrets you can only tell a stranger." She leaned against the painted gray wall and tilted her head. Considered me. "I don't care what you think of me—I made the right choice for my life and I don't regret it. If you think I'm a horrible person and a murderer and that I'm going to hell, we never have to see each other again. But it would hurt my parents if they knew, and Jamie—he's awesome, and the most loyal person I've ever known. But he's a little . . ." She scratched her nose, "He's judgmental. Self-righteous. I love him to death, but he has this black-and-white worldview. Like, he likes you a lot, but he was ragging on you earlier for being with Noah even knowing you're going to have your heart broken—he holds onto stuff *forever*. Noah definitely has his assaholic moments, and there's a lot of darkness there; I've heard he's done some seriously fucked-up shit. Maybe he will break your heart, I'm no oracle." She shrugged. "But in the fallacious case of Noah Shaw vs. Stephanie Roth? He's not guilty," she said, heading for the door. She put her hand on the handle. "I just—watching you out there, with your brother—" she started. Dropped a shrug. "I just wanted you to know."

"Wait," I said, and her hand fell to her side. "Why don't you just tell Jamie now? It's been years."

"He's got other crap to deal with, and he's taking this whole Horizons thing pretty hard. Or rather, he's taking the fact that our parents don't believe a word he says pretty hard."

I knew what that was like.

"Plus, he's adopted, and I think it might bother him."

I shook my head. "I don't think so. I think he'd want to know the truth."

"There is no truth," Stephanie said mysteriously. "Only perspectives. Philosophy 101," she said with a wink.

But despite her light tone, I could see that she was biting the insides of her cheek.

"I don't want him to know, okay?" she said after a pause. She looked me in the eye. "So don't tell him." And then Stephanie walked out the door.

I stared after her. Jamie thought he was being loyal by hating Noah, who had actually only helped. And Stephanie wasn't upset about her choice; she was just afraid of what her brother would think of her for making it.

Was I so different?

I used to think there was nothing I could do to change the way my family saw me. There was nothing I couldn't say.

But now I knew that wasn't true. I'll walk forever with stories inside me that the people I love the most can never hear.

35

I SURVIVED MY FIRST WEEK AT HORIZONS WITHOUT killing anyone or getting killed myself, and by the time Friday afternoon arrived, I was relatively thrilled. Noah called and asked if I wanted him to spend the weekend, which, obviously, I answered in the affirmative despite the fact that he still sounded a bit off. So he convinced Ruth to go out of town and had her call my mother to ask if she would host him. Mom said yes without hesitation—I was surprised, but gift horses and mouths. You know.

Half the family was in and half was out when Daniel and I got home from our sibling session at Horizons, and since nothing much was planned and I had nothing to do, I picked up *New Theories in Genetics,* which was conveniently sitting on my desk, and took it to the family room to read.

"Mara?"

Daniel's voice. Daniel's hand on my shoulder. I opened my eyes to find that my cheek was smushed against the sixth page.

I fell asleep. Fantastic.

I wiped my mouth in case I'd been drooling. "What time is it?"

"Not even five. Interesting choice of pillow. Title?"

I handed Daniel the book. He squinted at it. Then at me.

"What?"

"Nothing. Just seems like an unusual selection."

"For me, you mean."

"I didn't know you were interested in genetics, that's all."

I sat up and folded my legs beneath me. "What happened to the 'I wish Mara knew she was just as smart as me' business?"

"Nothing. Still true. But what sparked the sudden interest?"

"Noah said something about genetic memory and it made me curious. He said he read about it in there." I tipped my head toward the book. "But the only things I picked up in the introduction were references to Euhemerism and Jungian archetypes—"

"*Euhemerus*, wow. Way to trigger an eighth-grade honors English flashback."

"Seriously—"

"You had O'Hara too, right? Did she make you guys do that project where you had to choose a myth and invent a 'historical' interpretation?"

"Yeah—"

"I think I ended up doing something about Aphrodite and heteronormativity—I don't really remember much except that it was brilliant, even for me," he said with a smile. "Why are you reading this again?"

"To achieve enlightenment about genetic memory. I have only six hundred plus pages to go."

Daniel made a face, and scratched his nose.

"What?"

"Not to, like, discourage you or anything, but genetic memory is science fiction, not science fact."

I shot him a weary look.

"Sorry, but it is. It can't be peer reviewed or tested—"

"That doesn't mean it's impossible."

"It means it's unprovable."

I thought of everything I had been through and all the things I was *still* going through, none of which I could prove. "Just because you can't prove something doesn't mean it isn't real." I reached for the book.

Daniel dodged out of arm's length and flipped it open to the first page. "Maybe I'll give it a read anyway."

I reached for it again, flexing my fingers. "You can borrow it after me."

"But you're not reading it. You're sleeping on it. I'll put it in my room—you can get it whenever you want. Oh, and ask Mom about Jung, she'll like that."

"Daniel—"

"THERE IS AN ALLIGATOR IN MAX'S POOL!" Joseph shouted from the foyer. He came running into the living room, his face lit with excitement.

"How big?" Daniel asked, and shifted the giant book behind his back.

"Big," Joseph said, eyes wide. "Really big."

My turn. "Did you see it?"

Joseph shook his head. "He e-mailed. They're calling that guy to come over and get it out."

"What guy?" Daniel asked.

"Wait, that guy from Animal Planet?" I asked.

Joseph nodded furiously. "He invited me over to watch. His mom is freaking out because they have an outdoor cat and they haven't found her yet."

Ice slid through my veins as I remembered—

The still body of a gray cat lay inches from where I'd been standing, its flesh torn open, its fur streaked with red.

My mother appeared in the kitchen. "Max's cat is missing too?"

Daniel arched an eyebrow. "Too?"

I had to stay calm. Had to keep up the show.

"The Delaneys just asked me if any of us have seen *their*

cat." Their house bordered ours in the back. "She's been missing since Sunday."

Since I came home.

Joseph's eyebrows lowered. "That's when Jenny's dog ran away."

Who's Jenny? I mouthed to Daniel.

"Angelo," Daniel said. "Across the street and to the left."

Joseph looked back at Mom. "Mom, will you take me to Max's?"

"I'm kind of tired, honey."

Joseph looked at Daniel and then at me. We simultaneously said, "Not it."

Joseph clasped his hands together in mock prayer. "PLEASE take me! I will never ever ask for anything ever again, I swear."

"Mara has to stay and help me with dinner," my mom said.

My turn to make a face, even though I was spectacularly relieved. "I do?"

"Daniel, take him please?" she asked. Daniel was already reaching for her keys.

"Thanks."

Joseph fist-pumped, but turned to me before he left. "You're coming to the carnival tonight, right?"

I raised an eyebrow. "What carnival?"

"There's a fair out in Davie," Mom said. "I thought it would be fun if we all went."

"Be back soon," Daniel said as he left the kitchen and left *New Theories* on the counter. Then popped his head back in for one final *you owe me* look.

I did owe him. Remembering the cat unsettled me, even though I knew John was outside, watching our house. Jude hadn't appeared since John had been here and the missing animals could be a coincidence, but they made me nervous and—

And my mother was looking at me.

I smiled at her. Widely. "What can I do?" I asked, all enthusiasm and cheer.

"Would you mind setting the table?"

"Sure!" I began unloading the dishwasher while my mother started rummaging in the pantry.

"How's everything going at Horizons?" she asked.

So *this* is why I was granted a reprieve. "It's great!"

"What kinds of things are you doing there?"

Aside from making new enemies? "Um, in drama therapy yesterday we chose monologues from old books and then performed them."

"Did you like it?"

I nodded seriously. "I did."

"Really?"

"It's fun pretending to be someone else."

"What book did you pick?"

"Um, *Jekyll and Hyde*."

"What part did you play?"

Hyde. "Jekyll."

She put something in the oven, hiding her face. "How are things with Noah?"

Ah. That was what she *really* wanted to talk about. "They're good." I think. "The same, you know?"

"What do you guys do together?"

Aside from evading my stalker and burning dolls? "We talk."

"About what?"

Genetic memory. "Books." Possession. "Movies." Jude. "People we don't like."

"Do you talk about what's going on with you?"

I tried to remember the conversation I overheard between my parents, right after my psych ward stint. Mom said it was good for me to have someone who listened—

"He's a good listener," I said.

"Do you talk about what's going on with him?"

What? "What do you mean?"

She turned to face me, her features neutral and her stare direct. She searched for something in my eyes, but whatever it was, she didn't find it because she went on. "Noah's parents are going out of town this weekend and they sent his sister to a friend's house, so I said he could stay here."

I nodded. "I know. . . ." I waited for the other shoe.

"I just want to make sure I don't have to worry about you two."

I shook my head emphatically. "Nope. No worries."

She mixed something together in a bowl and then set it down on the counter. "How serious are you?"

"Not serious enough for you to worry," I said with a light smile, scrambling for a way to distract her before the conversation got seriously awkward. "Hey, Mom," I started, remembering my conversation with Daniel. "What do you know about Jungian archetypes?" Best segue ever.

She looked appropriately surprised. "Wow, I haven't thought about that since college. . . . I could tell you more about Jacques Lacan than Carl Jung—he was more my speed, but let's see," she said, drawing out the word as her eyes flicked to the ceiling. "There's the Self, I remember, and the Shadow," she ticked them off on her fingers, "the Persona . . . I'm blanking on the other two main ones . . . There are other archetypal *figures*, though—the Great Mother, the Devil, the Hero . . ." Her voice trailed off for a second before her face lit up. "Oh! And the Sage and the Trickster, too—and I'm remembering something about Oedipus, but he could be creeping in from Freud? And Apollo, maybe—" she said before being interrupted by a knock on the door.

I was already on my way out of the kitchen when she asked me to see who it was.

I opened the door to find Noah standing there in a long-sleeve plaid shirt and dark jeans, with sunglasses on that masked his eyes. He looked perfectly disheveled and perfectly blank.

He only ever shows you what he wants you to see.

"Where is everyone?" he asked evenly.

I pushed Stephanie's words away. "Mom's in the kitchen," I said. "And Daniel and Joseph went to go watch someone remove an alligator from a pool."

Noah's brows rose above the dark lenses.

"I know."

He sighed. "I suppose I'm going to have to wait."

"For?"

Noah glanced at the kitchen. Not a peep from my mother. He shook his head. "Fuck it." He reached into his back pocket and handed me a piece of paper.

No. Not a piece of paper. A picture. A faded color photograph of two girls; one blond and vibrant, wearing Noah's half-smile, and the other—

"Holy shit," I whispered.

The other was my grandmother.

36

NOAH," MY MOTHER SAID, EMERGING FROM THE kitchen and wiping her hands on a towel. "We missed you."

I stuffed the picture in my back pocket as furtively as I could.

"Thank you for having me," Noah said. "I have something for you, from my parents—"

Mom smiled and shook her head. "Totally unnecessary."

"It's just in the car, I'll go get it," Noah said. He left and I ran to my bedroom and hid the picture before my mother saw it or I spilled water on it or it spontaneously burst into flame.

When I came back, Noah and my mom were talking in the kitchen.

"So where in London did you used to visit?" he asked her as he stirred what I thought might be salad dressing.

"Oh, you know, the usual." She shrugged from the sink. "Buckingham Palace, Big Ben, that sort of thing."

"Your mother grew up there?"

A hundred points for Noah Shaw. I almost mimed a high five.

Mom nodded.

"What did she do?"

"She was a student," she said, her voice clipped.

"That's so interesting—what university?"

My mother set the salad bowl in front of Noah. "Cambridge."

Our eyes locked.

"Darwin College," she went on. "She was in school for her PhD, but she never finished. I think that always bothered her. All right, you two," she said, grinning at us. "Thanks for helping, you're free to go."

This was the one time ever in my life that I would rather be talking to my mother than taking my boyfriend to my room.

"It's no trouble," Noah said. He apparently felt the same way.

My mother dusted her hands off. "I'm finished. There's nothing more to do. Go on," she said, waving us away and shutting the conversation down. It *would* happen that she'd extend a grand gesture of trust when what I really wanted was more answers from her. But Noah and I had been dismissed and if we didn't leave, she might get suspicious.

Once we were alone in my room, I closed the door almost all the way, turned to Noah and said, "Holy shit."

"Well put."

I was completely overwhelmed, and backed up onto my bed. "Where'd you find it?"

"A random box of my mother's things."

I rubbed my forehead. "So they knew each other."

"Seems that way. Where's the picture?"

I went to my desk and took it out from the drawer, then handed it to Noah. "How did you know it was my grandmother?" I asked him.

He looked up at me, clearly perplexed. "Seriously?"

"Yeah . . ."

"You don't see the resemblance?"

I glanced over at the picture again. Something bothered me about it, but it wasn't that.

"When was this taken?"

He flipped the photograph over. "1987." He paused. "My mother would have been in university," he said. "At Cambridge."

"Wait," I said as an idea dawned. "Your parents went there together, didn't they?"

"Yes," Noah said slowly.

"Can you ask your dad? Maybe he remembers this." I indicated the picture.

"He won't talk about her." Noah's voice went flat.

"But—"

"He won't," he said again. Then, "I could try Ruth, maybe. She was there also."

One look at him told me I wouldn't get any further, not unless I pushed, and I wasn't sure if I should. Not about his family.

I looked back at the picture in my hands. Then wandered out of my room and into the hallway. Noah followed. I glanced down at the photograph and up at my grandmother's portrait that hung on the wall and then I realized what was off.

"She looks exactly the same," I said.

Noah's eyes followed mine. It was a long time before either of us spoke.

"They couldn't have been studying there at the same time," I said, once we were back in my room. I sat back down on my bed. "My grandmother would've been living in the States when *your* mother was in school."

"But she used to go to London every year when your mum was growing up. Maybe they met on one of those trips?"

"I guess, but they seem kind of . . . familiar, don't they?" I said, staring at the photograph. "Like friends."

"Everyone seems that way in pictures."

I rubbed my forehead. "Why take a picture with someone you barely know at all, then? It's weird."

Noah's eyebrows knitted together. "Is it possible she may have gone to London more than your mother knew?"

I sighed. "At this point, anything's possible," I said, and paused. "Maybe she was immortal."

At that, Noah cracked a smile. "I was going to suggest 'time traveler,' but, sure." He stretched his arms casually behind his head, exposing a sliver of stomach above the low waist of his jeans.

Torture. I cleared my throat and looked back at the photograph. "My mom said the portrait is the only picture she has of my grandmother. She'd die if she saw yours."

Noah's smile vanished. His expression made me want to talk about something else.

"Do you still have the pendant?" I asked.

"Yes." The planes of his face were smooth. "Do you want it back?"

I did not. "It's safer with you," I said. "I'm afraid I'd lose it." Or throw it away. "I was just wondering if maybe you found out anything else?"

He gave a single shake of his head before asking, "What's your mother's maiden name?"

"Sarin, why?"

"I'm going to have Charles look into this," he said, indicating the picture.

"And Charles would be . . ."

"The private investigator."

"Did he turn up anything on Jude?"

Noah looked away. "Dead end after dead end. Did you find the answers you were looking for in that book?"

"I haven't had a chance to read it yet," I said nonchalantly.

A half-smile tugged at Noah's mouth. "You fell asleep, didn't you?"

I lifted my chin. "No."

"What page?"

"I didn't fall asleep."

"What page?"

Busted. "Six," I said. "But I was really tired."

"No judgment. I could barely make it through that obscenely pompous introduction."

"What about the Lukumi situation?" I said, changing the subject. "Any luck?"

Noah's voice brightened a bit. "I did in fact return to Little Havana while you were at Horizons, and I canvassed the botanicas, just as you asked."

"Well?"

"Well," he said slowly. "Imagine for a moment how receptive they were when *I* walked in there and started asking questions."

"What? Your Spanish is perfect."

He arched an eyebrow. "One look at me and their jaws

visibly clamped shut. One owner thought I was with the Health Department and started showing me around the place, repeating 'No goats, no goats.'"

I smirked.

"Glad to amuse you."

"I get my kicks where I can these days. Speaking of Horizons, I almost had an . . . incident."

"Of what nature?" Noah asked carefully.

"This girl, Phoebe—she keeps *pushing* me. I almost lost it with her." Remembering filled me with frustration. "What if someone pisses me off and I tell them to go jump off a bridge?"

Noah shook his head. "You'd never say that."

"Oh, really?"

"You'd tell them to go die in a fire."

"Helpful. Thank you."

Noah stood then, and joined me on my bed. "I only said it because I'm sure that's not how it works."

"How *does* it work?" I asked out loud, as my fingers curled into the blanket. They were nearly touching his. My eyes traveled up to his face. "How do you heal things?"

I thought I saw a faint tinge of surprise in Noah's expression at the sudden shift in the conversation but he answered evenly. "You know that everyone has fingerprints, obviously."

"Obviously."

"To me, everything has an aural imprint as well. An individual tone. And when someone—or something—is ill or hurt, the tone is off. Broken. I just . . . innately know how to correct it."

"I don't understand."

"Because you're not musical."

"Thanks."

He shrugged. "It's not an insult. Daniel would get it. If your mother wasn't in the kitchen, I'd show you."

"How?"

"You have a piano. Anyway, it's like . . ." He stared straight ahead, looking for words. "Imagine the melody to a song you know well. And then imagine one note of that song being changed to the wrong key, or to a completely different note."

"But how do you fix it?"

"If you asked a basketball player how to shoot a perfect free throw, he wouldn't be able to describe the physiological process that makes it happen. He just . . . does it."

I inhaled. "But there are so many people."

"Yes."

"And animals."

"Yes."

"It must get noisy."

"It does," Noah said, "I told you before, I learned to tune it out unless I want to focus on one sound in particular." He smiled. "I prefer," he said, trailing a finger down my arm, "to listen to you."

"What do I sound like?" I asked, more breathily than I intended. God, so predictable.

He considered his answer for a moment before he gave it. "Dissonant," he said finally.

"Meaning?"

Another long pause. "Unstable."

Hmm.

He shook his head. "Not the way you're thinking," he said, the shadow of a smile on his lips. "In music, consonant chords are points of arrival. Rest. There's no tension," he tried to explain. "Most pop music hooks are consonant, which is why most people like them. They're catchy but interchangeable. Boring. Dissonant intervals, however, are full of tension," he said, holding my gaze. "You can't predict which way they're going to go. It makes limited people uncomfortable—frustrated, because they don't understand the point, and people hate what they don't understand. But the ones who get it," he said, lifting a hand to my face, "find it fascinating. Beautiful." He traced the shape of my mouth with his thumb. "Like you."

37

His words warmed me through even as he pulled his hand away. I was sure my face fell.

"Your parents," he said, with a glance at the door.

I got it. But still. "I like hearing about your ability," I said, my eyes on his mouth. "Tell me more."

His voice was level. "What do you want to know?"

"When did you first notice it?"

When his expression shifted, I realized I had asked him that question before; I recognized that shuttered look. He was withdrawing again. Shutting down.

Shutting me out.

Something was going on with him, and I didn't know what it was. He was growing distant, but he wasn't gone yet. So I quickly said something else. "You saw me in December, after the asylum collapsed, right?"

"Yes."

"When I was hurt."

"Yes," he said again. To anyone else, he would have sounded bored. But I was learning, and now I recognized something else in his voice. Something that never fell from those reckless, careless, lips.

Caution.

I was pressing up against something raw, and I wanted to know what it was.

"You've seen other people who were hurt," I went on, keeping my tone even. "Four?"

Noah nodded.

Keeping my tone light. "Including Joseph."

He nodded again.

And then I had an idea. I pinched my arm. I watched Noah to see if there was any reaction. There wasn't, as far as I could tell.

I pinched it again.

He slitted his eyes. "What, exactly, are you doing?"

"Did you see me when I pinched myself?"

"It's a bit hard to ignore you."

"When you first told me you saw me," I started, "in

December, in the asylum—you said you saw what *I* was seeing, through *my* eyes. And when Joseph was drugged, you saw him through someone else's eyes—the person who drugged him, right? But you didn't have a—a vision just now, did you? So there's some factor besides pain," I said, studying his face as I spoke. "Don't you want to know what it is?"

"Of course," he said indifferently.

"Have you tested it?"

His eyes sharpened, then. "How could I? You're the only one I've seen that knows."

I held his stare. "We can test it together."

Noah shook his head immediately. "No."

"We have to."

"No." The word was solid and final and laced with something I couldn't quite identify. "We don't. There's absolutely nothing at stake except information."

"But you're the one who said that whatever is happening to me is also happening to you—that was your argument for why I can't be possessed, right?"

"Also because it's stupid."

I ignored him. "So figuring out how your ability works could help me figure out mine. And no one would get hurt—"

Noah's expression grew very serious, and his voice grew dangerously quiet. "Except you."

"It's *science*—"

"It's madness," he said. He was completely still but

completely on edge. "I've never regretted telling you the truth. Don't make me start."

"Don't you want to know what we *are*?"

Something flickered behind his eyes, there and gone before I could identify it. "It doesn't matter what we are. It matters what we do." His jaw tightened. "And I won't let you do that."

Let? "It's not just up to you."

There was nothing but apathy in his voice when he finally spoke. "I'll leave."

"I've heard *that* before." The second the words left my mouth I wished I could take them back. Noah's expression was as smooth and colorless as glass.

"I'm sorry," I started to say. But then a few seconds later, when Noah's expression still hadn't changed, I said, "Actually, I'm not. You want to go because I don't agree with you? There's the door." I flung my hand dramatically, for emphasis.

But Noah didn't leave. My outburst thawed whatever had frozen him, and his gaze slid over me. "I wish you had a dog."

"Oh yeah?" I raised my eyebrows. "Why's that?"

"So I could take it for a walk."

"Well, I'll *never* have a dog, because dogs are either terrified of me or hate me and you won't help me figure out—"

"Shut up." Noah's eyes closed.

"*You* shut up," I said back, quite maturely.

"No—stop. Say that again."

"Say what again?"

"About dogs." His eyes were still closed.

"They're either scared of me or hate me?"

"Fight or flight," Noah said as something clearly fit into place for him. "That's it."

"That's what?"

"The difference between the humans and the animals that you've—you know," he gestured. "When we went to the zoo and the insects died, it was because I nearly forced you to touch the ones that terrified you most. But once they were dead, I couldn't push you anymore."

Flight.

He ran a hand over his mouth. "In the Everglades, you were terrified we wouldn't reach Joseph in time, and so you eliminated what was in your way—you reacted—without needing to think." He ran his fingers through his hair. "You were pushed, and unconsciously you pushed back."

I knew what was coming next and preempted it. "But with Morales . . ."

"You weren't afraid," he said.

"I was angry." *Fight.*

"There are different biochemical reactions that occur in response to different emotions, like stress—"

"Adrenaline and cortisol, I know," I said. "I took ninth grade bio too."

Noah ignored me. "And they're processed differently by the brain—we should read more about this."

"Okay," I said. But I was still frustrated; Noah once again managed to turn the conversation back to me, thereby avoiding what I wanted to know about him.

So I said, "I still think we should test your ability."

Noah's eyes went sharp—he was uncomfortable again. "You want to do this scientifically? Here," Noah said, and stood. He crossed the room and picked up a bottle of Tylenol that I left on my bookshelf. Placed it on the floor. "We'll use the scientific method: My hypothesis is that you can manipulate things with your mind."

Deflecting again. He didn't actually believe I could do it; he was just trying to distract me. I went along with him—for now. "Telekinesis?"

"I don't think so, exactly, but in order to figure out what you *can* do, it would be helpful to know what you can't do. So here, move this."

"With my mind."

"With your mind," he said calmly. "And I'll know if you're not trying."

I glared at him.

He gave me a nod. "Go on."

Fine. I'd do this and then it would be my turn to make *him* do something. I dropped to the floor, crossed my legs and hunched forward, staring at the bottle.

About twenty seconds of fruitless silence later, Daniel knocked and pushed my bedroom door open all the way.

"I'm here to announce that we're departing for the carnival in approximately twenty minutes." He paused. I felt him look down at me, then up at Noah, then back at me. "Uh, what are you doing?"

"Mara is trying to move a bottle of Tylenol with her mind," Noah said casually.

I glared at him, then back at the bottle.

"Ah, yes," Daniel said. "I tried that once. Not with Tylenol, though."

"What did you use?" Noah asked.

"A penny. I also tried that 'light as a feather, stiff as a board' game—the levitation one, you know?" he said to Noah. "And Ouija boards, of course," he said to me, adding a melodramatically meaningful look.

"You played with a Ouija board?" I asked slowly.

"Of course," Daniel said. "It's a childhood rite of passage."

"Who did you play with?"

"Dane, Josh." He shrugged. "Those guys."

"Was it yours?" I felt nervous without quite knowing why.

Daniel looked taken aback. "Are you kidding?"

"What?" Noah asked.

"I would never keep one in the house," Daniel said, shaking his head vehemently. "Conduit to the spirit world, Mara, I told you."

Noah cracked a wry grin. "You don't actually believe that, do you?"

"Hey," Daniel said. "Even men of science such as ourselves

are entitled to get the heebie-jeebies now and again. Anyway," he said, a smirk creeping onto his lips as he gestured to the Tylenol bottle, "nice to see you giving *something* the old college try, Mara. Though, my brain is bigger, so if *I* didn't have any luck—"

I refocused on the bottle and said, "Go away."

"Any progress on the vampire story?"

"GO AWAY."

"Good luck!" he said cheerfully.

"I hate you," I said as Daniel closed the door.

"What vampire story?" Noah asked.

I was still staring at the bottle. The bottle that hadn't moved. "It was his other theory about my fake alter ego," I explained. "An alternate to possession."

"Well, you are awfully pale."

I exhaled slowly. Refused to look up.

He reached for my bare foot and squeezed my toes. "And cold."

I pulled my feet away. "Bad circulation."

"You could always bite me, just to test."

"I hate you, too, by the way. Just so you know."

"Oh, I do. I would suggest make-up sex, but . . ."

"Too bad you have scruples," I said.

"Now you're just being cruel."

"I like pushing your buttons."

"You'd enjoy it more if you undid them first."

Save me. "I think you should go and help Daniel."

"With what?"

"Anything."

Noah stood. There was a mischievous smile on his lips as he left.

I stared at the bottle of Tylenol for another few minutes and tried to envision it moving, but it went nowhere and I gave myself a headache. I popped it open and took two, then trudged into the kitchen and plopped down at the table across from my mother, who was sitting with her laptop. I rested my head on my arms and sighed dramatically.

"What's up?" she asked.

"Why are boys so annoying?"

She chuckled. "You know what my mother used to say?"

I shook my head, still in position.

"Boys are stupid and girls are trouble."

Truer words were never spoken.

38

DELIGHTED SCREAMS PIERCED THE AIR AS carnival rides swirled and blinked and swung over my head. I walked with my older brother through the crowd of people; it had been years since we were last at a fair, and the second we arrived, our dad dragged our mom onto the Ferris wheel and Joseph absconded with my boyfriend to conquer some ride, leaving me and Daniel alone.

I was flooded with sounds and scents; artificial butter and giggles. Frying dough and swelling shrieks. It felt good to be out like this. Normal.

"Just you and me, sister," Daniel said as we milled around between booths. "Whatever shall we do?"

A little kid walked by carrying enough balloons to make me wonder how many it would take for her to lift off. I smiled at her, but the second she met my eyes, she darted away. My smile fell.

We passed beneath a row of hanging stuffed animals. "I could win you a teddy bear," I said to him. My feet crunched over discarded popcorn and I dodged a giant puddle left by an earlier drizzle.

He shook his head. "The games are rigged."

Noah and Joseph reappeared from the multitudes, then. My little brother looked pale and shaken. Noah's blue-gray eyes were lit with amusement.

"How was the ride?" I asked.

Joseph lifted his chin and shrugged. "It was okay."

"He was very brave," Noah said. A smile tugged at the corner of his mouth.

The four of us meandered until Joseph stopped us and pointed up. A huge menacing clown face towered over the entrance to a garishly painted building.

"Hall of Mirrors! Yes!"

No.

Daniel must have noticed my unease because he put his arm around Joseph's shoulder. "I got this," he said to Noah and me. "You guys have fun."

"Don't do anything I wouldn't do!" Joseph called back, and the crowd swallowed them up.

A slightly wicked smile appeared on Noah's lips. My favorite. "It seems we're on our own," he said.

It did. "It does."

"What shall we do with this newfound freedom?"

The twinkling lights accented the angles of his high cheekbones. Noah's chestnut hair was a tousled, gorgeous mess.

I'm sure we can think of something, I thought. I was about to say so when I heard a voice behind us.

"Would the young lovers like their fortunes told?"

We turned to find a woman wearing the traditional costume: long and flowy printed skirt, check. Peasant blouse, check. Wavy black hair spilling out of a head wrap, check. Too much makeup, check. Regulation gold hoop earrings, check.

"I think we'll pass," I said to Noah. No need to tempt fate. "Unless you want to?"

He shook his head. "Thanks anyway," he told her as we headed away.

"You must not go out there," she called out after me.

I felt a rush of familiarity as her words tickled the back of my mind.

"What did you just say?" I'd heard those words before.

The fortune-teller peered at me with guarded eyes, her expression mysterious. "Come with me and I will explain."

Noah sighed. "Look—"

"It's okay," I said, glancing up at him. "I want to go."

Noah raised an eyebrow, his expression darkly amused. "As you wish," he said to me, and we began to walk.

We followed the woman as she wove a path through the people to a small striped tent. She held the flap open; there were twinkle lights and crystals, flocked tablecloths and hanging tapestries. They adorned the little space without irony. Noah and I stepped in.

The fortune-teller shook her head at Noah. "You may wait outside," she said to him. "My daughter will show you where. Miranda!" she called.

A sullen-looking girl with a pink streak in her hair appeared from behind a beaded curtain.

"Please offer this young man some tea. Show him where to sit."

The girl, who was about thirteen or fourteen, seemed like she was about to roll her eyes until she noticed Noah; the long line of him leaning carelessly against the frame, the slight sarcastic smile on his perfect mouth. Her demeanor changed instantly and she drew herself up.

"Come on," she said to him, and tipped her head toward the curtain.

He looked to me.

"I'll be okay," I said, nodding. "Go."

Once they were gone, the fortune-teller gestured to a plastic folding chair beside a round card table that was swathed in cheap fabric. I sat. There was a deck of cards in front of me. Tarot, I presumed.

"Money first," she said, and held out her hand.

Of course. I reached into my pocket and withdrew her fee. She tucked the cash into the folds of her skirt and then stared at me for a beat, like she was expecting something else.

I had no idea what. When she didn't stop staring, I said, "So do I cut the deck, Miss . . ."

"Madam."

"Madam . . . what?"

"Madam Rose."

"Madam Rose," I said with mock seriousness. I glanced up at a crystal ball sitting on a shelf. "Is the pseudonym thing a requirement too?"

Her expression was grave. "There is power in a name."

The words filled my heart with ice. They echoed in my mind but in someone else's voice. I blinked, and shook my head to clear it.

"Do you have a question?" she asked, breaking the silence.

I swallowed and refocused on Madam Rose. "What do you mean?"

"A question you seek an answer to."

A bitter smile twisted my lips. I had tons of questions. All I *had* were questions. *What's happening to me? What am I?* "I have lots of questions," I finally said.

"Think carefully," she warned. "If you ask the wrong questions, you will get the wrong answers." Then she nodded at the deck.

I reached for it but paused before my fingers made contact. My heart thundered against my ribs.

Madam Rose noticed my hesitation and dipped her head, catching my eyes. "I can do a different type of reading, if you like."

"Different how?"

"Give me your hands," she said. I reluctantly placed mine in hers, palm up. She shook her head and her earrings swung with the movement; she flipped my hands over, palm down. Then she rolled her neck, her long hair draping her face like a veil. She said nothing. The silence stretched on uncomfortably.

"How long—"

"Hush," she hissed. The fortune-teller drew her head up and examined my hands. She studied them for a few moments, then closed her heavily shadowed eyes.

I sat there while she held my hands and waited—for what, I didn't know. After another length of time, I don't know how long, her red lips parted. Her eyelids twitched. She tilted her head slightly up and to the left, her forehead creased in concentration. Her fingers twitched around mine and then tightened. I was getting freaked out and I nearly pulled away, but before I could, her eyes flew open.

"You must leave him." Her words cut the air.

A few seconds passed before I found my voice. "What are you talking about?"

"The boy with the gray eyes. The one outside."

"Why?" I asked warily.

"The boy is destined for greatness, but with you, he is in danger. You are linked, the two of you. You must leave him. This is what I have seen."

I grew frustrated. "Is he in danger *because* of me?"

"He will die before his time with you by his side, unless you let him go. Fate or chance? Coincidence or destiny? I cannot say." Her voice had turned soft.

Soft and sad.

A fist closed around my heart. I tried to let him go once before. It didn't work.

"I can't," was all I said to her, and quietly.

"Then you will love him to ruins," she said, and let my hands go.

39

SHE WITHDREW THE CASH FROM HER POCKET AND offered it back to me. "I cannot take this from you, and you must not tell him what I said."

"That's convenient," I muttered under my breath.

"If you leave him, tell him," she said with a shrug, "by all means. But only if you let him go. If he knows of his destiny and the two of you remain together, it will seal his fate." She gestured to the door.

I didn't move. "That's it?"

"I cannot help you further," she said.

My nostrils flared. "You didn't help at all." My voice was sharp, but then it thinned. "Isn't there something I can do?"

She crossed the small space and stood by the door. "Yes. There is something you can do. You can let him go. If you truly love him, you will let him go."

My throat tightened as I looked at her. Then I marched out of the tent.

Noah was waiting outside and matched my pace as I stomped down the dirt path.

"Bad news?" he asked, clearly amused.

I wiped my eyes with the back of my hand and kept walking.

"Wait," he said, reaching for my hand and spinning me around. "Are you crying?"

I pulled away. "No."

"Stop," Noah said, and stood in the path. I hurried along and increased my pace to a jog. Before I knew it I was running.

We were nearly back by the Hall of Mirrors when Noah caught up with me. I felt a hand on my shoulder and whirled around.

"Mara," he said softly. "Why are you running from me?"

And that undid me. The tears came faster than I could wipe them away. Noah took my hand and pulled me behind one of the game booths, then wrapped me in his arms. He stroked my hair.

"What did she say?"

"I can't tell you," I said between quiet sobs.

"But it's the reason you're crying, yes?"

I nodded into his soft shirt. He felt so solid beneath my cheek. I didn't want to let go.

But Noah took a slight step back, pulling away, and tilted my face up with his hand. "This is going to sound mean, but I don't mean it that way."

"Just say it." I sniffed.

"You're gullible, Mara," he said quietly, and his voice was kind. "An easy mark. A few weeks ago it was hypnosis and Santeria. Now it's possession and tarot."

"She didn't do a tarot reading."

Noah sighed and dipped his head. "It doesn't matter what she did. What matters is what you *believe*. And you're highly suggestible—you hear something offhand and suddenly you think it's an all-embracing explanation."

I glared at him, but there was no heat behind it. "At least I'm trying to find one."

Noah's eyes closed. "I've been trying to find one for years, Mara. It hasn't led me anywhere. Look," he said as he opened his eyes, taking my hand and lacing his long fingers through mine. "We'll go straight back to her and I'll double her money to admit the truth and she'll tell you she made the whole thing up. To put on a good show. I'm not letting some con artist upset you this way."

"She didn't take my money," I said quietly. "She didn't have anything to gain by lying."

"You never know what another person stands to gain or lose by anything." He pulled me back onto the path. "Let's go."

When we made it back to her tent, a sign was hung over the entrance that said BACK IN ONE HOUR. Noah ignored it and pushed the flap open.

The fortune-teller's daughter sat in a small overstuffed armchair reading a magazine. There was a Ouija board on the table in front of her. I looked away.

"Where's your mother, Miranda?" Noah's eyes roamed the small tent.

The girl cracked her gum and looked at me. She blew a fat pink bubble, then sucked it back into her mouth. "She got you good, huh?"

Noah arched an eyebrow at me.

"What do you mean?" I asked her.

"You bought her Madam Rose crap?" she asked me. "Look, her real name is Roslyn Ferretti and she's from Babylon, Long Island. You'd get better predictions from a Magic Eight Ball," she said to me. Then turned back to her magazine.

Noah tilted the page down with one finger. "Where can we find her?"

Miranda shrugged. "Getting high probably, behind The Screaming Dead Man."

"Thanks," Noah said, and we left the tent. He held my

hand and walked like he knew where we were going. "See?" he said gently. "It isn't real."

I didn't respond. I didn't trust my voice.

An intimidatingly tall tower rose in front of us, right next to the Ferris wheel. A small car ascended slowly into the air; I assumed it would eventually fall in one drop. We hooked back behind the ride, searching for the woman as we walked. Noah led me around a patch of dirt; we wandered until it became grass and then, finally, we saw her.

Madam Rose, aka Roslyn Ferretti, was sitting perched on a small rock, the hem of her skirt pooled at her feet. Smoking a joint, just as her daughter predicted.

"Hey," Noah called out.

The woman coughed and hastily moved her hand behind her back. Her eyes were bloodshot and unfocused. When she recognized me, she shook her head. "I already gave you your money back."

"Why did you say those things?" I asked quietly.

Her eyes roamed over the two of us. She lifted the cigarette back to her mouth and inhaled deeply. "Because they were true," she then said, exhaling the words in a cloud of cloying smoke. Her eyes began to close.

Noah snapped his fingers in her face. She pushed his hand away. "Listen closely," he said. "I'll give you a hundred dollars to admit you made it up."

She looked at me then, her eyes suddenly sharp. "Did you tell him?"

I opened my mouth to insist that I didn't, but Noah spoke before I had the chance.

"A thousand," he said darkly.

She gave him a long look. "I can't take your money."

"Don't fuck with me," Noah said. "We know you're a fraud, Roslyn, so please do yourself a favor and admit it."

Her head dropped, and she shook it. "That girl, I swear."

"Roslyn."

She lolled her head back, like this was some kind of giant inconvenience. "He paid me, okay?"

The hair rose on the back of my neck. Noah and I exchanged a glance.

"Who paid you?" I asked.

She shrugged. "Some guy."

"What did he look like?" Noah pushed.

"Tall. Dark. Handsome." She smiled, and tried to take another puff. Noah plucked the joint from her fingers and held it in front of him, just out of her reach.

"Be specific," he said.

She shrugged lazily. "He had an accident."

"An accident?" Noah asked. "A limp? A prosthetic limb? What?"

"Talked funny."

Noah rolled his eyes. "An accent. Right. What sort of accent?"

"Foreign," she said thickly, and began to giggle.

"This is useless," I said. But at least she hadn't described Jude. A small relief, but still.

"We're not leaving until she tells us exactly what happened," Noah insisted. "Was his accent like mine?" he asked her.

She shook her head.

"What did he say to you?"

She sighed. "He told me to bring you into my tent," she said to me. "He told me what to say to you." Then she lifted her face up to Noah. "And he said you'd offer me money and that I couldn't take it."

"When was this?" I asked her.

"About ten minutes before I saw you."

Noah ran his hand over his jaw. "I don't suppose he gave you a name?"

She shook her head.

"Are you sure?" he pressed. "There's *no* amount of money I could offer you to tell us?"

A sad, brittle smile appeared on her lips. "God knows I could use it, sweetheart, but I can't take money from either of you."

"Why not?"

Her gaze drifted off into the darkness. "He told me I couldn't."

"So what?" Noah asked. "Why listen?"

Her voice grew quiet. "Because he's the real deal." Then

she reached out her hand. Noah gave back her joint, and she stood.

"I'm truly sorry," she said to me as she passed by, leaving Noah and me alone. The tower above us was just about to fall; but even though everyone in it knew what was coming, when it dropped, they still screamed.

Noah fit his hands to the curve of my waist. "Tell me," he said.

He looked inhumanly beautiful under the lights. It almost hurt to look at him, but it would have hurt more to look away.

"Tell me," he said again. There was need in his voice, and I didn't have the strength to refuse.

"She said I have to let you go."

He drew me closer. Brushed a strand of hair from my face, trailed his fingers along the curve of my neck. "Why?"

I closed my eyes. The words ached as they left my throat. "Because you'll die by my side if I don't."

Noah slid his arms around me and fitted me against him. "It isn't real," he whispered into my hair.

Maybe it wasn't. But even if it was . . . "I'm too selfish to leave you," I said.

Noah pulled back so I could see his smile. "I'm too selfish to let you."

40

WHEN WE MET BACK UP WITH MY FAMILY, I put on my happy face. I was still haunted by what Roslyn had said and the idea that someone paid her to say it, but when I managed to sneak a minute alone with Noah after we got home, he said he'd have Investigator Guy look into it, kissed my forehead, and left it at that. My face fell, but Noah didn't see it.

Or he ignored it.

Noah *would* try to find out who paid her off, I knew. I trusted him. But I wasn't sure he trusted me.

I was suggestible, he said, and Noah was the opposite.

Eternally skeptical and arrogant about it. Yes, he went along with anything I wanted, no matter how strange—the Santeria stuff, burning that doll. And tonight, with the fortune business; he gave in to me too, even though he thought Roslyn was just high, that her words had no more weight than a horoscope. Noah indulged my every whim, but they were more than that to me.

Which made me wish I had the freedom to look for answers myself.

I knew I should be grateful not to be locked up in a mental hospital already and I was, but it was hard not to feel like a prisoner in my own house instead. And I wasn't just under my parents' observation—I was under John's, too. I wanted him watching me and the house, absolutely. But even though I felt safer now, I didn't feel free. That wasn't his fault, and it wasn't Noah's.

It was Jude's.

Noah did ask me to come to his room after everyone fell asleep that night, and even though I was frustrated and tired and still thinking about my crappy fortune, I went. Obviously.

When I opened the guest room door, Noah was in bed—still clothed and reading.

"What book?" I asked, closing the door and leaning against it.

He showed me the title: *Invitation to a Beheading.*

I smiled, but it didn't reach my eyes. "I recommended that to you."

"You did."

"And?"

"It's sad," he said, placing the book on the bed.

My brows knitted together. "I thought it was funny."

"Cincinnatus is in a prison of his own making. I find it sad." He tilted his head at me. "You're still upset."

It wasn't a question, but I nodded anyway.

"In that case, I have a proposal."

"I'm listening."

"You've been doing exposure therapy at Horizons, yes?"

"Yes . . ."

"To overcome your fears."

I nodded again.

"And one of the things you're afraid of is hurting me."

"Killing you," I said quietly.

"If we kiss."

If I lose control. "If we stay together," I said, thinking of Roslyn's words.

"You want to do both?" Noah asked evenly.

So much. "Yes."

"Then my proposal is this: that we approach it the way you would any other fear. First, you'll imagine an encounter with the source of the phobia." A half-smile appeared on his lips.

I saw where he was going with this. "You want me to imagine kissing you?"

"I'll guide you through it."

"Then what?"

"Then," he said, "you'll get closer to the source, but you won't confront it yet."

"And how exactly will that translate?"

"I'm sure I'll think of something." The timbre of his voice woke me up.

"When do you want to start?" I asked.

He looked up at me from the bed. "Come here."

I obeyed.

Noah sat me down opposite him so that we faced each other. His eyelashes nearly swept his cheekbones and he bit his bottom lip and my breath caught as I stared.

Easy, there.

"Close your eyes," Noah said, and I did.

"I want you to imagine us somewhere you love."

I nodded.

"Somewhere safe."

The room evaporated around us as he spoke. I walked through the hallways of my mind and opened the door to the house I grew up in. Where I played with my old toys on the floor. Where I had sleepovers with Rachel and laughed at her jokes and told her my secrets.

"Where are we?" he asked, his voice soft.

"My old bedroom."

"Describe it."

"There's old, dark wood furniture that used to be my

mom's when she was younger. It's antique. Pretty, but a little scratched-up."

"What else?"

"The walls are pink, but you can't see much of them under the sketches and drawings and pictures."

"Pictures of . . ."

"Me. My family. Rachel," I said, my voice nearly hitching. I took a deep breath. "Landscapes and stuff. I tacked everything to the wall." I remembered it perfectly. "The papers flutter when I open or close the door, like the walls are breathing."

"Tell me about your bed," Noah said, the hint of a smile in his voice.

"It's a twin," I said, the hint of a smile in mine. "Oak, like the rest of the furniture. A four poster."

"Blanket?"

"A really heavy quilt. It was my grandmother's. Goose down and really thick."

"What color is it?"

"Ugly." I grinned. "A weird brown and black and white geometric print from the sixties, I think."

"Where are you in your room right now?"

"Just . . . standing in the middle of it, I guess."

"All right. If I were in your room, where would I be?"

I saw it with vivid clarity: Noah in my doorway. "Standing there, in the doorway," I said, though our bodies now were just inches apart.

"I'm there, then," he said in that warm, slow, honeyed voice. "It's dark outside—night. Is there any light in your room?"

"The lamp on my nightstand."

"All right. I walk into your room. Should I close the door?"

Yes. "Yes," I said, my breath quickening.

"I close the door. I cross the room and meet you in the middle. What then?"

"I thought you were the one guiding me through this."

"I think you should have some agency too."

"What are my options?"

"You could read obscure poetry while I play the triangle, I suppose. Or we can smother ourselves in peanut butter and howl at the moon. Use your imagination."

"Fine," I said. "You take my hand and back up toward the bed."

"Excellent choice. What then?"

"You sit down, and pull me down with you."

"Where are you?" he asked.

"You pull me onto your lap."

"Where are your legs?"

"Around your waist."

"Well," Noah said, his voice slightly rough. "This is getting interesting. So I'm on the edge of your bed. I'm holding you on my lap as you straddle me. My arms are around you, bracing you there so you don't fall. What am I wearing?"

I smiled. "The T-shirt with all of the holes in it."

"Really?"

"Yeah, why?"

"I thought I'd be wearing a tux in your fantasies or something."

"Like James Bond? That sounds like *your* fantasy," I said, though the image of Noah in a crisp tuxedo with his artfully messy hair—his bowtie undone, hanging around his collar—I swallowed. My blood burned beneath my skin.

"Katie hates it."

"The T-shirt?"

"Yeah."

"She's your sister."

"So I should keep it?"

"Yes."

"All right. I'm wearing the T-shirt. And below that?"

"What do you usually wear to bed?" I asked.

Noah said nothing. I opened my eyes to an arched brow and a devious grin.

Oh my God.

"Close. Your. Eyes," he said. I did. "Now, where were we?"

"I was straddling you," I said.

"Right. And I'm wearing . . ."

"Drawstring pants," I said.

"Those are quite thin, you know."

I'm aware.

"Whoa," he said, and I felt the pressure of his hands on my shoulders. I opened my eyes.

"You swayed a bit," he said, dropping his hands. "I thought you might fall off the bed."

I blushed.

"Maybe we should take this to the floor," he said, and stood. He stretched, and it was impossible to ignore the strong line of him, standing just inches away. I rose too quickly and wobbled on my feet.

He grinned and took a pillow from the bed and placed it on the floor, indicating that I should sit. I did.

"Right," he said. "So what are you wearing?"

"I don't know. A space suit. Who cares?"

"I think this should be as vivid as possible," he said. "For you," he clarified, and I chuckled. "Eyes closed," he reminded me. "I'm going to have to institute a punishment for each time I have to tell you."

"What did you have in mind?" I asked archly.

"Don't tempt me. Now, what are you wearing?"

"A hoodie and drawstring pants too, I guess."

"Anything underneath?"

"I don't typically walk around without underwear."

"Typically?"

"Only on special occasions."

"Christ. I meant under your hoodie."

"A tank top, I guess."

"What color?"

"White tank. Black hoodie. Gray pants. I'm ready to move on now."

I felt him nearer, his words close to my ear. "To the part where I lean back and pull you down with me?"

Yes.

"Over me," he said.

Fuck.

"The part where I tell you that I want to feel the softness of the curls at the nape of your neck? To know what your hipbone would feel like against my mouth?" he murmured against my skin. "To memorize the slope of your navel and the arch of your neck and the swell of your—hey."

I felt his warm hands on my shoulders. I opened my eyes. I must have been moving toward him while my eyes were closed, because I was almost in his lap.

"You should stay on your pillow," he said.

But I don't want to. "I don't want to," I said back. My fingertips ached with the need to touch.

"We shouldn't rush this."

But I want to. "Why not?" I asked.

He stared at me. At my mouth. "Because I want to kiss you again," he said. "But not if any part of you is still afraid. Is any part of you still afraid?"

That I might hurt him? Kill him? If we kissed? If we stayed together?

"I'm not afraid of *you*, Noah," I said out loud.

"Not consciously."

"Not at *all*," I said, shifting back and crossing my legs.

He tilted his head. He didn't speak.

"I'm afraid of . . . myself," I clarified. "I don't—I don't feel like I'm in control with you."

His brow creased. I could see the gears turning in his mind.

"What are you thinking?" I asked.

"Nothing."

"Liar. You're never thinking nothing."

"I'm wondering what would make you feel as though you're in control. What could make you trust yourself with me."

"Any luck?"

"I'll let you know."

"Well." I glanced at the clock. "We have a few hours before we have to be up again."

"We should sleep," he said, but didn't move back to his bed.

I grinned. "We should go back to my room."

That was when he stood. "Which is right between Joseph's room and your parents'. And I thought I just told you I didn't think we should rush anything?"

I rolled my eyes. "I meant my old bedroom."

"Ah."

I stood and wove my fingers into his. "Noah," I said, my voice soft.

He turned and looked down at me. The shadow of a smile touched his mouth. "Tomorrow," he said.

I must have been unable to hide my disappointment, because he placed his finger beneath my chin and tipped it up. "Tomorrow," he said again, and I could hear the promise in the word.

I nodded. As the adrenaline dissolved in my blood, Noah pressed his lips to my forehead and led me to his bed. I wished with everything in me that I could sink into the feeling of Noah wrapped around me as I slept. But despite his words tonight, all I heard were Roslyn's as I lay in his arms, awake in the dark.

You will love him to ruins.

If I did, it would ruin us both.

41

MY EYES FLUTTERED OPEN. THEY WERE unfocused, my vision hazy as I stared at the ceiling. Not the guest room ceiling.

Noah's ceiling.

I was in Noah's house. I was in his bed.

I was dreaming, I realized. And then the mattress shifted beside me.

The word *nightmare* came to mind unbidden, and suddenly, I was afraid.

But it was only Noah, facing away from me, staring at the rows of books that spanned the length of his room. What little light filtered in through the curtains shaded his beautiful face in sharp angles.

He could never be a nightmare.

I knelt up gingerly, afraid that the wrong movement would make the dream dissolve. I reached out and cautiously pushed his hair back. It felt so real, even though he didn't move, didn't respond, to my touch. I ran my fingers through his hair because when I was awake, I was scared I would do it too much.

But this wasn't real, so there was nothing to be scared of. I ran my finger, my hand, along his jaw, enjoying the scrape against my skin. Touching him felt natural but possessive, and I wasn't sure how far he would let me go.

Not far, apparently. Noah looked down at me with translucent eyes. His stare was desolate and hopeless.

"What's wrong?" I whispered, but he didn't answer. His expression frightened me. Looking at his face and into his eyes, all I wanted was to make him feel something else.

With a boldness my waking self didn't have, I took his face in my hands, tilted him toward me, and kissed him. Not deeply. Light. Fresh. Soft.

He didn't move toward me, not at first. He closed his eyes, shut them tight like I had hurt him. I blushed, stung, and backed away.

But then. He pulled my hair back from my face, brushed it behind my shoulders. With the flat of his palm, he pushed me down against the mattress very softly. He moved over me, pressed soft kisses against my skin, teased me with his mouth. I heard him whisper in my ear but I couldn't hear his words—my own breath was too loud. He slid his hands into mine then, and kissed my lips lightly, one last time. Then he withdrew, leaving something behind in my open palm.

It was heavy but soft and fit perfectly in my hand. I couldn't see what it was in the dark, so I cradled it to my chest. Followed him out onto the balcony, out of his room.

But when I stepped outside my feet touched nothing. I was weightless. I turned back to look at Noah's house, but dark vines crawled over it. Trees burst from the ground and cracked through his roof.

I didn't want to see this. I closed my eyes. *Wake up*, I told myself. *Wake up*.

But I opened them just in time to watch the bay soak into the ground. Buildings were crushed and crumpled in seconds beneath the weight of the forest. The jungle had been let in, and now there was nothing I could do.

I closed my eyes and twisted inside myself. I willed the nightmare to end.

But then I heard voices. Footsteps. They were approaching, but my eyelids were filled with lead; they wouldn't open. Not until I felt the brush of a feather on my cheek. My lungs filled with breath and my eyes opened, drenching my world in color. When I woke, I was not myself.

A man knelt before me; he looked familiar but I did not know his name. He withdrew the feather from my cheek and placed it in one of my hands. My thumb caressed the edges. It was so soft.

"Show me what is in the other," he said kindly.

I obeyed him. Uncurled my fingers to reveal what was inside.

It was Noah's heart.

I woke up in the kitchen, facing the dark window above the sink. Noah was next to me. I had sleepwalked again but I was flooded with relief as I glanced at his chest—it was very much whole, and he was very much alive.

The nightmare wasn't real. Noah was all right.

But when I looked up at his eyes, they were desolate. Hopeless. It was the expression he wore in my dream, before he gave me his heart.

"What's wrong?" I asked him, panicked.

"Nothing," he said, and his hand found mine. "Come back to bed."

Noah woke me a few hours later and urged me into my own bed before the rest of the house woke up. I left because I had to but I was unsettled and didn't want to be alone.

I felt sick. My muscles were tight and sore and my vertebrae crackled when I stretched my neck. My skin felt hot and the brush of my clothes against my skin seared my flesh. I felt wrong, like someone had poured me into a different body overnight.

What was *happening* to me?

I walked into my bathroom and turned on the light. I was shocked by what I saw.

Looking at myself in the mirror was like looking at a picture of myself in the future, like I had aged a year in an hour—I was still me, but not quite the same. The curves of my cheeks seemed hollow, and my eyes looked hollow too.

Was I the only one who could see it?

Did *Noah* see it?

"All you can do is watch," I had said to him, in his bed but lying alone.

"I have been, Mara."

If that was true then he *had* to see me changing, and whatever he saw I had to know. Noah seemed so haunted when I woke up in the kitchen: I'd sleepwalked before, but he never looked at me that way before. . . .

I was profoundly uneasy. I climbed back into bed, but it was a long time before I finally fell asleep.

"Morning, sleepyhead," my mother called, her face peeking out from behind my door. "It's almost noon."

My eyes felt like they were pasted shut. I pushed myself up on my elbows and groaned.

"You feeling okay?"

I nodded. "Just tired."

"You want to go back to bed?"

I did, but I shouldn't. "No, I'll be out soon."

"Should I make you some lunch? Breakfast, I mean?"

I wasn't really hungry, but knew I should eat anyway. "Thanks."

My mother smiled, then left. I stood slowly and leaned against my dresser, arching my back.

I kept seeing Noah in my mind. The way he looked last night, in the kitchen and in my dream. Something was really wrong. We needed to talk because I couldn't make sense of it by myself—the dream, the pendants, my grandmother, the picture. I was falling apart, and all my pieces were scattering to the wind.

When I dressed and made my way to the kitchen, Joseph was eating a sandwich, but aside from my mother, he was the only one.

"Where's—everyone?" I asked. Didn't want to be too obvious.

"Dad's playing golf," Joseph said between bites.

Next.

"Daniel went to hear Sophie rehearse for a recital she has in a couple of weeks."

Next.

Except neither of them mentioned Noah. I sat down at the table and poured myself some juice. I glanced at the phone. I'd call.

"Noah went to pick something up at his house," my mother said, a smile in her voice. "He'll be back later."

So I *was* that obvious. Excellent.

"Toast?"

"Thanks," I said.

"What do you want to do today?" she asked me.

"Horseback riding," Joseph answered, mid-bite.

"I'm not sure I'd even know where to go for that."

"Noah does," Joseph said. "He knows everything."

"I see we have a bit of hero worship happening here." My mother handed me a plate of toast as she shot Joseph a knowing look. "I think maybe we should let Noah have some space today and do what he wants to do. Why don't we see a movie?"

My brother sighed. "Which one?"

"Whichever one you like—"

Joseph flashed a mischievous smile

"That's rated no higher than PG-13."

His expression fell. Then brightened again. "What about *Aftermath*?"

My mother squinted. "Is that the one about the plague?"

Joseph nodded vehemently.

My mother looked at me. "Okay with you?"

I didn't particularly want to go anywhere. In fact, I could think of nothing I'd rather do than have the house to myself for a while. Maybe try to read more *New Theories*, or research the pendant symbols, the feather—something.

But my mom would never agree to leave me alone, and if I said I didn't want to go out, she might wonder why. And wondering would lead to worrying, which would only make her less likely to release me from captivity anytime soon. So I assented. I could make Joseph happy, at least.

The movie didn't start for over an hour, so I found myself with time to kill. I nearly called Noah to ask him about last night, but my mother was right. He deserved some space.

Which is why my insides squirmed with guilt when I found myself standing in the doorway of the guest room. I didn't know what I was looking for until my eyes found it.

I didn't touch his things. I didn't dig through his black nylon bag. The room was as neat as if it had never been slept in, as if no one had ever been inside. Everything of his had been carefully put away. But just before I turned to leave, I noticed the corner of something peeking out from the crack between the wall and the bed.

A notebook.

Noah didn't take notes.

I took a step into the room. Maybe it wasn't his. Maybe Daniel or Joseph had left it there and forgotten, or maybe it belonged to one of their friends? I could look at the first page. Just to check.

No. I marched out of the room and picked up the phone to call Noah. I'd ask if it was his and if it was he'd know that I found it but didn't betray his trust by looking inside.

This was my inner monologue as I dialed his number, as his phone continued to ring. Eventually, I heard a click, but it was only his voice mail. He didn't pick up.

Within moments, I found myself back in the room.

The notebook probably wasn't even his. I'd never seen him with one, ever, and anyway, there was no reason for him to bring one to my house. On spring break, no less. I would just flip through it to see whose it was; I wouldn't read whatever was inside.

A Gollum/Sméagol conundrum. Would evil or good prevail?

I took a step toward the bed. If the notebook was Noah's, the law of the universe dictated that I would get caught.

But it's easier to ask forgiveness than permission. I took another step. Another. Then I reached for the notebook, swallowed my guilt, and began to read.

42

So begins the unillustrious record of the observations and musings of one Noah Elliot Simon Shaw insofar as they relate to one Mara (middle name as yet unknown, must remedy) Dyer and her purported metamorphosis.

Mara has just left. We have just immolated her grandmother's doll, which seems to have been (distressingly) stuffed with human hair, as well as a pendant identical to the one I own. Both of us are justifiably disturbed by this development, though it has provided a new avenue of exploration as to why the fuck both of us are so deeply weird.

Also, I kissed her. She liked it.

Naturally.

If there was anyone to speak to, I would have been speechless.

I blinked, hard, and then stared at the page, at the words, in his handwriting, just to make sure they were actually there.

They were. And I knew when he'd started writing then. It was after I told him I was afraid of losing control. Of losing myself. After telling him—

That all he could do was watch. My own voice echoed harshly in my ears.

"Tell me what you see. Because I don't know what's real and what isn't or what's new or different and I can't trust myself, but I trust you."

He had closed his eyes. Said my name. And then I said—

"You know what? Don't tell me, because I might not remember. Write it down, and then maybe someday, if I ever get better, let me read it. Otherwise I'll change a little bit every day and never know who I was until after I'm gone."

My throat felt tight. He was writing this for me.

I could stop reading now. Put the notebook back, tell him I found it and admit to reading the beginning. I could tell him I just wanted to check to see who it belonged to and once I saw it was his, stopped reading right away.

But I didn't. I turned the page.

Ruth informs me that when my father returns home, I'll be expected to return to school and attend classes without fail. I listen patiently but I can feel myself detach as I see it in exquisite, miserable detail:

I stare listlessly behind the teachers' heads as I listen to them drone on about things I already know. I cut class and stretch out on a picnic table beneath the tiki monstrosity and lie there, completely still.

A group of girls walks by, peering over the edge of the table. I am envious of chameleons. I open my eyes, squinting, and the girls dart away. They titter and giggle and I hear one of them whisper, "too perfect." I want to shake them for their ignorance and scream that their Sistine Chapel is filled with cracks.

In my previous life, for it seems that way though it's barely been a few months, I would flirt, or not, with anyone who seemed remotely interesting on any given day. There'd be one candidate, if I was lucky. Then I would count down the hours and minutes and seconds until another pointless day would finally end.

And then I'd go home. Or go to a new club with Parker or some other asshole who wears a cardigan around his shoulders and pops the collar on his fucking polo. I would stumble out, two gorgeous, faceless girls clutching my waist, the dull thud of soulless house music matching the dull throb in my temples, evident even through the slight haze of ecstasy and alcohol, and I would drink and feel nothing and laugh and feel nothing and stare at my life for the next three, five, twenty years, and loathe it.

The image of it bores me so deeply that I'm willing to die, right now, just to feel something else.

When the words ended, I realized that I was no longer standing; I had backed onto the bed. The notebook, the journal, was spread open against it, and my left hand had covered my mouth. I heard Noah's voice when I read his thoughts but there was a bitterness to them that I couldn't ever remember hearing out loud. I turned the page.

The best money can buy is nothing. Nothing on Lukumi or whoever the hell he is, and nothing on Jude. Even the search for his family has proven fruitless; nothing on Claire Lowe or Jude Lowe or parents William and Deborah since the collapse. There was an obituary in the Rhode Island paper with donation instructions and such, but the parents moved after the accident—or incident, I should say. And even with Charles's PI connections, zero. People can disappear—but not from people like him. It's as though the longer I reach, the further the truth gets. I hate that there's nothing more I can do. I'd go to Providence myself, but I don't want to leave Mara behind.

I might say something when I see her, though at present she seems preoccupied with some psycho at Horizons. I'm not the only one who doesn't play well with others. Perhaps that's why we get on so well.

Those were the first words that made me smile. The next ones made it vanish.

I sift through my dead mother's things. It's been years since I've bothered and I feel empty as I explore the full boxes, mostly brimming with battered, dog-eared, highlighted books. Singer and Ginsberg and Hoffman and Kerouac, philosophy and poetry and radicalism and Beat. The pages are worn, well-read, and I skim through them. I wonder if it's possible to know someone through the words they loved. There are photographs stuck in some of the books. Mostly people I don't recognize, but there are a few of her. She looks fierce.

*A book that doesn't seem to belong catches my eye—*Le Petit Prince. *I open it and a black-and-white picture slips out—her from the back, looking down, holding a blond boy's hand. My hand, I realize. My hair grew darker as I grew up.*

A spot of red bleeds through the picture and spreads, covering her fingers, mine. I hear shouting and screaming and a boy's voice begging her to come back.

The text ended there and didn't pick up again until the following page. My throat ached and my fingers were shaking and I shouldn't be reading this but I couldn't stop.

Another fight.

I was already annoyed by the Lukumi-fraud situation when I heard some random on Calle Ocho say something vaguely insulting to the girl he was with. I said something profoundly insulting back. I desperately hoped he'd swing.

He did.

There is an unparalleled freedom in fighting. I can't be hurt and so I'm afraid of nothing. They can be, so they're afraid of everything. That makes it easy, and so I always win.

Mara calls. She's hopeful for answers but I have none and I don't want her to know.

He must have written the entries on Thursday, when he didn't come over. After I called him and he hung up and I worried, wondered why he sounded so distant. I was riveted.

When I don't see her, her ghost wanders my veins. And when I see Mara today after a day apart, she is different.

The word seeps into my blood.

It is subtle—so subtle that I hadn't quite noticed it myself until she mentioned it; perhaps I'm too close. But now, the time apart throws the changes into relief and I watch her closely, so I can remember. She is still beautiful—always—but her cheekbones are more prominent. Her collarbone is diamond sharp. The softness I love is slowly being filed away by something inside or outside, I don't know.

I don't want to tell her. She came undone over nothing at the fair, after some hack fed her lines about destiny and fate. Things are precarious enough as it is.

He wrote that yesterday.

I tried to piece together the things he thought with the moments he may have thought them, moments he was with me. The words picked up again on the bottom of the same page.

I can't forget the kiss.

It's laughable. I barely touched her but it was distressingly intimate. She arched up toward me, but I placed my hand on her waist and she stilled under my palm. I don't think she's ever looked so perilously beautiful as she did in that second.

She isn't the only one changing. Every day she shapes me into something else.

I am definitely a pussy.

Sharing a bed with her is its own exquisite torture. I twine around her like moss on a limb; our heartbeats synchronize and we become one twisted, codependent thing. She brings me to heel with one look and I hear an aching violin, a cello's low swell. It hums beneath my skin; I want nothing more than to devour her, yet I do nothing but clench my jaw, press my lips to her neck, and savour the tremor in her chord. After a while, it softens at the edges as she slips into sleep. Her sound is a siren's song, calling me to the rocks.

She thinks I don't desire her and it's almost ridiculous how wrong she is. But she has to fight her demons before I can prove it, lest I become one of them. She hears Jude's name and her sound tightens, rises; her breath and heart quicken with fear. He fractured something inside of her and God knows, I will make him pay.

I can't slay her dragon because I can't find him, so for now I stay close.

It's not enough.

My dragon. My demons.

Noah thought what Jude did to *me* was what made me afraid to kiss *him*. That if I was still fearful and Noah let things go too far, it would haunt me the way Jude does now.

He didn't trust me when I said I wasn't afraid of him. He didn't understand that I was only afraid of myself.

Then there was nothing for five, seven pages. On the thirteenth page, there was more:

My theory: that Mara can manipulate events the way I can manipulate cells. I have no idea how either of us can do either thing, but nevertheless.

I try to get her to envision something benign but she stares and concentrates while her sound never changes. Is her ability linked to desire? Does she not want anything good?

Nightmare:

The sun slants through my bedroom windows, backlighting Mara as she draws in my bed. She wears my shirt—a shapeless black and white plaid thing that I wouldn't normally notice but with her inside of it, it is beautiful.

The skin of her bare thigh glances against my arm as she shifts in my sheets. My hand holds a book: Invitation to a Beheading. *I'm trying to read it, but I can't get past this passage:*

"In spite of everything I loved you, and will go on loving you—on my knees, with my shoulders drawn back, showing my heels to the headsman and straining my goose neck—even then. And afterwards—perhaps most of all afterwards—I shall love you, and one day we shall have a real, all-embracing explanation, and then perhaps we shall somehow fit together, you and I . . . we shall connect the points . . . and you and I shall form that unique design for which I yearn."

I can't get past it because I keep wondering what Mara's thigh would feel like against my cheek.

Her graphite pencil scratches the thick paper and it is the soundtrack to my bliss. That, and her sound—dissonant, aching. Her breath and heartbeat and pulse are my new favourite symphony; I'm beginning to learn which notes will play when, and to interpret them. There is wrath and contentment and fear and desire—but she has never let the last get too far. Yet.

The sun sings in her hair as her head tilts, dips toward the page. She arches forward, her shape slightly feline as she draws. My heart beats her name. She glances over her shoulder and smirks like she can hear it.

Enough.

I toss the book on the floor—a first edition, I don't care—and I lean into her. She coyly moves to block her sketchbook. Fine. It isn't what I want, anyway.

"Come here," I whisper into her skin. I turn her to face me. She knots her fingers in my hair and my eyelids drop at her touch.

And then she kisses me first, which never happens. It is light and fresh and soft. Careful. She still thinks she can hurt me, somehow; she doesn't grasp yet that it isn't possible. I have no idea what's going on in her mind but even if it takes her years to let go, it will be worth it. I would wait forever for the promise of seeing Mara, unleashed.

I pull back to look at her again, but something is wrong. Off. Her eyes are glassy and blurred, shining with tears.

"Are you all right?"

She shakes her head. A tear spills over, rolls down her cheek. I hold her face in my hands. "What?"

She glances at the sketchbook behind her. Moves out of the way. I lift it.

It's a sketch of me, but my eyes are blacked out. I narrow mine at hers.

"Why would you draw this?"

She shakes her head. I grow frustrated. "Tell me."

She opens her mouth to speak, but she has no tongue.

When I wake, Mara is no longer in bed.

I lie alone, staring at the ceiling, then at the clock. Three minutes after two in the morning. I wait five minutes. After ten, I get up to see where she's gone.

I find her in the kitchen. She is staring at her reflection in the dark window with a long knife pressed against her thumb, and suddenly I'm not in Miami but in London, in my father's study; I am fifteen and completely numb. I skirt the desk my father never sits in and reach for his knife. I drag it across my skin—

I blink the memory away and whisper Mara's name in desperation. She doesn't respond, so I cross the kitchen and take her hand and gently put down the knife.

She smiles and it is empty and it freezes my blood because I've seen that smile on myself.

In the morning, she remembers nothing.

It is March 29th.

I couldn't breathe when I read the date. March 29th is today.

43

I WAS A SEETHING CAULDRON OF THOUGHTS, NONE OF which I could process before I heard Daniel calling my name.

I rushed to put the notebook back where I found it and slipped out of the guest bedroom and into the kitchen. Daniel was twirling his keys.

"We're going out," he said.

I glanced at the hallway. "I don't really feel like—"

"Like staying home. Trust me." Daniel flashed a cryptic smile. "You'll thank me later."

I doubted that. I needed to sit still, by myself, and just think. About what I would say to Noah when I finally saw him. What I would tell him after what I read.

The entries about me were one thing. Noah wrote them for me, meant for me to see them, someday.

But the rest. The rest was his. *His.* I felt sick.

"I got you out of seeing that awful-looking movie with Mom and Joseph. Come on," Daniel said with an exaggerated arm-wave. "COME ON."

He was relentless so I followed him sulkily into the car. "Where are we going?" I asked, trying to sound casual. Trying to sound okay.

"We are going out for your birthday."

"Hate to break it to you, but you're a little late."

He stroked his chin. "Yes, yes, I see how it may seem that way from your unenlightened perspective. But in fact, seeing as how your technical birthday resulted in what we shall henceforth call your 'Dark Period', it was discussed and then agreed that you should have a do-over."

I shot him a sidelong glance as he turned onto the highway. "Discussed and agreed by . . . ?"

"By everyone. Everyone in the *whole world*. There *is* no other topic of discussion other than Mara Dyer, didn't you get the memo?"

I sighed. "You're not going to tell me where we're going, are you?"

Daniel mimed zipping his lips.

"Right," I said. It was hard not to smile, even though I wasn't in the mood. My brother was trying to make me happy. It was my fault that I was miserable, not his.

We eventually stopped at a marina, which, obviously, I did not expect. I got out of the car, my feet crunching on the gravel, but Daniel stayed put. I looped around to his window and he rolled it down.

"This is where I leave you," he said with a salute.

I glanced back at the entrance. The sky was beginning to change, and silver-pink clouds appeared low over the tall masts. No one was there. "Am I supposed to do anything?"

"All shall be revealed in time."

There was a plan, clearly, a plan that likely involved Noah, which made me want to smile and cry at the same time. "Does Mom know?" was all I asked.

"Sort of . . . not really."

"Daniel—"

"It's worth it, you deserve this. Hey, look behind you!"

I turned. A man in a nautical-ish uniform was walking from a long dock into the parking lot, a garment bag draped over his arms. When I looked back at Daniel, he'd rolled up his window. He winked through it and waved.

A lump formed in my throat as I waved back. I didn't deserve *him*.

The uniformed man spoke. "If you would be so kind as to come with me, Miss Dyer, I'll bring you to the boat."

I smiled, but it didn't reach my eyes. I thought Noah would catch me reading his journal, maybe. He'd get angry.

We'd fight. I'd explain, we'd make up, we'd move on.

But now as I walked toward what was sure to be a grand gesture of the grandest sort, it was polluted by my betrayal. I had to tell him; the longer I waited, the worse it would be.

The man introduced himself as Ron and led me toward the end of the dock. The air smelled of brine and seaweed and water lapped beneath our heavy steps. We finally came to a stop before a sleek, stunning boat. I was helped up the steps and asked to take off my shoes; the blond wood deck gleamed beneath my bare feet, shining and spotless.

Once we were on board, Ron turned to me and asked if I'd like anything to drink. I said I was fine, even though I wasn't.

A flurry of activity began behind me. Knots were being untied and it looked like we were getting ready to leave.

"Where are we going?" I asked him.

"It won't be a long trip," he said with a smile. I looked at the sky; it was nearly sunset now, and I wondered when Noah would appear.

Ron handed me the garment bag. "I've been instructed to tell you that you don't need to change, but that this was made for you if you'd like to wear it. Either way, it's yours to keep."

Something fluttered in my chest and in my mind as I took the bag from him gingerly.

"But if you'd like to, I can show you the cabin?"

I thanked him and he led me down a small, narrow half-staircase, half-ladder situation. We climbed down into an abbreviated hallway that sprouted off into a few separate rooms; a man in a chef's hat worked in the galley, and we passed two bedrooms before he showed me into the third. I looked for Noah in all of them. He wasn't there.

"Let me know if there's anything you need," he said.

"Thanks."

He inclined his head and closed the door behind him, leaving me alone.

I could have been in a boutique hotel. Plush white bed linens adorned the bed that anchored the room, and twin swing-arm sconces flanked either side of the tufted leather headboard. There was a small bar built into the wall below a row of round windows. I spread the garment bag onto the bed and unzipped it.

A sliver of dark blue, almost black cloth peeked out, and when I lifted the strapless dress—the gown, really—out of the bag, the fabric felt like water beneath my fingers. It was extraordinary; so soft and perfect it didn't feel real. I slipped on the dress, and looked in the mirrored wall.

It was like I was wearing night itself. The color made my skin look like cream; flawless, instead of just pale. The dress gently skimmed every curve as if it had been taught how by someone who knew every line and dip and arch of my frame. The act of wearing it was intimate, and my skin flooded with heat.

But most astonishing of all was that when I looked at my

reflection, it seemed more familiar to me than it had in weeks.

When I finally tore my eyes away, I opened the closet to see if there were shoes. There weren't. I searched in a few places I thought shoes might be, but I didn't see a box.

Or, more precisely, I didn't see a *shoe*box. As my eyes roamed the room, I noticed a small box on the built-in nightstand that was part of the bed. A small, black, velvet box.

A jewelry box. It rested on top of a cream colored envelope. I opened it with trembling fingers and unfolded the note inside as carefully as I could. My breath caught in my throat as I read the words in Noah's script.

This belonged to my mother, but it was meant for you.

My heart thundered against my rib cage and my pulse fluttered beneath my skin as I put down the note and finally looked inside.

44

THE DARK JEWEL WAS THE COLOR OF MIDNIGHT and it glittered with fire. A hundred diamonds or more surrounded the sapphire in a loop and extended into a long strand, which uncoiled into my palm. I had never held anything so precious. I was almost afraid to put it on.

Almost.

I glanced at the door. I half-expected Noah to appear to clasp it around my neck, but he didn't so I did it myself. The necklace was heavy but the weight felt right, somehow, around my throat.

I tied my hair back in a knot, then left the room. My bare

feet found purchase on the narrow ladder as I climbed up to the dock where I knew I'd see Noah. My heart was beating fast and I bit my lip as I emerged.

He wasn't there.

Perplexing. I slowly let out the breath I didn't realize I'd been holding and looked around. We were far from the marina now, floating in a large, dark turquoise expanse of water dotted with many other boats. Tangles of seaweed floated by on the surface, the foam from another boat's wake clinging to the water. There were people, too; some drifting in tubes, others flying kites off the decks of their boats. An old man floated by us on an orange foam noodle, with neon green sunglasses on his reddened face and a neon pink beer cozy in his hand. A preppy college student in plaid shorts and a dumb little straw hat manned a shiny yacht that blasted the air with inane lyrics and a pulsing, officious beat. He tossed his cigarette butt in the water. Ass.

And then, as we sailed under a beautiful, old-fashioned white drawbridge dotted with street lamps, the landscape around us changed. We passed a golf course peppered with palm trees on one side, and beautiful homes lined the opposite shore. The backyards were thick with peach and olive trees, or rose gardens with arbors surrounding full tennis courts. A lonely frame ladder stood in one yard, there to trim a menagerie of hedge animals into their respective shapes. The house beyond the yard was enormous, Tuscan style, with tiered arches spanning the length of the floor to the ceiling.

I leaned my arms against the prow, taking in the lavish mansions; the modern glass and steel monstrosities and the attempted charm of the sprawling older homes. The boat rocked gently beneath my bare feet. I spent so much time feeling sick these days that I was mildly surprised at *not* feeling sick on the boat.

A blast of loud music assaulted my ears and I looked up. Someone in one of the homes had turned on a massive outdoor speaker system. I heard the angry wail of guitars and crashing electronica in the background, and a growling singer yell about damage and abuse and saving yourself.

We passed an enormous boxlike house, a throwback to the sixties, I guessed, and then floated by a grand, white mansion with soaring windows that faced the water. Greek statues bordered the intricately landscaped lawn, and something about it felt—

Familiar.

Because it was Noah's house. I almost didn't recognize it from here; I had always been on the inside looking out, but now I was out, looking in.

But I didn't see or feel any sign that we were stopping. That apparently wasn't where we were going. Curious.

The houses soon gave way to forest. An enormous banyan tree bent away from its roots, saturated with Spanish moss that kissed the water. The dying sun reflected off the surface, casting rippling shadows beneath the tree. Palm trees on either side of us bent and swayed, heavy with coconuts. Then the forest became less dense. We passed pylons with nothing tethered to them, their weathered wood exposed at mid-tide. A palm tree with the top cut off stood at attention to our right, just a tall stump that punctured the air.

And then, finally, I saw where we were headed. A small island appeared in front of us—we had passed many, but I felt, I knew, that Noah was on this one. Waiting for me.

We sailed around to a narrow dock that jutted out into the ocean. The crew anchored the boat and Ron helped me step off, but didn't join me. He just nodded to the end of the small pier, and I began to walk.

The wind had untied my hair and now it hung loose in dark waves over my bare shoulders. The wood beneath my feet was smooth, worn down by air and water. I lifted the hem of the dress—I would die if I tripped—and wondered where I was going.

I didn't have to wonder very long; at the end of the dock, small torches rose out of the ground, and their flames guided my way. I followed them down the beach until finally, I saw him.

It was hard to appreciate how beautiful the silent, secret beach was with Noah standing there, looking like sex in a slim-cut tux, lean and tall and extravagantly gorgeous. I dropped the hem of the dress, along with my jaw and my thoughts and everything else.

"You're here," he said.

The sound of him, the *sight* of him, stole my words away.

Noah gracefully crossed the sand and dipped his head to meet my eyes. "Mara?"

Still speechless.

Noah smiled that crooked smile of his and I thought I might dissolve. "Should I be concerned?"

I managed to shake my head.

He took a slight step back and considered me. I felt his eyes slide over my skin. "You'll do."

I broke into a brilliant smile. "You too," I said, my voice strangely hoarse.

"You mentioned a tux in your fantasy, so . . ."

"Actually," I managed to say, "I believe *you* mentioned a tux in *your* fantasy."

Because I was too limited to comprehend what he would look like in one. I adored Noah's I-can't-be-bothered-to-care wardrobe of worn shirts and destroyed jeans, but this . . . there were no words.

"Hmm," he said thoughtfully. "Perhaps you're right."

My smile widened. "I am right."

"Well," he said, his voice even as he glanced back at the dock. "I suppose if you'd rather go back to your house . . ."

I shook my head vehemently.

"This will do, then?"

Would it ever. I nodded.

"Excellent. Oliver will be pleased."

"Oliver?"

"The tailor I rarely have the occasion to use. He was thrilled when I called, even though he had to drop everything to make it in two weeks."

"Sounds expensive."

"Five grand, but for that look on your face, I'd have paid ten. Shall we?"

I followed the line of Noah's gesture down the length of the beach. There was a blanket anchored farther down the expanse of white sand, surrounded by torches. A piece of bright fabric was swathed between two trees.

He walked toward the ocean and stood at the edge where the waves licked the sand. I followed him almost all the way, careful to avoid the water. The sunlight was all gone and gray clouds chased one another across an inky, perforated sky.

"This is what I should've given you for your birthday," he said, his voice velvet, but shot through with something I couldn't name. Then he turned to me and his eyes dropped to my throat. He took a step closer, nearly aligning my body with his. His elegant fingers moved to my neck. They wandered over the jewel. "And this."

They traced my skin, dipping below the necklace, then up.

"And this," he said, as they came to rest below my jaw, tipping my face up to his. His thumb followed the curve of my mouth, and his beautiful, perfect face angled down toward mine.

"And this," he said, his lips just inches from mine.

He was going to kiss me.

He was going to trust me.

Somewhere between the boat and the dress and the beach and the sky I had forgotten what I'd done. But now it roared back loudly in my ears; if I didn't tell him now, I never could. Lies make us look like someone else, but with Noah, I had to be myself.

The words burned in my throat. "I—"

Noah drew back slightly at the sound of my voice. His eyes translated my expression. "Don't," he said, and pressed one finger to my lips. "Whatever it is. Don't say it."

But I did. "I read it." The words took my breath with them. Noah's hand left my skin.

They lie, you know. It's not easier to ask forgiveness. Not even a little.

45

I'M SORRY," I STARTED TO SAY. "I DIDN'T—"

"Yes, you did," Noah said, his voice cold. He looked at the ocean. Not at me.

"I just thought—"

"Must we? Must we do this?"

"Do what?" I asked softly.

"*This.*" The word was a splash of acid. "This—whatever." His voice had slid back into flatness. "You told me to write what I see. I did. Then you read it without asking. Fine." He dropped a viciously indifferent shrug. "I suppose part of me wouldn't have left it there if I hadn't wanted you to. So, done. It's over." He stared ahead into the darkness. "It doesn't matter."

"It does."

He turned to me with predatory grace. "All right, Mara." His voice lacerated my name. "You want to hear how I first learned about my ability? About being told that we were moving into yet another miserable home two days before we left by my father's secretary, because he couldn't be bothered to tell me himself? About feeling so numb to it and everything that I was sure I couldn't actually exist? That I must be made of nothing to feel so much nothing, that the pain the blade drew from my skin was the only thing that made me feel real?"

His voice grew savagely blank. "You want to hear that I *liked* it? Wanted more? Or do you want to hear that when I woke up the next day to find no trace of any cut, no hint of a forming scar, all I could feel was crushing disappointment?"

There was nothing but the sound of deceptively tranquil waves and my breath in the stillness before he shattered it again.

"It became a kind of game, then, to see if there was any damage I could actually do. I've chased every high and low you can imagine," he said, underscoring the word *every* with a narrow look to make sure I understood what he meant. "Completely without consequence. I wanted to lose myself and I couldn't. I'm chasing an oblivion I will never find." And then he smiled; a dark, broken, empty thing. "Have you heard enough?"

He was terrifyingly cold, but I wasn't afraid. Not of him.

I took a step toward him. My voice was quiet, but strong. "It doesn't matter."

"What doesn't matter?" he asked tonelessly.

"What you did before."

"I haven't changed, Mara."

I stared at him, at his expression. *I still want to lose myself,* it said. And I began to understand. Noah craved danger because he was never in it; he was careless because he didn't believe he could actually break. But he wanted to. He wasn't afraid of me—not just because he believed I couldn't hurt him, but because even if I did, he'd welcome the pain.

Noah was still chasing oblivion. And in me, he found it.

"You *want* me to hurt you." My voice was barely above a whisper.

He took a step toward me. "You can't."

"I could kill you." The words were edged in steel.

Another step. His eyes challenged mine. "Try."

As he stood there in his exquisite clothes, his flawless features staring me down, he still looked like an arrogant prince. But only now could I see that his crown was broken.

The air around us was charged as we stood opposite each other. Healer and destroyer, noon and midnight. We were silently deadlocked. Neither of us moved.

I realized then that Noah would never move. He would never back down because he didn't want to win.

And I wouldn't lose him. So all I could do was refuse to play.

"I won't be what you want," I said then, my voice low.

"And what do you think that is?"

"Your weapon of self-destruction."

He went still. "You think I want to *use* you?"

Didn't he? "Don't you?"

Noah inhaled slowly. "No, Mara." My name was soft now, in his mouth. "No. I never wanted that."

"Then what *do* you want?"

"I want—" He stopped. Tore his fingers through his hair. "Never mind what I want." His voice was quieter, now. "What do *you* want?"

"You." Always you.

"You have me," he said, his eyes meeting mine. "You *inhabit* me." His face was stone but the words issued from his lips in a plea. "You want to know what I want? I want *you* to be the one wanting me first. Pushing me first. Kissing me first. Don't be careful with me," he said. "Because I won't be careful with you."

My heart began to race.

"You can't hurt me the way you think you can. But even if you could? I would rather die with the taste of you on my tongue than live and never touch you again. I'm in love with you, Mara. I love you. No matter what you do."

My breath caught in my throat. *No matter what.* The words were a promise, a promise I didn't know if anyone could keep.

"We're only seventeen," I said quietly.

"Fuck seventeen." His eyes and voice were defiant. "If I were to live a thousand years, I would belong to you for all of them. If we were to live a thousand lives, I would want to make you mine in each one."

Noah knew what I was and what I'd done and he wanted me anyway. He *saw* me. All of me. With my skin peeled back, my heart bare. I was inside out for him, and trembling.

"All I want is you," he said. "You don't have to choose me now or ever, but when you choose, I want you *free*."

Something inside me stirred.

"You're stronger than you believe. Don't let your fear own you. Own yourself."

I turned the words over in my mind. *Own myself.* As if it were that easy. As if I could walk away from grief and guilt and leave fear and everything behind.

I wanted to. I wanted to.

"Kiss me," I whispered.

Noah's fingers traced the column of my spine, exposed in the dress. Heat bloomed beneath my skin.

"I can't. Not like this."

Noah started this chase and I stood before him, waiting to be caught. He could have me, but he refused to move.

Only now did I realize why.

He wanted to be caught. He was waiting for me to chase *him*.

I lunged for his shirt and pulled him to me. Against me. My

hands became fists in the cloth but his were stone on either side of my rib cage; they rose and fell with each hard breath I took but didn't move. Mine did. My fingers wandered beneath his dress shirt; his breath quickened when they met his pale gold skin. They traveled over ridges of muscle and sinew, hard and hot beneath my palms. I tried to reach his mouth with mine, but he was too tall and he wouldn't bend.

So I backed down onto the sand. And I pulled him down with me.

The hem of my dress touched the water but I didn't care, not then. The earth gave way beneath my body as Noah moved over me and slid his knee between mine, stoking my flame. His arm slipped beneath my back and his mouth moved over my neck, his lips brushing my collarbone and the hollow beneath my ear. My arms twined around his neck, my fists curled in his hair. My heartbeat was wild. His was still calm.

And then I slid over him. Above him. His ribs moved under *my* hands, now. His waist was between my legs. I was breathing hard and feeling reckless. Noah watched me, and if I didn't know him as well as I did, I wouldn't have known that there was anything unusual about this. But I *did* know him, and still though he was, there *was* something different about the way he looked at me now.

I placed my hands on his chest. His heart beat faster. His control was slipping.

Chase.

I leaned closer, my hands moving lower down his stomach, my back arched above him. I kissed his throat. I heard a sharp intake of breath.

I smiled against his skin, moved my lips along his jaw, his throat, marveling at the point where the rough became smooth. My hands wandered slowly to his waist and he slid my dress up, his fingers hot on my bare skin, making me breathless. Making me ache. I pressed into him harder, my body bent, bowstring-tight over his. His mouth was just millimeters from mine.

"Fuck," he murmured against my lips. The feel, the word, sent a hot little shock through my spine. It skittered through my veins, danced through every nerve.

And then I brushed his lips with mine.

I knew Noah worshipped Charlie Parker and that his toothbrush was green. That he wouldn't bother to button his shirts correctly but always made his bed. That when he slept he curled into himself and that his eyes were the color of the clouds before it rained, and I knew he had no problem eating meat but would subtly leave the room if animals started to kill one another on the Discovery Channel. I knew one hundred little things about Noah Shaw but when he kissed me I couldn't remember my own name.

I was starved for him, for this. I was a creature of need—soaked in feeling and breathless. There was a pull, furious and fierce, and part of me was frightened by it but another part, low and deep and dark, breathed *yes*.

Noah whispered my name like a prayer, and I was free.

I moved his jacket off of his shoulders. Gone. Unfastened the buttons on his shirt in seconds, loosened the tie at his neck. His skin was on fire under hands that traveled the slender muscle and bone beneath them of their own volition. Over his abdomen, his chest. Over two slim lines of silver that rested against his throat—

Colors burst in my mind. Green and red and blue. Trees and blood and sky. The sand and ocean vanished; they were replaced by jungle and clouds. There was a voice, warm and familiar but it was far away.

Mara.

The word filled my lungs with a rush of air and I breathed in sandalwood and salt. Then there was strong pressure on my hips, shifting me away. Down. Gray eyes pinned me to the earth and the sky changed again above them; the blue chased by black, the clouds chased by stars. Noah was above me, his breathing quick, his pupils blown. He looked down at me.

Differently.

My thoughts were hazy, and it was difficult to speak. "What?" I managed to say.

Noah's eyes were lidded, and there was a storm beneath them. "You—" he began, then stopped. "I felt—"

"What?" I asked again, louder this time.

"I believe you," he finally said.

Heat rose beneath my skin as I understood what he meant. "Did I hurt you?" I asked in a rush. "Are you okay?"

A slight smile turned up his mouth. "I'm still here."

"What happened?"

He considered his words. "You sounded different," Noah said slowly. "I was listening for a change and I heard it but didn't know what it meant; I've never heard you like that before. I said your name but you didn't respond. So we stopped."

I didn't know what it meant either and I didn't care. "Did I hurt you?" I asked again; that was what I cared about. That was what I needed to know.

Noah helped me up and we rose from the sand together. His words and eyes were soft. "I'm still here." He laced his fingers through mine. "Let's go home."

Noah led me along the water, looking forward, not at me. I studied him closely, still unsure if he was all right.

When I arrived on the beach, Noah was flawless. Now his tie was loose, his cuffs were undone, sand and sea had ruined his five-thousand-dollar suit, and his hair had been ravaged by my hands. His gray sapphire eyes were blazing and his velvet lips were swollen from mine.

This was the boy I loved. A little bit messy. A little bit ruined. A beautiful disaster.

Just like me.

46

IT FELT LIKE THE WEIGHT OF MY WORLD DISSOLVED with that kiss.

It wasn't feather-light, like the others. It was wild and dark. It was incredible.

And Noah was still here.

I wore the goofiest grin on the ride back to the marina; I couldn't stop smiling and didn't want to. After both of us had changed into our normal clothes and I returned his mother's necklace so that it would stay safe, what we decided was this:

I was right. Something changed in me when we kissed.

But Noah was also right. I didn't hurt him the way I was sure I would.

I didn't know if it was because he was listening for something this time, for that change, maybe, or if it was because I really *couldn't* hurt him, just like he said. I was thrilled that he was okay, obviously. Deliriously so. But it shook my confidence in my memory a little—I couldn't help but wonder if maybe, after all this, I *had* dreamed or imagined or hallucinated that first kiss in his bed. I told Noah as much, but he took my hands and looked into my eyes and told me to trust myself, and to trust my instincts, too. I tried to coax more out of him but then he kissed me again.

I could spend the rest of my life kissing him, I think.

I was buoyant the rest of the weekend. We had answered one question out of a thousand, but it was a *happy* answer. I wanted to believe that after everything I'd been through, I deserved it.

Noah seemed different, too. He told me he brokered a deal to buy the security tapes from the carnival people to resolve one way or another whether Roslyn Ferretti *was* bribed, and if so, by whom. He also wanted to fly to Providence and try to find out more than his investigator, to see if he could learn more about Jude himself. I was happy to let him go. Nothing had happened since John started watching the house, and I didn't need to be attached to Noah every second. The fake fortune-teller's words mattered less to me now that I knew I couldn't hurt him, and so

I in turn cared less about them. I didn't feel afraid.

I felt free.

Noah's hands lingered on my waist when he kissed me good-bye on Sunday night, and I smiled at the two charms that now hung around his neck. I loved that he was wearing mine for me.

My good mood was obvious to everyone, including my parents, apparently.

"We're really proud of you, Mara," my father said on the drive to Horizons on Monday morning. "Your mom and I were talking about the retreat this week and we decided that if you don't want to go, you don't have to."

The Horizons retreat; part of the evaluation I was signed up for—to see if I would be better suited to the residential program than the outpatient one. I'd forgotten all about it, but I guess now it didn't matter because I didn't have to go.

I was shocked but thrilled by this development. "What brought this on?"

Dad shook his head. "We never wanted you to live somewhere else. We love having you home, kid. We just want you healthy and safe."

A worthy goal. I had no protest.

The thing about happiness, though, is that it never lasts.

When I walked into Horizons I was handed a worksheet, which turned out to be a test. A sociopath test, if the questions were any indication. It was obvious which answer you were supposed to provide when prompted to choose—those tests always are—so I answered benignly, growing slightly uncomfortable about the fact that most of my real answers were not particularly nice.

`Do you lie or manipulate others when it suits your needs or to get what you want?`

`A) Sometimes`

`B) Rarely`

`C) Often`

`D) Never`

Often. "Rarely," I circled.

`Do you feel that the rules of society don't apply to you, and will you violate them to accomplish your goals?`

Sometimes. "Never," I chose.

`Do you easily talk your way out of trouble without guilt?`

Often. "Rarely."

`Have you killed animals in the past?`

Sometimes, I was loath to admit. "Never," I chose.

And on it went, but I tried not to let it sour my mood. When I sat down for Group, I was able to maintain my golden bubble for a little while longer, even though everyone's tiny miseries kept pressing up against it. I clenched my mouth against the snark and made sure my inner monologue stayed inner; I didn't want anything to derail my Get Out of Inpatient Treatment Free pass.

Jamie looked like he was having as hard a time with all the sharing today as I was after one of Adam's standard narcissistic diatribes, so when we broke for snack time I edged over.

"I hate that guy," I said, grabbing a cookie.

"Yeah," was all I got out of him, quite uncharacteristically. He filled a glass with water and sipped it very slowly.

I sat on the couch beside him. "Who died?" I asked.

There was a thin film of sweat on his forehead, which he wiped with the back of his sleeve. "Anna Greenly."

"Wait—*Croydian* Anna?"

"The very same."

I stared at him for a beat, waiting for the punch line. Then realized there was none.

"Seriously?" I asked quietly.

"Careened off an overpass. Drunk."

"I'm . . ." But I didn't know what I was. I had no idea what to say. You say you're sorry when someone loses a person they love. Not a person they hate.

"Yeah," Jamie said, though I hadn't said anything. He did not look well.

"You okay?" I asked softly.

He shrugged. "I have a stomach thing. Don't get close."

"Well, now you've spoiled everything," I said casually, working hard to fake it. "I was planning to seduce you in the broom closet." I pointed. "Right there."

A joyless smile appeared on Jamie's lips. "We are far too

screwed-up for a goddamned love triangle."

That's my Jamie.

After a minute of silence, he said, "You know how every now and then there's a news story about kids being bullied into suicide?"

I did.

"Someone always says, 'Kids are mean.' 'Kids will be kids.' Which implies that the kid bullies will grow out of it someday." The muscles in his jaw tightened. His stare was unfocused and far away. "I don't think they do. I think kid bullies turn into adult bullies and it pisses me off that I'm expected to feel sad because one of them is gone. Anna was like . . . like a social terrorist," he said, staring at the floor. "Aiden too." His nostrils flared. "I was in that cesspool of douchebaggery with them for seven years and there was a lot—whatever. Let's just say beating the shit out of me and having me unjustly expelled from school wasn't the worst of it." A wave of something passed over his face but he said nothing else.

I tried to catch his eye. "Misery's no fun if you keep it to yourself."

"Ain't that the truth," he said, but didn't look up. "My parents asked if I wanted to go somewhere else for ninth grade but"—he waved his hand—"you know it doesn't matter. There's always one or two or five of them and I was short and a nerd and a minority in every major way and that's more than enough reason to be picked on." He exhaled through his nose. "But you know what their real problem with me was? I never wanted to be one of them. That's what bothers bullies the most."

Jamie stared at the near empty glass in his fist, gripping it tightly. "Of course, you can't say any of this out loud, or people will clutch their pearls and call you a monster."

I thought of my less-than-honest answers on this morning's assignment and nudged my friend with my shoulder. "Not me. I took the sociopath test this morning. I only got three out of ten non-sociopath results."

"That's plenty." Jamie flashed a weak half-smile, deepening his dimple, then went on. "I'm sure she had a redeeming quality or two and her family and sycophantic friends will miss her dearly. And if she were sitting here now talking about *me*, I'd probably feature in her narrative as a Moor out to steal all da white ladies." He shrugged a shoulder. "I just can't muster up the energy to feel shitty. I don't really want to. She wouldn't want my pity, even if she had it. You know?"

"I do," I said, because I did.

He looked at the wall in front of us, at a ridiculous motivational poster with an eagle skimming the water, triumphantly clutching a fish in its talons. "A little dark for dear little Jamie?"

"No," I said.

"No?"

"Your love of Ebola tipped me off," I explained. "And you're not so little, either."

He inclined his head slightly, with a smile to match. Then he stood. "I am going to go throw up now. Enjoy your cookie."

Jamie left but I just sat there, feeling vaguely nauseated myself.

His words unlocked something inside of me and images of corpses bobbed up in my mind.

Morales. Would I have killed her for failing me if I knew what I was doing? No. But was I sad that she was dead?

The brutal, honest answer was no. I was sorry that *I* might've killed her, but I barely thought about her at all.

And Mabel's owner. If he was alive, she wouldn't be. Or she'd be suffering still, with gaping wounds in her neck infested by maggots as her body consumed itself, as she died slowly in the miserable heat. But because he was dead? She was spoiled and fat and happy and loved. Her life was worth more than his.

And then, of course, there was Jude. Who trapped me. Pushed me. Forced me. And tortured me, now that he wasn't dead after all.

I wasn't sorry that I tried to kill him. I was sorry he was still alive. I would kill him again if I had the chance.

47

JAMIE WAS SENT HOME EARLY AFTER ONE OF THE counselors heard him throwing up in the bathroom. I was not so lucky. At lunch, I sat down next to Stella, who picked idly at her loaded sandwich. I started inhaling mine; the cookies from snack time were stale and store-bought, but the food they served in the dining room was addictive.

But then Phoebe sat across from us and began watching me intently. She scribbled in her journal, chewing on her fingernails as she scratched away, creating a little pile on the table.

Appetite gone. "That's gross, Phoebe."

"It's for the voodoo doll," she answered, her smile spreading like a stain. "It looks just like you."

You can't respond to a statement like that. There's just nothing to say.

A weird look settled over Phoebe's weird face and she leaned forward. "Gimme your hair," she said to me.

Stella stood suddenly, and pulled me away from the table.

"I'm telling my boyfriend!" Phoebe shouted after us.

It was all so screwed up that it was almost funny. I told Stella as much and she dropped my arm. That was when I noticed the bruise. An oil slick of colors, peeking out from beneath her sleeve.

"You okay?" I asked her, staring at it. She tugged her sleeve down, and when I met her eyes, her face was a mask.

"It's nothing," she said blankly. "Are *you* okay?"

I must have looked confused, because she nodded at the table. "Phoebe—" she said.

"Oh. I'm getting used to her shenanigans, I think." I shrugged.

Stella didn't say anything. Then, "She was getting intense."

"Phoebe's definitely not one of my favorite people."

Stella looked at me for a beat and said, "Be careful, okay?"

I was about to ask what she meant, but Dr. Kells appeared behind us and called out my name.

"Mara. Just the person I wanted to see." She looked from me to Stella and then back to me. "Are you busy at the moment?"

Stella offered a small wave, and walked away. Damn.

"No," I said. Wish I was.

"Can you step into my office for a sec?"

Let's get this over with.

"I wanted to check in with you," Dr. Kells said with a benevolent smile. "How are things?" She lowered herself into her chair.

"Fine." I said nothing more. She said nothing more. A common psychologists' trick, I knew—she who speaks first loses. I was an expert at this game now.

I felt the urge to yawn. I tried to stifle it, but eventually biology took over.

"How are you sleeping?" Dr. Kells asked.

"Okay." It was kind of true. I'd woken up in my own bed two days in a row. That should count for something.

She studied my face. "You look pretty tired," she said.

I shrugged. A non-answer.

"And thin. Are you dieting?" she asked me.

I shook my head.

"Maybe you're having difficulty adjusting? Do you think you could use something to help you rest?"

I wanted to throw my head back and groan. "I'm already on a lot of pills."

"You need your sleep."

"What if I become addicted?" I challenged her.

It didn't work. "The pills I'll prescribe for you are non-habit forming, don't worry. How are your other medications working out for you, by the way?"

"Great."

"Any hallucinations?"

None that I'm going to tell you about.

"Nightmares?"

None that I'm going to share.

Dr. Kells leaned forward. "Nothing unusual at all?"

"Nope," I said, smiling. "Completely normal." A complete lie.

"And what about being here at Horizons? How do you like our program?"

"Well," I said, feigning thoughtfulness, "I *really* like Art Therapy."

"That's wonderful, Mara. Have you been writing in your journal?"

The journal I couldn't even remember receiving? Admitting that meant admitting to losing time. Blacking out. Big red flags that I Am Not Okay. I might as well tattoo my forehead with the words INSTITUTIONALIZE ME.

So I told Dr. Kells it was lost. Normal people lose things all the time. No big.

"Have you been more forgetful lately?" she asked.

"No," I said, acting surprised by the question.

"Well, some of the medications could be responsible for that. I want you to pay attention and see if there's anything else like that that you've noticed." She pushed her glasses up on her nose. "Even if you don't think something is important. I think maybe I will adjust some of your dosages," she said, writing that down on her notepad. "What about emotionally?"

"What do you mean?"

"How are you getting along with the other students?"

"Good."

Dr. Kells leaned back in her chair and crossed her legs; her nude pantyhose crinkled over her knees like a second, artificial skin. "How about Phoebe?"

So that was where this line of questioning was going. I sighed. "I wouldn't say we're friends."

"Why do you say that?"

"Does Phoebe *have* any friends?" I asked her.

"Well, Mara, I'm more interested in hearing why you and she don't get along."

"Because she's certifiably insane. And she's a liar."

"It seems like you don't like her very much."

I rubbed my chin. "That's pretty accurate, yes."

"Phoebe said you threatened her."

"She said *I* threatened *her*?" I told Dr. Kells about the sinister *I see you* note Phoebe left in my bag, but, "I'll have a talk with her," was all Dr. Kells said.

Then she asked, "How about Adam?"

I shifted uncomfortably. I couldn't stand him, either.

"Have you made any friends here, Mara?"

The air conditioning clicked on as the silence stretched out. "Jamie," I suggested.

"You two knew each other from Croyden, right?"

"Yeah . . ."

"How about Tara?"

Who the heck was Tara?

"Megan?" Dr. Kells asked hopefully.

Megan. Megan of the bizarre phobias. We'd barely spoken to each other, but when I saw her I said hello—I decided to nod in response to Dr. Kells's question, and tossed out Stella's name for good measure. Dr. Kells didn't seem particularly impressed.

"All right," she said then, and waved her hand at her office door. "You're free to go. Let's talk again before the retreat."

"Actually," I said, drawing out the word. "I might not be going." I tried not to sound smug.

"That's too bad." Dr. Kells looked disappointed. "Our students tend to find it rewarding. Maybe you'll join us on the next one?"

"Definitely," I said before grabbing my bag, thanking her for the chat, and making my escape.

It would have been nice if Anna's death and Phoebe's fingernails had been the worst parts of my day.

Dad drove me home and the house was quiet when we reached it—school had started again for Daniel and Joseph, and they weren't home yet. Mom was probably still working. With Noah in Rhode Island until tomorrow, I found myself confined in the house with nothing to do.

So I settled on research. I passed my grandmother's portrait in the hallway on the way to my room and resolved to give *New Theories in Genetics* the old college try, as Daniel had said. Six hundred pages be damned.

But it wasn't on my bookshelf.

Or in my closet.

I started taking down boxes from my closet shelves, wondering if maybe I put it in one of them to keep it safe and just didn't remember. But even after I emptied their contents on the floor, nothing.

I grew increasingly frantic until I remembered that the last time I saw it was in the family room before the carnival, and that before I left it there, Daniel insisted on borrowing it. It was probably just in his room. I felt a little relieved and a little crazy for freaking out. Normal people forget things like that all the time.

I went into Daniel's room and scanned his shelves; there were some books missing from one, leaving the remaining spines slanted against one another at a sharp angle.

I wouldn't have noticed the composition notebook otherwise. Wouldn't have noticed the fact that my handwriting was on the front cover. Spelling out my name.

The notebook was completely, utterly unfamiliar to me, and the realization etched my mind with fear.

I remembered Brooke's words:

"Mara, where's your journal?"

"I never got a journal."

"Of course you did. On your first day, don't you remember?"

I didn't, but now I was looking right at it. I opened it up.

There was nothing on the first page, and I almost felt relief.

But then I flipped it over.

Panic rushed in, tidal and fierce and tugging me away. My knees almost buckled beneath me. I sat on Daniel's bed, folding into myself as I stared.

Each line on the second page was filled with words. Hundreds of words on thirteen lines, arranged into the briefest of sentences.

Help me help me help me help me help me help me help me help me
help me help me help me help me help me help me help me help me help
me help me help me help me help me help me help me help me help me
help me help me help me help me help me help me help me help me help
me help me help me help me help me help me help me help me help me
help me help me help me help me help me help me help me help me
help me help me help me help me help me help me help me help me help
me help me help me help me help me help me help me help me help me
help me help me help me help me help me help me help me help me
help me help me help me help me help me help me help me help me
help me help me help me help me help me help me help me help me
help me help me help me help me help me help me help me help me help
me help me help me help me help me help me

The words stopped in the middle of the line. I passed out.

48

BEFORE

Port of Calcutta, India

I followed behind the Man in Blue, my small legs hurrying to match his long stride. Seven days had passed since he first brought me to the empty village, since I began to live with Sister in the hut. I was happy to be out again. I was happy to see the ships again, standing tall and crawling with men.

But I missed Sister. I wished she was here. I clutched the doll to my chest. I had not yet chosen her name.

The Man in Blue brought me to a big building, and we went inside to meet a white man with glass discs on his nose. The Man in Blue handed him a small black pouch. The white man filled it and then handed it back.

"Is she speaking?" the white man asked in a new language I was beginning to learn. He pushed the glass circles higher on his face.

"Not to me," the Man in Blue said. "But she speaks in Hindi and Sanskrit to my daughter."

"No other languages?"

"We have not tried."

"What's that, there, she's holding?" he pointed a bony finger at my doll.

I squeezed it tightly. The white man saw, and wrote something down.

"My daughter made it for her and she will go nowhere without it now. She is attached."

"Indeed." The white man wrote something else. His eyes shifted back and forth between the paper and me, until finally, the Man in Blue was allowed to take me outside, back into the smoky sunlight.

"I have business I must do before we leave," he said to me. "But as long as you do not lose sight of me, you may explore the port." He extended his arm along the bustling stretch of land near the water.

I nodded. He waved his hand, sending me off.

I ran. I had been confined for too long and I delighted in the freedom. I absorbed every scent—mud and brine, spice and musk—and my eyes drank in the colors of the people and the buildings and the ships.

I ran until I heard a reedy sound repeat itself in a rhythmic, hypnotic melody. It slowed my steps and drew me to the source.

An old man sat cross-legged before a basket, blowing on a long stick that swelled into a bulb. People ringed the basket, staring as a snake rose out of the depths, swaying back and forth. The people clapped.

I did not understand their delight. Did the animal live in the basket? Was it trapped there, to live in the dark?

I crept closer. I was small enough to push through the crowd without being noticed. I drew nearer until anxious whispers rose to a loud murmur, until the old man stopped his music and shouted for me to get back.

I understood him but did not listen. What did I have to fear from snakes? I marveled at the animal's soft armor, at the ruby tongue that flicked out to taste my scent. As I extended my arm out to touch it, it arched its long body back—

"Stop!" the Man in Blue shouted. My skin stung from his slap. He grabbed my sore wrist and led me quickly away. My arm hurt in his grasp, but after a measure of distance, he let me go.

"Are you mad, child?"

I did not know how to answer.

He softened at my confusion. "You like animals?" he asked, his voice warm, now. Gentle.

I nodded. Yes.

His cheeks folded into a smile and his grip on my wrist loosened. He fit his fingers in mine and led me down the length of the port. We came to a stop before one of the great ships, but that was not what stole my breath.

Hundreds of animals were trapped inside a row of gleaming cages. "Keep your hands away from the bars," he said, as we passed chattering, screaming birds that beat their wings but couldn't fly. A sullen monkey, large and brown, gripped the bars of its cage with human fingers. Stared at me with human eyes. A giant snake was tucked into a ball, withdrawing from everything, withdrawing from life.

The sight refused to make sense. I was born watching monkeys skip through treetops. I was lulled to sleep by the sound of a bird's call. They did not belong here, in this place of smoke.

We were not the only watchers. A cluster of jeering boys rattled long sticks along the biggest cage. A snarling tiger paced inside, its orange and black stripes rippling behind the bars.

The tiger threw its powerful body against the cage, at the boys, but they laughed and danced back.

"Now," the Man in Blue said, kneeling down. "You must stay here. The animals will entertain you?"

Entertain. I did not know the word.

"I will come back shortly. Do not cause trouble," he said, then left.

I edged over to a thin boy with small, darting eyes at the fringe of the group.

"Help me," I whispered to him.

His black eyes considered me warily. Maybe he did not understand? I tried another tongue. "Help me," I said again.

"Help you what?" he asked.

I pointed to the animals. "Get them out."

49

When I opened my eyes, I was in my brother's bedroom, still holding the notebook as he knocked on his door.

"This is kind of backward," he said, clearly wondering why I was there.

The contours of the dream-memory-blackout shivered in my mind. I tried to hold on to it.

"Mara?"

I blinked and it blurred away. I couldn't remember where I'd gone.

"Yeah," I said, standing woozily. I was still holding the notebook—I couldn't have been out for long. Maybe minutes?

Seconds? I was sweaty, and my clothes stuck to my skin.

"Did you take the book?" I asked my brother, trying to keep my voice even. "I was looking for it."

"The genetics one? Yeah." Daniel went to his closet and opened it. "Sorry, I put it in here; I didn't want it to get mixed up with my things. You okay?" He peered at me.

Fake smile. "Yes!"

Strange look. "You sure?"

I hid the composition notebook behind me. Why had I put *that* in his room? "No, yeah, I really am," I said, standing up. "Can I have the—"

"Is that the story?" Daniel said, glancing at the notebook behind my back.

What story? I looked down at it. "Um."

"How's the assignment going? Constructive? Cathartic?" He winked.

Ah. He thought it was the Horizons story. The assignment that I invented to get his help. I looked at the notebook, then back up at Daniel. I had no idea why I'd put it in his room or when, but I was lucky he hadn't noticed it, considering what was inside. My insides twisted. I needed to talk to Noah.

But my brother was waiting for an answer. So I said, "She's not possessed."

Daniel waited. Listened.

"Someone else is—there's someone else with a—a

power," I said. "And he never played with a Ouija board."

Daniel pondered this for a second. "So the Ouija board was a red herring." He nodded sagely. "Hmm."

"Gotta go," I said, darting for the door.

"The book." Daniel extended his hand and offered it to me; it dragged down my arm. I smiled before fleeing to dump *New Theories* and my notebooks in my room. Then forced myself to walk calmly to the kitchen, where I grabbed the phone and took it to my room and dialed Noah's number with trembling fingers. He picked up on the second ring.

"I was just about to call you—" he started.

I cut him off. "I found something."

Pause. "What?"

I couldn't bring myself to open the notebook. "So, at Horizons, they gave me a notebook to use as a journal."

"All right . . ."

"But I didn't *remember* them giving one to me."

"Okay . . ."

"But I just found it in Daniel's room. The cover had my name. And I wrote in it, Noah. It was my handwriting."

"What did you write?"

"'Help me.'"

"I'll be back tomorrow morning. I'll come straight to you—"

"No, that's what I *wrote,* Noah. 'Help me.' Again and again for almost a full page."

Silence.

"Yeah," I said shakily. "Yeah."

"I'll try to get a flight tonight—" He paused. I could imagine his face; his jaw tight, his expression careful and calm, trying not to show me how worried he was. But I could hear it in his voice. "There are only two more flights out of Providence today, and I won't make either of them now. But there's one from Boston to Ft. Lauderdale at midnight. I'll be on it, Mara."

"I'm feeling—really . . ." I couldn't finish the sentence. I struggled for words but nothing else came.

Noah didn't patronize me by telling me not to panic, or saying that everything would be okay. It wasn't, and he knew it. "I'll be there soon," he said. "And John just checked in with no news. Everything else is fine, so just stay with your family and take care of yourself, all right?"

"Okay." I closed my eyes. This wasn't new. I had blacked out before. Lost time. Had weird dreams. This wasn't new. I could live with this.

I could live with it if I didn't think about it. I changed the subject. "You were going to call me?"

"Yes."

"Why?"

"I just . . . missed you," he said, a lie in his voice.

That brought a tiny smile to my lips. "Liar. Just tell me."

He sighed. "The address you gave me, for Claire and

Jude's parents? I cross-referenced it with what Charles—the investigator—found and I went there to talk to them. To see if anything seemed . . . off."

I'd been holding my breath. "And?"

"There was a car in the driveway, so I knew someone was home. I knocked, there was no answer, and then I rang the bell. A man opened the door and I asked if he was William Lowe. He said, "Who?" I repeated myself, and he said his name was Asaf Ammar, which, obviously, is not at all the same."

"Well, we know the Lowes moved after—after what happened, right?"

"Right. So I asked if he knew where William and Deborah Lowe lived and he said he'd never heard of them. Which I told him was strange, because as of four months ago, they were living in that house." Noah swallowed. "He laughed and said that was impossible. Unamused, I asked him why that would be." Noah paused. "Mara, he said they bought the house from his wife's mother, Ortal. Eighteen years ago."

I backed up onto my bed. My throat was tight. Sealed so I couldn't speak.

"It's a mistake, obviously," Noah said quickly. "It's the wrong address."

"Hold on," I said to him as I carried the phone to my closet. Pulled down my boxes from Rhode Island. Pulled out a notebook from my old history class at my old school.

Rachel had passed me a note one day, telling me to meet

her at Claire's after school. I handed her my notebook as the teacher droned on, and she scrawled an address inside.

1281 Live Oak Court

"What was the address you went to?" I asked him.

"One two eight one Live Oak Court," Noah said.

The address wasn't wrong. Something else was.

50

I TOLD NOAH EXACTLY THAT.

"Your parents went to the funerals, yes?" he asked. "See if your mother knows anything."

I tried so, so hard not to lose it.

"People don't disappear," he said.

"What about Jude?"

Noah went quiet. Then said, "I don't know, Mara. I wish—I wish I did. But John is across the street right now. Nothing is going to happen to you or Daniel or Joseph or anyone, all right?" His voice was strong. "I promise."

I squeezed my eyes shut. "Anna died," I said after a too-long silence.

"I know."

"It wasn't me," I said.

"I know. Hang on, Mara."

"My parents think I'm getting better," I went on. "They said I don't have to go to the retreat to be evaluated for the residential program."

"Good," he said, sounding calm again. "They're impressed with you. You're doing well."

"Except for the fact that it's a *complete lie*. I'm not getting better. I thought maybe I was but I'm not."

"You are *not* insane." He barely concealed his anger. "All right? Something *is* happening to you. To us. I—I saw someone today," he said quietly. "Some asshole grabbed a girl, twisted her wrist. I thought he was going to break it. He nearly did."

"Who was she?"

"Don't know. Never saw her before in my life," Noah said. "But she's all right. I wouldn't have said anything except—you aren't alone in this, Mara. You aren't alone. Remember that."

It was hard to breathe. "Okay."

"I'll be back soon. Hang on, Mara."

"Okay," I said, and we hung up.

I stared at the phone for five, ten seconds, then forced myself to do something else. I filled a cup of water from my bathroom sink. Drank half. Sat on my bed until Joseph burst in.

"You coming?" he asked breathlessly.

I took a deep breath and carefully composed myself. "Where?"

"Dinner."

I rubbed my eyes and looked at the clock. "Yeah," I said, much more brightly than I felt. I stood up and started to leave.

Joseph stared at my feet. "Um, shoes?"

"Why?"

"We're going out."

I just wanted to go to sleep and wake up with Noah back in Miami, back in my arms. But my parents thought I was getting better, and I needed to make them believe it. Otherwise I'd be sent away for problems I *didn't* have. I was taking their drugs, drawing their pictures, passing their tests and it would all be for nothing if I was sent away now. I couldn't bear that. Not when it would separate me from the one person who believed me. The one person who knew the truth.

I set the cup down. I put on my shoes and a big, fake smile. I laughed on the outside while I screamed on the inside. My body was in the restaurant but my mind was in hell.

And then we went back home. Daniel and Joseph were talking, my parents were joking, and I felt a little better, until I entered my room. I drank some more water from the cup I filled before we went out to eat and got ready for bed, trying not to be afraid. Fear is just a feeling, and feelings aren't real.

But the disc I found under my pillow that night was.

My fingers curled around it in the dark. I began to hear the sirens of panic wail in my brain but I forced myself to shut them out. I stood slowly and turned on my light.

The CD was plain and unmarked.

Noah's security guard, John, was outside.

Maybe I made the disc myself? And just didn't remember? Like writing in the journal?

That had to be it. I glanced at the clock: It was midnight. Noah would be on the plane. My whole family was home and in their rooms, if not asleep. I couldn't vaporize the healthy normal teenager facade by waking them and losing it, so I drained the cup of water, gritted my teeth, and put the disc in my computer. I could not panic. Not yet.

I moved the mouse and hovered over the file icon hoping for a flash of recognition, but it was just a series of numbers—31281. I double clicked, and a DVD application opened up. I pressed play.

The screen was grainy and black, and then a flash of light illuminated—

"It's supposed to be in here, come on," said a voice from the computer.

Rachel's voice. My mouth formed her name but no sound came out.

"We could be in the wrong section?" Claire's voice, from behind the video camera. "I don't know."

I leaned in close to the screen, the air vanishing from my lungs as the asylum appeared. The paint on my bedroom walls began to peel, curl, and flake off around me like filthy snow. My bedroom walls seemed to melt and new ones, old ones, sprang up in their place. The ceiling above me cracked and the floor beneath my feet rotted away and I was in the asylum, right next to Rachel and Claire.

"What if there's no chalk?" Claire asked. The light from her video camera swung wildly over the hallway. No focus. No direction.

Rachel smiled at Claire, and held something up in her glove. "I brought."

Muffled footsteps kicked aside old insulation. Another light flashed—it was Rachel, taking a picture. My eyes brimmed with tears and I couldn't look away.

"Wait—I think it's this one." Rachel smiled wide and a thousand needles pierced my chest. "This is so creepy."

Oh God oh God oh God.

"I know." Claire followed Rachel into the room, her light resting on an old, enormous chalkboard, covered in names and dates written by dozens of different hands.

"I told you," Rachel said smugly. "Wait—where's Mara? And Jude?"

The image on screen jostled. Claire must have shrugged.

I tried to scream but no sound came out.

"I should get her," Rachel said, moving out of the frame.

I gagged. I gasped for air, pushed back the hair from my face, covered my mouth with my hands and kept trying to talk, to tell them, to warn them, to save them, but I was mute. Dumb. Silent.

"I'll go—write my name, okay? Take the camera."

Rachel winked. "You got it."

I fell to my knees.

Then she took Claire's video camera—I couldn't see her anymore—and pointed it at the blackboard. Scanned all of the names. She began to whistle. Her breath was white steam.

The sound echoed off the cavernous walls and filled my ears and mind. I crouched on the floor and hugged my knees to my chest, unable to breathe or speak or scream. The scrape of the chalk on the filmy, worn blackboard mingled with Rachel's whistle and my mind processed nothing else until footsteps approached. The shot swung back away from the board to face Claire.

"The lovebirds are enjoying some private time."

"Really?" Rachel asked. The camera tilted away from Claire. More jostling and chaos, then it pointed at Rachel again. "Mara's okay?"

"Mmm-hmm."

"Bad girl," Rachel said suggestively.

A laugh. Claire's.

And then a crack, so loud I could feel it.

"What was—" A panicked whisper. Rachel's.

There was a metallic groan. Then the ringing, successive slam of thousands of pounds of iron fitting into frames.

"Oh my—" Panting. Screaming.

Interference and dust clouded my vision and the hiss and rush of static filled my ears. White letters appeared in the darkness that arranged themselves into the words FILE CORRUPTED. Then silence. The image on the screen went black. The scene in my mind went dark.

But just when I thought the footage was over, I heard the soft lilt of laughter. Unmistakably mine.

I didn't know how much time passed. All I knew was that when I screamed again, there was sound but it was muffled. I tried to force my eyes to see, but I was trapped in darkness; there was no floor beneath my feet, no ceiling above my head.

Because I was not in the asylum. I was not in my room at home.

I was bound and gagged and in the trunk of someone's car.

51

I don't know how I got there.

One second I was in my bedroom, watching footage from Claire's camera, hearing myself laugh, struggling to stay grounded and not let the flashback wash me away. And the next, I was covered in shadow as rough fabric scraped against my cheek, as my lungs were stifled by heat.

But I did know this: Jude was the only person with any reason to want to hurt me, and he had tried before.

Which meant he must be driving.

When the car hit a pothole I bit my tongue. Blood filled my mouth. I tried to spit but my mouth was covered: by what, I didn't know. I sent messages to my arms and legs, begging them to move, to struggle, but nothing happened. I imagined myself contorting my limbs, arching and twisting against whatever restrained me, but I was loose and limp. A doll tossed around in a bored child's toy chest, powerless to move.

He must have taken me from my home—my room—while my family slept, unsuspecting.

What had happened to John?

Tears squeezed out of the corners of my eyes. The texture of the trunk's interior made my skin itch and burn. The muscles in my arms and legs wouldn't move, which meant I must be drugged.

But how? We ate at the restaurant, not at home. I rewound the past hour in my mind but my thoughts were blurry and I couldn't remember. I couldn't.

The car stopped. *That* was when my slow, sluggish heart finally charged to life. It beat against every inch of my skin. I was soaked in sweat.

A car door slammed. Footsteps crunched on gravel. I lay there, helpless and hopeless, slimy and miserable. Fear made me an animal and my primitive brain could do nothing but play dead.

The trunk opened; I heard it and felt it and then realized that I still couldn't see, which meant that I was blindfolded. I listened—there was water around us. It lapped against something nearby.

I felt big, meaty hands on my body, which was completely limp. I was shackled by terror. I was lifted out of the trunk and I felt bulging, thick muscles against my flesh.

"Shame," a voice whispered then. "It's so much more fun when you fight."

It was Jude, absolutely.

There was pressure in my head—I must be upside-down. I moaned weakly, but there was nowhere for the sound to go.

And then I was set right side up, propped and arranged in a chair with my arms behind me, chafing against the back. My knees, thighs, calves ached. Smells and sounds—brine and salt, rot and water—were sharp, but thoughts were difficult.

My blindfold was slipped off, then, and I saw him. He looked older than I remembered, but otherwise the same. Bright green eyes. Dirty blond hair. Dimples. And two whole, intact hands. So harmless.

My eyes drank in the details of my surroundings and absorbed them like a sponge. We were in some kind of boathouse. There were life preservers stacked against one wall, two kayaks lying across another, and an old, rusty sign that read IDLE SPEED, NO WAKE propped up in a corner. It was well maintained, with a thick coat of grey paint slapped on, obscuring any flaws. There was one door. Jude was in front of it.

I scanned the room wildly for some kind of weapon. Then I remembered: I was one.

It was him or me. I imagined him being gutted, a slash

of blood stretching across his stomach. I imagined him in agony.

"So," Jude said.

I wanted to spit in his face at the sound of his voice. I would, I decided, if he ripped the gag off.

"Did you miss me? Nod for yes, shake your head for no." His smile was an open sore.

A sour taste coated my tongue, but I swallowed, and imagined my fear going with it.

Jude sighed then, and his shoulders sagged with the movement. "This is the problem. I would like to talk to you, but if I rip the tape off, you'll scream."

I sure as shit will.

"There's no one around who would hear you, and I'd get a kick out of it once, it's true, but it would get on my nerves after a while. So what do I do?" He looked up at the ceiling. Ran his hand over his chin. "I could say that if you scream, I will slit Joseph's throat in his bed when we're finished here?" He withdrew something from his pocket. A box cutter. His watch glinted in the low light.

It was as if I'd been punched in the stomach. I coughed.

"Easy there, tiger," he said, and winked.

He needed to die. He *had* to. I turned the image over in my mind. Jude, bleeding out, dying. I rewound it, again and again. *Please.*

"Yeah, that should work." He took something out of

his other pocket—a key. He held it up. "For good measure, remember that I can get into and out of your house whenever I want. I can drug everyone in your family and kill them while they sleep. Or make your parents watch me kill Daniel and Joseph? Anyway, I don't know, there are a lot of options and I hate multiple choice. So let's just say—there's a lot I *could* do which I *will* do if you scream, and taking you was so easy I could laugh." A smile appeared and a wholesome dimple deepened in his baby-smooth cheek.

I was disgusted by him and disgusted by myself. How did I get here? How did I let this thing in human skin chew his way into my life? How did I miss this? How could I not know?

"You understand? Nod yes if you understand."

I nodded, my eyes brimming over with tears.

"If you scream without my permission, you will kill your family. Nod yes if you understand."

I nodded and felt bile rise in my throat. I was going to choke.

"Okay," he said smiling, "here we go. This might hurt a little."

And then he ripped the duct tape from my mouth. I retched onto the slatted floor: that was when I noticed there was water beneath it. The ocean? A lake?

The ocean. I smelled salt.

Jude shook his head. "Gross, Mara." He looked at me the

way you would at a puppy for soiling a newspaper. "What am I going to do with you?" Jude looked around the room. His eyes settled on something. A mop. He stood up and cleaned the mess from the weathered wooden slats.

Trying to kill him was useless. He lived through the collapse somehow and anything I tried would fail. Jude realized it, because when he looked at me, he wasn't at all afraid.

But even if I couldn't kill him, I wasn't powerless. I heard Noah's defiant voice echo in my mind.

"Don't let your fear own you," he had said. *"Own yourself."*

Jude wanted something from me, otherwise I'd be dead already.

Whatever it was, I couldn't let him get it.

"I asked you a question," Jude said, when he was finished. "You can answer."

He wanted me to answer, so I stayed silent.

Something hardened in his face and I was glad, because he finally looked the way someone who bound and gagged and kidnapped someone was supposed to look.

"What am I going to do with you?" he asked again, his voice quieter and infinitely more horrifying. "Look at me," he said then.

Own yourself. I looked away.

Then he came close and pinched my cheek. "Look at me."

I closed my eyes.

"You look pretty good, Mara," he said softly.

Please, please let him die. *Please.*

"Your opinion," I whispered, "means very little to me, Jude." I opened my eyes. I couldn't help it.

Jude's smile had spread. He rocked back in his chair. "I bet that mouth gets you into all sorts of trouble."

He exposed more of the blade he was holding, smiling the whole time, and a primal, instinctive shiver ran through me. He raised his hand, staring at the wickedly sharp edge.

"What do you want?" I was surprised by the strength in my voice. It fortified me.

Jude looked at me like I was a puzzle he was trying to work out. "I want Claire to not be dead."

I closed my eyes and saw the words he left for me in blood.

FOR CLAIRE

My bones hurt and my mouth and arms ached from my position. "I want Claire to not be dead too."

"Don't say her name." His voice was edged with razor blades. But then, seconds later, it was calm. "Are you going to bring her back?"

He knew what I'd done. That I killed her. And now he was punishing me; he'd been punishing me all along. This was revenge.

I had no idea what to do. I didn't see a way out; I was tied up and trapped and I'd tried to kill him before but he didn't die.

Should I lie? Pretend I didn't understand? Or admit what I did since he already knew it? Apologize?

I couldn't decide so I ignored the question. "I thought you were dead too." I swallowed. Looked at his hands. "How are you alive?"

He rocked forward in his chair this time, until he was inches away from me. I felt his breath on my face.

He wanted me to flinch, so I kept still.

"Disappointed?" he asked.

He wanted me to say yes, so I said, "No."

His eyebrows lifted. "Really?"

I couldn't help it. "No."

At that, a toxic grin spread across his mouth. "There we go," he said softly. "Some honesty, finally. Don't worry, I don't hold *that* against you."

"It was an accident," I said, before I even knew that I'd said it.

Jude considered me for a moment, then gave a single shake of his head. "We both know that's not true."

"The building was old and it collapsed," I said, trying like hell not to sound so desperate and fake.

He tsked. "Come on, Mara. You don't believe that."

I didn't, but how did *he* know what I believed?

"I don't believe that either," he said. "You saw the video." He shook his head. "God, that laugh, Mara. Really creepy."

"How did you get it?" I asked him. "How did you get out?"

"How did you trigger the pulley system?" he asked me,

moving closer. "How did you get the doors to close? Did you just think it and it happened?"

Was that how I did it?

"I heard the levers shriek and then ran to the doors, but they closed on my hands," he said. His eyes studied my face. "You actually smiled at me when I turned to look at you. You *smiled.*"

The memory flickered in my mind.

One second, he had pressed me so deeply into the wall that I thought I would dissolve into it. The next, he was the trapped one, inside the patient room, inside with me. But I was no longer the victim.

He was.

I laughed at him in my crazed fury, which shook the asylum's foundation and crushed it. With Jude and Claire and Rachel inside.

"What kind of person does that?" he asked, almost to himself.

Own yourself. My lips were dry and sour. My tongue was sandpaper, but I found my voice. "What kind of person does *this*? What kind of person forces himself on someone else?"

His nostrils flared. "Don't pretend you didn't want it," he said sharply. "You wanted me for months. Claire told me." Jude crouched next to me, his cheek close to my ear. He held up the box cutter in front of my eye. "This could happen two ways. One, you do it yourself. Two, I do it for you. And if you make me do it for you, I am going to take my time."

The blade was so close to my eyes that I squeezed them shut reflexively. "Why are you doing this to me?"

"Because you deserve it," he hissed in my ear.

52

HELPLESSNESS AND FEAR WARRED WITH hatred and defiance—I didn't know what to do or say, but the longer I kept him talking, the longer I would stay alive.

"They have you on camera," I said, grasping for anything. "They'll know you did this."

He laughed. "At the police station? Did you tell them it was *me*?" He took my chin in his hand. "You *did*. I can tell just by looking at you. Let me guess—they have a guy on camera who was wearing long sleeves, baggy clothes, and a baseball cap. And you thought they'd believe it was your dead boyfriend? No wonder they think you're crazy." He sucked in his lower lip. "And let's be honest, you kind of are. But it does make this easier," he said, glancing down at the box cutter. "Less messy."

He stood from his chair and my veins flooded with adrenaline, bringing everything into sharper focus. I felt wrung-out and picked clean, but my wrists were less numb. My legs were less limp.

The drugs were wearing off.

"Why'd you come to the police station? To school?" I asked. Begged.

"I wanted you to know I was alive," he said, and I was so grateful just to hear words issue from his mouth that I could have cried with relief. "I thought you saw me at—What's it called?"

"What?"

"Your old school."

"Croyden," I said.

He snapped his fingers. "Right. You ran," he said with a smirk. A snake smile, reptilian and cold. "And the precinct? I didn't know why you were going. But I was—" he paused, considering his words. "Concerned. I wanted to distract you."

It worked. "You could have killed me a hundred times before now. Why wait?"

Jude smiled in response. Said nothing. Lifted the blade.

Oh, God. "What about your family?" I whispered. Talk, Jude. *Talk.*

"Claire was my family." Jude's voice was different now. Less harsh. He swallowed and took a deep breath. "You know what they found?" he asked evenly as he moved behind me. "She was so badly mangled they had to have a closed casket."

"Rachel too," I said in a low voice.

It was the wrong thing to say. Jude crouched next to me, his cheek close to my ear. "*Please,*" he said, and grabbed my hand.

And this feeling, this terror, was something new. Like nothing I'd ever experienced—not earlier, in the trunk, or in the asylum.

"Why should I help you kill me?" My voice was barely more than a breath. Barely a whisper.

He was close again. So close. Behind me, next to my ear. "You can choose, Mara. Your one life, or two of your brothers'." He reached around and held the blade against my cheek. Reminding me what he could do.

And reminding me of something else.

His watch, his Rolex, the same one Noah saw in his vision, was inches from my face. "Nice watch," I whispered. *Keep talking. Keep talking.*

"Thanks."

"Where'd you get it?"

"Abe Lincoln," he sneered.

"Why did you take Joseph?"

Jude said nothing.

"He's *twelve.*" My voice sounded like a wail.

Jude's stare was ice. "A brother for a sister."

My hate grew, a formless, shapeless mass that devoured my fear. "You used to talk about football with him at my house."

Jude laughed then, and the word that reverberated in my mind was *sick*.

"I had this whole *plan*," he said, sounding exasperated. "I was going to bring Daniel over for a party—don't worry, I wasn't going to hurt him either. You were."

I would've shaken my head, but the blade was too close. "I'd never hurt him."

"Never say never," he said seriously. His voice turned quiet. "I can make you do anything I want." Then he sighed. "But *someone* had to go and be a hero," he rolled his eyes. "And now here we are."

"I'm not a—"

Jude chuckled. "You think I mean *you*?" he said, wrinkling his nose and moving closer. His breath was in my ear, tickling me. "You are no hero, Mara Dyer. You'd do anything to get what you want. Which makes you just. Like. Me."

Then he moved in front of me so that I could see him. Stood up to his full height. He was broad and enormous and immovable before me. His eyes scanned my body. "Kind of a waste." He ran the back of his hand down my bare arm, and my flesh died.

Make him talk. I grasped for words, for anything. "Why'd you take Joseph to the Everglades?"

"I told you already. And if you're going to dispose of a

body in Florida, there's really no better place."

But the shed—the property was owned by my father's client. By Leon Lassiter. "Why *there*?"

"It was a suggestion."

I was reeling. "From who?"

"A mutual friend," he said, as he inspected my wrists. Turned them over. Glanced at the blade.

My family might believe that I would kill myself. After everything that happened, it was possible. But, "Why would I come here?" I asked urgently. *Tell me where we are.*

"You wouldn't want them to find you at home, would you? Where Joseph could be the one to find your body? No, you'd do it somewhere out of the way. Somewhere you'd be found pretty quick, but not by anyone you knew. You took Daniel's car tonight, by the way."

He sounded so proud of himself. It made me want to cut out his tongue.

Jude moved behind me. Dragged my chair to the back of the room, which was when I noticed that there was, in fact, another door; it was painted the same color as the walls and there was no knob, so I didn't notice it until he pushed it open, dragging me through.

"You know, I always thought that once I had you like this, what I would want most would be to kill you for what you did. But I wonder if there might be something worse?" His eyes slithered over my skin.

I couldn't bear him staring at me that way. I squeezed my eyes shut.

He shook the chair and my teeth chattered. "Hey." Shake. "Look at me." He was right in my face and he took my chin in his hand. "Look at me."

There was nothing I could do. I was alone. My eyes opened.

But as I stared right into Jude's—unnaturally dark, considering the bright lights in the boathouse—words seared through me, words that weren't mine.

"You aren't alone in this."

Noah's words, spoken to me just hours before. Noah found Joseph when he'd been taken—by Jude, I knew now—when my brother was drugged and in danger. He felt an echo of what Joseph felt, and knew where Jude had taken him because Noah saw it through Jude's eyes.

Noah heard me when I was hurt and trapped in the asylum. I trapped myself, so he saw what I saw through *my* eyes.

If I hurt myself now, he might see through them again.

He wasn't in Miami, so he couldn't save me. But I could make sure he knew the truth.

I bit down on my tongue so hard that I moaned. *See me,* I wished.

"Are you going to do this," Jude breathed into my ear, "or am I?"

Blood filled my mouth and silent sobs wracked my chest. Water stretched out in front of us, black and endless. We were at the end of a dock. I turned my head to try and find anything that would give me a clue as to where I was—a sign, something—but my vision swam. From the pain? From tears?

Yes, from tears. When they cleared a little, I saw that the dock veered off to our right in a narrow path toward a grouping of blurry, faraway boats.

But no people. No one.

Jude gripped my head hard in one of his hands, palming it like a basketball. He looked down into my eyes. "You're not motivated enough."

I had no idea if Noah could see this. I remembered that it wasn't just pain that made him see; there was something else. But we never figured out what.

As I spat blood out onto the dock, Jude smacked me. Not hard enough to leave a bruise, but hard enough to sting. "Do not. Do not fuck everything up. You will kill your family, Mara." He leaned down. "Look at me and tell me I'm lying."

See me, I begged silently. *Help me help me help me help me help me help me help me help me.*

"Okay," I said out loud. "Okay, I'll do it. I'll do what you want."

"Just like that?"

"Yes."

"If you try to run, don't forget I have the key to your house."

"I won't," I whispered.

"And I could always cut the brakes on Daniel's car. Or your parents'."

I couldn't breathe. A sob escaped from my throat. I was beyond terrified for them. Beyond reason.

"You control whether they get hurt, you understand?"

"Yes," I said. He gripped my head harder. "Yes," I moaned.

I could do anything for them, as long as they would be okay. Even this. "I'll do it."

Jude sliced the duct tape from my feet and my wrists. He held me by the waistband of my jeans, just the way he used to.

"Give me your hand."

My thoughts were a roar. I could barely stand. His blade touched the inside of my wrists, tracing a vein. Then it bit into my skin. I cried out.

"Quiet."

The blood welled and flowed and the coppery scent made my stomach roil. He drew a horizontal line of blood along my wrist, not deep. Then handed me the blade.

"Cut deeper, exactly where I cut. Then your other hand. Don't forget what I'll do to Joseph."

But the line was horizontal.

Not vertical.

Not fatal.

My heart soared for all of a second.

Until I looked back at Jude and realized—

He knew.

53

JUDE DIDN'T WANT TO KILL ME. HE WANTED something else.

Something I couldn't imagine as I freed the blood from my body, the metallic smell mingling with the salt of the water beneath us, around us, in front of us. Jude stood in front of me, holding my forearms steady as I cut, holding me up. I could not look away from the deepening gashes on my wrists. I was shaking and weak and I let out a low whimper.

"Hello?"

My head snapped up at the same time as Jude's. My vision blurred—from dizziness, now, not tears—but a lighter shape approached us.

I tried to scream but nothing came out. I was weak and scared and I could barely see and I couldn't even cry out for help.

Jude let go of one arm and took my face in one large hand. "Don't even think about it." He took the blade from me, hid it, and shifted himself so that he stood between me and the voice.

"What's going on over here?"

The man's voice was getting louder. Closer. I heard rushed footsteps clap on the wood to my right.

"Everything's fine," Jude said calmly.

Clap clap. "Do you need—"

A pause. A gasp. "Oh my God," the stranger said.

"Everything's under control," Jude said, turning on the full force of his charm. He was transformed—I could hear it. If I didn't know about the rot inside, it would have reminded me why I was attracted to him in the first place.

The man's voice changed—imbued with authority.

"Did you call an ambulance?"

I tried to speak, to form words, but I had no voice.

"They're on their way," Jude said.

My vision cleared a bit as more tears fell. The man reached for something at his hip. "I can have them here in minutes. Cop," he said.

And then something shifted beneath Jude's expression. He withdrew the box cutter and my mind roared with terror. The cop had just turned on his radio when Jude flicked the blade open.

The man's eyes widened. "What are you—"

Jude was going to filet him open. He twisted the box cutter in his hand just as the cop lunged for it.

And then Jude stabbed himself in the side.

I couldn't process what I was seeing.

Neither could the cop. He wrested the box cutter from Jude's hand.

"What in the hell—what's *wrong* with you?"

Jude fell to his knees, wincing. The cop turned on the radio. "Dispatch, send backup to—"

But the man dropped the radio before he could finish his sentence. An expression of exquisite pain swallowed his confusion. Then he dropped Jude's box cutter.

Just a few feet away.

I slumped down and crawled toward it because I was too weak or too scared to stand. Pain chewed through my nerves. My vision was edged in black and red. I crawled anyway.

"Don't . . . bother," Jude wheezed. He just knelt there, half bent, staring down, his head heavy and his arms limp.

I moved toward him even though everything in me was utterly repelled. I wanted to stop. I kept going. There was groaning—but it wasn't mine or Jude's. It was the man, the cop. I couldn't see him or hear what he was saying or see what was happening. I had one thing on my mind and that was the blade. I reached for it but my muscles weren't under my control; they shook and I was weak and when my fingers nudged the plastic handle, it fell through the slats of the dock.

It was over.

I was done. My legs and shoulders collapsed and I couldn't move myself up or anywhere. My eyes were open still and I was still conscious but there was so much pain I wished I wasn't.

I felt the vibration of a body hitting the dock. It was the cop; I could see him out of my peripheral vision. His eyes were open. Glassy. His breathing was shallow. I heard a tinny voice somewhere to my left. His radio? The only other sound was the water beneath me. The wood was rough against my cheek. I looked down. The water slapped the pylons as the tide slowly came in. It was louder than I would have expected. The moonlight lit the surface of the water. Peaceful.

But then I noticed shapes down there. The shapes, the things, were slapping wetly against the pylons. It wasn't just the waves.

In a burst of focus before I lost consciousness, I realized that the water wasn't empty.

It was filled with hundreds of dead and dying fish.

54

TIME DIDN'T EXIST FOR ME ANYMORE. IT could have been seconds or years before I heard another sound.

Beep.

I tried to open my eyes, but the world was bleached of color. Someone had scraped it all away.

Hiss.

"It's so much more fun when you fight."

Jude's voice in my ear. I tried to kick out but I was tangled in something. Caught and helpless, still.

"She's waking up." A new voice, strange and foggy and unfamiliar. I tried to speak but gagged instead.

Footsteps approached rapidly. "Shh, now. Just relax." A

hand on my shoulder, heavy and somehow reassuring.

My eyes flew open and light seared my vision. I closed them for a minute, or maybe five. Then tried again.

A woman leaned over me, blurred at the edges, not looking in my eyes. I caught the underside of her jaw, her neck, and her large chest as she reached over me.

"Who are you?" I asked hoarsely, in a voice that didn't sound like my own.

I thought I caught a smile. "Name's Joan, sweetie."

"Wait—is she—Mara, oh God, Mara, are you awake, honey?"

My mother's voice rushed in, plunging me in warmth. Something clawed and tore at my chest and it was hard to breathe—then I realized it was a sob. I was crying.

"Oh, honey." Her hands on me, delicate but solid.

I tried to focus. It was like looking at the world through smudged glass, but I finally, finally saw where I was.

Industrial ceiling tile. Florescent overhead lights. Machines. The hospital.

The second I thought it, more feelings announced themselves; the tube under my nose. The pressure in my hands, my arms, where more tubes branched out from my skin. I wanted to rip them out and scream but everything was so *tight*; my chest, my arms, everything. I couldn't move.

"Why can't I move?" I asked. I looked down at my body, which was covered completely by a scratchy-looking blanket.

My mother appeared in my view. "It's to keep you safe, baby."

"From what?"

My mother glanced up at the ceiling, searching for words. "You don't remember," she said, as if to herself.

I remembered Jude taking me from my room and bringing me to a dock to open my veins. I remembered him threatening to kill my family if I didn't obey.

My mother withdrew something from her pocket then. It was a piece of paper, folded very small; she opened it in front of me. "You left this in your room before you took Daniel's car," she said, then showed me the piece of paper. "It was in your journal."

The journal I didn't remember keeping. A page of words I didn't remember writing:

Help me help me help me help me

My mother's face was broken. She was ashen and drawn and she looked like she'd been crying for a hundred years. "You slit your wrists, Mara," she said, and choked back a sob. "You slit your wrists."

"No," I shook my head fiercely. "You don't understand." I tried to sit up and move but I couldn't. I was still trapped, which poisoned me with panic. "I want to sit up," I said with desperation.

My mother nodded and the woman I didn't know—Joan, a nurse, apparently—came over and pressed a button, elevating the bed. I wanted to adjust the pillow under my head but from my new vantage point saw why I couldn't.

My chest, arms, and legs were bound. In restraints.

"What *is* this?" The words were caught between a wail and a curse.

My mother walked up to my bed, pulled down the sheets. She glanced at the nurse, who nodded, then unbuckled the cloth cuffs that bound my wrists.

They were wrapped in white gauze. And, as if on cue, I noticed that they *hurt*.

I breathed deeply, trying not to come apart at the seams but it was hard. So hard.

"Everything okay in there?"

My eyes shot to the door, which was now open. An officer—or security guard?—loomed there, his hand at his waist.

"Just fine, officer," Joan said, sounding exasperated. "Got it all under control."

My eyes darted frantically between her and my mother, but my mom could barely look at me.

I must have looked like I felt—like I was about to scream—because the nurse began to loosen the restraints from my legs, my chest. They were complicated. "You lost quite a bit of blood last night, honey, and you were mostly unconscious. But after the transfusion, you woke up and with all the drugs we were pumpin' into you? You went a little wild. But you're okay now."

"Why is there a cop outside?"

Joan paused, hesitated, just for a moment, then busied herself with checking the monitors beside my bed.

"Someone else was brought in with you from the marina," my mother said.

The world stopped. A man? My mother knew what Jude looked like. Why didn't she just say Jude's—

"A middle-aged man. White hair, heavyset." Her eyes searched mine. "Did you know him, Mara?"

The memory seared my mind.

The man dropped the radio before he could finish his sentence. An expression of exquisite pain swallowed his confusion.

I shook my head, registering the stiffness in my neck, the ache in my mouth. How did he die? "What happened?" I asked.

"We don't know," my mom said softly. "He wasn't—he was—gone—when the police got there. They want to ask you some questions, when you're ready."

What about Jude? What about *Jude?*

My mother closed her eyes. "Jude is dead, Mara."

I must have spoken out loud. For a second my heart threatened to explode with joy.

"He died in the asylum."

She didn't understand. "No. *No.*"

"The building collapsed."

I remembered her saying those same words in another hospital room, in another state. A scream was building in my throat.

"Jude didn't make it. Neither did Rachel or Claire."

"No, just *listen*—" My words were frantic and they singed my throat.

"Dr. Kells is going to be here soon," my mother said, "They're going to take care of you."

"What?"

"At Horizons, honey." My mother sat gingerly on the side of my bed, and her stare broke my heart. "Mara, baby. We love you too much to let you hurt yourself. This family needs you."

I shook my head violently. "You don't understand."

"Calm down, sweetheart," Joan said. Her eyes met my mother's.

"I didn't do this," I pleaded, holding up my wrists. Joan was a blur of motion next to my bed. She took my arms gently but I flinched. Her hold tightened. "Don't *touch* me."

My mother recoiled. Covered her mouth with her hand.

"You're not *listening* to me!" White noise pulsed in my ears. I hunched forward.

"We are listening. We are listening, honey."

The room began to fade. "Just let me explain," I said, but the words were slurred. I tried to look at my mother but I couldn't focus, couldn't meet her eyes.

"Take a deep breath, that's a good girl." Someone rubbed my shoulders.

My mother was leaving the room. Joan held my head. "Breathe, breathe."

They wouldn't listen to me. Only one person would.

"Noah," I whispered into the thunder.

And then a shadow darkened the window in the hospital room door. I looked up before the black tide rolled in, praying silently that it would be him.

It wasn't. It was Abel Lukumi, and he was staring directly at me.

55

THE NEXT TIME I AWOKE, THE TUBES WERE disconnected from my skin. I was still in the hospital—in a different room, though. And I was unrestrained.

A day had passed, I learned. Doctors and nurses and psychologists swept in and out of the room in a blur of tests and questions. I went through the motions, answering them the best I could without looking in their faces and screaming about Jude. About the truth. About Lukumi.

How did he find me?

Why?

I couldn't let myself think about it because one question

led to more and I was drowning in them and I couldn't panic because I wouldn't be allowed to see Noah if I did. The drugs and the tubes made me lose it, always, but without them now I could compose my face into an expressionless mask to hide the seething beneath. Good behavior would buy me time, I had to remember. With my father's help, I was even able to talk with a detective about the cop who was found dead on the dock right by me. He had a stroke, it turned out. Not my fault.

Even if it had been, I wasn't sure I would have cared. Not then. The only thing I wanted was Noah. To feel his hands on my face, his body wrapped around mine, to hear his voice in my ear, to listen to him say he believed me.

But another day passed, and he still didn't show up. Joseph didn't come, either. He wasn't allowed, Daniel told me when he finally visited. He sat hunched over a can of soda, flipping the tab back and forth.

"What about Noah?" I asked quietly.

Daniel shook his head.

"I need to talk to him." I tried not to sound desperate.

"You're on another hold," Daniel said, his voice weak. "They're allowing immediate family only. Noah came straight here from the airport when he found out you were admitted and didn't leave until a few hours ago."

So he was here and gone. I deflated.

"You scared the hell out of us, Mara."

I closed my eyes, trying not to sound as infuriated as I was. This was Jude's fault, but they were the ones who had to pay. "I know," I said evenly. "I'm sorry." The apology tasted foul, and I felt the urge to spit.

"I just keep— What if the police found you an hour later?" Daniel rubbed his forehead. "I keep thinking about it." His voice shook, and he finally broke off the tab on the soda can. He dropped it inside and it landed with a *clink*.

His words made me wonder. "Who called them?" I asked. "Who called the police?"

"The caller never left a name."

There's this look people give you when they think you're insane. On the ferry to the Horizons Residential Treatment Center on No Name Island the following morning, I got it.

The wind snapped at my skin and tumbled my hair in front of my face. I smoothed it back with both hands, exposing the twin bandages on my wrists. That's when the captain, who had been chatting with my father about the ecology of the Keys, realized he was taking us to the glorified mental hospital, not the resort that shared the island. A slow wariness crept into his expression, mingling with fear and pity. It was a look I was going to have to get used to; the doctors told me that my wrists would scar.

"We don't have too far to go," the captain said. He pointed at some indistinguishable clump of land in the open ocean, and I felt obscenely small. "No Name Island right there, to the east. See it?"

I did. It looked . . . desolate. I recalled Stella's words.

Lakewood is . . . intense. It's in the middle of nowhere, like Horizons—practically all RTCs are.

"Do you like astronomy?" the captain asked me.

I hadn't really thought about it.

"Look up at night, at the stars. The island is off the power grid, though the electric company is lobbying hard to change that. Most of the No Name residents don't want it, though."

I couldn't imagine not wanting electricity. I couldn't imagine not *having* it. I said as much. He just shrugged.

I must have looked panicked, because my mother reached over and smoothed her hand over my back. "Horizons is powered by solar energy and generators. There's plenty of electricity, don't worry."

As we approached the island, a small dock appeared before us, with just a few boat slips and a sign:

LAST FERRY DEPARTS SIX PM, NO DEPARTURES IN INCLEMENT WEATHER

The captain looked up at the iron sky and squinted. "Might be changing things up today," he said. "Those clouds aren't friendly."

"That's what the cabin's for," my mother said to him, nodding in the direction of the covered part of the boat. She didn't like being told she'd have to leave me before she was ready. She looked at me, and I could tell how much it hurt her to leave me at all.

The captain shook his head. "It's not the rain, it's the waves. They get choppy in the storms. Best be getting on, otherwise you'll be spending the night."

"Thank you," my father said to the captain. "We'll be back soon." We disembarked, my parents quietly toting the luggage I didn't even get to pack myself as we left the ferry.

I didn't get to see Noah before we left, either. It would be twelve weeks before I saw him again.

The thought turned my stomach. I pushed it away.

It was then that I noticed a golf cart idling near the dock. The Horizons admissions counselor, Sam Robins, nodded condescendingly at me. "Well, Mara, I wish I were seeing you again under different circumstances."

Under no circumstances.

"Come on," he said to my parents. "Hop in."

We did. The golf cart whizzed around a paved path surrounded by tall reeds and grass. We stopped in front of a cluster of whitewashed buildings with bright orange Spanish roof tiles. There was lovely, wild landscaping in the courtyard, evoking my mom's issues of *Cottage Living*. Purple hibiscus and white lilies edged a small pond filled with goldfish that drifted lazily near the surface. There were neat hedgerows lined with some kind of pink wildflowers and yellow daisies everywhere. It felt inappropriately cheerful and I hated it.

The four of us walked into the pristine building—the main one, I guessed, since it was in the front. The walls were white stucco and the floor was white tile. Pedestals with a statue or figurine on top dotted the occasional corner, and terra cotta pots filled with manicured topiaries flanked the doorways. But other than that, the space and decor echoed Horizon's outpatient counterpart almost exactly.

"Hermencia will check your suitcases and your clothes, Mara. And lucky you, it's the retreat weekend, so all of your friends are here."

The retreat. I ended up on it after all.

At least Jamie would be here to launch me into my mandatory sentence before he got to go home. That was something.

My parents went off to sign paperwork and I was ushered into a room by a woman who wore a neutral expression beneath a thick, short mop of dark hair.

The woman nodded curtly. "I need to check for anything dangerous."

"Okay."

"Are you wearing any jewelry?"

I shook my head.

"I need you to take off your clothes."

I blinked stupidly.

"Okay?" she asked me.

I just stood there.

"I need you to take off your clothes," she repeated.

My chin trembled. "Okay."

She stared at me, waiting. I unzipped my hoodie and shrugged it off of my shoulders. I handed it to her. She put her arms through it and placed it on a table. I looked down at the floor and lifted my tank over my head. It landed softly on the tile.

I stood there, breathing hard in just my bra and my jeans. My spine was bent and my arms had unconsciously wandered over my chest.

"Your pants, too," the woman said.

I nodded but didn't move for one minute. Two.

"Do you need help?" she asked.

"What?"

"Do you need me to help you?"

I shook my head. I pressed the heels of my palms into my eyes and inhaled. Just clothes. They were just clothes.

I unzipped my jeans and they fell around my ankles. I stood still, exposed to the air as the room began to slowly spin. She inspected my clothes with her hands and my body with her eyes and asked if I had any piercings she couldn't see. I didn't. Finally, she placed my clothes back into my hands. I clutched them against me and then almost tripped as I rushed to put them back on.

When we were done, my parents had signed the paperwork and then I had to sign *more* paperwork, acknowledging the rules and regulations that hemmed me into my new life. Three months with no outside contact. Phone calls to family were allowed, but only after thirty days. I signed, and felt like I was bleeding on the page.

Then it was time to say good-bye. My mother squeezed me so tightly. "It's temporary," she said, trying to reassure me. Or reassure herself.

"I know," I whispered as she pulled me even closer. I wanted to hold on to her and push her away.

She smoothed my hair down my back. "I love you."

My throat burned with the tears I wanted to cry but wouldn't. I knew she loved me. She just didn't believe me. I understood why, but it hurt like hell just the same.

56

AFTER MY PARENTS LEFT, I WAS GIVEN A TOUR of the compound; four buildings that connected with a Zen garden in the center. I wandered through the rooms without paying much attention; the layout didn't matter, and I didn't really care. I was here. Noah and my family were out there. *Jude* was out there. He could do whatever he wanted.

I prayed he already had.

Because my family was at his mercy. I had no idea what happened to John; how Jude was able to take me without him knowing. But I had to believe that somehow, Noah would make sure my family was safe. The alternative—

I couldn't think it.

I was scheduled for intensive therapy immediately, and answered all of the new counselor's questions by rote. Between my cognitive behavioral therapy sessions and a meeting with the Horizons nutritionist, I thumbed through the small self-help library in the common room while the rest of the Horizons "students"—the permanents, with sentences of three months or longer, like me—and the temporaries, like Jamie, Stella, and Phoebe, unfortunately—went about their indoor team-building activities or whatever. I was excused from most of them, thanks to my "suicide attempt." Sweat and stitches don't mix. Lucky me.

Barney, one of the residential staff counselors, watched me from a short distance away. He was big, like most of the male staff—easier to restrain us, perhaps?—but seemed friendly when he tried to engage me in conversation. He wasn't condescending, like Robins, or inappropriately enthusiastic like Brooke. He was nice; I just didn't want to talk.

I idly turned the pages of a bizarre book entitled *What's Normal?* when my compatriots filtered in. They had come from some sort of game, it looked like, because they were split into three groups wearing differently colored T-shirts: white, black, and red. Megan was in red. Her pale cheeks were flushed, and wisps of blond hair curled up around her face, creating a messy halo. She begged for the bathroom and was sent with a buddy. Adam entered next and he was also wearing red. His bulging forearms were crossed over his puffed-out chest, looking like he'd just lost whatever game it was, and sorely.

Then Jamie waltzed in, dressed in black. He saw me and made a beeline.

"This is your fault."

I closed the book. "Hi, Jamie. Nice to see you too."

He shot me a glare. "It's not nice to see you, actually, considering why you're here."

"Thanks for not sugarcoating anything. I've been really sick of everyone treating me with kid gloves."

"The sarcasm, it burns!"

I rolled my eyes.

Jamie shrugged and said, "Look." He leaned forward. "I refuse to acknowledge your suicide attempt because it screws with all of my preconceived notions about you, okay? Though I *am* happy to see that you still have your sense of humor, at least."

I grinned—couldn't help it. "There is that. So," I said, glad to not have to talk about my fraudulent reason for being here, "what did I do this time?"

"Interesting choice of words," Jamie said, and looked over his shoulder at the doorway. I followed the line of his gaze, and saw—

Noah.

Here.

He stood about twelve feet away, his gray T-shirt damp

and clinging to his lean, muscular frame, droplets of rain falling from his guitar case onto the pristine tile floor.

When Noah met my eyes, I was without words.

He turned away. "Where should I put this?" he asked Barney, lifting the case slightly.

"This way," Barney said. "I'll show you your room."

And then Noah walked right past me. Like I wasn't even there.

I sat catatonically in the lounge. Seats filled up and good old Brooke sat down opposite me, her bangles jingling with every gesture. She straightened her head wrap and said, "We'll be starting in five minutes, guys. If you want to get a drink of water or make a quick bathroom run, now's the time." Then she leaned forward to say a gentle hello to me and patted my arm with a pitying look before leaving to fetch some water herself.

Then Noah walked in. He ran his fingers through his still-wet hair and sat nowhere near me, his long legs languidly stretched out in front of him as he slouched in a too-small plastic chair. He didn't say a word—to me, or anyone else. He seemed—different.

I studied him, trying to figure out why. He looked perfectly imperfect in destroyed jeans and a vintage T-shirt, his hair a beautiful mess above his unreadable face. Everything about him was the same, except—

His necklace. It was gone.

I rubbed my eyes. Noah was still there when I opened them.

Jamie acknowledged him. Barney did too. That normally would have been enough to convince me that he was real.

But when everyone tells you you're crazy and no one believes you when you swear you aren't, a small part of you will always wonder if they're right.

So when Stella stood to get a drink, I stood with her. "Hey," I said.

She brushed the hair back from her olive skin as she pulled the tap on the water cooler. "Hi."

What *is* the appropriate way to ask someone if you're hallucinating the appearance of your boyfriend in your glorified mental hospital?

"Do you see that guy over there?" I asked, nodding slightly at Noah, who had now crossed his arms behind his head.

Stella wound a curl around her finger as she looked back and forth, from him to me. "The hot one?"

That would be him, yes. "Yeah," I said.

Her full lips split into a smile. "The really, *really* hot one?"

Indeed. I looked over at him, but he didn't meet my eyes. "Yes."

Stella looked, too. "Tall, with dark brown, *perfect* hair." Someone said something to Noah, provoking an arrogant grin. "Unbelievable smile," Stella said as he looked in our direction. "Blue eyes?"

"Yes," I said, still staring at the inexpressibly gorgeous boy who told me he loved me a few days ago, and who didn't acknowledge me now.

"Yeah, I see him," Stella said, and took a sip of water. "I'm not sure I'd mind seeing more of him. Wait," she said, cocking her head at me. "Do you *know* him?"

I considered my answer. Can you ever really know someone? "I don't know," I said.

She peered at me, then sat back down. I did too, still dazed. Jamie dropped down in the chair next to me and poked me in the arm.

"Ow," I said, rubbing it.

"Oh, good, you're alive. I was afraid I'd have to do CPR." He cut his eyes at me. "If I didn't know better, I'd say you were surprised by this development."

It took a monumental effort to answer Jamie when I still couldn't take my eyes off of Noah. I thought I wouldn't see him for months. That I'd have to wait to tell him what Jude did and about Lukumi in my hospital room and about the footage from Claire's camera that Jude had left for me.

But now Noah was here. I wouldn't have to wait at all, and I could have cried with relief.

"Surprised," I finally said. "Yes."

"As if you didn't know he was joining us on the island of misfit children?"

"What?" I tore my eyes from Noah and met Jamie's. "I didn't."

"Right," Jamie said. "They're making me room with him, Mara. I hate you."

"You think *I* did this?"

"Please." Jamie shot me a withering look. "As if he could resist a damsel in distress."

"I didn't tell him to come," I said, but I had never been happier to see him in my life. "And before you complain about *your* roommate, I was informed by Mr. Robins that *I* have to sleep in the same room as *Phoebe*."

Jamie looked appropriately horrified.

"Yeah," I said. I complained about it immediately, of course, but was told I'd have to take it up with Dr. Kells. And she wasn't at the retreat today—she only came a few times a week, they told me, to supervise the residential staff. So until I saw her again, I was stuck.

Brooke clapped her hands. "All right, everyone back? Great! Well, it looks like we have another new member of the Horizons family, everybody! Let's give a big welcome to Noah Shaw."

"Hi, Noah," everyone said in chorus.

"Noah's here for the retreat this weekend, to see if it suits. Why don't you tell everyone about yourself, Noah?"

"I was born in London," he said with complete disinterest. "My parents moved here from England two years ago."

My mouth parted.

"I don't have a favorite color, though I strongly dislike yellow."

Unbelievable.

"I play the guitar, love dogs, and hate Florida."

And then Noah finally met my eyes. I was expecting a trademark half-smile, but when he looked at me his eyes were empty. My heart cracked.

"It's so nice to meet you, Noah. Would you feel comfortable telling us why you're here?"

He grinned, but there was no warmth in it. "I've been told that I have an anger management problem."

Everyone shared their fake feelings for an hour, and then we broke for lunch. Noah caught up with me in the hallway. He looked down at me.

He looked broken.

"You're a hard girl to get a hold of," he said quietly.

I barked out a laugh, but Noah covered my mouth with a gentle hand.

My lids dropped at his touch. I could *feel* him. He was real.

All I wanted in the world was to hold him and be held. But when I lifted my hands to his waist he said, "Don't."

I blinked, and then I thought I might cry, and Noah must have seen it because he rushed to speak. "They don't know we're together. If they find out, they'll take care to separate us and I won't be able to bear that."

I nodded beneath his hand and he lifted it, looking over his shoulder. The hallway was clear, but who knew for how long?

"How did you get in?" I asked.

The ghost of a smile touched his mouth. "It's a long story that involves copious quantities of alcohol and Lolita."

My brows knitted in confusion. "The book?"

"The whale."

He made me smile, despite everything. "Do I even want to know?"

"Probably not," he said tonelessly. He avoided my eyes.

Something was wrong. I wanted to ask what it was, but I was nervous so I asked where his necklace was instead.

Noah sighed. "I had to take it off during that delightful near-strip search they offer here. Hermencia quite enjoyed it, I think. I'll be sending her a bill."

I smiled again, but Noah didn't. I didn't know what had changed or why, but I needed to. Even if I might not like the answer. "What happened?" I asked him.

He lifted my hand, my wrist, and held it out in answer.

"They think I tried to kill myself," I said.

Noah closed his eyes. For the first time ever, he looked like he was in pain.

"Do you?" I asked him.

The muscles in his throat worked. "No," he said. "I saw—I saw everything. I saw Jude."

When he opened his eyes, his expression was vacant again. A smooth, unreadable mask. I was reminded of a different conversation we shared under very different circumstances:

"And what if something happens and you're not there?" I had asked him, miserable and guilty and horrified after we returned from the zoo.

"I'll be there," Noah had said, his voice clear and sure.

"But what if you're not?"

"Then it would be my fault."

Was that what this was? I looked up at him now and shook my head. "It's not your fault."

"Actually," he said with unparalleled bitterness, "it is."

But before Noah could say anything else, a counselor interrupted us, and we were ushered away.

57

WE HAD NO TIME ALONE THE REST OF THE day. Noah was shuttled from pointless thing to pointless thing with Adam, Stella, Megan and the other temporaries as I was left to endure more talk therapy and generally languish in solitude. I met a few permanents, who didn't seem obviously disturbed. Not as bad as Phoebe, anyway, by a long shot.

When we finally sat down for dinner, I dropped down into a seat across from Noah. A few boys I didn't know well shared the table, but they weren't too close.

I was desperate to talk to him. I had so much I wanted to say.

He was so close, but too far away to touch. My fingertips ached with the need to feel him, solid and warm and real under my hands.

I said his name, but Noah gave a single shake of his head. I bit my lip. I could scream from frustration and I wanted to. I felt like I was drifting and needed him to tether me to the earth.

But then he scribbled something on a napkin with a crayon—he must have stolen it from the art studio they had here—and handed it to me.

I glanced up, then around, then down at the message as discreetly as I could.

Music studio. 1 a.m.

"But—" I whispered.

Trust me, Noah mouthed.

I did.

I wished the sunlight away as I finished dinner that evening across from a silent, unusually sullen Stella. She picked at her food and every now and then, her eyes would sweep the room. When I asked her what was wrong she excused herself, leaving me alone.

I couldn't wait for night to fall and I gazed out the thick, distorted windows at every opportunity. The darkness nipped at the heels of the sunset, waiting to swallow it.

The sounds of silverware clinking against ceramic dishes died away as the sun sank below the horizon. Counselor

Wayne came around with everyone's evening meds in tiny little paper cups, just like in Miami.

Stella swallowed hers in front of me, her white T-shirt riding up slightly with the movement. I glanced up and saw Jamie, who downed the contents of his makeshift shot glass too. His Adam's apple bobbed, and Wayne moved on.

Then it was my turn. There were two additional pills inside my cup today. Oval and blue.

"You know the drill, Mara," Wayne said.

I did. But I couldn't have been more unenthused about taking them. What if they made me tired? My eyes flicked up, trying to find Noah in the small sea of faces in the dining room. He wasn't there.

"Mara," Wayne said, warmly but with a touch of impatience.

Damn it. I took the cup in my hands and swallowed the pills, chasing them with a gulp of water.

"Open," he said.

I opened my mouth and showed him my tongue.

Wayne smiled and moved on to the next person. I grudgingly stood and brought my dishes over to the counter, then followed the line of girls walking down the hallway to their respective rooms. I grabbed my little tote with my shampoo and soap in it, helpfully packed by my mother as if she'd sent me off to summer camp, and headed to the girls' bathroom for a shower. There were stalls, thankfully, but we had to avail ourselves of the spa-like bathroom in groups or pairs. My other half was Phoebe, of course. At that point, I was too used to my life sucking to care.

When I finished, my limbs felt weak with exhaustion and I almost dropped my towel before slipping on my robe. I managed not to embarrass myself, barely, then followed Phoebe's stupid steps out of the bathroom and back down the hall. She opened the door to our unadorned white room, occupied by a pair of identical white twin beds. Phoebe sat on one at the far end of the room, leaving me the bed closest to the door.

Perfect.

Phoebe was quiet. She hadn't said anything to me all day, in fact, and I counted myself fortunate. She watched me for a minute, then stood and turned out the main light while I rummaged in my recently-filled dresser for something to wear to bed, even though I had no plans to sleep. I shot her an annoyed look, which she either didn't notice or ignored. Then she slipped under her covers and I changed and slipped under mine.

Each room had a schoolhouse clock positioned on the wall between both of the beds. Ours read ten o'clock, then ten thirty, then eleven. The seconds ticked away as I listened to Phoebe snore.

Then, in the darkness, two words:

"Get up."

A harsh, female voice reached into my brain. I wanted to stab it.

My eyes opened slowly. Phoebe hovered near my bed. I started to sit up, but was surprised to find I was already sitting.

I was more surprised to find that my feet were on the floor, the slick tile surface cool beneath them.

"You were getting out of bed," Phoebe said mechanically.

"What?" My voice was thick with sleep.

"You woke up," she said to me. "You were going to get out of bed."

I rested my forehead in one hand. My eyes traveled to the clock.

Four a.m. I missed it. Missed Noah. I was too late.

"Want to get some water?" Phoebe asked.

My throat was sour, my mouth and tongue coated with film. I nodded, not quite sure why Phoebe was being so uncharacteristically nice but not really with it enough to ask. I stood on unsteady feet and followed Phoebe out into the dimly lit hallway. We made our way soundlessly to the bathroom, passing Barney who was now at his console desk.

"We're going to the bathroom," Phoebe announced. He nodded at us, smiled, and returned to his book. *Silence of the Lambs.*

Once inside, Phoebe turned on the faucet. I was desperate for water; I lurched forward to the sink and cupped a handful, raising it to my mouth. I drank deeply, though most of the liquid spilled through my fingers, and quickly darted to catch another mouthful, and another. I didn't think I could ever drink enough until, finally, the staleness in my throat softened, and the burn died away. I looked up in the mirror.

I was pale and my skin was damp. My hair hung limply around my face, my eyes staring blankly into the silvered glass. I didn't look like myself. I didn't feel like myself.

"Bloody Mary," Phoebe said.

I jumped. I'd almost forgotten she was next to me. "What?" I asked, still focused on the stranger in the glass.

"If you say 'Bloody Mary,' three times after midnight, she'll come to you in the mirror and scratch your eyes and throat out," Phoebe said.

I stared at her in the mirror. She was looking at the ceiling.

"I just said her name twice." She smiled. The faucet dripped.

"She had miscarriages," Phoebe continued. "They said it made her crazy, so she would steal other women's babies. But then they would die too. She killed them." Phoebe met my eyes in the mirror, thoroughly creeping me out.

What was I supposed to say? I cupped one last handful of water and splashed it on my face instead of in my mouth.

"Who did you kill?" Phoebe said. Her voice was chilling and clear.

I froze. The water dripped from my face and my fingers onto the tiled floor.

"When you got out of bed, you said you didn't mean to kill Rachel and Claire. But you weren't sorry about the others. That's what you said."

"It was a nightmare." My voice was shaky and hoarse. I turned the faucet off.

"It didn't seem like a nightmare," she said.

I ignored her and turned to leave. Phoebe stepped in front of me.

"Who are Rachel and Claire?" she asked, piercing me with her eyes. They looked hollow in her white moon face.

"It was just a nightmare," I said again, staring back at her. I tried hard not to give any outward sign that what she repeated had any basis in reality, but inside?

Inside I was crumbling.

"You said you were glad you killed the man, that you wished you could have crushed his skull with your own fingers."

"Stop it," I said, starting to tremble.

"You told me about the asylum," she said, backing up slightly. "You told me *everything*." The corners of her mouth turned up in a disturbed smile. "I know about *him*," Phoebe said, her grin spreading. "How much you want him. How much you love him. How desperate you are. But he doesn't love you back," she said in a singsong voice.

Did I tell her about Noah? I closed my eyes and my nostrils

flared. I wanted to scream in her face, to tell her to shut her too-wide mouth, but I couldn't. Not without giving myself away. "I'm going back to bed," I said, stepping around her. My voice trembled when I spoke. I hoped she didn't notice.

Phoebe followed close behind me. Too close.

We made our way back to our room without speaking. Phoebe climbed into bed, wearing a satisfied smile. I wanted to smack it off of her face, but in the back of my mind, I knew that the person I was most furious with was me.

Losing time, writing in notebooks—it was frightening, yes, but it hadn't hurt me. Not yet. And as long as I didn't tell anyone, maybe this *would* just be temporary, and I could get out.

And find Jude. Make sure he could never hurt me again.

But Phoebe couldn't know those things she said unless I told her. Which meant that my already tenuous self-control was slipping.

I drew the blanket up to my chin and stared at the wall. My mind wouldn't quiet, and I couldn't sleep.

And so I laid awake until the darkness turned to daylight, and then at seven a.m., stood up to face the day.

Phoebe started to scream.

"What is *wrong* with you?" I hissed at her.

She wouldn't stop.

Residents began to cluster by the door. A counselor broke through just as I met Noah's eyes.

Wayne squeezed by until he stood just inside the doorway to our room. "What's going on here?"

Phoebe somehow seemed to shrink back against the wall and lurch forward with her accusation at the same time. "She was standing over me while I slept!"

Wayne's shifty eyes shifted to me.

I raised my hands defensively. "She's lying," I said. "I was just getting up to change."

"I woke up and she was standing right *there*," Phoebe keened.

I fought off a wave of fury.

"She was going to hurt me!"

"Calm down, Phoebe."

"She's going to hurt me if you don't stop her!"

"Can everyone just back up a second? Barney! Brooke!" Wayne called, his eyes on me the whole time.

"We're here," Barney's deep voice boomed from somewhere behind me.

They entered. I was rooted to the spot, just a foot away from my bed.

"All right, Phoebe, try and relax," Brooke said, floating over to her and sitting beside her on the bed. Phoebe had started to rock back and forth. "I want you to do the breathing exercises we talked about, okay? And the counting."

I heard Phoebe begin to count to ten. Meanwhile, Wayne

and Barney were both focused on me. Wayne had taken a step closer.

"What happened, Mara?" Wayne asked.

"Nothing happened," I said, and I was telling the truth.

"I can't live with her!"

"Phoebe," Wayne said, "if you don't stop screaming, we're going to have to take you to the room."

She shut up instantly.

Brooke looked up at me from Phoebe's bed. "Mara, please just tell me what happened last night? In your own words?"

I fought the urge to lift my eyes to the doorway and search for Noah. I swallowed. "I ate dinner with everyone else."

"Who did you sit with?" she asked.

"I—" I didn't remember. Who *did* I sit with? "Stella," I said finally. I looked to the doorway and she edged in next to Noah. He looked down at her and a strange expression passed over his face.

Brooke said my name and drew my eyes back to hers. "So you had dinner with Stella. Then what happened?"

"I took a shower and then we came back to our room. I put on my pajamas and went to bed."

"Both of them got up at about four," Barney said.

I nodded. "Phoebe came with me."

"Don't say my name," she murmured quietly. I rolled my eyes.

"That's all?"

"Yes."

"Have you ever sleepwalked before?" Brooke asked me.

I didn't answer her, of course, because the answer was yes.

58

AFTER A STRICT INSTRUCTION TO SPEAK TO Dr. Kells at my next appointment with her, Brooke left us to change before meeting up in the common room for an impromptu group session.

I rounded on Phoebe once we were left alone. "Why are you lying to them?"

She smiled at me. I wanted to hit her so badly.

I almost did.

I closed my eyes and breathed deeply instead, trying to shake her off. When I left the room, Noah was hanging back near one of the studios that flanked the hallway.

"What happened?" he asked, his voice low and wary.

"I overslept," I said. I wanted to kick myself. "Phoebe woke me up in the middle of the night. She says I—I told her about Rachel and Claire. About everything."

Noah didn't comment. He just asked, "Who is that girl?"

I followed his eyes until they landed on Stella, who had folded herself into a chair in the common room. She cracked her knuckles and then rubbed absently at the faded left knee of her jeans.

"Stella," I said. "She's nice. A little moody sometimes, maybe. Why?"

"I saw her," Noah said.

"Saw her—"

"Someone hurt her." His gaze dropped to my hands. "Grabbed her wrist. Nearly broke it."

My throat felt dry. "Why her?"

Noah rubbed his forehead. "I don't know."

"That's how many?" I asked him.

"Five, now."

"Me, Joseph, the two you don't know, and now—"

Stella.

"Come on in, everyone!" Brooke called.

Noah and I shared one more look before settling into the room. I sat down next to Jamie, who was oddly quiet.

Brooke nodded to Wayne and they drew nearer to the periphery of the circle. "Okay, everyone," she said to us. "We all know there was a little event this morning. Not a big deal, but we decided that it would be a good day to do some trust exercises."

Loud groaning. Stella muttered a few of the only words I seemed to remember in Spanish, which were delightfully inappropriate.

"It doesn't matter how many we do," Phoebe called out. "You can't trust Mara."

Jamie began to chuckle silently. I stepped on his foot.

"Phoebe, I think we got a sense of your feelings about this earlier, so unless you have anything specific you'd like to share, I'd like to move along."

Phoebe zeroed in on me as she spoke to Brooke. "I do have something specific I'd like to share."

I didn't like the sound of that.

"You all think Mara's this innocent girl who's just had really bad luck. She isn't. She wants to hurt me. She wants to hurt all of us."

Jamie lost it completely. His laughter would have been contagious. But despite Phoebe's melodramatic presentation, what she said was disturbing. Not because it was true.

Because it was calculated. She was insane, but shrewd. Phoebe was saying these things on purpose *for* a purpose, and I couldn't figure out what it was.

"Phoebe, why do you think Mara wants to hurt you?"

"Because she says so in her sleep."

Shit.

Brooke looked at me, and then looked back at Phoebe. "When was this, Phoebe?"

"Last night."

Okay, it *was* possible. She was gross and annoying and limited, but smart in that evil, demon-child way. But while I might have muttered something about killing her, maybe, I didn't actually *want* her dead. Not like the others. I didn't *envision* it. Not consciously.

Unconsciously?

Could I have dreamed about her death? What would happen if I wanted it while I slept?

Would she die?

"I can't room with her, Brooke," Phoebe said softly. Her chin began to tremble.

Here we go.

"I'm scared," she added, for good measure.

"That's why we're going to do these trust exercises, Phoebe."

"They won't help!"

"They won't if you don't give them a chance," Brooke admonished. "All right, everyone, I want you to stand up— Wayne, can you read the list of partners for this?"

Wayne read off the pairs. I was paired with Phoebe, to no one's surprise. Jamie was with Noah. A girl I recognized from Horizons Miami was with Megan, and Adam was paired with a permanent. The pairings seemed like they were all roommate-roommate. Maybe to stave off a patient revolution?

"Okay, guys. The first thing we're going to do is called a trust fall. We're going to start in alphabetical order—that means if your name begins with a letter that comes earlier in the alphabet than your partner, you get to "fall" first, and your partner will catch you."

Everyone started moving into their pairs. I noticed then that they'd moved floor cushions and yoga mats into the common room. Insurance, perhaps?

"When I count to three, the first person from each pair is going to fall."

That would be me. I glanced at Phoebe behind me. She was smirking. This wasn't going to go well. "You'd better catch me, Phoebe," I whispered.

She ignored me.

"One," Brooke began.

"I'm serious," I said, as I backed toward her.

"Two."

Phoebe had her arms out, and still hadn't answered me.

"Three."

I fell. On my ass.

"Motherf—!"

"She said she was going to slit my wrists!" she wailed to Brooke. "She whispered it when you weren't listening!"

Brooke glanced at me and sighed. "This isn't productive for your rooming relationship."

Phoebe began to cry. Big, fat crocodile tears. "I can't stay with her. I just can't."

I stood and glanced at Jamie, who shot me a sympathetic look. Noah was studying Phoebe. He knew something was up with her too.

Brooke was frustrated herself. And then she said something I didn't expect to hear.

"Would anyone be willing to switch rooms and be Mara's new roommate?"

Crickets.

I raised my hand.

"Yes, Mara?"

"I think I could manage without a roommate, Brooke."

"No dice," she said, her eyes flicking to my wrists. "I'm sorry. Guys, are you sure none of you would be willing to switch? I think it would help things out a lot . . ."

No one raised their hand. I tried to catch Stella's eye, but she completely avoided my gaze and gave me the stare ahead in response to my visual pleading.

It was like being picked last for dodgeball, only *so much worse.*

Suddenly, there was a crash of ceramic hitting stone behind us.

I turned. Phoebe was standing near a toppled pedestal;

a vase had shattered on the floor. Her face was red and her damp hair stuck in sweaty tendrils to her cheeks. You could hear a pin drop. Everyone was absolutely silent as Phoebe gulped in a few breaths, then reached for one of the shards.

"Phoebe!" an adult voice shouted. Soon, there were more adults in the room than I ever remembered seeing at Horizons individually.

"No one's listening to me," she wailed, but before she could grab one of the pieces of the smashed vase, Wayne had managed to get hold of her. He lifted her up and away.

"Page Kells, then get her journal," I heard Brooke whisper to him. Phoebe was thrashing wildly but then Barney showed up and stood in front of her, blocking my view. Phoebe's cries died away. When I saw her next, she was rag-doll limp in Wayne's arms. He carried her out.

Jamie and I made eye contact.

"Weirdo," Jamie said.

"Understatement," I replied.

Jamie leaned in and whispered, "How's your ass?"

"I'll survive."

"Saw that coming a mile away."

"Me too. But that roommate thing? Worst. Ever."

He raised an eyebrow.

"I'm the creepy girl. In a *mental hospital.*"

He grinned. "Nobody's perfect."

59

THERE WAS A DEFINITE ADVANTAGE TO PHOEBE'S sedation: For the rest of the day, I wouldn't have to listen to her talk. And tonight?

I wouldn't have to worry that she would wake up.

I passed Noah a note, mimicking his from yesterday:

Tonight at one by the music studio? Make it happen?

When I caught his eye during dinner, he nodded yes. Each second fell away as the clock slipped forward. I wished, I *needed*, everyone to sleep. I conjured mental images of empty hallways. Of Barney in the common room, asleep in front of the television with his headphones on. Of Brooke in bed.

No one needed to use the bathroom. No one felt like they had to monitor the halls. I imagined I could hear the sounds of everyone else turning over in their beds, rustling in their sheets, breathing quietly into their pillows.

And then it was time. I slipped off my blanket and slipped on my hoodie. I pulled it over my head and zipped it up to quiet the sound of my ferociously beating heart. When I shifted to stand, the mattress groaned and my eyes darted to the other side of the room.

Phoebe was sleeping.

I tiptoed to the door and opened it as softly as I could. The second I did, someone somewhere coughed and my heart leapt into my throat. I waited there in the doorway for what felt like hours.

Nothing.

I left the room. I walked down the hallway. And each time I passed another doorway, my heart stopped. When I rounded the corner by the common room, directly in front of the counselor's desk, I mentally prepared myself to be directed back to bed.

But no one was there.

I practically ran the rest of the way to the studio. Where was everyone? The bathroom? Sleeping?

It didn't really matter and I didn't really care, because Noah stood in the silent corridor waiting for me, and I wanted nothing more than to fly into his arms.

I didn't. I stopped.

"You made it," he said with a smile.

I returned it. "You too." I reached for the door to the music room, but I noticed the keypad.

"Are you serious?" I whispered through gritted teeth.

Noah hushed me, then pressed a series of numbers on the pad. I looked up at him incredulously.

"Everyone has a price," he said, as the door in front of us clicked open. He held the door open for me, and I walked through.

The dark was impenetrable. Noah's fingers twined around mine as he led me forward, and then down to the carpeted floor.

My eyes began to adjust somewhat to the darkness in the room. There was a small window at the far corner, letting in a sliver of moonlight that illuminated the planes and angles in his expressionless face.

He sat with his back against the wall, statue-still and cold. He withdrew his hand from mine.

I reached out to take it back, but he said, "Don't." His voice was laced with contempt. Poisonous.

"Don't what?" I asked flatly.

His jaw locked, and he stared at me with empty eyes.

"What's *wrong*?"

"I don't—" he started. "I don't know what to—" He glanced down.

At my wrists.

So that's what this was about. Noah wasn't furious with me. He was furious with himself. It was hard to recognize still, because I was the opposite. I turned outward with anger. Noah turned in.

I put my hands on either side of his face, not gentle and not soft. "Stop it," I said, my voice harsh. "You aren't the one who hurt me. Stop torturing yourself."

Noah's expression didn't change. "I wasn't there."

"You were trying to help," I said. "You were trying to find answers—"

His slate blue eyes looked like iron in the darkness. "I swore I would be there for you and I wasn't. I swore you would be safe, and you weren't."

"I'm—"

"You were terrified," he said, cutting me off. "When you called me, I'll never forget your voice."

"Noah."

"You told me about the notebook you didn't remember writing in and I had never heard you—I'd never heard you sound like that." His voice grew distant. "I scrambled to get to Boston to make the other flight the second we hung up. I did, and I was trapped on that fucking plane while he forced you—"

Noah didn't finish his sentence. He nearly vibrated with rage, with the effort it took not to scream. "I felt you dying beneath my skin," he said, his tone hollow. "I called Daniel from the plane—I dialed again and again until he woke up." Noah met my eyes. "I told him you were going to kill yourself, Mara. I didn't know how else to explain—what I saw." His face was drawn in fury.

I wanted to draw something else.

My fingers traced the fine, elegant bones in his face. "It's okay."

"It is *not* okay," he snapped. "They had you *committed*. They sent you here because of what I told them."

"Because of what *Jude* did."

He laughed without humor. "Your mother said I couldn't see you—that you had to deal with this as a family now, and that they were going to send you somewhere for proper help. I couldn't comprehend it—that the last time I heard your voice for months, it would be riddled with terror as you begged for your life." He closed his eyes. "And I wasn't there."

"You were at the hospital," I said, brushing my thumb over his beautiful mouth. "Daniel said you didn't leave."

Noah opened his eyes but avoided mine. "I managed to see you, once."

"Really?"

He gave a short nod. "You were unconscious. You were—they had you in restraints." He said nothing for what seemed like a very long time.

We didn't have enough of it. There was so much he still didn't know.

"I saw Abel Lukumi," I said.

Noah's brows drew together. "What?"

"In the hospital. On the second day, I think. When I woke up—my mother told me why I was there and I . . ."

Freaked out. I freaked out, and they sedated me. "I tried to explain to her what happened, with Jude, but I—I lost it," I said. "Before the drugs kicked in, I saw Lukumi by the hospital room door."

Noah was silent.

"It wasn't a hallucination," I said firmly, because I was afraid he was thinking it. "You didn't see him in the building, did you?"

"No" was all he said.

Of course not. I went on to tell Noah about everything else that happened that night—about finding the unmarked disc in my room, and what was on it. I told him about seeing Rachel, watching her through the lens of Claire's video camera. Watching the asylum collapse.

I left out the part about hearing my laughter after it did.

When I finished, Noah said, "I should never have left you." He shook his head. "I thought John would be enough."

"You trusted him. He watched the house for days, and everything was fine." I paused, then asked, "What happened?"

"He had a stroke. Just sitting there, in the car."

I felt like I'd been bathed in ice. I tried not to sound as freaked out as I felt. "So did the officer."

"What officer?"

"When Jude—at the dock," I said, choosing my words carefully. "At the marina, before I passed out—there was a man, an off-duty cop, who came to help when he saw me hurt. He tried to call for help but then Jude—"

Jude stabbed himself in the side.

I still couldn't make sense of it—the images in my memory bled into one another, and the feelings, too. Terror and rage, fear and panic. So I described what happened on the dock to Noah—he had seen it, but from a different perspective. Maybe together, we could connect the points.

"There were dead fish under the dock," I said to him as his eyes sharpened. "Just floating in the water."

Like the Everglades, I thought, remembering Noah's words. We had been trapped in the creek. I had to get to Joseph but couldn't. There were only two choices: fight or flight, and I couldn't flee. I was backed into a corner. So without thinking, my mind fought.

My fear killed everything in the water around us. Alligators. Fish. Everything. And I was afraid at the marina, too. I was terrified of Jude. *He* didn't die, but in trying to kill him, did I kill everything around me too?

Did I kill the police officer? The one who tried to help?

My throat burned with the thought and my stomach twisted with guilt. But then I remembered—

John. He also died of a stroke. And I hadn't even seen him that night. I might be responsible for the rest of it, but not him.

My mind churned, trying to work through it. I glanced up at Noah, wondering what he was thinking, so I asked.

"I wasn't there," he answered, with that same vacant look.

I moved toward him then. Slid my arms around his neck and drew him against me. Noah winced at the contact. I ignored it. Now that we were this close, I could see what I missed before.

Noah acted like he felt nothing because he felt everything. He seemed not to care because he cared too much.

I smiled against his lips. "You're here now."

60

Noah's voice sliced the air like a razor blade when he spoke. "I'm here because you're alive, Mara. If he had killed you—"

"He didn't," I said, and the words lingered in my mouth. "He didn't kill me," I repeated, and edged my back up against the wall as the words transported me to the marina. I saw myself prone and bleeding on the dock.

I could not look away from the deepening gashes on my wrists.

Not fatal.

But Jude knew. I could tell by the way he was staring at the cuts as he held my forearms, studying them. To make sure I bled, but not too much. He didn't want to kill me. He wanted something else.

"Jude left me alive," I said out loud. "On purpose. Why?"

Noah ran a hand over his shadowed jaw. "To live so he could torture you another day?" He smiled, and it was full of malice. "If only I'd had enough time in central holding to make friends."

I looked up, surprised. "You were in jail?"

Noah shrugged, his shoulder moving against mine.

"When was this?"

"When I found out they were sending you here and there was nothing I could do. The situation demanded something . . ." Noah searched for the right word. "Outlandish. I had to convince my father that I would be an embarrassment to him—a public one—every second I couldn't be with you."

"Wait—was this after the Lolita incident?"

Noah gave a brief nod.

"Noah," I said cautiously. "What did you do to that poor whale?"

He cracked a real smile, then. Finally. I wanted to make him smile like that for the rest of my life.

"She's fine," he said. "I only pushed someone into her tank."

"You didn't."

"A little bit, yes."

I shook my head in mock disdain.

"He was encouraging his budding sociopath child to bang on the glass," Noah said, his voice matter-of-fact.

"What were you even *doing* there?"

"Looking for a fight. I needed something that would make the news."

"Oh my God, it did?"

"I was this close," he said, and held his thumb and forefinger a fraction apart. "Edged out by a corrupt politician."

"You were robbed."

"Indeed. My father paid them off, I think."

I watched Noah closely when I asked my next question. "So your father knows about us, then?"

"Yes," Noah said evenly. "He does."

"And?"

Noah raised his eyebrows. "And what?"

Boys. So impossible. "What does he *think*?"

Noah looked like he didn't understand the question. "As if that matters?"

Ah. He understood the question, he just didn't know why I was asking. "It does matter," I said. "Tell me."

"He thinks I'm a fool," Noah said simply.

I tried not to show how much that hurt.

Apparently I failed, because Noah took my hands in each of his. It was the first time he touched me like this, like it mattered, since before Jude took me. His touch was impossibly gentle as he unwrapped the bandages on my wrists, but it still hurt and I began to protest. He hushed me. He lifted my hands to his mouth. His petal-soft lips brushed over my knuckles, then my palms. Noah looked into my eyes and owned me.

And then he kissed my scars.

"It doesn't matter," he murmured against my skin. His fingers traced the cuts, healing the veins beneath them. "There's only one thing that does."

"What?" I whispered.

He looked at me through his long, dark lashes, with my hands still in his. "Killing Jude."

61

Noah's hands were gentle and his voice was soft, which made his words somehow even more chilling.

I wanted to kill Jude. I'd thought about it many times. But those words in *his* mouth sounded wrong.

Noah let go of my hands. "I made arrangements before I came here to have more people watch your family, but I don't think Jude's going to go after them," he said, staring straight ahead. "Everything he's done—it's been to get at *you*. He said he took Joseph because he wanted to make *you* hurt him yourself, knowing that's exactly what would torture you the most."

I swallowed. "But now I'm in here. And so are you."

Noah was silent for a moment. Then said, "Not forever."

Something in his voice scared me, and drew my eyes to look. Noah was beautiful—always—but there was something dark now beneath those perfectly carved features. Something new.

Or maybe it was always there, and I had just never seen it.

My pulse began to race.

Noah turned to me, the movement fluid and graceful. "The girl I saw—Stella, yes?"

I nodded.

"What do you know about her?" He sounded like himself again, and I felt relieved without quite knowing why.

"Not much," I admitted. "Jamie said something about her almost passing for normal, but I don't know what she's in here for." I felt a little bad now that I hadn't bothered to find out, but in my defense, I'd been a bit preoccupied. "Why?"

Noah ran his fingers through his hair. "Have you noticed anything different about her?"

"Different as in . . ."

"Like us."

"Nothing obvious," I said, with a shrug.

Noah arched an eyebrow. "Our abilities aren't exactly obvious, either."

True. "So you think she's like us?"

"I wonder. There has to be some kind of reason I've seen you and her. Think about it—there are millions of injured and sick people everywhere. But I've seen only five. The only thing I can think of that connects us is—"

"But that would mean . . . Joseph." I could not fathom him sharing this misery.

"I think whatever we have is acquired," Noah said carefully; he must have guessed my fear. "If Stella's here, she has a file like everyone else, and it will mention her symptoms. Maybe she shares some of yours?"

And my grandmother's.

But if my grandmother and I were both different in the same way, it *had* to be hereditary, which meant Noah was wrong. All of this could happen to Joseph, too.

Noah ran a hand over his jaw. "It might show some kind of connection—something we're missing."

Something we're missing. The words sparked an image of Phoebe crying and rocking on the floor while Brooke reassured her, then smiling behind Brooke's back. "We should check Phoebe's, too," I said, though the idea of her being like us was a horrifying thought.

And I had an equally horrifying thought—if Stella and Phoebe were like me and Noah, there was another thing we had in common.

We were all here.

I glanced at the tiny window in the music studio. Branches were thrashing in the wind, but despite the chaos outside, the room was quiet. The sky was still dark.

"We should go now," I said to Noah, and we rose from the floor together. "How are you going to get their files?"

"The same way I got us into this room," he said, flashing his crooked grin. "With a bribe."

Noah led me up and out of the studio and into the hall. I didn't want to risk a whisper, especially not in front of Dr. Kells's door. It had an identical keypad, I noticed. But what if she was in there?

Noah shook his head when I asked my question out loud. "She's only here a few times a week—and she definitely wouldn't be in there at this hour." He pressed a series of different numbers this time. Fewer. The door opened with a click.

"Well, well, what have we here?"

I nearly jumped out of my skin. Noah and I turned at exactly the same time.

To see Jamie standing in the hallway, just a few feet away.

"If it isn't Noah Shaw," he said in a low voice, mimicking Noah's accent. "Seducer of virgins, fresh from making beautiful music with his beautiful conquest in the music studio. METAPHOR," he stage-whispered.

"Jamie—" I hissed. He was going to get us caught.

"Which is fine," he said, holding up his hands defensively. "Free country. But unless you're about to engage in some executive-secretary role-play—"

"Jamie."

"Or, oh my God, psychologist-patient role-play? Please tell me that is not what you were about to do, or I will throw up in both your faces. Simultaneously."

"You're disturbed," I said sharply.

"That's what they tell me," Jamie said with a wink. "So, no role-play?"

"None," Noah said.

"Then I want in."

"Fine," Noah said. "But for God's sake, shut up." He pushed open the door, and the three of us found ourselves in Dr. Kells's lair.

"What are you looking for?" I asked Jamie as Noah pushed the door closed behind us.

"My file," Jamie said, as if it was obvious. Then he cocked his head at me. "You?"

"Seems as though we have a similar agenda," Noah lied.

Jamie moved gingerly in the dark room. He sat on the edge of Dr. Kells's desk. "Who'd you pay off?"

"Wayne," Noah said.

Jamie nodded sagely. "He seemed like the type."

"There's very little money can't buy," Noah said, as his eyes roamed over a tall file cabinet in the corner.

"Ain't that the truth," Jamie said. "Have you broken into the room *without* a keypad yet?"

I looked over at him. "What room?"

Jamie shook his head. "What kind of juvenile delinquent

are you, Mara?" he asked. "I tried picking it," he said to Noah, "but no luck. If we could get our hands on the master key and a bar of soap and a *lighter*, Noah, we could make a copy of it."

Noah didn't respond—he was already gently opening drawers. Jamie and I took the hint and followed his lead.

My eyes scanned the hanging file folders for names, but all I saw were numbers. Years, maybe? I withdrew one of the manila folders and opened it.

Financial records of some kind. Huh. I put the folder back.

We worked in the dark room in silence for a while, with nothing but the sound of drawers and folders opening and closing in the background. It would have been so much easier with some light, but under the circumstances, that probably wouldn't have been wise.

"Bingo," Jamie said, startling me. "They're organized chronologically." He held up three files in his hands. "Dyer," he said, and handed me mine. "Shaw," he said, placing Noah's into his hand. "And Roth." He hugged the last file close to his chest.

I looked down at mine. If only that was what I really wanted. Noah took Dr. Kells's chair and flashed a lazy smile at me, pretending to go along with this. I moved to sit on his lap.

"Get a meadow," Jamie muttered.

I grinned and Noah smiled and neither of us moved. He opened his file, but I just stared at mine. I wasn't entirely sure

I wanted to know what it said, but considering I might not get another chance—

Screw it. I flipped it open. On the first page were my stats. What I was interested in was on the second page:

The patient admits to having past and present thoughts of harming herself or others, as well as to experiencing auditory and visual hallucinations. The patient did not hesitate to describe the circumstances that led to her episode at the Metro Dade Police Department. Her thoughts were organized and coherent. The patient admits to having specific phobias, namely of blood, needles, and heights. She denied having specific obsessions or compulsions. She admitted to having problems concentrating.

Hallucinations and nightmares appear to be stress and fear induced. Patient also experiences extreme insomnia and panic attacks. She has had recurring thoughts and incidents of self-harm (see records attached) and according to the patient and her family, suffers from extreme guilt, possibly stemming from her dual trauma; a sexual assault on the night of the PTSD event (building collapse) and the PTSD event itself. Patient was the sole survivor of a collapse in which her best friend, boyfriend, and boyfriend's sister died. Patient claims that the boyfriend assaulted her, and she is preoccupied with the delusion that he is still alive. The patient has a psychiatric history of hearing voices that others can't and exhibits paranoid ideation. Patient exhibits social avoidance: has a demonstrable lack of close friends or relationships other than with first-degree relatives, though she appears to be friendly with male patient J. Roth. Heightened animosity observed between the patient and female patient P. Reynard. Absence of flat affect. Possible indications of heightened superstition, magical thinking, and preoccupations with paranormal phenomena lead to probability of:

PTSD with possible co-occurring Mood Disorder (Bipolar: Severe with Psychotic Features)

Schizophreniform Disorder (1-6 months in duration)

Schizophrenia (if symptoms persist until eighteen years of age) as distinguished from Delusional Disorder.

Will continue to observe before final diagnosis.

"Mara."

I heard Noah's voice close to my ear. I half-turned in his lap. Noah brushed my cheek with his thumb. I was shocked to feel that it was wet.

I'd been crying.

"I'm okay," I said in a strangled voice. I cleared my throat. "I'm fine."

He tucked a strand of hair behind my ear. "Whatever it says in there, it isn't you."

Yes, it was. "You haven't read it," I said, looking away from him. Jamie was preoccupied with his own file. He was quiet.

Noah traced a pattern with his finger on my side, under my ribs and over my T-shirt as he held me on his lap. "Do you want me to?"

I wasn't sure. "I'm not sure," I said. Noah watched me go through so much, and he was still here. But seeing it on paper like this, seeing what everyone else thought . . .

"Do you want to read mine?" Noah asked. His voice was low but warm.

I couldn't lie; I did. And the fact that he was willing to show me meant something. I felt strangely nervous as Noah handed me the folder. I opened it to the first page.

62

PATIENT NAME: Noah Elliot Simon Shaw

AGE: Seventeen

The patient presented as a healthy teenage male of above average height and lean, muscular body build. He appeared somewhat older than his stated age. Rapport was not easily established. Patient was not matter-of-fact or helpful.

Patient has an ongoing pattern of uncooperative, defiant, hostile, and aggressive behavior toward authority figures and peers, according to family and educators. Atypically, it has not affected the patient's performance in school, where the patient has maintained a perfect GPA. Patient demonstrates neither hyperactivity nor anxiety but has engaged in multiple violent confrontations with others. Parents have reported several callous-unemotional traits and patient has rated highly on all three sub-scales. However, parents state that the patient has never exhibited any cruelty to animals and is in fact an exceptional caregiver to them, demonstrating a particular facility with feral and dangerous animals at his stepmother's veterinary practice, negating Antisocial Personality Disorder and other sociopathic types as potential diagnoses. Both the patient's father and the school have reported the patient's intentional destruction and vandalism of property in the past, however, as well as deceitful behavior (lying) and flouting of social norms. School restrictions are repeatedly ignored and punishments are demonstrably ineffective. Stepmother reported past incidences of alcohol and drug abuse, but nothing in recent history.

When confronted with reports from his parents and educators, questions were met with arrogant, cynical, and manipulative responses, and educators report history of sensation-seeking (renowned sexual reputation) and impulsivity. Patient demonstrates arrogant self-appraisal and superficial charm; inability to tolerate boredom; is self-assured, voluble, and verbally facile.

Continue to monitor for probable Oppositional Defiant Disorder; possible eventual diagnosis of Conduct Disorder or Narcissistic Personality Disorder.

I closed the folder without ceremony and handed it back to Noah.

"Why do you have two middle names?" I asked.

"That's your question? After reading that?" Noah drew back, searching for something in my eyes. Disgust, maybe. Or fear.

"It's not you," I said to him, and softly.

The corner of Noah's mouth lifted in a slow smile. A sad one. "Yes. It is."

We were both right, I decided then. Our files were part of us—the parts that people wanted to fix. But they weren't *all* of us. They weren't who we were. Only we could decide that.

I swung my leg over Noah's waist and straddled him. "Maybe the uncooperative part's true. You're very"—I brushed my lips against his—"frustrating."

Jamie cleared his throat. I nearly forgot that he was there.

"You okay?" I asked him.

"If okay means 'pessimistic, unstable, and manipulative,' then sure," Jamie said cheerfully. "'Patient demonstrates extreme sarcasm and enduring bitterness; sees things in terms of extremes, such as either all good or all bad. His views of others change quickly, leading to intense and unstable relationships,'" he recited from memory. "'Patient demonstrates conflict about sexual orientation and is pre-occupied with the sexual histories of others. Demonstrates a classic pattern of identity disturbance—an unclear, unstable self-image—as well as impulsivity and emotional instability,'" he said, suddenly sounding tired. He closed his file, chucked it like a Frisbee at the opposite wall, and leaned back with his arms above his head. "Ladies and gentlemen, Jamal Feldstein-Roth."

I blinked. "Wait, *Jamal*?"

"Suck it," he said with a grin. "My parents are liberal Jews from Long Island, okay? They wanted me to have a connection to my *heritage*." Jamie made air quotes with his fingers.

"I'm not judging—my middle name is Amitra. I'm just surprised."

"Amitra," Noah mused. "Mystery solved."

"What is that?" Jamie asked me.

"Sanskrit? Hindi?" I shrugged.

"Randomly?"

I shook my head. "Mom's Indian."

"What does it mean?" Jamie asked me.

"What does Jamal mean?" I asked him.

"Point taken."

"I probably have about as much connection to my Indian heritage as you do to your African heritage," I said. "My mother's favorite food is sushi."

"Latkes." Jamie smiled for a second, but then it faltered. "This is bullshit," he said suddenly. "We're teenagers. We're *supposed* to be sarcastic."

"And preoccupied with sex," I chimed in.

"And impulsive," Noah added.

"Exactly," Jamie said. "But we're in here and they're out there?" He shook his head slowly. "Everyone's a little crazy. The only difference between us and them is that they hide it better." He paused. "It . . . kind of makes me want to burn this place down?" He raised his eyebrows. "Just me?"

I grinned. "Not just you."

Jamie stood and chucked me on the shoulder. Then yawned. "Rain check? I'm beat. You guys staying?"

I looked over at Noah. We hadn't gotten what we came for yet. When our eyes met, it was obvious that he was thinking the same thing.

"Yeah," I said.

Jamie picked up his file and dropped it back in the appropriate drawer. He reached for the door. "Thanks for the fun. Let's do it again soon."

I waved. Jamie closed the door behind him.

And then Noah and I were alone.

63

NOAH LEANED BACK IN DR. KELLS'S CHAIR and watched me. I was still in his lap.

And suddenly self-conscious. "What?" I asked as I blushed.

"Are you all right?"

I nodded.

"You sure?"

I thought about it, about what was in my file and what it meant. "Not entirely," I said. Not being believed about Jude would always hurt. Noah's arms tightened around me, solid and warm.

"You can read it," I decided.

He shook his head, his hair tickling my skin. "I showed

you mine with no expectations. You don't have to show me yours."

I looked up at him. "I want to."

Noah's hand wandered over the folder on the desk behind my back, and then he leaned back in the chair to read with me still in his lap.

We were silent. His fingers wandered beneath my T-shirt, drawing invisible pictures on my skin. Distracting me, I realized with a smile. I was grateful.

Then he said my name, bringing me back. "Mara, did you see this?"

I leaned over to look. Noah flipped the file around so I could read it. Under my stats, the ones I'd skimmed, there was a handwritten notation beneath a section called CONTRAINDICATIONS that read:

Sarin, orig. carrier; contraindication suspected, unknown; midazolam administered

My heartbeat thrummed in my ears. "Sarin. My mother's maiden name."

My grandmother's last name.

I wasn't sure if Noah heard me. He handed me the file and shifted me up, off of his lap. He was up in an instant.

The rush of blood was loud in my ears. "What does it—what's a contraindication?"

"It's like," Noah started to say as he began opening drawers. "It's like if you have a penicillin allergy, the contraindication is penicillin," he said. "You shouldn't take it unless the benefit outweighs the risk."

"Like a weakness?" I asked. "What's midazolam?"

"They use it at the clinic," Noah said, thumbing through file folders. "They never told you they were giving it to you?"

"Wait, what clinic? The *animal* clinic?" I asked, my eyes widening.

"Most veterinary drugs started as human drugs, not the other way around. If it's what I think it is, they use it for sedation, presurgery."

"Why would I need to be sedated?" The idea made me shiver.

Noah shook his head. "I'm not sure," he said. "Unless there's a human indication I'm unaware of, which is possible." He glanced at the clock. "They're going to start waking up soon," he said. He was silhouetted in the dark. "You look for Phoebe's file, I'll look for Stella's."

I looked without words because I couldn't find any, not then. I kept searching, careful as I could be not to disturb anything as I tunneled through file cabinets and scoured the desk drawers. In the bottom-right one, on top of a pile of papers, I found something. But not what I had been looking for.

I withdrew the fine black cord with the silver pendants—mirror images, mine and his—that should have been hanging around Noah's neck.

"Noah," I said. "Your necklace."

He turned to me, placing a manila file folder on the desk. *Benicia,* the label read—Stella's last name.

I handed Noah the necklace and he fastened it around his neck. Then helped me search for Phoebe's file.

I opened every drawer, looked under every pile of paper. There were a bunch of notebooks all stacked on a shelf—I looked between those, too, taking each one out and flipping through it—maybe her records had been stuffed inside?

He slid into Dr. Kells's chair then. "Keep looking," he told me, as he turned on the computer monitor on her desk. I willed myself to hold it together despite the panic that scratched below the surface, and resumed the physical search as Noah began an electronic one.

And then, just as my eyes found a notebook with Phoebe's scrawl on the front, I heard Noah say my name in the most haunted voice I had ever heard.

His skin was pale, illuminated by the monitor's light, which flickered over his face as he watched something on the screen, utterly riveted. I gripped Phoebe's notebook and moved next to him to see what it was.

What I saw, framed in the glossy white monitor, was us.

An extremely high quality video on Dr. Kells's computer screen of me on my bed. In my bedroom. At home. Of Noah straddled in my desk chair, looking at me. Talking to me.

I saw his artful smirk. My answering smile.

And a date in the corner, where a counter ticked.

It was filmed last week.

Noah did something, clicked on something, and I watched in horror as our on-screen selves appeared and disappeared in fast motion as seconds, minutes, hours of footage passed.

Noah clicked again and a window opened up, containing more files with more dates. He opened them in rapid succession and we saw my kitchen. Daniel's bedroom. The guest bedroom.

Every room in my whole house.

Another click. The sound of Noah's voice reached out from the speakers and out from the past.

"I won't let Jude hurt you."

Noah inhaled sharply. He fast-forwarded again and we watched his lean frame disappear. We watched me speed in and out of my bedroom, and then finally change and get ready for bed. And then we watched Jude walk into my bedroom that night. Watched him watch me as I slept.

Jude had hurt me, again and again and again. Noah blamed himself because he wasn't there, but it wasn't his fault. He was just as lost as I was, just as blind in this as me.

Dr. Kells wasn't blind, though. She saw it all. She saw everything.

"She knew he was alive," I said, my voice sounding dead. "She knew he was alive the whole time."

64

NOAH WAS COMPLETELY SILENT.

My eyes hardened as I stared at the screen. "Evidence," I said, and Noah looked at me, his expression chilling. "We need to copy the files, then tell everyone what's going on."

Noah clicked an icon and an electronic window opened—a picture of a yellow triangle around an exclamation mark appeared on-screen along with the words:

UNABLE TO CONNECT

"Fine, then," Noah said, and kicked out of the chair. He took my hand. "We'll leave."

But we couldn't. "Not without proof," I said, thinking of

my file. Delusions. Nightmares. Hallucinations. "If we have no proof that Jude's alive, that she knew, and we get out—I could just be sent *back*."

My voice cracked on the word. I tried to swallow away the tightness in my throat and handed Noah Phoebe's journal so I could keep rifling through the desk. For CDs, a thumb drive, any way to record this.

But Noah's voice stopped me cold.

"Jesus," he whispered, staring inside Phoebe's notebook. I leaned around to see.

I could barely read her chicken scratch, but I did see my name in several places, along with sketches of a crude likeness of myself with my insides spilled out.

"Not that," Noah said. He pointed instead to the inside cover.

Where Phoebe had drawn hearts with the initials J+P inside. Where she had written in flowery, cursive script:

Phoebe Lowe

Phoebe's last name was Reynard. *Jude's* last name was Lowe.

J + P.

Phoebe's words rushed back to me—what she said after she planted the note in my backpack, the one that said *I see you.* They tumbled and spun in my brain:

"I didn't write it," Phoebe had said, then lowered her eyes back to her journal. She smiled. *"But I did put it there."*

I heard her voice in my mind again as bile rose in my throat.

"My boyfriend gave it to me," she said in a singsong voice.

"Who's your boyfriend, Phoebe?" I asked.

But I never believed she actually had one. I just thought she was playing some crazy game. When she never answered, when she started singing, it made me think I won. But now I knew I hadn't.

Jude did.

"He was using her," I said, the fear fresh and raw. "He was *using* her."

Dr. Kells knew Jude was alive and knew his connection to me. Jude was meeting with Phoebe, telling her who-knew-what and giving her frightening notes to pass along. Phoebe and I were Horizons patients. Dr. Kells was the Horizons director. And Jude?

What the hell was *he*?

"Fuck this." Noah snapped Phoebe's notebook shut and took my hand. "We're leaving *now*." He pulled me, tugged me toward the door. I could barely make my leaden legs move.

"What are they *doing*?" I whispered.

"We'll figure it out, let's just go—"

My mind was shutting down in fear and confusion and shock. I wouldn't have known what direction to go in if Noah didn't lead me. I followed him out of Dr. Kells's office—the door closed behind us with a click. The halls were still empty and all of the dormitory room doors were still closed. None of the counselors had woken up yet. We might be able to slip out before they did.

Did they know everything too?

As we rushed through the hall, though, I noticed that there was, in fact, one door still open. One that I made sure I closed earlier on my way out.

My door.

I jerked to a stop in front of it, halting Noah along with me. "My door," I whispered to him. "I closed it, Noah. I closed it."

"Mara—"

I pushed the door open—a dim rectangle of light fell on the wall, by Phoebe's bed.

Where there were letters.

Letters that formed words.

Words that were written in something dark and wet.

The salt-rust smell assaulted my nostrils and turned my stomach. Noah flipped the light switch but the light didn't turn on. He moved deeper into the room, but did not let go of my hand.

Phoebe was tucked into her bed, the covers up to her chest. Her arms were by her side, and two dark, red balloons of blood burst from her slashed wrists, staining the white blanket on either side of her body. And on the wall, written in blood, were three words.

I SEE YOU

Jude was here.

The room was sucked of all sound. I tried to swallow, to scream, but I couldn't. It was an infinity before I heard my name whispered in the most familiar voice I knew.

Noah's arms wrapped around me, vise-tight and perfect. He folded me into him. He lifted me up, the warmth of him warming me through my sweat-damp shirt. I wrapped my legs around him and buried my face in his neck and sobbed without sound.

He didn't say anything as he carried me. Noah stalked swiftly and silently, through the hall with me in his arms; I didn't know how he was doing it and I didn't care. If he put me down, I wasn't sure I would be able to stand on my own.

We reached the front entrance then. And he leaned back and looked up into my eyes.

"The resort is maybe twenty minutes, if we run. Can you run, Mara?"

Could I run?

The wolf was at my door and there was fire at my feet. I had to run. I would.

I nodded, and Noah set me down, my hand still in his grasp. He reached for the door.

But what about—

"Jamie," I whispered, looking behind us. Looking back. "Jamie was with us in the office, Noah. He was with us."

I was being watched and tortured. Phoebe was being used and had been killed.

Neither of us had been safe. Both of us were here.

Which meant Jamie wasn't safe either. None of the other students were.

But of them, Jamie was the one I cared about the most. If I had to choose, he was the one I had to get out.

"We have to get Jamie," I said, my voice clear.

Noah nodded once, his expression hard. "I will, I swear it, but I need to get you safe, first."

Noah was choosing me.

I didn't waver. "We can't leave him."

"Mara—"

"We can't leave him," I said, and tried to pull away.

"We won't," Noah said. But he placed his hand on the doorknob anyway, and he wouldn't let me go.

It wouldn't have mattered if he had, though, because the door didn't open. The knob didn't even turn.

We were locked inside.

"We're trapped," I whispered. I hated my voice. I hated my fear.

Noah pulled me away from the door and headed left. His strides were long and fast and I could barely keep up. I had no idea where we were going; the place was like a maze. But Noah's perfect memory served us well—he led us to the empty dining room, which looked out over the ocean. The edge of dawn had begun to creep over the black horizon through the window. Noah tried the door that led to the kitchen.

It was locked too.

He swore, and then he was back by my side. He looked out at the dark water. Looked at the tables and chairs.

"Move," he said to me, urging me away from the window.

I backed away as Noah lifted a chair. Launched it in fury at the glass.

It bounced off.

"All right," he said calmly to the air, to no one. Then to me he said, "Let's wake them up."

Jamie. Stella. Everyone, he meant. We outnumbered the adults, and together, maybe we could do something that alone, we couldn't. Maybe together, we could all find a way out.

We ran back to the patient rooms. Noah tried to open the first door. Locked. He banged his fist once, ordered whoever was inside to wake up.

He was met with silence. We tried another door.

Another locked door.

That was when I realized I'd never seen any locks on *any* of the patient doors. There *were* no latches to turn. No buttons to press.

That didn't mean there were no locks. It just meant that we, the patients, weren't able to lock them.

But now we were locked inside.

Trapped, my mind whispered.

We hadn't seen or heard another living soul since we left Kells's office. No counselors. No adults. They left us here.

Why?

My mind bent in confusion as Noah pulled me to his room, the one he shared with Jamie. The door was open.

Jamie was not inside.

My legs were string—I couldn't stand anymore. I sank, but Noah caught me. He pulled me close, so close against him and wrapped himself around me until every point of my body made contact with his. Forehead to forehead, chest to chest, hips to hips. He loosened his arms and pushed the matted, damp hair from my face, from my neck. He tried to hold me together, but I still fell apart.

After my pointless sobs softened into silence, I spoke. "I'm so scared," I said.

And so ashamed, I didn't say. I felt so *weak*.

"I know," Noah said, his back against the frame of his bed, his arms wrapped around me still. His lips brushed my ear. "But I have to go find Jamie."

I nodded. I knew. I wanted him to. But I couldn't seem to let him go.

It wouldn't have mattered, though. A few seconds later, we heard the scream.

65

IT CUT OFF AS SHARPLY AS IT BEGAN.

"That wasn't Jamie," Noah said strongly against my temple. He tucked my head beneath his chin, my cheek against his chest.

He was right. The voice had been female.

We listened, fitted against each other in the dark. The silence was thick, shutting out everything but my heartbeat. Or Noah's. It was impossible to know.

Another scream issued—from the compound's center. From the garden? I couldn't tell from here.

"Stay here," Noah said to me, his voice firm and clear.

He couldn't not go. But I couldn't leave him.

"No," I said, shaking my head. "We're not splitting up." My voice sharpened. "We're not splitting up."

Noah exhaled slowly. He didn't answer, but he took my hand and lifted me up.

Our footsteps echoed in the silent halls and I gripped his fingers tightly, wishing we could become one thing. Holding on to him, I noticed, my wrists didn't even hurt.

The early morning sky was still very dark, the black brightening only to a deep purple. Lightning flickered through the windows that wouldn't release us and made monsters of our shadows against the wall.

Another scream.

We were corralled by it. Drawn to it. That was the point.

We walked into my nightmare together.

Jude stood in the Zen garden, broad and imposing in the sand. He stood between harmoniously arranged stalks of bamboo and sculptured bonsai trees. Jamie and Stella Adam and Megan were kneeling, arranged in the sand. Heads bowed. Hands bound. Positioned among the rocks.

Another girl—I couldn't see her face—was lying on her side, unmoving. Her white shirt was soaked in blood, coloring it red.

There was a storm outside. It raged through the skylight. But the garden was quiet. No one struggled. No one said a word. Not even Jamie. The tableau was surreal. Deranged. Utterly terrifying.

Then Jude's voice polluted the air. "Did you try the doors first?" he asked us, and smiled. "The windows?"

No one spoke.

Jude clucked his tongue. "You did. I can tell." His gaze wandered over each of the bodies in the sand. When he looked up, it was at Noah. "While I'm glad we're able to finally meet," he said, "I did want to avoid this."

Nothing in Noah's posture or expression showed that he'd even heard him. He was as still and smooth as one of the stones in the sand. The sight of bound and kneeling teenagers didn't appear to unsettle him at all.

Which appeared to unsettle Jude. He blinked and swallowed, then met my eyes. "I tried to find you, Mara, but you were hiding. So I had no choice. You made me take them."

"Why?" My voice shattered the quiet. "What do you *want*?"

"I want Claire back," he said simply.

"She's dead," I said, my voice quivering. "I killed her and I wish I hadn't but I did and she's dead. I'm *sorry*."

"He thinks you can bring her back," Stella said, her husky voice barely above a whisper.

Seven pairs of eyes focused on her with eerie precision.

"What?" I asked her.

Jude crouched down in front of Stella, a coiled snake.

She ignored him, didn't look. She looked, instead, at me. "He thinks you can bring her back."

Jude smacked Stella across the face.

Jamie flinched.

Megan started to cry.

Adam watched Jude with keen interest—not fear.

Noah took a step forward, brimming with quiet violence.

But when I saw Jude hit Stella, something inside of me rose up from the dark. I held on to Noah still, but I stopped shaking.

"Bring Claire back," I said slowly.

Stella nodded. "That's what he thinks."

"How do you—" I began to ask. Then stopped, because I knew.

Stella was like us. Different. I looked at her, at the expression on her face, and realized how.

She knew what Jude was thinking. She could hear his thoughts.

If Jude believed that I could bring Claire back from the dead, Claire who was mangled and crushed to pieces, who was buried in a closed casket in Rhode Island under six feet of earth, he was absolutely detached from reality. Completely delusional.

The only way out of this would be to act like his delusion was real.

"Jude," I said, my voice pleading. Practiced. "I want to bring Claire back. Tell me how to bring her back."

The muscles in his face twitched. "You have to be motivated," he said mechanically. Then smacked Stella again. Hard.

The muscles in Noah's arms went rigid, tense beneath my grip.

Jude's eyes raked over Noah and a smile formed on his lips. "Yes, join us," he said to him. "You can help."

Something changed in Noah, then. He relaxed. "And how, precisely, would I do that?" His voice had become more than just blank. It was bored.

Stella coughed. Bowed to the ground, spat blood on the sand. Then looked up at me, her stare direct. "You have to be scared," she said to me. "If you're afraid enough, he thinks, you'll do it."

So Jude did want me afraid. Everything he did was designed to terrify me. Showing up at the police station so I would know he was alive. Stealing Daniel's key so he could come and go whenever he wanted, so he could take pictures of me while I slept, so he could move my things around, like the doll, and I would know he had been there, violating the place I should have felt safe.

He killed the cat and told me why with a message in blood.

But that wasn't enough. He didn't want me to feel safe anywhere, with anyone. Not with my father—so he nearly ran us off the road. And not at Horizons—so he used Phoebe to scare me. He gave her the picture and had her scratch out my eyes, he wrote that note and had her deliver it. He played me like an instrument and used Phoebe like a tool, to unsettle me, to push me, to make me afraid when he couldn't be around to do it himself.

I thought it was all for revenge. For Claire. To punish me for what I'd done to her and to him. And no doubt that was part of it. But in his mind, it was also a means to an end.

An end I couldn't possibly deliver.

I had to be motivated, he said. If I was afraid enough I'd do it, he thought.

But I *was* afraid. I was terrified. And Claire was still never going to come back.

I didn't know how to pretend otherwise anymore. "Jude," I said. "I swear, I would do it if I could. I'm sorry."

He cocked his head at me. Studied me. "You're not sorry," he said plainly. "But you will be."

Then, in a movement so sudden I almost couldn't make sense of it, he grabbed a fistful of Stella's thick curls, lifting her up and bending her back at once.

Megan screamed. Jamie looked away. Adam made a surprised noise.

Noah was on edge again, I could feel it. But he didn't move from my side.

I was seething. "You think if you torture her, I'll bring Claire back?" I asked, my voice rising in fury. "If I could do it I'd have done it already—"

Jude let Stella fall back to her knees. He looked down at her.

"Oh, *God*," she whispered.

A smile crept across Jude's mouth.

The way she sounded, the way he smiled, set my nerves on fire. "What?"

Jude looked up at me, and his grin grew wider. "Tell them," he said to Stella. When she didn't speak, he tugged on her hair. "Tell them."

"She—" Stella screwed up her face, and her eyes flicked to Jude as he crouched beside her. "She knew," Stella whispered, looking straight at him. "Jude's part of it. She knew—oh my God, she *knew,* about all of us, the whole time—he's part of it, she promised him you'd bring Claire back if he brought you here, she told him how to make you do it, and she left the rest of us here to see what you would do, oh God—"

"She?" Jamie whispered.

"Kells," Noah said.

"Jude's part of *it?*" I asked, my voice brittle and breaking. "He's part of *what*?"

What *was* he? What were *we*?

"I can't *hear*," Stella wailed, "there are too many voices!" Then Stella whispered and mumbled; I could only catch one word. It sounded like "insurance."

"How do we get out?" I asked quickly. That was what I needed to know, before Stella lost it. How to get out.

"You can't," Stella moaned.

"I was let in," Jude said calmly.

I felt like I'd been kicked in the chest.

Dr. Kells had let Jude in. The adults were all gone. There was no one to help us, no one who would come.

"He killed Phoebe," Stella said, her shoulders shaking. "But it looks like you did it, Mara—that's what they're going to say. They need you—"

Jude slapped her cheek. Stella sucked her full lips into her mouth and looked down at the sand. She wasn't going to say anything else.

I couldn't make sense of most of what she *had* said, but one thing I caught was this: Dr. Kells promised Jude I would bring Claire back if he brought me here tonight. And she was lying.

She wanted me here for some other reason and I couldn't begin to fathom what it was. I couldn't play along with Jude's delusion, but maybe if I could show him that he was just a piece, a pawn in whatever twisted thing was happening here, there might be a chance, however small, that he would let us go.

I didn't see another way. So I said, "Dr. Kells is lying to you."

"No," Jude said to me, "you are."

Then he grabbed Stella's wrist and broke it. We all heard it snap.

Megan screamed like an animal. Jamie swore. Adam smirked. I churned with rage.

But Noah. Noah didn't make a sound. He didn't step forward.

He didn't even tense. After a minute, he said, "You might want to let her go," as if he were pointing Jude in the direction of the nearest gas station.

The muscles in Jude's face twitched. He didn't understand why Noah wasn't reacting, why he didn't seem to care, and until that second, neither did I.

Jude wanted us off balance. He *wanted* us afraid. He needed those things from me most of all, and I thought he was hurting Stella to try and scare me even more.

But it wasn't working. I wasn't scared. I was *angry*, and Jude saw it. Which is why he wasn't trying to use Stella to provoke *me*—he was using her to try and provoke *Noah*. Thinking he couldn't resist a damsel in distress.

He wanted Noah to take her place.

But it wasn't working. Noah didn't move.

Jude dropped Stella's wrist, then. She fell back against the bloody sand and I felt a split second of relief—

Until Jude pinched the back of Jamie's neck.

Everything changed. My stomach curdled with fear.

"I'll let this one go," Jude said with a wholesome smile, "if Mara takes his place."

I let out the breath I didn't realize I'd been holding. Jude had me before, at the marina, and didn't kill me then. He came into my room and ruined my life but I was still here. I was still alive.

Jude *couldn't* kill me, Stella had said—he thought he needed me to get his sister back. If I took Jamie's place it wouldn't matter that it wasn't possible; Jude would be busy with me, giving the rest of them a chance to get *all* of us out.

I let go of Noah's arm.

66

NOAH FLASHED ME A LOOK THAT FROZE MY blood. "Don't you dare."

Then Jamie spoke. His voice was like the edge of a diamond, brutally sharp and compelling. "Let me go," he said to Jude.

And to my enormous shock, Jude did.

I watched Jamie drop to in slow motion, but just before he hit the ground, Jude gripped his neck again, pulling him up.

Then landed a brutal kick to Jamie's stomach. Jamie curled in the sand.

"Don't speak again," Jude said.

I shook with rage and hatred. Jude looked at me with clinical interest. "Here's how this is going to work," he said, against the background of Megan's now-constant sobs. "The longer you make me wait, Mara, the more you will make them suffer."

"This has *nothing* to do with them," I spat.

Jude nodded. "Exactly," he said. "So are you going to make *them* pay for what *you* did? All you have to do is take their place." He smiled like a reptile and looked at me like I was a rat. "Otherwise you'll kill them slowly, and I will make you watch."

Noah placed a hand on my stomach very softly, keeping me back. "You aren't killing anyone, Mara," he said to me. Noah looked straight at Jude. "He is."

That shadow had crept back into Noah's voice, into his face. I had never, ever seen him lose it, but I had a feeling I was about to.

It was frightening.

Jude trailed his finger along the crown of Megan's sweat-damp blond head. The sand beneath her darkened with urine. "Who will you choose first?" he asked me.

I was mute. Transfixed. Jude knelt down to Megan slowly.

Then Noah shifted me gently, subtly behind him.

Jude took Megan's face in his large hand and as he did, Noah moved so silently and fast I almost missed it.

Noah was in the garden. His fist met Jude's face with a sickening crack.

Megan and Adam let out a double, inharmonious gasp, but I didn't turn to look. I was riveted, spellbound by what I saw: Jude used his size like a wrecking ball, inflicting carnage with heavy hands and feet. But Noah was incisive and swift, lithe and fierce. He knew instinctively what would hurt most, and that's what he did. Noah hit Jude again and again and again and I couldn't look away.

But then I heard my name—in Megan's voice. Just before she and Adam slumped forward at exactly the same time.

A memory flashed—Jude stabbing himself, dropping to his knees on a wooden dock.

I was assaulted with memories then. The man at the marina who died when he tried to rescue me from torture. John, my bodyguard, who died in his car from a stroke. I remembered dead fish beneath the dock and dead birds that fell from the sky.

Not my fault. But not random, either.

"Noah," I whispered, looking back and forth between Megan and Adam and Jude. I finally, finally understood.

Jude could heal himself like Noah—by killing things, like me.

He didn't have to touch anyone to kill them. He didn't even have to think it. He just had to be hurt himself, and if he was, anything and anyone around him would die.

Like John. Like the off-duty cop. Like the fish.

I was lethal, but Jude was worse. And animals could sense

it—our neighbors' pets disappeared the day I came home from the psych ward—the same day Jude began haunting my house.

Noah had Jude prone and locked to the sand. He pressed his forearm to Jude's throat and leaned over his face. "I will murder you," he said calmly. "And before you die you will beg for her forgiveness."

Jude might have made a noise but I couldn't hear it because Megan and Adam groaned in anguish.

Insurance, Stella had said.

Jude's chest heaved and his shoulders shook. He was *laughing*.

"He'll kill them," I said, my voice rough and miserable. "If you hurt him, they'll die."

"If you don't kill me," Jude said, his voice hoarse, "I'll slice Mara into pieces so small you won't—"

Noah released Jude's throat. And shattered his kneecap in one brutal move.

There was a scream—from Jude, this time. It fractured the air. Jude twisted onto his side, but after a minute, he was laughing again. Still.

His laughter and my heartbeat were the only sounds I could hear. "You want revenge?" Jude asked. His words echoed in the quiet space. He nodded his head at Megan and Adam. "Take it."

My eyes darted toward them—they were unconscious now, but still breathing. Her hair was mixed in with the sand—

almost exactly the same color, too. Bits of it stuck to Adam's buzzed head.

Jamie and Stella, however, were both awake. They were silent, but their eyes glittered with awareness. Taking it in, just like me.

Just like me.

I was unaffected. They were unaffected. Which meant that if Noah could keep Jude engaged—maybe I could get them free. I looked around frantically for a weapon, a tool, something sharp—

"She's right," Jude said, nodding at Stella. "I don't want to kill Mara." His voice was raw, but laced with delight. "Torturing her is too fun."

Noah kicked him again; flattened him onto his back. Knelt. Pressed his forearm against his throat again.

Which was what Jude wanted. Adam made a wet-sounding noise; the tattoos on his arms stood out against his now-pallid skin. Megan didn't make any sound at all.

"You're killing them," Stella said loudly.

Noah looked deceptively, chillingly calm but I knew he was out of control. He could only think of Jude dead and me safe, not the price he or anyone else would pay for it. If Jude had threatened anyone else, Noah could hold himself back. But he couldn't not react when Jude threatened me.

I was his weakness.

Noah would never forgive himself if he gave in.

I said his name.

Noah's expression had been viciously hollow as he waited for the oxygen to leave Jude's lungs, but at the sound of my voice something changed. He leaned back, just slightly, releasing some of the pressure on Jude's throat, enough so he could breathe.

I looked around the space hoping to find something, anything, to help us. But the garden was in the center of the compound and the walls around it were bare and sparse. No furniture, just a scrolled pedestal in the corner holding a green porcelain urn.

The object triggered a memory—of Phoebe smashing a vase to the ground.

And then I had an idea. "Hold him," I called to Noah as I rushed to the far corner of the room. I tipped the pedestal forward and the urn smashed on the stone tile. I snatched one of the shards—maybe I could cut them loose with it? Was it big enough?

But then Stella screamed, shattering the scene in the garden, scattering my thoughts.

Jude was standing. Noah's side darkened with blood.

A slow, lacerating smile appeared on Noah's lips.

The two of them were locked in a silent stalemate and those of us who were still conscious watched. I was hypnotized in my private hell. Even knowing Noah could heal, even seeing his savage smile and knowing the pain didn't bother him, that it *electrified* him—seeing him hurt still dipped me in acid. My hands curled into claws and I felt a sharp pain in my palm—

The shard. I was still holding it.

I forced myself to tear my eyes away from the boy I loved and darted forward to help my friends. Jamie was closest.

"This is so fucked," he said under his breath as I began sawing at the zip-tie that bound his wrists. The jagged piece of porcelain was cutting my skin but I kept sawing until Stella shouted Noah's name and then I had to look up.

Jude had repositioned himself so that he was now nearer to me than Noah was; he moved when *I* moved to try and cut Jamie loose.

"Run," Noah said to me, his voice almost a whisper. It was soft and desperate.

I couldn't leave him. It would have been smart, maybe, but I couldn't do it.

And I couldn't leave Jamie and Stella trapped either. So I ignored Noah's plea and attacked the tie on Jamie's wrists and feet with an even greater fervor.

They came free. Jamie sprang up on startlingly quick feet and Jude dove forward, toward me, just as Noah lunged for him.

Jude knocked me down. The shard fell from my hands.

"Get them out!" I screamed to Noah as Jude's arms snaked around my body. As a steel blade pressed against my skin. It would take nothing to break the flesh. To plunge it into my neck and bleed me out like an animal in front of Noah.

Noah, who watched me with an expression that others would take for rage. But I knew better.

It was terror.

A hot tear slid down my cheek as Jude lifted me up and held me tightly against him, my back against his broad, awful chest. I stared at Noah, his perfect face frozen, his limbs radiating tension as he stared back at us, motionless.

But Jamie had set Stella free and they stood. Stella cradled her broken wrist. Megan and Adam were unconscious, but alive. Jamie hauled Megan up beneath her arms, dragging her toward one of the hallways with Stella by his side. We were still locked in the building, but Jude would leave them alone now that he had me.

"Go," I said to Noah, even knowing that he never would. His jaw was iron and his stare was fierce. I would miss it.

I was saying good-bye, I realized.

Noah saw it in my expression and shook his head slowly. His voice was calm and strong, just for me. "You're going to be fine," he said.

I will fix this, he meant.

But Jude's grip tightened, and the blade pressed into my neck. The breath I was holding escaped and he gripped me tighter. A trail of warm blood trickled down into my shirt.

"I will give you anything," Noah said to Jude. His voice was quiet. "Anything."

Jude spoke to Noah, but his lips were at my ear. My flesh rotted beneath them. "There's nothing you have that I want. Not anymore."

I met Noah's eyes and watched as something in him died.

I couldn't take it. I wasn't afraid anymore for myself; just miserably, desperately sad. "He won't kill me," I lied to Noah. "I'll be okay."

Jude inched us up against a white, bare, empty Horizons wall, crushing me in his arms. He edged us slowly toward the hallway, flanked by patient rooms on each side. I was trapped by him again.

Trapped. The word triggered a memory. I remembered—

A different hallway. Illuminated by the flash of Rachel's camera.

Jude and I walked together behind Rachel and Claire, sticking to the middle of the cavernous hall. Patient rooms flanked it, and I didn't want to go anywhere near them. When Rachel and Claire disappeared behind a corner I sped up, terrified to lose them in the labyrinthine passageways.

I had been trapped before.

And I *escaped* before.

With nothing more than a bruise on my cheek, which wasn't even from the collapse. I remembered seeing the blossoming purple stain on my cheekbone in the hospital mirror. It was from Jude. From when he hit me.

I brought the asylum down, but I made it out unharmed. Safe.

But Jude escaped, too, my mind whispered.

His arms gripped me tighter and I knew his eyes were locked on Noah's. The blade edged into my skin and I felt a rush of warmth and pain. Jude was eliciting every last drop of malicious glee from hurting me and being able to make Noah watch.

I wanted to hurt him back.

And maybe I could. Yes, Jude escaped—but without his hands.

Which meant I could *hurt* him, but not kill him; I'd tried so many times to kill Jude before and it never worked, but I did escape. I brought the asylum down and maybe if I brought *this* building down, I could get free.

And Noah. He might be injured if the building collapsed but he was different, like me—so he would survive like me. Even if he was hurt when the building collapsed, he would heal. He always did. Noah would be safe.

But Jamie? Stella? They were different like us, too. Like Jude. Which meant they would probably survive, but they might be wounded.

Noah could heal them, though. He healed my father. If I hurt Jamie and Stella by trying to get us out, he could fix them.

Jude's hot breath tickled my neck, making me turn my head before we edged into the shadows. I saw the blood-soaked girl in the garden. I saw Adam lying in the sand.

Me and Jamie and Stella and Noah would survive. But we weren't the only ones here.

Adam was probably still alive. Megan was when Jamie dragged her away. There might be others locked in their rooms behind their doors, too.

If I brought this place down like the asylum, anyone who wasn't different would die like Rachel and Claire. Adam. Megan. Anyone else, anyone normal.

But they could die anyway, I told myself. Jude might go through each one of them until they—we—were all gone.

My skin tightened and the blood rushed in my ears and I felt Jude inching us farther away. If he turned the corner, Noah would be out of sight.

I was running out of time. I would have to choose even though neither option was good. Maybe a hero could see another way out of this, but I was not a hero.

You always have a choice, Noah had said once.

I made mine.

I used every bit of force I had to slam us both into the wall.

Jude wasn't expecting it. His head cracked obscenely and I imagined fissures spidering from where it hit up to the ceiling and down to the floor, to below, to the foundation. The arms around my chest loosened as Jude fell to the ground.

But I didn't run.

I whipped around to face him. I could hear nothing but my breath and my heartbeat and pulse and they were loud and fast but not with fear. With pure, cold, rocking fury.

I felt a strong, disturbing tug in my mind, but I gave in to it and something came free. I pushed Jude's slack body up, up against the wall. Pinned him, crushed him against it so firmly that bits of plaster seemed to shake off and fall to the floor. I was stronger than I knew. I couldn't kill Jude with my mind but I would kill him with my body and he deserved to die.

I knew Noah was behind me but he didn't move to help. He saw I didn't need it.

Jude was unconscious and limp and time seemed to slow down as spots of black and red crowded into my vision, as a colorless scent invaded the air. I crushed Jude's throat with graceful hands that didn't feel like my own. The sight brought a rush of savage joy. I felt myself smile.

Mara.

I heard my name whispered in a loved, familiar voice, but it was far away and I didn't listen. I would not stop until this thing beneath my grip was dead—I would not allow it to escape or heal. I wanted to watch it die, to turn it to meat. The thought filled me with hot pleasure. The doors were still locked and I was still sealed inside but I would bring this place down, I would claw at it with my mind and my fingers if I had to. I would get the boy I loved out. I would set myself free.

That was the last thought I had before everything went black.

67

BEFORE

Port of Calcutta, India

THE CROWD GREW AND THICKENED AROUND the wild creatures at the port, where they did not belong. A loud blast sounded from one of the ships and small monkeys chittered and screamed. One man hit the top of a cage with his fist—a large, bright-colored bird shrieked inside. He smiled and peered closer as the bird beat its wings against the bars and jewel-colored feathers fell to the ground.

Another man poked a stick through a different cage at the large, brown monkey. It pulled its lips back and bared its fangs.

The small boy with small black eyes I had asked for help had darted back to the others, who kept running sticks along the tiger's cage and kept dancing back. The largest boy, clothed in dull red, spit at the tiger. It roared.

The people laughed.

My breath was quick and my small chest rose and fell with it. My heart was beating fast, and I crushed the doll in my fist.

The large boy bent down. He picked up rocks—one, two, three. The rest of the children did the same.

Then each of them hauled their arms back and threw the stones at the tiger. Rattled its cage. Struck its fur.

I swelled with loathing, brimmed with it. Dark thoughts swirled in my mind and time slowed to a crawl as the tiger snarled and shrank back against its cage. The boys laughed and the people cheered.

The animal did not deserve this. I wished it could get out and I saw it in my mind: Bright metal bars falling to the earth. Claws and teeth meeting skin instead of rocks meeting fur. I closed my eyes because that was the picture I would rather see.

A scream pried them open.

The creature had pushed up against the back of its cage—which fell. I watched as it lashed out at the nearest boy, the biggest one. Its claws split open his side in a widening red gash.

The other boy, the one with small eyes, had gone white and still. He was not looking at the tiger. He was looking at me, and his mouth formed the shape of the word that would one day become my name.

Mara.

The tiger pushed the large boy down and he screamed again. It moved over him, grabbed his throat in its mouth, and bit down. The boy's screaming stopped.

Others began, but it did not matter. The animal was free.

68

AFTER

I awoke on the morning of some day in some hospital to find Dr. Kells sitting in my room.

Everything was clear: the IV stand towering over my bed. The rough, bleached cotton sheets. The commercial ceiling tiles and the embedded fluorescent lights. I could hear them hum. But it was as if I was looking at the antiseptic room and everything in it through glass.

And then, in a flood, everything came back.

Jude, limp while I drained the life out of him with my hands.

Stella and Jamie, hurt and bruised and dragging Megan away from the torture garden.

And Noah, watching him die inside while I lied to him, when I told him that I would be okay.

But it wasn't a lie. I broke out of Jude's arms and Noah was near me, beside me, before I blacked out. He called my name. I heard it. I remembered it.

Where was he now? Where were they? Where was *I*?

I tried to sit up, to get out of bed, but something held me back. I looked down at my hands, which rested on top of the light blue cotton blanket covering the bed and tucked in over my feet, expecting to see restraints.

But there were none. My hands still wouldn't move.

"Good morning, Mara," Dr. Kells said. "Do you know where you are?"

I felt a splintering fear that I would look up and see words on the wall informing me that I was in a psychiatric unit somewhere. That I had never left. That none of the past two weeks, six weeks, six months, had happened. That was the one thing she could say to me, after everything I survived, that would make me break.

But I was able to turn my head both ways and look around. There were no windows in this room. No signs. There was nothing except the IV stand, and a large mirror on the wall behind Dr. Kells's head.

I may not have known where I was but I remembered what she did. I watched her sit there placidly in the plastic chair next to the bed and flipped through memory after memory of her lying to my face. I saw images of Jude in my room, watching me as I slept while Dr. Kells recorded it. She had known he was alive. She knew what he was doing to me. She let him into Horizons and she put all of us through hell.

Her expression hadn't changed, but I saw her with new eyes.

"Do you know who I am?" Dr. Kells asked.

You're the person who betrayed my trust. You're the person who fed me lies and drugs pretending to make me better when all you really wanted was to make me worse. I know exactly who you are, I tried to say. But when I opened my mouth, all that came out was the word, "Yes."

It was like I was pressed between two panes of glass. I could *see* everything, I could *hear* everything, but I was removed from myself. Detached. Not paralyzed—I could feel my legs and the scratchy sheets that brushed my skin. I could lick my lips and I did. I could speak, but not the words I wanted to say. And when I tried to order my mouth to scream and my legs to kick, it was like the desire was impossible to reach.

"I have some things I'd like to talk with you about, but first, I want to let you know that you've been given an infusion of a variant of sodium amytal. Have you heard of sodium amytal?"

"No," my poisoned tongue replied.

"Colloquially, they call it truth serum. That's not entirely accurate—but it can be used to help relieve certain types of suffering. We sometimes use it in experimental psychiatry to give patients a respite from a manic or catatonic episode." She leaned in closer to me, and said in a softer tone of voice, "You've been suffering, Mara, haven't you?"

I seethed in that bed, in my body, and I wanted to spit in her face. But I couldn't. I said, "Yes."

She nodded. "We think the variant we've developed will help with your . . . unique issues. We're on your side. We want to help you," she said evenly. "Will you let us help you?" She glanced over her shoulder at the mirror.

No, my mind screamed. "Yes."

"I'm glad." She smiled, and reached down to the floor. When she raised her hand, there was a remote in it. "Let me show you something," she said, and then called out to the air. "Screen."

A thin white screen lowered mechanically from the ceiling while a portion of the wall near the mirror retracted, exposing a whiteboard that bore a scrawled list.

"Monitors," Dr. Kells called out before I could read it. I heard something beep beside my head, matching the pace of my heartbeat.

"Lights," she said again, and the room went dark. Then she raised her hand and the remote, and pressed play.

I watched shaky footage from Claire's camera as she swung and panned over the asylum, over Rachel. I watched the scene that Jude left for me in my bedroom for me to watch before.

The image went dark. I heard myself laugh.

But where the video stopped before, the image now shook. Jude's footage was spliced. On *this* footage, *this* screen, I now saw that someone was lifting the camera. And just before the image cut out, there was a flash of light.

Illuminating the face of Dr. Kells.

She had been at the asylum. She was *there*.

My mind wanted to throw up, but my body was perfectly still as the lights came on.

Dr. Kells pointed at the whiteboard. "Mara, can you read what's written there?" I skimmed the words as my blood pounded in my ears. The machine, the monitor, beeped faster.

Double-Blind

S. Benicia, manifested (G1821 carrier, origin unknown). Side effects(?): anorexia, bulimia, self-harm. Responsive to administered pharmaceuticals. Contraindications suspected but unknown.

T. Burrows, non-carrier, deceased.

M. Cannon, non-carrier, sedated.

M. Dyer, manifesting (G1821 carrier, original). Side effects: co-occurring PTSD, hallucinations, self-harm, poss. schizophrenia/paranoid subtype. Responsive to midazolam. Contraindications: suspected n.e.s.s.?

J. Roth, manifesting (G1821 carrier, suspected original), induced. Side effects: poss. borderline personality disorder, poss. mood disorder. Contraindications suspected but unknown.

A. Kendall: non-carrier, deceased.

J. L.: artificially manifested, Lenaurd protocol, early induction. Side effects: multiple personality disorder (unresponsive), anti-social personality disorder (unresponsive); migraines, extreme aggression (unresponsive). No known contraindications.

C. L.: artificially manifested, Lenaurd protocol, early induction, deceased.

P. Reynard: non-carrier, deceased.

N. Shaw: manifested (G1821 original carrier). Side effects(?): self-harm, poss. oppositional defiant disorder (unresponsive), conduct disorder? (unresponsive); tested: class a barbiturates (unresponsive), class b (unresponsive), class c (unresponsive); unresponsive to all classes; ~~(test m.a.d.),~~ deceased.

Generalized side effects: nausea, elevated temp., insomnia, night terrors

"You've been a participant in a blind study, Mara," Dr. Kells said. "That means most of your treating doctors and counselors have been unaware of your participation. Your parents are unaware as well. The reason you've been selected for this study is because you have a condition, a gene that is harming you."

Carrier.

"It makes you act in a way that is causing you to be a danger to yourself and others."

Side effects.

"Do you understand?"

"Yes," my traitor tongue responded. I understood.

"Some of your friends are also carriers of this gene, which has been disrupting your normal lives."

Stella. Jamie. Noah. Their names were on that list, right by mine.

And by J. L. Jude Lowe.

I had wanted to know what we were and now I did. We weren't students. We weren't patients.

We were subjects. Victims, and perfect ones. If we cried wolf, Dr. Kells would cry crazy, and there were hundreds of pages of psychological records to back her up. If any of us told the truth, the world would call it fiction.

The asylum, Jude, Miami—the people I'd killed, the brother Jude had taken. It all led to this moment.

Because it had been calculated that way. It was planned.

I wasn't sent to Horizons—I'd been *brought*. My parents had no idea what this place was; they just wanted to help me get better and Dr. Kells made them believe I would. When they thought I *was* getting better, they decided not to make me go to the retreat; they would eventually pull me out of the program entirely.

And the day they decided not to make me go was the night when Jude made me slit my wrists. But not to kill myself.

To get me sent back.

I heard Stella's voice, just a whisper in my mind.

"They need you."

They? Dr. Kells and Jude?

Dr. Kells interrupted my racing thoughts. "Your condition has caused pain to the people you love, Mara. Do you want to cause pain to the people you love?"

"No," I said, and it was the truth.

"I know you don't," she said seriously. "And I am truly sorry we weren't able to help you before now. We had hoped to be able to sedate you before you collapsed the building. We tried very hard to save all of your friends."

My heart stopped. The room was silent for seconds before the monitor beeped again.

"We didn't anticipate that things would happen quite the way they did—as it was, we were lucky to be able to extract Jamie Roth, Stella Benicia, and Megan Cannon before they were seriously harmed. We just couldn't get to Noah Shaw."

I heard her wrong.

That was it. I calmly, slowly looked back at the board, and forced my mind to turn the letters into words, ones I could understand, ones that made sense. But all I could process when I read them now was:

Deceased.

Written under Noah's name.

My mind repeated the words of the woman Noah had once called a liar.

"You will love him to ruins."

All the pain I had ever felt was just practice for this moment.

"The roof caved around you, but not on you, Mara. Noah was too close, and he was crushed."

"He will die before his time with you by his side, unless you let him go."

"I'm very, very sorry," Dr. Kells said.

What she was saying was impossible. Impossible. Noah healed every time he was hurt, always. He swore I couldn't hurt him again and again and again. Noah didn't lie. Not to me.

But Dr. Kells did. She lied to me about Jude. She lied to Jude about me. She lied to my parents about Horizons. She lied to everyone, to all of us.

And she was lying to me now.

A tear escaped anyway. Just one. It rolled down my alien cheek.

"We want to make sure nothing like that happens again, Mara, and we think we can, if you consent."

Dr. Kells waited for my response, as if I had the ability to say anything but yes. She knew I couldn't consent, which meant this was some kind of display, some kind of show. For someone's benefit, but not mine.

I was raging.

"We want to help you be better, Mara. Do you want to be better?"

Her words brushed the dirt off of a memory.

"What do you want?" Dr. Kells had asked me, on my first day in her care.

"To be better?" I had answered her.

My answer then had been honest. After the asylum, I was gnawed by grief. After Jude came to the police station, I was tyrannized by fear. Grief and guilt, fear for my family and for myself. *Of* myself. It ruled me.

Dr. Kells manipulated that. Jude did too. I didn't know

what part he was playing in this, or what Dr. Kells stood to gain by terrorizing and torturing and lying to me. I didn't know why they needed me or why I'd been brought here or where *here* even was or whether I was alone. But I was no longer afraid. There were other names on that list, and if they were here with me, I would get them out and we would see the people we loved again.

I would see the boy I loved again. Everything in me knew it.

Dr. Kells repeated her question. "Do you want to be better, Mara?"

Not anymore.

Something dormant kicked to life inside me. It reached up, stood up, and held my hand.

"Yes," my tongue lied. My answer drew a plastic smile from her painted lips.

This is what I knew: I was trapped in my body, in that bed, at that moment. But even as I looked out through the windows of my eyes, through the bars of my prison, I knew I wouldn't be trapped forever.

They rattled my cage to see if I'd bite. When they released me, they'd see that the answer was yes.

end of volume two

Turn the page for a sneak peek at the thrilling conclusion to Mara's story.

THE EXAMINATION OF MARA DYER WAS TAKEN ON [redacted] at the Horizons Residential Treatment Center for Behavioral Health. 31821 No Name Island, Florida. Video transcript time: 2:13 p.m.

Examination by: Dr. Deborah Kells

Also present: Mr. [redacted]

KELLS: Hello, Mara. My name is Deborah Kells, and this is Mr. ____. We're here because your family says that you have agreed to residential treatment at the Horizons Residential Treatment Center for Behavioral Health on No Name Island,

Florida, just off No Name Key. Is that correct?

[Silence]

KELLS: How much Amytal did you give her?

MR. ____: Forty ccs.

KELLS: Anemosyne?

MR. ____: One hundred micrograms.

KELLS: And the midazolam?

MR. ____: Fifty milligrams. Same as the others. She won't remember any of this.

KELLS: God, she's like a zombie. Mara, Mara—are you awake? Do you understand me?

MARA: . . . Yes.

KELLS: Great. Thank you. Is it correct that you agreed to being treated here?

MARA: Yes.

KELLS: Thank you. Now, if at anytime you don't understand what I'm asking you, just let me know and I'll try to make it clearer, okay?

MARA: Okay.

KELLS: Now, you'll notice that there's a video camera in the room here with us. We want to record this just so we have a record. Is that okay with you?

MARA: Yes.

KELLS: Excellent. Okay, Mara. Let's start with the basics. What is your full name?

MARA: Mara Amitra Dyer.

KELLS: And how old are you?

MARA: Seventeen.

KELLS: Where were you born?

MARA: Laurelton.

KELLS: Where is that?

MARA: Outside Providence.

KELLS: Rhode Island?

MARA: Yes.

KELLS: Thank you. Can you tell me a little about why you're here?

[Silence]

KELLS: She's struggling with the open-ended questions. Can we counteract the Anemosyne?

MR. ____: She might not be as cooperative.

KELLS: Well, she's not exactly cooperative now, is she?

MR. ____: I'll have to do it intravenously—

KELLS: Obviously. Just—

MARA: I hurt people.

MR. ____: Do you still want me to adjust—

KELLS: No, let's see where she goes. Mara, who did you hurt?

MARA: My teacher.

KELLS: What was her name?

MARA: Morales.

MR. ____: Her file says that her teacher, Christina Morales, died of anaphylactic shock in reaction to fire ant bites on [date redacted].

KELLS: Let me see.

MARA: Also a . . . a man. He hurt a dog. I—I—

KELLS: It's okay. Take your time. Just tell us what you remember.

MARA: Rachel.

MR. ____: Rachel Watson, deceased, died Wednesday [date redacted] in Laurelton. Remains discovered at six a.m. with those of—

MARA: Claire.

MR. ____: Claire Lowe, yes, as well as her brother, Jude Lowe—

Mara: Noah.

MR. ____: Noah Shaw? I don't—

KELLS: Quiet.

MR. ____: Sorry—whoa. Did you see that? She just—

KELLS: What else is she on?

MR. ____: The hundred milligrams of Zyprexa, as prescribed prior to intake. It shouldn't interfere.

MARA: [speech unclear]

KELLS: What did she say?

MR. ____: I don't know. Jesus, look—

KELLS: Is she on anything else?

MR. ____: I don't—

KELLS: Is she on anything else?

MR. ____: No. No.

KELLS: Does she have a history of epilepsy?

MR. ____: I don't think so.

KELLS: Well, do you think or do you know?

MR. ____: No— Jesus Christ. Is that a seizure? Is she seizing?

KELLS: Turn off the camera.

MARA: [speech unclear]

KELLS: What did you say, Mara?

MR. ____: I'm going to call—

KELLS: Don't call anyone. Turn off the camera. What, Mara?

MARA: [speech unclear]

MR. ____: Did she just say our names? Did she just say—

KELLS: TURN OFF THE CAMERA.

MR. ____: Oh, God—

[End video examination, 2:21 p.m.]

THE FIRST FACE I SAW WHEN I OPENED MY EYES WAS my own.

The wall in front of the iron bed was mirrored. So were the walls to my right and left—there were five mirrors, or six maybe. I smelled nothing, heard nothing, saw nothing but me.

During the past several months, I hadn't spent much time looking in mirrors, for reasons. Now that I was forced to, I couldn't quite believe that the girl I was seeing was me. My dark, thick hair was parted in the middle, and it hung limp and dull over thin shoulders. My lips were almost the same color as my skin—that is to say, white. There were angles to my face that I'd never noticed before. Or maybe they hadn't existed before. I was looking at a ghost, a shell, a stranger. If my parents saw me, they would never know who I was.

But they never did see me. That was part of the problem. That was why I was here.

"Yeah, we look like shit," said a voice.

Said *my* voice.

But I hadn't spoken. My lips hadn't moved.

I bolted upright, looking at my infinite reflections. They stared back, looking panicked and wary at once.

"Up here."

The voice was above me. I craned my neck—the ceiling was mirrored too. I saw my reflection in it, but this one, this reflection, was smiling at me. Even though I wasn't smiling.

So. I'd finally lost it.

"Not yet," my reflection said, looking amused. "But you're close."

"What—what is this?" A hallucination?

"Not a hallucination," my reflection said. "Guess again."

I dropped my gaze for a moment, glancing around the room. Every other reflection turned when I did. God, I hoped I was dreaming.

I looked back up at the reflection above me. The girl in the mirror—me, I guess—tilted her head slightly to the left. "Not quite. You're in that kind-of-unconscious-kind-of-not space. Which should make you feel better about your sanity."

Marginally.

"Also, you should know that there are sensors monitoring our pulse and heartbeat, so it would be better for both of us if you'd lie back down."

I swung my head, looking for the monitors, but didn't see any. I listened to the girl anyway.

"Thanks," she said. "That Wayne guy comes in and examines us whenever our heart rate spikes, and he really creeps us out."

I shook my head, the papery pillowcase crinkling with the movement. "Don't say 'us.' That creeps *me* out."

"Sorry, but it *is* us. I'm you," my reflection said, arching an eyebrow. "I'm not exactly your biggest fan either, you know."

I've had weird dreams. I've had weird hallucinations. But weird didn't even begin to touch this, whatever this was. "So, what are you? My . . . my subconscious or something?"

"You can't talk to your subconscious. That's stupid. It's more like—I'm the part of you that's aware even when you don't know you're aware. She's been giving us a lot of drugs—a *lot* of drugs—and it's dulled our—sorry, *your*—awareness in some ways and heightened it in others."

"'She' being . . . ?"

"Dr. Kells."

The machine beside me beeped loudly as my heart rate spiked. I closed my eyes, and an image of Dr. Kells rose in the blackness, looming above me, so close that I could see tiny cracks in her thick layers of lipstick. I opened my eyes to make her go away, and saw myself instead.

"How long have I been here?" I asked out loud.

"Thirteen days," the girl in the mirror answered.

Thirteen days. That was how long I'd been a prisoner in my own body, answering questions I didn't want to answer and doing things I didn't want to do. Every thought and memory was fuzzy, as if they were smothered in cotton; me, locked in what looked like a child's bedroom, drawing picture after picture of what used to be my face. Me, extending my arm obediently while Wayne, Kells's assistant in therapeutic torture, drew my blood. And me, the first day I woke up here, held captive by drugs and forced to listen to words that would change my life.

"You've been a participant in a blind study, Mara."

An experiment.

"The reason you've been selected for this study is because you have a condition."

Because I'm different.

"Your condition has caused pain to the people you love."

I've killed them.

"We tried very hard to save all of your friends. . . . We just couldn't get to Noah Shaw."

But I did not kill Noah. I could not have killed him.

"Where are they?" I asked my reflection. She seemed confused, then looked at the mirror on my right. Just a normal mirror, I thought, but then the glass went dark.

An image of a girl, or something that had once been a girl, materialized out of the blackness. She was kneeling on carpet, her black hair falling over her bare shoulders as she leaned over something I couldn't see. Her skin glowed bronze, and shadows flickered over her face. She was blurred and indistinct, as if someone had spilled a glass of water over a painting of her and the colors had started to run. And then the girl lifted her chin and looked directly at me.

It was Rachel.

"It's just a game, Mara." Her voice was scratchy. Distorted. When she opened her mouth again, the only sound that came out was static. Her smile was just a smear of white.

"What's wrong with her?" I whispered, looking at Rachel's flickering image in the glass.

"Nothing's wrong with her. I mean, aside from the fact that she's dead. But there *is* something wrong with your memory of her. That's what you're seeing—your memory."

"Why does she look like—" I didn't even know how to describe it. "Like that?"

"The flickering? I think it's the candles. The three of us lit them before taking out the Ouija board. Don't tell me you've forgotten that?"

"No, I mean she's—she's—distorted." Rachel's arms moved in front of her, but her hands were dipped in shadow and I couldn't see what she was doing. Then she lifted one of them to her nose. Her arm ended at her wrist.

The girl in the mirror shrugged. "I don't know. Not all of your memories are like this. Look left."

I did, expecting the new mirror I was staring at to go dark too. It didn't—not at first. I watched my reflection as the ends of my hair bled from dark brown to red, until it was red to the roots. My face filled out and rounded, and the eyes that stared back at me from the glass were Claire's.

Claire sat up, and her image split off, separated from mine. She walked out of the white surgical gown I wore, and black threads wove around her pale, freckled body, until she was clothed in the dark jeans and puffy coat she'd been wearing the night we went to the asylum. The bright light in the mirrored room flickered and went out. Roots cracked the concrete floor beneath my bed. They grew into trees that scratched the sky.

Claire looked over her shoulder at me. "Oh my God. She's freaking out already."

When Claire spoke, her voice was normal. She wasn't blurry, and she didn't flicker or warp. She was whole.

"I don't know what it means either," the reflection above me said. "Jude is the same."

My mouth went dry at the sound of his name. I glanced up and followed her gaze to the mirrored wall to my right; Jude appeared in it. I saw him standing in the center of a manicured Zen garden, with huddled, hunched people arranged around him like rocks. Jamie and Stella were among them. He held

Stella by her shining black hair. I could see the veins in his hands, the pores in his skin. Every feature, every detail of him was clear. Sharp. I felt a flare of rage.

"Don't," my reflection said. "You'll wake us up."

"So what?" I said. "I don't want to see this." I never wanted to see him again. But when I looked again, there was a different image of him in the mirror. He was pushed against a bare white wall, a hand gripping his throat. The hand belonged to me.

I looked back up at the ceiling and the girl in it. I didn't want to remember Horizons, or what had happened to me since. I looked down at my wrists, at my ankles. No restraints. "Just tell me how to get out."

"They don't need restraints to keep us chained up," she said. "The drugs do that for them. They make us compliant. Willing. But they're changing us too, I think. I don't know how yet, but it has to mean something, that your memory of Rachel is broken but your memories of Claire and Jude aren't."

"What about my brothers? My parents?" *And Noah*, I thought but didn't say.

As I spoke, images of each of them filled the mirrors around me. Joseph was wearing a suit with a pocket square, rolling his eyes at someone. Daniel was laughing in his car, making a face at me from behind the wheel. The image of my mother showed her sitting on her bed, laptop on her lap, her face drawn and worried. My father was sitting up in his hospital bed, eating a contraband slice of pizza. And Noah—

Noah's eyes were closed, but he was breathing. Sleeping. One of his hands was curled in a loose fist by his face, and his T-shirt, the one with the holes in it, was twisted, exposing a sliver of skin above his boxers. This was how he looked the morning after I told him what was wrong with me. After we figured out what was wrong with us.

I couldn't stop looking at them—the people I loved, laughing and talking and living behind silvered panes of glass. But as I did, I realized something wasn't right. I looked closely at Noah. He was sleeping, not moving, which made it easier for me to finally see. His edges were faded. Blurred. I glanced back at the images of my parents, my brothers. Their edges were soft too.

"We're losing them, I think," the girl said. "I don't know why, but I think Kells does, and I think she's doing it on purpose."

I was only half-listening. I couldn't stop staring at the mirrors.

"I'm never going to see them again, am I." It wasn't a question.

"My sources say no."

"You know," I said to her, "you're kind of an asshole."

"Well, that would explain why we're so popular. Speaking of, Jamie and Stella are here too. In case you were curious."

"Have you seen them?"

She shook her head. "But Wayne mentioned 'Roth' once, and 'Benicia' twice, to Kells. And he talked about them in the present tense."

I swelled with relief. My throat tightened and ached and I felt like I might cry, but no tears came. "What about Noah?" I blurted out the question before I could think about whether I really wanted the answer.

The girl knew. "Kells mentioned him once."

But my question had gone unanswered. And now I had to know. "Tell me what she said."

"She said—" The girl didn't finish her sentence. Something hissed and clicked behind me, and she went still.

"What?" I asked. "What did she say?"

She didn't answer. When she spoke again, her voice shook. "They're here," the girl said, and then she was gone.